HARRIET
and
ISABELLA

P ATRICIA O'B RIEN

A TOUCHSTONE BOOK
Published by Simon & Schuster
New York   London   Toronto   Sydney

Touchstone
A Division of Simon & Schuster, Inc.
1230 Avenue of the Americas
New York, NY 10020

For information about special discounts for bulk purchases,
please contact Simon & Schuster Special Sales
at 1-800-456-6798 or business@simonandschuster.com.

Designed by Jan Pisciotta

Manufactured in the United States of America

10   9   8   7   6   5   4   3   2   1

Library of Congress Cataloging-in-Publication Data

O'Brien, Patricia.
   Harriet and Isabella / Patricia O'Brien.
      p. cm.
   1. Stowe, Harriet Beecher, 1811–1896—Fiction. 2. Stowe, Harriet Beecher, 1811–1896—Family—Fiction. 3. Hooker, Isabella Beecher, 1822–1907—Fiction. 4. Sisters—Fiction. 5. Women abolitionists—Fiction. 6. Suffragists—Fiction. 7. Women authors—United States—Fiction. I. Title
   PS3565.B73 H37 2008
   813'.54—dc22   2007001686

ISBN-13: 978-1-4165-5220-8
ISBN-10:   1-4165-5220-0

For Margaret Hall Cohoe
I still hear her laugh.

PART ONE

✢ CHAPTER ONE ✢

Brooklyn Heights
March 7, 1887, 7:00 a.m.

A PERSISTENT SKITTERING SOUND from the darkened space between floor and baseboard pulls Isabella from an uneasy sleep. She sits up, shivering in her thin cambric nightgown, scanning the room. The bed in which she lies, no more than rusting scrap iron, creaks ominously as she hugs her knees to her chest.

Her gaze travels from an old sideboard with broken drawer pulls to the green curtains hanging like seaweed from the window, resting finally on a scattering of black pellets that confirm the origin of the sound coming from the floorboards.

Mice. She hates mice.

What is she doing here? She wonders if she is insane after all.

But the day has begun, and there's no use crouching in a ball feeling sorry for herself, wishing only that she could drift back to sleep and pick up the threads of her dream. She had been a child again, with Henry's large hands gripping hers, swinging her by the arms, both of them laughing; she, knowing he would not let go, knowing it was safe to throw her head back and not worry that her feet were nowhere near the ground.

Fully awake now, Isabella presses her fists into her eyes to stop sudden tears. At this moment a few houses away, Henry lies in his own bed, cut down by a stroke. Everyone from President Cleveland to Queen Victoria is keeping a death vigil for Henry Ward Beecher, for his eloquent preaching has enthralled the country for decades. But she, his sister, uneasy occupant of a garret room, is keeping vigil for the brother who played with her as a child, the one who hasn't spoken to her in fifteen years.

"Why?" John Hooker's voice had been more exasperated than astonished when she told him she was going to Brooklyn. His face had that worried look which she had come to know so well through the long years of their marriage. "You've got this vague idea that he wants to see you. If you show up now, that family of yours will pull you apart. You're making a mistake."

"I want to see him before he dies. He's my brother; I love him."

"He's in a coma."

"He'll know I'm there."

"What is it you want, Bella? An apology?"

"I want . . . mutual forgiveness."

"You are fantasizing," John said somberly.

"I have to try," she said.

She knows the words ring hollow. Persuading Henry's wife to let her see Henry will not be easy. Eunice does not forgive.

Isabella swings her feet to the floor, searching with her toes for her slippers before padding to the window. People are gathering on the sidewalk. There are some with heads bent, praying silently, probably Henry's parishioners from Plymouth Church. But most are men milling about, talking in low voices, stamping their feet to warm them on this frosty morning. They wear bowler hats, cheap black ones, which mark them as reporters. Maybe it is the angle of the hats—jaunty, pushed back—but she knows there is more going on down there than a death watch. Those men are salivating for a meal long gone cold. They want to revive what twelve years ago they dubbed the "trial of the century." Henry's trial. They want it back in all its lurid detail: the accusing, cuckolded Theodore Tilton raging for justice; his waiflike wife, Elizabeth, alternately confessing and denying her guilt; Henry, insisting he, as a man of God, would never commit adultery.

Twelve years now since the scandal that tore her family apart. Twelve years since she and her brothers and sisters were said to wobble on their national pedestal of moral virtue. The Beecher family, shaken by accusations of Henry's human frailty—that was the story reporters fed on, and it was true.

She knows the scandal still courses under the surface, emerging from time to time in jokes and ditties sung on the streets and in the saloons. And she knows that even though Henry continued to preach on Sundays from the pulpit of Plymouth Church, his voice was never again quite as strong or his demeanor quite as confident.

Had those snickers and snatches of song bothered him? Or did he come so to believe his own recounting of events that he became detached from the pain and the lies that destroyed so much? Isabella wonders where that calamity lives in his heart. She knows where it is in hers.

She draws back into the room. She can't afford to let anyone see her yet, particularly her sister Harriet, who arrived in her carriage late last night. It was Harriet, after all, who sent the chilly note reminding her she was not welcome in Henry's home. Sitting back in Hartford with that note on her lap, staring at the formality of its stiff phrasing, parsing each word for hidden meaning, Isabella had made her decision: enough of deferring to the nurtured wrath of her family. She would go to Brooklyn.

She walks now over to the chest and picks up a pink tortoiseshell hand mirror, stroking the garnet beads that frame the back in a graceful, curving line. How many times has she done this? Hundreds of times.

"They aren't real," Hattie had said quickly when Isabella, with a cry of pleasure, pulled the mirror from its wrappings on her fifteenth birthday.

"Why would I care? It's beautiful, Hattie, it's the most beautiful thing I own. Thank you, thank you!" She threw her arms around her older sister.

"I wanted you to have something elegant," Hattie whispered, hugging her back. "I wanted you to see how lovely you are. But be sure to keep it in your room. Father would disapprove."

Isabella had nodded silently. Lyman Beecher was a towering figure of moral authority, both at home and throughout the nation, and he would call this a vain, frivolous gift, a bauble flouting modesty, an occasion for the sin of pride. It awed her to realize Hattie was willing to risk his displeasure.

"I would like to be a writer someday, like you," Isabella had said shyly as Hattie leaned over to pick up the wrapping paper crumpled on the floor. Harriet glanced up with a smile, and then said something Isabella would never forget: "You are a dear girl, Bella, and just as smart as anyone in this family, and you will find your own way. I want you to start by enjoying the gifts God has given you."

So long ago . . . Isabella stares down at the mirror in her hand. She has never reached the level of Hattie's fame, but she has made a name for herself. She has traveled the country, speaking and organizing women to fight for suffrage and legal rights, trying to instill in them a passion for what should be theirs. She has tried to stay true to her values. Would that Hattie valued her for that.

Why has she kept this old treasure all these years? And why did she bring it with her?

Slowly she turns the mirror and stares into the glass. She no longer sees the surface image—the dark hair and smooth skin that still draw attention. She would like to find some clue as to who she really is, but the mirror won't tell her that. So what is she looking for? Hattie, of course. All her life, she has looked for resemblance to the vibrant, brilliant sister she loves most, straining to see more similarity than could ever have been possible with two different mothers. How exciting it had felt as a young woman to stand proudly and say, "Yes, my sister is Harriet Beecher Stowe, and yes, she is indeed the author of *Uncle Tom's Cabin*." How thrilling to realize her big sister had awakened the nation to the evils of slavery and shaped the focus of the War Between the States, an amazing achievement, all with the imagined story of one humble man.

"Hattie, where *did* you go? Where are you?" She listens to the sound of her own voice in the empty room, hearing it more as an echo deep from the past. From when?

She closes her eyes. It was that first summer in Cincinnati, after Lyman Beecher moved the entire family west to establish a new seminary. She was ten years old. She can feel the spongy wood of the old dock under her feet, smell the acrid, soupy air, hear the water sloshing against the rotting piles.

The weather was burning hot, but she didn't care. She loved being with Hattie on any venture, and going down to the river was the most fun. It seemed to her this time that the crowd of grown-ups around her were jostling one another too much, and Harriet explained they were impatient for the late-arriving mail boat. Just like me, she said with a smile. If I get the big batch of student applications I'm hoping for, our new school can open and we can all make some money. Isabella smiled back and held on tight to her sister's hand as they pressed to the front of the crowd.

But it wasn't a mail boat steaming up the Ohio River to the dock. It was a vessel with the name *The Emigrant* painted on the bow. Its deck was jammed with people, most of them half-naked, the hot sun glistening off the sweat of black skin. They seemed to sway in unison with the vessel as it approached across the lapping waves. Isabella guessed there were a hundred of them.

"Hattie? Who are those people?" she whispered, tugging at her sister's sleeve.

"Slaves," Harriet said, pulling her little sister closer, squeezing her hand.

The boat docked amidst shouts from the crowd on the wharf. "About time!" yelled one. "We've got eight escaped ones for you!"

"Bella, let's go," Harriet said, sounding alarmed. "This isn't the mail boat." But the crowd was pushing forward, and they couldn't retreat. Isabella lifted a hand to keep her hat from being knocked off, still staring at the people on the deck as the vessel docked.

They were close up now. There were men and women, and there were children too. She saw a girl about her own age and impulsively waved. The girl slowly raised an arm but kept it motionless, as if to shield her eyes from the sun. Only then did Isabella see an iron cuff on her wrist. From it swung a chain of iron links, one looped through another, like the daisy chain of paper Isabella had made that very day at home for her mother. Her eyes followed the links to a woman standing next to the child, to a band on her wrist. And from there to a man, and from there to another child. They were all chained together.

"Hattie—" Isabella turned to her sister, but she wasn't there. A man's arm pushed her aside. A corridor had been improvised through the crowd, and eight people with dark skin were walking single file to the boat, their hands cuffed in front of them, each held to the others by the same heavy chains. One had white hair; he looked a little like Father, except for his skin color. His head hung heavy, and his arms shook under the weight of the iron.

"Where are they going?" Isabella yelled to the man on the boat who had just tied up at the dock.

"To market, child," he said with a cheerful grin. "Know anyone who needs a good colored? We grow 'em ripe in Kentucky."

A commotion broke out back in the crowd, and a man pushed forward. "You can't take that one!" he shouted at the boat captain. "That big buck there, he's mine. I own 'im! Took me a month to track him down!" He pointed at a man with sturdy shoulders and a long scar cut ragged across his nose and right cheek.

"You'll have to prove it on the other side," the captain said, a careless thumb pointing toward the Kentucky shore. "I paid a bounty hunter for him, fair and square."

The man asserting ownership was standing now next to Isabella. His eyes were furious. "He's my property, damn it. I own him, not you. And I'll prove it." He turned, pointing at the man with a scar. "Silas, you kneel!" he yelled. "I'm your master, and you know it. Kneel!"

Isabella watched, transfixed, as the man with the scar stared straight ahead. He seemed turned to stone.

"Kneel, damn it!"

The man with the scar didn't so much kneel as buckle at the knees. The movement jerked the chain shackling him to the others, causing a slightly built woman in front of him to stumble back and almost fall.

Someone laughed.

"You haven't proved anything, you just scared the son of a bitch," the captain said with a chuckle. "All right, climb on. We'll hash it out on the other side."

The man was still on his knees, his head hanging down between his arms, which were pulled taut by the connecting chain. He looked like he was praying, Isabella thought.

"Get up," said the captain. He yanked on the chain, pulling the slave to his feet. The line moved on again. When the man shuffled past Isabella, she smelled something strange and acrid, a very different smell from that of sweat on a hot day. What was she smelling? Suddenly panicked, Isabella began flailing against the legs of the men pressing forward.

"Hattie, Hattie, where did you go?" she wailed. *"Where are you?"*

Someone shouted that a child was alone on the dock. Men who had been focused on the escaped slaves began looking down at her, which only made her scream louder. One tried to pick her up, and she punched out at him, refusing touch or help. But then suddenly Hattie's familiar arms were wrapped around her.

"I thought I lost you, I thought you fell in the water," Harriet said, holding her tight, her voice shaky with relief.

"I'm sorry, I'm sorry," Isabella sobbed. "I'm sorry I let go."

Later that night, back at home in Walnut Hills, they lay in bed, hugging each other. "Hattie, what did I smell when those poor people in chains were going onto the boat? What was it?" Isabella asked.

Harriet pulled her so close, she could feel the thumping of her heart. "You smelled fear, Bella," she said. "The fear of people who are never free. It's wrong, it's wrong."

Isabella would remember that talk with Harriet as her first lesson on the dark contradictions of human souls. Good people turned away from slavery because they felt no moral obligation to interfere, Harriet said, her voice trembling with anger. They wanted trade with the South, so they kept quiet. Hypocrisy was the enemy of truth, she said. It was the coward's way out, and don't you forget it, Bella.

In the boardinghouse, she wipes her eyes, reminding herself that brooding only feeds the strange pleasure of melancholy, and she cannot afford that anymore. She has to believe that Harriet suffers too, otherwise their love for each other could not have been real, and that would be a travesty. The big sister who taught her to read at the age of five by holding up word cards, who patiently coaxed her through learning her sums, who walked her to school each day for those precious few years she was allowed to attend—could she truly be gone? No, it wasn't possible.

But the truth is, her family is gathering today in a house that has no room for her. In this neighborhood of elegant homes graced with mellow brownstone stoops and finely wrought iron balustrades, she sits in a room with mouse droppings. On the sidewalk, the reporters think of her as the shunned daughter of the famed Beecher family. The pariah. What an irony that her banishment came for telling the truth.

"I am not crazy," she whispers into the air. "No matter who says so."

She hears something new from outside, a different sound. A snatch of song? Isabella goes back to the window and gazes across the street in the direction of Plymouth Church. She glances again at the sidewalk in front of Henry's house and sees the bowler hats watching a strange-looking creature perform some kind of dance. She rubs her eyes. It cannot be. But yes, a man dressed as a caricature of Uncle Tom, his face darkened with lampblack and burnt cork, his lips wide, thick, and painted a gleaming white, is prancing before the Beecher home.

> Beecher, Beecher is my name—
> Beecher till I die!
> I never kissed Mis' Tilton—
> I never told a lie!

"Go away, you stupid fool!" she screams before she can stop herself. She sticks her fist out the window and shakes it, venting her rage, only to see the figure in blackface dance away down the street, followed by the guilty chuckles of the bowler hats.

A right turn from this dreary rooming house onto the sidewalk leads down the street, past three houses, and across the road directly to 124 Hicks Street. Henry Ward Beecher's home is tall and sturdy, built solidly of dull brick. The windows are elegantly corniced, capable of providing ample sunlight to the interior, but the shutters inside are tightly drawn. A sleepy-looking newsboy stands at the corner, waving newspapers at the few carriages now bumping across the cobblestones, pulled by horses expertly keeping their balance, lifting their hooves high over the familiar terrain. HENRY WARD BEECHER IN COMA, reads the headline of the paper in his grubby hand. Below it, RENOWNED AMERICAN FAMILY GATHERS FOR VIGIL.

The carriage occupants stare at the Beecher home. He's dying, they whisper to one another. The old man is dying. The most brilliant preacher in America, that's what everyone says. Even more than his father was . . . What was his name? Lyman. Lyman Beecher. A family of preachers, all of them. Except for the women.

Inside the house, dust hangs in the air. The windows have not been opened in days. The walls of the parlor to the right of the front door are covered in very expensive satin paper, purchased for three dollars a roll (thirteen single rolls to do the job) but unfortunately in a snuff brown color that Eunice Beecher insisted upon because she was sure it would fade and she didn't want to start with something too light. It has not faded.

The stairs are steep, and any visitors today will be met at the top with the mix of sweet and acrid smells of the sickroom: tallow, various medicinal syrups, slops, perspiration. In the presence of illness, Eunice does not believe in excessive ventilation.

There is, unsurprisingly, little light in Henry's sickroom. A coal fire not stoked for hours has burned out, leaving white ash in the fireplace. The room is cold, so cold. At the foot of the bed stands the small figure of a woman with slightly sunken cheeks and dark eyes that seem too big for her face. But Harriet Beecher Stowe stands erect, projecting a strength that commands the room as she crosses her arms, tucking her fingers under the armpits of her compact body for warmth. She wears one of her usual severe black dresses, a tacit acknowledgment that the mourning of one loss quite quickly blends into the mourning of another, and sometimes it is too much effort to change one's wardrobe. Her hair is pulled back into a tight bun.

Henry lies motionless, his body, sheathed in a white blanket, an imposing hillock rising from the bed. His inordinately large head takes up the entire pillow, but without animation his face looks oddly loose and fleshy. His long, white hair lies tamed, tucked behind his ears, and his eyes are closed.

It makes Harriet uneasy to stare at him when he looks so vulnerable. Her eyes turn in the direction of the oak armoire, where her sister-in-law is rummaging for something in a large trunk under the windowsill.

"What are you looking for? Can I help?" she asks.

"No, I've found it." Eunice pulls out a black silk dress and briskly shakes it. "I'll have the girl air this out and iron it. I'll need a hat and veil. A heavy veil."

Harriet tightens her arms across her chest and looks away. Eunice is preparing for Henry's funeral, actually planning her wardrobe as he lies in his bed, still breathing.

"You find what I do inappropriate?" Eunice turns and faces Harriet, her long, thin face looking even more sallow than usual.

"I judge you in no way, Eunice. You have a great deal on your mind right now and a great burden to bear. I understand."

Eunice lets the dress fall heavy in her hands, the skirt touching the floor. "Well, you don't really, but you're trying to say the right thing. In truth, you think I'm detached." Her gaze shifts to the bed. "The person lying there"—she nods to the still figure in the bed—"that isn't really Henry."

"Eunice—"

"Fiddlesticks." Eunice's voice is matter-of-fact. "Henry has no time to die. He'll be rushing through the door any minute, tugging at his collar, saying he's hungry, imploring me to sit and listen to his latest brilliant sermon, as if I didn't have anything better to do. And then he'll be gone, hardly having seen me, hugging the maids and patting the shoulders of neighbors on the street and never once touching me." She gestures toward the window. "And then I'll stand here and watch him as he strides across the street to where he really lives. His church."

Harriet breathes deeply, trying to shape a response. All these years of puzzling over this difficult sister-in-law. What came first, her dour approach to life or Henry's desire to flee? It is far too tender a question to speak about openly in the family, but there have been whispers about her refusing Henry his marital rights. What are her secrets? Once Henry told Harriet that Eunice's father threw a tureen of hot soup on his daughter when, as a young girl, she wore a slightly low-cut dress to dinner. Harriet tries to imagine not only the shock of such a physical scalding but the shame and humiliation the poor woman must have felt. It makes a charitable response easier.

"This is his home, Eunice. With you," she says.

Eunice makes no reply.

The nurse suddenly appears at the door. "Where have you been?" Eunice demands.

"Taking my breakfast, ma'am."

Harriet sees the dislike in the nurse's eyes as she glances at Eunice and then approaches the bed. She has seen the same expression on the faces of several servants in the short time she has been here. There is more than one reason why this house is so cold.

Her gaze travels to her brother. He hasn't spoken a word since his stroke two days ago. Is she imagining it, or is his breathing more shallow than last night? The doctors know nothing. They stand around the bed and clear their throats and say he is a very sick man, and the outcome is doubtful, although, well, he *might* regain consciousness.

He "might"? How could that be, when only a few weeks ago, on her last visit, he had entered the parlor in his great melton coat, the cape thrown over one shoulder, a slouch hat covering his long, flowing hair, laughing and having his usual convivial exchanges with friends while she and Eunice provided refreshments? How could someone larger than life be brought down so fast?

"Is there no improvement?"

"No, Mrs. Stowe, I don't see any, but you never know. I've had patients who came back—sometimes only for an hour or so, but they talked away and sometimes they recovered."

Harriet bends to stroke her brother's forehead and senses Eunice stiffening. She steps back, quick to cede position. Eunice lifts her husband's head and begins briskly plumping up his pillows.

"Don't shake him, Mrs. Beecher," warns the nurse. "It's not good."

"I'm *not* shaking him."

Harriet hears the chanting outside first. Moving swiftly to the window, she opens it before Eunice can object.

> Beecher, Beecher is my name—
> Beecher till I die!
> I never kissed Mis' Tilton—
> I never told a lie!

Eunice turns from the bed and put her hands to her ears. "Close that window," she demands and whirls on the nurse. "Call the police, do you hear? I want that scum outside removed! Now, do you hear? Now!"

The nurse pales, and Harriet can see the indignation—and then the uncertainty—in her eyes as she hurries from the room, eager to be gone as fast as possible. Eunice rushes out after her, running downstairs, her hands still over her ears. Harriet sees her pause only briefly at the polished hardwood telephone box that hangs in the hall. She can imagine the berating the nurse will get on the ground floor for not having used Mr. Bell's telephone to call the police, but Eunice, clearly, is not interested in making the call herself. Harriet's pity for her sister-in-law is dissipating rapidly.

Harriet slams the window shut and presses her forehead against the glass. She is having a hard time drawing a deep breath, but not because of that prancing fool in blackface. The angry yell spiraling up from the street, that was Isabella. She knows her sister's voice.

She moves to the side of her brother's bed and sinks to her knees. Will she have to protect him against yet another assault? Just remembering him up on that stand in the Brooklyn courthouse, facing mocking lawyers and treacherous friends—it is too much. Bella had no judgment then, and certainly would have none now. What did she hope to accomplish by coming to Brooklyn Heights? She had to be here to put herself somehow at the center of Henry's dying, that's what she was about. She was trying once again to force herself to center stage.

Henry moans, and his eyelids seem to flutter. Harriet catches her breath. Will he open his eyes? Look at me just once more, she pleads silently. But his eyes remain closed.

Harriet stands up and pulls a chair close to the bed, still hearing in her head the coarse chant from the sidewalk. There is no way to erase what the trial did to Henry's life. He has come through it and lived honorably, but the press will be delighted to drag the details out again. There will be no stopping them, of that, she is sure.

Harriet takes a folded washcloth from the bedstand, moistens it with water from a small earthenware pitcher, and presses it to Henry's cracked lips. It is perhaps a futile gesture, but she has to do something. How much care is he getting from the nurse, she wonders. Or, more to the point, from Eunice.

A memory flashes: Bella turning to her on one occasion when Eunice's disapproving presence had flattened out a family evening and whispering, "Save us from the sourpuss." Harriet had giggled into her napkin, delighted with her sister's mischievous streak. The Bella she remembers from those years would certainly have had something pithy to say about Eunice already planning her wardrobe for the funeral.

But not anymore. Bella's sense of mischief turned destructive long ago, and what she is most capable of now is something melodramatic and harmful. Had Calvin been right? Harriet cannot forget his comment about Bella's shocking behavior before the trial. "Hattie, don't expect anything from Bella. Separate blood breeds separate loyalties," he had said.

"Are you implying we are not true sisters?" she'd demanded.

"You have different mothers. I'm saying that means different natures." He had looked tired, as if unwilling to go another round with his strong-willed wife.

"That's absurd. She's a Beecher, and Beechers stand together."

"Well said. But it isn't happening."

He was right, of course. But why then, as she sits next to Henry's shrouded, still form, bracing for his imminent death, does the sound of her sister's voice almost move her to tears?

Deep in memory, something else stirs, the sound of another angry, spiraling wail. She closes her eyes and grabs again at the flailing fists of thirteen-year-old Bella, trying to hold her close. Poor child, her mother gone. The beautiful, melancholic stepmother who cared not a fig for her stepchildren, but whose death had left Bella bereft. It was strange to soothe her little sister that day, strange to feel again a distant mourning for her own lost mother, and only detachment for the loss of this one.

"Hattie, help me. I'm trying to accept God's will, but I can't!"

"You don't have to." Harriet's voice caught.

"No, no, Papa says I grieve too much and it is a sin."

"He's wrong."

Bella's eyes widened at this apostasy. "But he never is," she whispered.

"Bella." Harriet cupped her sister's chin in her hands and looked her straight in the eye. Even as she spoke she felt her recklessness. Who was she, at twenty-four, to challenge the orthodoxy of her father? But it was what she and Henry talked about, somewhat guardedly, to be sure, for they did not want to hurt or outrage Lyman Beecher. Yet was his vision of a vengeful God the only one in this day and age?

"God will forgive you. Grieving is not a sin," she said.

How startling to realize, all these years later, why her eyes are indeed filling with tears. The look of gratitude on Bella's young face, the sense of having lifted a stone from that sister's heart, had forged a bond of love. Harriet had thought it would last for eternity.

⚜ CHAPTER TWO ⚜

March 7, 1887, 8:00 a.m.

"Hello up there!"

The voice Isabella hears from the street is relaxed, deep, confident; all she can hope for now is that the owner of that voice—and the rest of the bowler hats—did not recognize her when she shook her fist and yelled out the window.

"Hello!" comes the yell again.

A laugh, then a chuckle. "You think you'll coax her back for a friendly chat?" says a voice. "Good luck, fella."

She can hear other voices now, murmuring in unison from a distance. A prayer vigil for Henry must be under way on Orange Street. She tries to envision the church, hazily remembering a sprawling structure surrounding a placid courtyard. But the inside she remembers quite well. Shaped like an elongated bowl, with tiers of red-cushioned seats rising in a gentle curve almost to the elaborately decorated ceiling, it was richly warmed with ornate stained-glass windows. One could not be in it without feeling a sense of grandeur, especially when it pulsated with Henry's presence. She had told Henry once that it reminded her of a theater, and he was pleased. Was it still as imposing a place? She hasn't been inside since Lyman Beecher's funeral. But the event most vividly etched in her mind took place there in 1858—when Henry astounded his parishioners by auctioning off a young slave girl.

*　　*　　*

Henry was taking his usual sauntering stroll home from Plymouth Church late one Saturday afternoon that spring, surrounded by the usual crowd of adoring parishioners, neighbors, and tradespeople eager for his attention. Isabella watched from the front door of his house on Hicks Street as he came up the block, his arm draped over the shoulders of an elderly man with a cane, listening intently as the man talked. A health problem, perhaps? Whatever it might be, Henry gave the man his undivided attention and a few comforting words before turning to answer an eager question from a local shopkeeper. His laughter boomed out, carrying down the block to some children jumping rope, who stopped and ran toward him, knowing he always carried candies for them in his pocket. He paused at the foot of the stairs to his home, continuing his conversations, asking questions: How is your mother doing, Mrs. Turnbull? Did she get the blankets sent over from the church? He grasped a neighbor's hand in warm welcome, laughed at a joke, all the while lounging against the railing as if he had all the time in the world; as if there was nothing he wanted to do more than stand there and talk the evening away. He seemed as hungry for those crowded around him as they were for him.

"Father makes people feel important," a voice said from behind Isabella. She turned to see young Harry, the eldest son of Henry's nine children, looking proud and solemn. Behind him a little sister giggled; the boy flushed and walked away.

Indeed, Henry was a magnet for all. His speeches and editorials in *The Independent* were pored over by clergymen everywhere looking for guidance in the debate over slavery. Members of Congress sought his counsel; brokers on Wall Street came, hats in hand, for his moral advice. No one knit together emotion, religion, and politics better than Henry. It was hardly surprising that Horace Greeley was urging him to run for Congress. Her brother was a giant of a man, Isabella told herself—as much now in the limelight as Harriet. Her heart was full as he bounded up the steps, gave her a hug, and announced to her and their waiting brothers and sisters why he had insisted they come this particular weekend.

"Prepare to be amazed," he said, his handsome face lit with excitement. "I am holding an auction tomorrow—and I am going to make history!"

He laid out the details as they all sat down to dinner. A young mulatto girl would be dressed in white and brought to the podium to stand next to him. It would be a surprise—no one in the congregation would know what was about to happen until he declared she was up for "sale" to the highest bidder.

"You'll be criticized for cheapening your ministry with theatrics," warned their older brother Edward. All turned dutifully in his direction. It was Edward's job in the family to be cautious.

"There's reason to be careful, Henry. Some in your congregation think you're way too radical on slavery already," Tom said. His tone was more relaxed than Edward's, but even though he was the least aggressive of the Beecher brothers, his opinion held weight. Frowns passed around the table, coupled with worried looks.

"Nonsense. There's more danger in being *too* careful," Harriet said. Her voice had the extra edge of crisp authority she used to win family arguments.

"Exactly. Who cares if some of them don't like it?" Henry stabbed at the brisket on the plate before him, not once but twice, with the vigor of a man of considerable appetite. "We need to dramatize slavery. We need to make people know what it means to *sell* a human being. A child, a wife. Then we need to make them feel what it is like to *buy*—to wave money and win a piece of flesh."

"Why from the pulpit? Why not just write an editorial?" protested Edward.

"Not enough," Henry said, with a dismissive wave of his fork. "I guarantee you, this will bring them to their feet! Why? Because they will move from understanding the brutal power of buying to the shame of knowing what it means to *debase the soul*. It *must* be from the pulpit. Otherwise it means nothing. Right, Hattie?" He turned to Harriet, eyes expectant.

"Absolutely," she said.

"You see?" Henry smiled widely, taking them all in with his gaze.

"I have an idea," Isabella said, speaking rapidly so the others would take heed. Even though an adult, she was still one of the youngest and least significant of the Beecher clan, and her opinion was rarely sought by her older brothers and sisters. "Her hair—could it be bound up when she mounts the podium? And then released?"

Henry raised an eyebrow and smiled again in appreciation. "Very good, Bella—from constraint to freedom, I like that. You have a dramatic touch, little sister."

She beamed her pleasure at his praise.

The next morning Henry emerged from the vestry and climbed the steps to the podium with a deliberate, unhurried pace, ignoring the intricately carved chair placed there for him. He looked somewhat unkempt, artless. His pants hung loose on his frame, and his long hair curled over his collar. His face was smooth. He had often said a beard would make him look like other men, and that would never do. He paused, staring out at the packed church, all there waiting for his usual sermon. He turned toward the vestry door and clapped his hands. It opened. A slender mulatto girl dressed in a flowing white gown walked slowly up the stairs and took her place by his side.

"This child is from Virginia," Henry said. "You may wonder why she is here on this podium with me. Well, her white father wants to sell her."

The heads of those in the congregation on the edge of dozing jerked up. People began stirring in their seats, whispering to one another.

"Consider, my friends. For what purposes does he want to sell her, do you think?"

For a long moment, as the logical answer to this question sank in, Henry stood still, surveying his congregation. Then he clapped his hands. "So—we will do it for him!" he announced.

People exchanged puzzled glances.

Henry put his hand on the girl's shoulder. "Ladies and gentlemen, *what am I bid?*"

Was he joking? Men cleared their throats. One woman pulled out a handkerchief and wiped her eyes.

"This is real," Henry said. *"How much?* Will you allow this woman to go back to meet the fate preordained if her father sells her? If not, who bids? Who bids *to buy her freedom?"*

A prominent lawyer not known for his generosity stood and held up his wallet. "I do," he yelled. His wife stood next. She hesitated, then unfastened a gold brooch from her bosom and held it aloft.

It took only that for a fever to stir the crowd. Women, watching the girl—little more than a child—began to cry. Men pulled banknotes from their wallets, and some even pulled out pocket watches to toss into the collection baskets now hurriedly being passed around. Isabella herself felt like crying as she unfastened the tiny gold locket she wore around her neck and threw it into the basket. She knew it was the right thing to do, the right sacrifice to make. She then clasped the hands of her daughters, one on each side of her, and pulled them close. Mary was wiggling too much, her usual response to sitting still in church. But Alice was properly disciplined, although little Edward, clutched tightly in his sister's arms, had begun to whimper. But how glad she was the girls could witness this. Her constant worry was the character development of her children, and no lesson of generosity could be more eloquently taught.

Later, John Hooker called Henry's performance one of the greatest bits of theater he had ever seen. Isabella was annoyed with him; his amused tone had made Henry's gesture somehow smaller.

Through the next amazing half hour, the young girl stood still, her eyes cast down. Finally, with money and jewelry bulging from the collection baskets, Henry announced the girl's freedom was won. He held a heavy chain of shackles over his head. "Do you all know what this is?" he shouted. "You do, don't you?"

Harriet, sitting in the aisle ahead, turned to Isabella and smiled. She is remembering too, Isabella thought: the vessel filled with shackled slaves on the Cincinnati dock. For months after that day, Isabella had dreamed about the little girl trying to raise her arm. Had she been trying to wave back to the ten-year-old on the dock?

What had happened to her? In Isabella's dream, she was on that boat too, wincing into the sun, her arms hurting from the weight of the iron that seemed to tug her to the deck. To whom was she bound? She tried to see, but her vision was always foggy.

Henry threw the chain to the floor, causing Isabella to jump. "This is what we say about slavery!" he shouted again.

At that moment the girl lifted her eyes and smiled at the crowd, then reached up and released her hair. The auction was over.

There was still sobbing in the room, but Henry broke the spell by descending onto the floor to meet his audience, shaking hands, touching shoulders, murmuring, listening intently. The members of his congregation could not seem to get close enough to him. A young woman with violet eyes and a boater hat thrust forward, touching his lapel, saying something that made him throw his head back, hair flying, laughing heartily.

"We won't hear any more about Henry sending rifles to Kansas, will we?" It was a man's voice, pitched low. He was standing in the aisle ahead of Isabella, talking to a shorter version of himself, a man wearing heavy gray gloves—two frowning churchgoers who disapproved of their charismatic pastor, considering him an intemperate abolitionist. Shipping guns off to Northern radicals had been one of Henry's more exuberantly rash exploits in the last year, and the rumblings were only now quieting down.

"Don't think so," the second man said, his voice pitched even lower. "Saving pretty young slaves is much more palatable than being dubbed the Church of the Holy Rifles. Don't think the board liked that."

Isabella brushed past them, pretending not to have heard, sweeping past the baptismal font with her son in her arms, the girls rushing to keep up. She hated the cynicism in their voices. Henry, staging this event to blunt criticism of his political beliefs? Ridiculous.

From the corner of her eye, she saw Eunice moving toward Henry, plucking at her shawl with nervous fingers. If she was trying to get within her husband's range of vision, she was having little success.

Suddenly Harriet thrust herself forward, taking her sister-in-law's arm with one hand and grabbing the shoulder of her brother with the other. "Henry, Eunice and I think your sermon was splendid," she said, turning him away from the woman with the violet eyes. "Isn't that right, Eunice?"

Isabella couldn't remember how Eunice responded, all she could remember was the firmness of Harriet's tone. But she did recall turning her head and seeing Calvin Stowe begin to chat with the woman in the boater. She had removed her hat, releasing a cascade of titian curls, and Harriet's husband had a dazzled look about him as they exchanged pleasantries. He said later that she was a vapid child but eager to find God, and therefore redeemable.

"Hello up there! Won't you *please* come to the window?"

The voice from the sidewalk has taken on a lazy, teasing tone. Isabella doesn't like the idea of being seen as too timid to show her face, but there is no dignity standing in one's nightshift in front of strangers. She dresses quickly and moves back to the window, finally summoning the courage to look out.

Below her stands a tall man in a shiny black suit, his angular, beardless face tipped up. He catches sight of her and takes off his bowler, sweeping it before him in a mock bow. Then he straightens and grins.

"Hello, Mrs. Hooker. Remember me? Brady Puckett, down here. *Brooklyn Eagle.* Nice to see you again. Although under such sad circumstances."

Harriet waits until the flustered nurse is back at her station before leaving her brother's room. A lone policeman has shown up and talked to the crowd outside, the nurse reports. But he arrested no one, even though Mrs. Beecher demanded that he do so. Then he left and things were quiet again. But there is tension at the breakfast table, she says, and the maidservant named Anna has spilled the tea and Mrs. Beecher is very cross.

"Anna isn't a servant, she's my friend," Harriet says, annoyed.

"She came with me." Knowing Eunice, it was probably unfair to Anna Smith to have brought her to this house, but Anna had insisted. And, if truth be told, there was no sturdier friend to have by her side at this time than the woman who had helped raise her pack of unruly children. Anna was here to help, and she mustn't be treated like one of the Beecher servants.

"Yes, ma'am, not my business." The nurse manages to put a little crispness back in her voice, reminding herself she is beholden to no one here and they need her to tend to Reverend Beecher. She is not a servant either.

Harriet stops in the hallway to collect herself. She is exhausted yet unable to sleep as Henry's life slips away, unable to defuse the tensions of this strange house. Every waking moment seems a repetition of last year's lonely vigil for Calvin. The children worry about her, she knows. They think a year is long enough to mourn. But she wants to turn to him, to ask for advice, to apologize for every sharp word from her lips, every doubt. Not of love, never of love, but still . . . At another time, in another place, she would have talked this over with Bella. Now all she feels is a yearning to be back at Nook Farm, that dear community of friends, safe inside her house. Even though it is too dark and too filled with memories, there she can set up her easel and pull out her paint box. There she can put brush to canvas and enter another world.

She closes her eyes, seeing herself opening the box and picking up the tiny seashells stored inside. She will fill each one with a different color of paint and line them up again, her spirits lifted by the colors. It used to be just a pastime, a respite from writing, but now painting occupies much of her time. Spring is coming, and soon the lilies will be blooming and she will paint flowers once more.

Her Hartford home is too quiet now. When there, she can hear every creak as the house bends from the wind, every tick of the clock. Sometimes she hears her dead husband's step outside the parlor door. She freezes then, paintbrush in hand, unsure whether to turn around. Can the dead really visit the living? Such a silly thought; she knows better. What draws people to believe in such nonsense is beyond her. She will finally turn around and see nothing, and be left feeling only intensified hollowness.

"He's dead, and there's no coming back," her sister Mary said when Harriet shared this feeling with her. That put her head on straight again.

But who can she talk to now about Isabella's presence?

She will talk to Anna. Anna will have sensible advice.

The dark, narrow hall smells of illness, of medicines, bed linens, and fear. But it isn't Henry's dying that permeates this place, it is the sour smell of disappointment. Never once has she heard her much-traveled brother speak yearningly of home. Eunice is right; home has been Plymouth Church. That's where he caught the winds of change and became the truest spokesman for a kind and compassionate God. Isabella almost managed to rob him of that too. So his marriage is not a haven, his marital home not a comfort. But then neither were the homes in which they both grew up.

Harriet takes a firm grip on the balustrade and starts walking down. If she holds her breath and listens, she can hear again the whooping and hollering of her childhood, even remember the details of the nightly arguments around the dinner table at Walnut Hills after their move to Cincinnati, especially the challenge and anxiety of chewing one's food as quickly as possible while listening for a place to plunge into the conversation. Always there was Father at the end of the table, his head so large and kingly, his eyes so steady and stern, watching his throng of children fight for their legacy as Beechers. They had all struggled for his approval, but perhaps Henry had struggled the most.

"So, Son," Lyman said at the dinner table in 1834, the night Henry returned home to Cincinnati from Amherst, finally, after much play and lack of attention to his studies, with a college degree. "I await news of your plans. I assume you have them, of course?"

"A little rest at first, I suppose," Henry replied, flashing a grin. "For the brain, you know? Studying is quite taxing."

"Men of character don't waste time before pursuing their duties," Lyman replied with a frown. "Give us some news from the East. Is there much talk about colonization?"

"Colonization? Well, the idea of it is bandied back and forth, but the real topic of gossip in Boston now is pantaloons." Henry was clearly trying to keep a straight face.

"Pantaloons?"

"It's a sort of female undergarment—for women who want to dress like men, if you will."

"Undergarment?"

"Yes, sir." Henry's face was getting red.

The whole table fell silent as Lyman let his fork clatter to the plate. "I am astonished that such a garment would be a preferred topic over colonization," he said in the even tone that at one time or another had set every Beecher child's heart aflutter.

"What is colonization?" Isabella demanded. She was twelve at the time and hated being left out of dinner table conversation.

Father cleared his throat and turned to her, signaling an impromptu lesson for his youngest daughter. "The idea is to send slaves to form colonies in Africa. It is a possible answer to the slavery question; a quite sensible one, in my opinion."

"The Athenian Society debated colonization versus emancipation last month, Father," said Henry, wearing the pleased look of weighing in on the family conversation with a little more seriousness than usual.

"And what position did my son the debater take?"

This time it was Henry clearing his throat. "I argued that enforced colonization was no better than enforced slavery," he said.

"And which side won the debate?"

"The other side," Henry said with a shrug.

"For good reason," Father countered.

"Well, but I wasn't alone. I mean, I hear some of your students would argue the same way, Father."

Silence again fell over the table. Lyman's eyes widened, and Harriet wanted to shrink to the size of a pea on her plate. So Henry already knew what was happening at Lane Seminary. The trustees of Father's school had forbidden any talk of abolition among the seminarians, for fear of losing the financial backing of those in sympathy with the slave trade. The students were shocked when Lyman Beecher, worried that his school might go bankrupt, refused to support them. There was heated talk of abandoning Lane Seminary in protest.

"You would stab me with that?" Lyman pulled himself straight. "I oppose slavery and you know it. I would hope my son would be intelligent enough to realize evil cannot be expurgated by brute force and rude challenge. Have you learned nothing? We need *patience.*"

"Why?" Isabella suddenly demanded, banging her spoon on her plate for attention. Such a pretty little thing, with her dark, glossy hair and delicate features. She was Father's pet in those days and did not fear his sternness. "Why can't we shout and scream when bad things happen? I think Henry's right."

"Because it defeats the purpose," Father replied, then fixed his attention back on Henry. "Do you understand, Son?"

Henry slid down deep in his chair, avoiding his father's eyes. "It was just a debate," he said, casting a glance at Harriet. She was his usual champion, the one who could help bolster his courage. But this time she held back. Although he had prevailed, Father looked suddenly quite fragile, offering a swift glimpse of vulnerability that frightened her.

Harriet reaches the first-floor hall, remembering Henry's depression after that dinner. "He sees through me every time," he had said later that night as they talked alone. "I'm not sure of anything I think. Why didn't you support me?"

She tried to tell him how unbearable it was to think of Father as wrong or weak, and how important it was not to hurt him when he was under attack. She consoled her brother, praised him, told him what a fine man he was. And when Henry went off to his room, he was cheered. His swagger was back.

When Father's best students did indeed abandon him, in 1836, Henry was ready. He jeered at them, said they were crazy to risk their careers, and called them "a little muddy stream of vinegar, trickling down to Oberlin." That impressed Father.

"He might have the makings of a preacher after all," Lyman said to Harriet.

She held on to that accolade, giving it to Henry months later—when she thought he needed it, not before.

And yet, how strangely he responded—or so it seemed to her at the time.

"I'm delighted," he said slowly. "But Father may not stay so approving."

"Why not?"

"Hattie, let's be honest. Do you believe his creed of hellfire and damnation?"

"No," she responded. She had known this in her heart for years.

They looked at each other.

"Nor do I," he finally said.

This was not something Henry could admit to just anybody; only his most trusted sister would understand. He was not the bravest of young men, not ready for so daunting a move as openly defying his father.

But he had a plan.

"Get the young to love me," he wrote in a scratchy, urgent hand upon beginning his hardscrabble days as a preacher in Lawrenceburgh, Indiana. His sermons must touch the people, not spout dreary orthodoxy; that was the way to do it. Thank God for Eunice, who gave him the steady guidance that tamed his scattered message and kept it consistent. More than once, he declared to whoever was listening that he was lucky to have married her. At night when he was low and she had spent the day hauling wood and water to their two rooms above a livery stable, she would reassure him and bolster his spirits. He didn't mention to anyone his discomfort when, by late evening, her support would turn to a fretful complaint that he didn't spend enough time with her.

Henry was perfectly in tune with a changing world, and his power kept growing. He knew how to embrace the many pleasures and luxuries of modern life without being pained by the burrs of his Calvinist upbringing. He thrilled to the joys of the senses, be they the taste of savory food, the scent of flowers, or the shivery pleasure of seeing the rapt expressions of people drinking in his words. He needed to touch. If he was not gesticulating, mesmerizing an audience, he was reaching out with surprisingly soft fingers to touch a cheek, caress a hand, rub a shoulder.

From the pulpit, he reached out to the strivers of the world who filled his pews because he preached that God hated the sin but loved the sinner, with emphasis on the latter. To be loved was to be popular; to be popular—especially with the women of his congregation—was to be powerful.

Even back then, Harriet sensed that Henry represented the future. She suspected early on that eventually she and her brother would break the chains that held them to their father's religious and political views. They only needed the right moment to burst free—and that moment came in 1850, with passage of the Fugitive Slave Act. *That* jolted Northerners awake. There was no looking the other way anymore, no more uneasy mumblings about property rights. Not in the face of a law that allowed any Southern slaveowner to lay hands on any colored man or woman—be they free or escaped slave—on the street of any Northern town and haul them away, claiming the law of the United States of America gave them the right to snatch back these people as property.

Henry jumped on his horse when he heard the news and rode all night from Brooklyn to join his sister in Brunswick, Maine. He arrived at dawn, bedraggled, with bloodshot eyes. For hours the two of them paced and talked and gave vent to their fury, and from their shared anger came a vow: They would both fight for abolition with the tools they had. She had the power of the pen. Years of writing stories, essays, books, anything that would provide money for her family, had honed her skills and her confidence. She would turn these skills now to a greater good. Yes, she would write, he would preach; together they would change their world.

"If we Beechers can't do it, *who can?*" Henry cried.

Harriet steadies herself as she stands in the hall, struck suddenly with the fullness of what she is about to lose. She is about to be left without the one person who shared the most galvanizing moment of her life, the moment when she knew in her heart that not only *could* she do her part to change history but she *would*.

She sees Anna Smith's plump body bent over the hearth in the parlor, arranging a vast array of flowers, and notes that began to arrive before the sun rose. Neighbors and parishioners were trudging up the brownstone steps all day yesterday with offerings of food, flowers, and well-meant solace. None of the Beecher servants seems to know what to do with the sudden largesse, and cooked shanks of lamb have turned cold sitting in pots on the parlor carpet while bouquets of lilies lie crushed under baskets of bread. Anna has taken over, the way she did years ago to bring order to the chaotic Stowe family. Now she looks up at Harriet, her pale, matronly face going from cranky to concerned in an instant.

Harriet knows she is about to get a lecture on looking far too tired and in need of rest. "Isabella is here," she says quickly.

Diverted, Anna's hand goes to her heart. "Good Lord," she whispers.

"Be careful not to say a word to Eunice."

"I wouldn't dream of it. What are you going to do?"

"I don't know. It depends on what she does. What do you think?"

Anna clasps her arms together and opens her mouth, but nothing comes out. They stare at each other.

"Well, there's not much to do until she makes a move," Anna finally says.

"I could stand here and rail on about my crazy sister, but it doesn't do me much good, does it?"

"She never shirked," Anna says suddenly.

"What do you mean?"

"The time with the ear."

Harriet nods, patting her friend's shoulder and quickly moving down the hall to the dining room, not wanting to let on what Anna's words have unleashed.

Yes, 1852. The furor over *Uncle Tom's Cabin* had astonished her. Tens of thousands praised her name and bought her book, but she had never anticipated the level of fury that came from the South. Threats, epithets, hysteria. Might some crazy person hurt her or the children? Calvin soothed her fears. He made a special trip home from Cincinnati to share in the excitement, walking around in his favorite old ratty sweater with a stunned, delighted expression on his face. He told all who came by, quite truly, that he had predicted his wife's literary success all along. There had been spots of doubt along the way, but as a loyal husband, he didn't dwell on those. Neighbors and friends were coming and going, and the post each day brought heaps of mail and congratulatory gifts. Harriet could hardly think, let alone deal with such a deluge.

All this made the younger children harder to control than ever, which drove Harriet to distraction. She could not concentrate; she was not a maternal person, and that was the fact of it. The little ones baffled her half the time. Give them what they wanted, and they were sure to want something else. Spank one and praise another, and she would be doing the opposite in an hour, wondering how other mothers managed their children. Her words, praising and scolding, seemed to roll off them like water.

And then she opened the door and saw Isabella waiting on the steps, her own two girls, both of whom looked a little nonplussed when they heard the clamorous shouting of their cousins, in tow.

"Bella?" she said, astonished. Here was her youngest sister, the color high on her comely face, looking as delighted as she had as a child on Christmas morning.

"I heard you were falling into chaos, Hattie dear," Isabella said, clearly pleased with herself. "Actually, this is wonderful—I get to be the big sister for a change."

Well, there was no point in pretending she didn't need help. "I gladly give you the job," Harriet said gratefully.

Isabella barely had her gloves off before she spotted the baby on the hearth, happily stuffing his mouth with coal dust. She ran to scoop him up just as one of the twins mischievously tipped over the slop jar and pretended to wash her apron in it. Anna scolded the girl and hurried to fill a tub while Isabella peeled off the baby's clothes.

That done, Isabella hoisted the wailing child into the tub and began scrubbing him with a bar of tallow soap. She seemed not to notice the water seeping up her sleeves, staining her silk shirtwaist.

"Bella, your dress," Harriet said weakly.

"Oh, fiddlesticks, it will wash. Go deal with whatever you were doing; Anna and I will take care of this."

Harriet retreated to the kitchen and seated herself at the table. Finally, she could make some headway on the stacks of mail and packages. She began opening a small box on top of the pile. Through the door she saw Isabella lifting the newly scrubbed baby from his bath as she removed the lid of the box. Looking down, she let out a sharp cry.

Isabella and Anna rushed to the kitchen, Isabella holding the naked child in her arms. An inquisitive Mary clamored loudly to see, but Isabella blocked her daughter's path.

"What happened?" Isabella said at the doorway.

Harriet held the lid in one hand and sat frozen, staring at the contents of the box. She looked up, barely registering her sister's presence.

"I can't believe this," she said in a bewildered tone. "Tell me I'm wrong."

Isabella handed the baby to Anna and stepped forward. "What's in the box, Hattie?" she asked gently.

Harriet lifted it up, and Isabella looked inside. The three women stared at something dark and small resting in carefully folded paper. It looked like a piece of dried fruit. A fig, perhaps. A strange thing to send.

Then Isabella gasped. "Oh, this is despicable."

"So you see what I see. I suppose I'd better get used to being hated." Harriet was looking less shaken now, and her voice had lost its bewilderment. "Some poor soul paid a high price."

It was not a fig. It was a dried-up, black human ear. A slave's ear.

Harriet thrust her hand into the box and picked the thing up between two fingers. With a snort of disgust, she stood and threw it into the cookstove.

"No, Hattie, don't do that." Isabella jumped up immediately, grabbed a pair of tongs, and fished it out.

"Why not?" demanded Harriet.

"Because you want to keep it. Every time you look at it you'll remember why you wrote your book."

"That's ghoulish. It doesn't do the poor person who had it hacked off any good, and what if this is a signal? What if the person who sent this is capable of coming here, of doing something violent to me or my family? What if—"

"Hattie, stop and think. You're doing what they hope you will do."

Harriet heard the confidence in Isabella's voice and steadied herself, taking a deep breath. She could not bear looking at the awful thing, but Bella might be right; maybe her reaction was just what the sender wanted. Then the effort to terrorize her would have worked.

Harriet pushed a strand of hair from her forehead as she reached forward, took the tongs from her sister, and carefully deposited the ear back in the box. It wasn't easy to defer to her younger, headstrong sister, but this time it seemed warranted.

The three of them stared at the ear.

"It's a talisman, then," Harriet said.

"But not an ominous one," Isabella replied. "The time will come to throw it in the fire, but not while it makes you afraid."

Harriet reaches her brother's kitchen, feeling weary and drained. Why is her brain skittering around so, dropping her back in the past? The day has begun too harshly; she does need her tea and toast.

❧ CHAPTER THREE ❦

March 7, 1887, 9:00 a.m.

"BEG PARDON, MA'AM, but the nurse has quit."

The cook faces Eunice in the kitchen, her face gray with the solemnity of her announcement. "She just announced it on the stairway, and she's getting her coat now, and she wants payment."

Eunice's hand trembles slightly as she lifts a tea tray from the shelf, a tray impeccably polished. "She cannot do that," she says.

The cook looks even paler. "I'll convey that, ma'am." She disappears to the hallway.

"Don't you agree?" Eunice's voice has an edge as she turns to Harriet.

Harriet stirs her tea slowly, not ready for a test of wills between Eunice and the nurse. She does not feel ready for *anything* at this moment that requires weighing right and wrong and guiding a decision. She wants to drink her tea, to feel the warmth and comfort of the brew, unentangled by complications.

"I doubt if you could stop her," she says. "Could she have been unnerved by that strutting caricature out on the sidewalk?"

"She's unnerved by me," Eunice replies. "That cartoon character isn't new. Uncle Toms are everywhere."

Harriet keeps her gaze on the teacup, carefully spooning out a dollop of sugar from the sugar bowl on the tray. She needs to make allowances for Eunice's distraught state, so she will ignore this casual barb.

A clattering of footsteps and loud voices in the hall results in the sudden appearance of the nurse at the kitchen door, with the agitated cook immediately behind her.

"I am not waiting for my wages," the nurse announces. "I've earned my pay and I want it now."

"Well, I cannot give it to you," Eunice says. She stands braced against the stove, arms folded. This problem with restive servants is getting worse. Her own cook complains to her face that the immense old stove swallows coal by the bucket, as if that excuses her from getting it fired up early enough on cold mornings. The working classes don't know their place anymore, and her response will be firm. She may be invisible to the rest of her indifferent world but not to her servants.

It isn't as devastating as it once was. People searching for Henry have been looking past her for years. She is "the preacher's wife," and her role is to be strong and supportive and to cause no trouble, raise no controversy. If she has anything to say, few bother to listen. If she wears too fine a silk dress to church, she is extravagant; if she makes do with plain muslin, she is penurious. "I lost my husband when we came to Brooklyn," she once wrote an old friend, then worried that someone else would see the letter and there would be talk. She learned early it was not seemly to make such protests; in fact it wasn't seemly to have close friends; church members might see that as playing favorites.

The process of becoming invisible had been relatively painless. She quickly realized that church suppers required quiet industry, not much more. And receptions required polite smiles. She learned that no one wants to see the tears of the minister's wife who has lost a baby; that only reminds them of God's failure to save their own lost children. Not good at making common ground for mourning, Eunice was adept at catching the correct pitch of the tuning fork.

None of this saved her, of course, when the trial came along.

Now, twelve years later, she has her own rules and her own pleasures. Once in a while she pulls out her mother's silver pieces from their velvet bags and polishes them while sitting in the parlor, holding each fork and teapot up to the sun when she is done, then returning them to their resting places. Henry used to ask her to use them for receptions, but she resisted by agreeing and then doing nothing. Some things are to be kept for herself.

"My husband is dying. This is obviously a grave moment in this household, and the money which you are owed is not immediately available," she says.

"When will I get it?" The nurse's chin thrusts forward in somewhat wobbly fashion.

"More to the point, why? You exhibit an appalling lack of duty to leave my husband on his deathbed, and I see no reason why—putting aside the money—I should even give you a reference."

"Mrs. Beecher, I wouldn't be the first from this household who walked away without a reference from you. But I'm not nearly as beholden as most of the others, because people who are sick need nurses, and I've got two jobs to go to right now. You might treat the people who help you better."

Eunice freezes. The cook turns her face away.

Harriet stands and says in a mild voice, "I beg your pardon, but I don't know your name. Miss ———?"

"Sara Kelly. Mrs."

"Mrs. Kelly, come with me." Harriet reaches for her hand and moves toward the door. Startled, the nurse follows. Without another word Harriet leads her through the mud-colored entrance hall, a space that no amount of gaslight can enliven, and up the stairs. Still holding the woman's hand, she stops at the door to Henry's bedroom and pushes it open. His breathing is barely audible.

"This is a man in need of care," she says. "I'm sure you've seen many sickrooms, and there must be many grateful families who have benefited from your nurture and help."

"I'm a good nurse, ma'am. Do my best."

"I'm sure of that." Harriet gazes at her brother's still form. "It must be hard for you to imagine him as the vital man he was but a few days ago. Have you ever heard the Reverend Beecher preach?"

"No, ma'am. I'm Catholic." Mrs. Kelly's voice holds an edge of defiance.

"Of course. But forgive me, it's a pity you never heard him. He can pull every man, woman, and child in his church from their seats and make their hearts soar. I doubt if anyone fortunate enough to have had the opportunity will forget the experience of hearing him preach his gospel of love and acceptance."

"I've nothing against the Congregationalists," says Mrs. Kelly, stepping uncomfortably from one foot to another.

"We bend our knees before the same God," Harriet says, stepping farther into the room, touching Mrs. Kelly on the shoulder, drawing her forward. "Look at him," she says.

They stand in silence for a few seconds.

"My brother won't live long," Harriet says in a matter-of-fact tone. "Death may not come today or tomorrow, but it is coming. He needs the care of someone who will offer compassion and comfort, even under trying circumstances." She pauses, draws a breath, and faces the other woman fully. "If it were you lying there, Mrs. Kelly, I can assure you, my brother would take care of you."

Mrs. Kelly lifts a hand and wipes her eyes. "I know he's a good man, Mrs. Stowe."

"You aren't really going to desert him, are you?"

A deep sigh. "No, ma'am. I'm a nurse, and I'll stay at my post. It's just that—"

Harriet interrupts, squeezing her shoulder. She cannot let Mrs. Kelly elaborate on her complaints or she will appear to be complicit in vilifying Eunice. "I understand," she says. "And I'll make sure you get your money."

Mrs. Kelly slowly pulls off her coat, folds it neatly, and puts it on a stool next to the highboy. "I'll be needing some fresh linens for his bed this afternoon," she says in a bright, businesslike voice.

"I'll make sure you have them."

Harriet walks downstairs and into a silent kitchen. Eunice is still standing next to the oven, arms folded, as if to ward off a blow.

"Mrs. Kelly has decided to stay," Harriet says, sitting down at the table.

Eunice pauses only a second before turning to the cook. "Please get Mrs. Stowe some fresh tea," she says. "I have errands to run."

"Yes, ma'am." The cook retreats, her averted face hiding her expression. It wouldn't be long before the nurse's defiant speech was spread throughout the house. There was nothing to be done about it; Eunice reaped what she sowed.

Isabella stares down at the man on the sidewalk named Brady Puckett. She does recognize him. The intervening years have not changed the sharp jaw or the sardonic smile, although his hair is thinning and his bowler hat seems a little too big when he puts it back on. How could she forget him? He saved her reputation the night she lost her keynote speech at the National Woman Suffrage Association's convention in 1871.

She had been frantic that night, her self-confidence evaporating quickly as she searched for the speech, increasingly convinced the blithely heedless, ignorant woman she had remained for too long had reemerged. She was about to be unmasked.

At this moment? With her star rising in the women's movement? She could hardly breathe. There were many who were jealous of her high standing with Susan Anthony, and they would be quick to criticize. She was only favored because she was a trophy Beecher, people whispered; Susan couldn't snag Harriet for the cause, so she settled for Isabella. They scoffed at her as a latecomer.

It had taken a great deal of hard work to overcome those claims of favoritism. But as far as being a latecomer to the cause of suffrage, her critics were right. It wasn't as if she hadn't understood how differently women were treated, not after those quiet nights in the library early in her marriage, when John Hooker would read to her from *Blackstone's Commentaries*. She had been restive about marriage from the start, and it came as no surprise to hear Blackstone reaffirm the fact that women could not independently own property, that, in fact, a woman's identity disappeared at marriage. She could tighten with indignation, which she did, but life went on, and, as things were, she had a good marriage.

If it hadn't been for what happened in 1861, when the young Quaker abolitionist Anna Dickinson spoke in Hartford, how long would it have taken for her to face the uglier realities of a woman's life?

Anna Dickinson was only nineteen, but the Republicans had already dubbed her their Joan of Arc for her passionate defense of abolition. She was the magic speaker who could smite the Democratic opposition all through New England, even, they were sure, in a narrow-minded, conservative town such as Hartford.

Isabella had her doubts. No woman had ever spoken publicly in Hartford on any issue. It was ridiculous, of course, but there it was, and what good would it do to inflame the citizens of Hartford, diverting attention from the urgent need to defeat the Democrats who opposed abolishing slavery? But she and John, as staunch abolitionists, showed up that night to give their support.

"Look, there's the grocer, Mr. Sheehan, the one who always helps me with the bags," Isabella whispered as they passed a cluster of men and women milling outside the hall. "Have they come to hear Miss Dickinson?"

John tightened his hold on her arm. "I doubt it," he said. "They look unhappy to me."

The crowd parted as the couple approached the entrance; Mr. Sheehan, a heavy-browed man with large, ruddy ears, tipped his hat to Isabella and she smiled her thanks. Nothing rude or boisterous was said.

Once seated, Isabella forgot everything except the presence of the tall young woman with long black hair on the stage. Her self-possession was extraordinary as she argued for abolition with such fiery eloquence, one could see in the eyes of her audience that she was making converts. The Republicans were right.

Isabella dashed to the stage immediately after the speech and impulsively invited Anna Dickinson for dinner, an invitation that was quickly and graciously accepted. How young and tired she looks, Isabella thought. She's young enough to be my daughter. "You go ahead," she murmured to John, gently pushing him toward the entrance. "She has to talk to people here for a while. We'll take a carriage home."

It was after nine o'clock when Isabella and her guest made their way from the hall and began walking toward the carriage stand. Beside them were two women from the audience still eagerly chatting about Anna's speech, clearly reluctant to let her go.

Suddenly, from the shadows, a bulky male figure emerged. One of the two women, a redhead wearing a green velvet bonnet, whirled and cried out in fear.

"I told you not to go in there," the man said. With that, he grabbed the woman's arm, twisting it cruelly, and threw her to the ground.

"What are you doing?" Isabella screamed. The woman's companion sank to her knees and cradled the injured woman's head as Isabella and Anna stared in horror.

"She's my wife, and she disobeyed me," the man replied calmly. "If she does this again, I'm locking her in the house."

"How could you do such a thing? What terrible thing has she done?" Isabella protested. With relief, she saw a policeman running toward them from the direction of the hall. Even to be standing here, not knowing what to do, made her feel more than helpless—it seemed somehow an act of complicity.

At that moment, the man stepped closer, and she saw his face.

"Mr. Sheehan," she said unbelievingly.

"Mrs. Hooker."

He actually tipped his hat to her just as the out-of-breath policeman reached them.

"What happened?" the policeman demanded.

"Nothing important, Officer. I was reprimanding my wife. I told her not to go hear a woman speak."

"*Reprimanding* her?" Isabella gasped. "You don't reprimand like this!"

"Sheehan, if you punish too hard, there could be a problem," the policeman said quite matter-of-factly. He turned to Isabella. "I'm sorry you had to see this, Mrs. Hooker. But she was forewarned, it appears." He looked down at the two females on the ground. "Can she get up?"

The uninjured woman looked up and nodded, her face streaked with tears. "I'm her sister. I'll take her home," she said.

"You aren't going to arrest this man?" Isabella asked.

"Can't do that, ma'am. He is within his rights, you know."

Within his rights. Isabella was struck dumb. So this was how the dry language of the law translated into real life. Not just by not allowing women to vote or keep their children and home after a husband's abandonment but by allowing them to be treated as property themselves. How could she, a privileged woman, have not seen the parallel to slavery? Women were not held in iron chains and sold but soothed and cosseted and left uneducated and then auctioned off to men as wives. Except for her loving husband, that woman on the ground could be she.

Later that night, a visibly upset John repeated over and over at the dinner table that he should never have left them alone. He stopped only after Isabella impatiently interrupted him, saying "John—if you *had* been there, I wouldn't have seen what it means for a woman to have no rights!"

He sighed. "I can't dispute that," he said. Excusing himself to their guest, he stood and kissed his wife good night. She and Anna, in tacit agreement that sleep was impossible, retreated to the library to talk.

"My father managed to send six sons to school until they were twenty-two years old but never spent a hundred dollars a year on a daughter after she was sixteen," Isabella blurted out as they sat down.

"That's not a new realization, is it?" Anna asked.

"No. I've always been angry, but chose not to think about it." She was struggling. It wasn't her father she wanted to condemn. It was her own willful blindness. "I guess the same is true for facing how free that man was to hurt his wife. What recourse does she have?"

"She can leave him, but she won't have any money to live. And, as you saw, no help from the law."

"I have to do something," Isabella said.

The younger woman leaned forward, hair falling across her face, and took Isabella's hands in hers.

"I think I can help you with that," she said. She turned and reached into her knapsack of speaking materials and pulled out a copy of an essay. "Have you read this?" she said. "It's years old, but I carry copies with me because it so perfectly frames the problem. Harriet Taylor Mill—have you heard of her? No one has explained better how men are corrupted by their power in marriage."

"I looked at it once," Isabella says, suddenly embarrassed that she can't remember a word.

"It's worth rereading," Anna said with a smile.

"I'm not a radical, I don't want to get involved with radical women—"

Anna nodded. "It also describes how some women resist emancipation. They fear what they will lose if they are free and equal. Comfort, perhaps. Tranquillity. Mostly, protection." Her eyes, very bright, fixed on Isabella's without blinking.

Isabella looked away first. "Tell me more."

They talked for hours that night as the rest of the household slept. Isabella's indignation grew as she listened. How could there be so many laws and customs that left married women helpless? How could the courts be so indifferent?

"People want to hear me speak about abolition, because their consciences are wakening on slavery," Anna said. "But I wouldn't be the Republican Joan of Arc"—she said it mockingly—"if I were exhorting them to give women the vote and change repressive laws. *That* means donning a very different cap. Which I will, after we win this election. We have no power without the vote."

Isabella felt as if she were somehow emerging from a dark room as she continued through the night to listen and ask questions, marvelling at how much she was learning from a girl not much older than her own daughters.

Somewhere close to dawn, Anna began to tell her with mounting enthusiasm about Susan B. Anthony and Elizabeth Cady Stanton. "The two most notorious suffragists in America," she said cheerfully. "They make conservatives apoplectic. Have you heard them speak?"

Isabella shook her head. The papers jeered about this Susan B. Anthony, calling her "an ungainly hermaphrodite, part male, part female," and they were little kinder to the married Mrs. Stanton. "I'm afraid they are too radical for me," she said.

"They are the bravest," Anna murmured as the first rays of light broke over the horizon and cast a soft glow across the books on the library shelves. "You will see."

Shortly after that evening, Isabella pulled on her gloves and rode in a carriage to an organizing meeting of the New England Woman Suffrage Association, where she met Julia Ward Howe and Lucy Stone and gazed in awe on Frederick Douglass.

"So how was it?" John asked as she came into the house later that night.

Isabella waited for a long moment to answer as she peeled off her gloves.

"It will change my life," she finally said.

"Perhaps it already has," he said quietly.

She smiled, not even trying to control the elation in her voice. "Perhaps it has."

Isabella's reverie is suddenly jolted. "I guess you're too astonished to talk," Puckett says from the street. "Well, I'm going into town, too big a crowd here." He grins up at her. "I hear there's a nice tea shop, corner of Hicks and Montague. Perhaps you might feel like having a cup. Good day." With another slight bow, he turns and walks away.

She realizes she has just been invited to join him. Talking freely again to a reporter? She hasn't done that since the scandal, when every word she uttered had been magnified by these men into something larger and more lurid. Even before that, she had grown wary of them. No matter how she tried to convince them, they couldn't resist besmirching the women's movement with the "free love" label. She had been naïve to expect them to explain to the world that this was a cheap epithet flung by those out to resist reform of marriage and divorce laws. Who, she had argued, would march under a banner demanding the freedom to commit adultery? They didn't want to listen.

Nor, she found, did Harriet—another of her naïve stumbles.

It was in 1869, long past Isabella's initial embrace of the cause. Not quite understanding her own restiveness, she had left the more conservative suffragists and joined Stanton and Anthony's National Woman Suffrage Association, just as Anna Dickinson had gently predicted. She knew instantly she had found her home. So much so, in fact that, in typically exuberant fashion, she made the mistake of trying to transplant her convictions into the heart of her sister.

"You want me to write for this rag?" Harriet asked with astonishment as the two of them stood one day in Harriet's kitchen. She held aloft a copy of *The Revolution,* Mrs. Stanton's newspaper, which Bella had just handed her. "This woman supports divorce and has no problem with women committing adultery. She *says* so! How can you ask me to lend my name to this?"

"Because you have her all wrong, Hattie. Believe me; she's a motherly-hearted woman who supports divorce reform because she doesn't want children of bad marriages to suffer. She does *not* condone mindless personal gratification." Isabella tried to keep her voice calm. If Hattie brought her great stature and reputation to the movement, writing as passionately about women as she had about slavery, the country would listen. Wasn't it time? Wasn't it clear that nothing would change for women unless they fought for it? She had even offered to ask Mrs. Stanton to change the name of the newspaper so it wouldn't sound quite so radical—but Hattie was having none of it.

"Your New York group is too strident and radical, Bella. What a crew of harpies! For heaven's sake, your own *brother* is heading Lucy Stone's organization now. He's a suffragist! If you had to belong to a suffrage group, why didn't you stay with them? They are sensible women who don't try to provoke outrage. The vote? Fine, in due time. But not all these other crazy things."

Isabella bit down on her tongue to hold back her retort. Henry should never have let himself be talked into taking that figurehead position with Lucy Stone. My dear brother has much on his mind, but he is too cautious, she thought. Some of the most prominent people in the movement were saying he looked weak, and they were disappointed.

"I didn't stay with them because they won't fight hard enough for *all* the needed reforms," she answered.

Harriet gave a snort of impatience and pointed to an article in *The Revolution*. "Well, if your Susan Anthony wants to deflect claims that she's a supporter of free love, she isn't doing a very good job. Listen to this." She read aloud: "This howl comes from those men who know that when women get their rights they will be able to live honestly and no longer be compelled to sell themselves for bread, either in or out of marriage."

Harriet slapped the paper onto the table. "Howl?" she said. "*Howl?* Is this a way of putting respectable people's doubts to rest? Doesn't she realize she's insulting women too?"

"I wish I could convince you of the seriousness of our cause," Isabella said, her voice cracking slightly.

Harriet's demeanor softened. "I believe suffrage would be good—not necessary but good. I support a reasonable approach. But I do fear we women will *lose* stature, not gain it, if we heed the most strident voices. We don't have to agree on everything, Bella. You know that, don't you?"

"I do, but this is my life's work. I hate to see us differ on something so important."

"I admire your commitment; I can say that much. I truly mean that." Harriet's voice was now gentle. "I will always stand by my Bella, as I know you will stand by me." She reached out her arms and drew Isabella forward into a hug. Isabella hugged her back, knowing finally she would have to accept the fact that she might never be able to woo her sister to the fight for women's rights. I will live with it, she told herself. We can disagree, even on something as important as this. We love each other, and that won't change. Our bond goes deep.

She feels frozen at the window, unable yet to move, staring down at the street, thinking now about the man named Puckett.

She had ordered him out of the convention's afternoon meeting that January day in 1871 after a particularly heated argument over his inquisitive reporting. And yet when he found her speech he had brought it to her, asking for no return favors. If he was a man of honor then, perhaps he would be now. Should she go? She hesitates but decides he might be able to help her. After all, she is a risk taker, isn't she?

Isabella walks down the stairs as quietly as she can, stopping at the first-floor landing to get her bearings. She pulls the hood of her coat up over her hair, trying to decide whether she should walk briskly through the kitchen or wait for a moment when none of the servants are around to slip out. But if she appears to be sneaking out, the landlady might think she isn't going to pay her bill. Better to stand straight and walk out with a smile and a nod for all. It is the best she can do, so she strides through the kitchen, nodding at the startled cook, and exits as quickly as she can onto the narrow alley-way that runs behind Hicks Street.

"I'm going to see the solicitor," Eunice tells Harriet as she pulls on her black leather gloves and ties the strings of her bonnet tightly under her chin.

"Is this the right time to go?" asks Harriet. "People are coming, aren't they? Your children, Mary—"

"I must deal with some financial problems."

Harriet is nonplussed. She has heard rumors of Henry's profligate spending for years, but even though he was always a man who loved the good things of life, he did receive a lavish annual payment from Plymouth Church. Could they be short of money?

"Please don't ask me any questions." Eunice is opening the front door.

"But you'll be besieged out there."

"Yes, and tomorrow I will read that I am still as homely and thin-lipped as ever," Eunice replies. "It doesn't matter anymore."

Harriet closes the door only partway, watching Eunice descend the steps to the shouts of the suddenly enlivened reporters. Seven steps. Down three, four to go. Keep your head up, she urges silently with sudden compassion.

"Mrs. Beecher, we all offer our sympathy," booms a strong voice at the base of the stairs.

"Thank you," Eunice says, not pausing.

"We're hearing Mrs. Hooker is in the neighborhood, Mrs. Beecher. Is she coming here to see her brother? Is there a reconciliation in the offing?"

Eunice pauses, her foot hovering, and Harriet holds her breath. She should have realized she wouldn't be the only one to recognize Isabella's voice.

"I'm sorry, I cannot answer questions now. It is too distressful a time. Surely you understand." Five steps. Two to go.

One man pushes free from the rest. "Ma'am, is it true Reverend Beecher's nurse almost quit this morning? Sorry to pry, but we—"

"You're not at all sorry," Eunice says. "Now leave me alone, please." She draws her cape close and steps to the sidewalk, striding through the crowd, stopping for no one, not even the parishioners who step up to murmur their good wishes.

Quietly, Harriet closes the door.

She feels a tap on her shoulder less than a half hour later and looks up to see one of Eunice's maids standing at her side. She must have dozed off in the chair next to her brother's bed.

"Mrs. Stowe, a visitor downstairs. He came in through the back to avoid the reporters. I took him to the parlor." The maid curtsies and hurries off before Harriet, still disoriented by sleep, can ask her who the visitor is.

She knows immediately as she walks into the room, even though he stands with his back to her. It is Frank Moulton, once one of Henry's closest friends and a trusted confidant, turned accuser at the trial. He is here, in this house, the man who thought loyalty could be cut fine, claiming both Henry and Theodore Tilton as friends and presented himself as their liaison—the supposedly honorable man committed to trudging back and forth between an agitated Henry and an angry Tilton, carrying messages, orchestrating meetings, doing everything he could to broker a compromise that would keep the bubbling scandal out of the courts.

Until he took the stand to betray Henry. How dare he come here? The audacity of his presence takes her breath away.

"Mr. Moulton."

He turns around. His red hair and beard are undimmed by gray, his strong features unchanged by the passage of the years. He still has that grave, steady look that so impressed the jury when he declared on the stand that Henry had confessed to him the act of adultery with Elizabeth Tilton. What a travesty!

Had it all been part of an elaborate plot, as Harriet believes, to destroy her brother? It has been easier to believe that than to excuse Moulton for muddled good intentions. How could a man testify against a friend? It still angers her to remember some people declaring that a "moral" man had no choice but to tell the truth. There was nothing "moral" about Moulton, of that she was convinced. He spoke no truth.

"Mrs. Stowe." His voice is deep and calm. "Forgive me, I know I'm not wanted. Although I confess I waited until I saw Mrs. Beecher leave the house before approaching. You were the one I hoped to see."

Harriet is at a loss as to how to proceed. She would not dream of asking this man to sit down in Henry's home. "You can't possibly be here to see my brother," she says.

"Absolutely not." A weary smile flickers across his face. "I wouldn't do that to Henry. It would be an assault on a sick man. Robbing him of the right to throw me out."

"What do you want?"

"To tie up some strings," he replies. "I know Henry is dying. And I think the country is losing a good man, which may surprise you. I think he will be remembered, far more than I will be—or most any of us involved in that trial, for that matter."

Harriet gestures toward a chair. "Please sit down," she says. From the looks of him, he has prospered over the years. Is he still running warehouses? That is what she remembers; he was in trade. An exporter of goods.

Moulton sits down, unbuttoning his greatcoat. He makes no attempt to take it off. "I've seen Henry many times in the past several years," he says. "Brooklyn is too small a place not to run into people on the streets or in the horsecars. I've been tempted to approach him, but he never gives any indication of wanting that. I know many people think he was able to heal, but that isn't true, is it? To me, he seems diminished. Blurred in outline. Forgive me, that's what I've seen."

Harriet starts to protest, but she has seen the same. Henry, slumped in a chair, the buttons of his vest straining to hold in his expanded girth. But still charged with fire; always charged with fire.

"If you are implying that the trial destroyed him, you are wrong," she manages.

"I'm not here to relive the trial or imply anything. I'll mourn the man, Mrs. Stowe. I think I just wanted one Beecher to understand that acknowledging Henry's frailties does not destroy him or your family."

"Henry was innocent." Harriet's stomach tightens, and she clenches her fists inside the folds of her dress. She sees Moulton's motive now; he wants to give a parting shot as justification for his actions under some soulful guise of appreciating Henry. "I think you should leave."

He stands immediately and buttons his coat. "Mrs. Stowe, I'm not a religious man. I'm not looking for God's forgiveness or some heavenly future, so I can speak plain. You're the only Beecher I would approach. I will say this. There's only one person who was destroyed by what happened."

"I couldn't care less what happened to Victoria Woodhull." She finds it hard to even say the hated name.

He smiles at this reference to the woman whose attacks precipitated the collapse of Henry's reputation. "Oh, not her. She's done quite well, I'd say. Dropped her façade as a suffragist, moved to England, and married a British banker. Even invented a new past with royal lineage. People like Mrs. Woodhull manage to survive."

She waits, stubbornly set on his saying the name first.

"I mean Elizabeth Tilton, of course. She never quite seemed the type to become the fallen woman in all this, did she? When people began comparing her to Mr. Hawthorne's Hester Prynne, I found it fanciful at first. But I've come to believe it. She is sick and going blind, Mrs. Stowe, but the thing that hurts her the most is her excommunication from the church. I'm hoping her plight might stir some sympathy in you. You are a woman of great moral force, and your intervention could help reverse that."

Sympathy? There were days during the trial when Harriet, angry at the ethereal Elizabeth's hold on the public imagination, had been hardly able to look at the woman. Who could trust her? She had accused Henry, then rescinded her accusation, then accused him again—in the end, anger won. In the end, Harriet felt only contempt.

"How do you sympathize with someone who lied?" she says. "And how can you approach me with this at this time?"

He looks at her almost sadly. "Mrs. Stowe, surely you have other thoughts on this by now. Or perhaps not. I know this is an awkward time, but you are here in Brooklyn, and I had to try."

Harriet says nothing. This will go away, if she says nothing. But she cannot still her indignation. "I don't know why we're talking about Elizabeth Tilton. Her weakness is not my concern. You're the one who set out to destroy my brother."

He turns toward the door. "I see I shouldn't have come. As far as Henry is concerned, I told the truth as I knew it, and I have paid my own price." He pauses. "You know, what made Henry unique was that he didn't just study books, he studied people. He tried to walk in their shoes, feel their emotions. That was what made him a brilliant preacher. And then he forgot how to do it. He was swallowed by concern only for himself. A Beecher trait, it seems." Moulton opens the door, pauses with his hand on the knob, and looks back with a strange, exploring expression on his face. "I must say, I pity you. You have carried such a heavy burden on your shoulders for so long. Good day, Mrs. Stowe." Without another word, he steps over the threshold and departs, his face so grim even the reporters outside stay silent as they scribble the news of Moulton's presence in their notebooks.

Isabella is standing in front of the shoemaker's shop when she sees Eunice reflected in the glass, coming up behind her, walking rapidly to the corner, hands jammed into a fur muff. Eunice's lips are moving; she is talking to herself.

What should she do? If she turns right now, they will in another second be face-to-face. Or she can keep her head down and Eunice will pass by, none the wiser. Do nothing, she tells herself. This isn't the way to win access to Henry. But without Eunice's permission, what would? The truth of it all suddenly makes her tremble. *What is she doing here?* Her whole trip is absurdly quixotic, the kind of slapdash venture for which she is famous. Stupid, stupid. But berating herself has never made Isabella more cautious.

She turns around, ready once more for the quick gamble.

"Eunice? I've heard the news, and I am so sorry."

Eunice stops dead, staring at Isabella. Her face turns ashen, her lips part. What is in her eyes? Not anger, Isabella realizes. Fear. She's afraid of me. Is that what it is? It's as if I've impaled her.

"I'm sorry to surprise you like this," she says as her sister-in-law takes a step back and turns away. "Eunice, please wait a moment. I didn't expect to see you, but now that you're here, I must ask you most humbly for a kindness." Her brain races, trying to frame the words. "May I come see my brother? For one last time? Please."

"Your brother?" Eunice stops and faces her again.

"Henry." This is strange.

"You mean my husband. You want to see my husband." Something shifts and hardens in Eunice's eyes. This person facing her violated the one inviolable tenet of Beecher faith. She sways, and for an instant, Isabella wonders if she will have to grab her to keep her from falling. She starts to reach out and is startled when Eunice pulls a hand from her muff as if to slap her away.

"That's an outrageous request from a traitor," Eunice says. She turns and hurries away down the street, walking so fast she is almost running.

⚛ CHAPTER FOUR ⚛

March 7, 1887, 10:30 a.m.

MARY HAS ARRIVED. Harriet watches from the parlor window as her elder sister steps from the carriage and makes her way up the steps to Henry's door, amused by the puzzled looks of the reporters as she passes them by. They don't recognize her. Hardly anyone ever does, which is exactly the way Mary wants it. To be the anonymous Beecher was always her goal; a hard one for Harriet to understand, but one that has saved Mary a fair amount of grief. She is the conventional Beecher, not drawn to causes and crusades, but she is quite possibly the most content of them all with her life.

"Mary, dear," Harriet says, throwing open the door. In an instant she is encircled in Mary's plump, sturdy arms and finally able to shed her tears. The two sisters hold tight to each other for a long moment in the darkened hallway.

"Is he still with us?" Mary asks, eyes anxious.

Harriet assures her he is, as soothingly as she can.

"What happened?"

She explains. Eunice and Henry spent Wednesday shopping. They were looking for furnishings for the church parlor: new chairs, a porcelain clock, a chimney-glass mirror. Compulsively, Harriet gives details. Four chairs; two had to be Regency, which took longer. Henry was tired that night and went to bed early. He was nauseated the next morning, so he stayed in bed, telling Eunice it was nothing, just a sick headache. And then he slept through to the following day. Eunice didn't call for the doctor until four o'clock in the afternoon. Harriet hears her own criticism and bites her lip but knows Mary will be charitable. Mary is always charitable.

"And what did the doctor say?"

"They couldn't rouse him by then. He said Henry was dying of apoplexy."

"Poor man. It was ordained, Hattie. Not Eunice's fault, but you know that."

"I do, but I can't blame God." There, that was it.

"Come, let's sit together. We are here for him, that's all we can do," Mary says gently. "You know, dear, that new bridge is quite impressive. I felt hardly any sway when my carriage crossed. It must be a godsend for people."

It is a relief to talk about something else. "Mr. Roebling made sure none of us would have to stumble and slide across the ice again," Harriet replies. "Although Eunice is worried about a deluge of immigrants taking over Brooklyn."

"Well, they are everywhere," Mary says with a sigh. "How is she doing?"

"Distraught—and brittle, in that way of hers. She's out running errands right now."

Mary casts her sister a keen look. "I venture you mean she still manages to fill this house with tension. Yet how can we criticize? Her husband is dying. All the same, weaned on a pickle, I've always thought."

Harriet picks up her sister's valise, and together they begin to mount the steps to the second floor. What a relief it is to have someone here from the family with whom she can talk, who knows the subtext.

The stairwell is lined with the oil paintings in heavy gilt frames that Henry likes to show off to his friends and family. This, he enjoys announcing proudly, is a genuine—what? Perhaps a Dutch landscape. Or an Italian Renaissance portrait. He would announce to one and all what he had paid, a habit that seemed boastful to some but was really just the spillover of Henry's enthusiasm. He did love to buy. Even now, he and Eunice keep rich Oriental carpets piled four deep in the parlor.

"Mary, Isabella is here," Harriet says. "I heard her shouting from a window a few houses away this morning."

"Shouting? Good heavens."

"There was some fool prancing about in blackface singing doggerel about Henry—"

"And she yelled at him?"

"Yes."

Mary says nothing more until she reaches the top of the stairs, but her step grows heavier. "Ah me. Well then, problems are sure to follow." She takes the valise from Harriet and plunks it down. "Take me to Henry," she says.

Holding hands, they go directly to their brother's room and sit together in silence beside his bed. Mary touches his arm.

"Little boy, little boy," she finally says softly. As they leave, she wipes a tear from her eye and says, "It's like Catharine. Not sick a day in her life and then felled by a stroke, and I still can't believe that dear sister is gone. Now what will it be like without Henry? Ah, Hattie. It's the end of an era."

"Our era," Harriet replies.

"Do you have memories of Mother?"

"I like to think I do, but I'm not sure. My memory is of a saintly, beautiful person, but I can't quite see her face. I can't put the pieces together, no matter how I try."

"You were too young. And so was Henry. I remember coming home from the funeral and seeing that little boy trudge right out to the backyard, still in his best suit and collar. Father had told him Mother was buried in the earth so God could take her to heaven. He picked up a spade and began digging in the dirt. Catharine wanted to know what he was doing, preparing to scold him for getting dirty, of course. But he stopped us all with his answer. 'I'm going to heaven to find Ma,' he said." Mary fumbles for a handkerchief in the pocket of her skirt.

Tea is ready for them in the parlor, courtesy of Anna, Harriet is sure. Eunice's maid would not have bothered.

"Eunice has lovely china," Mary says, glancing at the fragile cups that Anna had found tucked away in the sideboard. "Better, of course, than what people get from those new mailing houses. But I've heard the one with the brown cover, the Montgomery Ward catalog, is amazing. They sell everything: dishes, banjos, guns, all sorts of clothing. Mostly to farm people." She sighs as she settles herself. "I can't believe we're able to talk about ordinary things."

Anna appears in the doorway, carrying cakes, looking quite solemn. Harriet smiles at her and tries to bring her into the conversation, reminding Mary of the long history she and Anna share. But Anna is in her servant mode, and there is no coaxing her out of it. With a curtsy and a few shared pleasantries, she deposits her burden and silently leaves.

"It's as if you put a bag over your head when other people are around," Harriet had once said to her in exasperation. "You're not a servant anymore."

"Some people feel, once a servant, always a servant, and they wouldn't understand," Anna had replied firmly. "There's a barrier, and that's the fact of it, and I'll be calling you Mrs. Stowe when others are present, and don't try to talk me out of it."

So Harriet had bowed to her friend's sense of propriety with slightly irritated resignation.

Whatever social barrier there might have been between them had begun to crumble almost immediately after they met in 1837, when Harriet first opened her door and saw a frightened sixteen-year-old on her doorstep, trying to look like the accomplished nurse-maid she was supposed to be.

Harriet's immediate reaction had been panic tinged with anger. Why hadn't she been warned the girl would be so young? She was a child and looked totally bewildered. Cincinnati was a dirty, noisy city in those days, and the sounds and smells that had greeted Anna at the station that day must have been appalling. But what Harriet needed was a helper who would take over, not a child who looked like a scared chicken.

"Are you my new nursemaid?" she demanded, hoisting the squalling infant she held in her arms from one hip to the other.

"Yes, ma'am," the girl said, her eyes darting from one direction to another. She was obviously taking in the debris scattered around the Stowe farmhouse and wondering how people who had reputations for intelligence and accomplishment could live this way, Harriet thought. And what do I look like to her? A frazzled woman with disheveled hair hanging loose and a button missing on her shirtwaist, that's what she sees.

"I'm not good at this sort of thing," Harriet said, glancing vaguely around the yard. "There's too much to do. My husband promised to clean up the trash before your arrival, but he no more wants to do it than I do."

"Children"—the girl tried to finish her sentence from an obviously meager store of experience—"consume time."

"What's your name?"

"Anna Smith." The girl held out an envelope. "My letters of recommendation, Mrs. Stowe."

What was there in the girl's eyes that moment that quelled her anxiety? Harriet has thought about it many times since. A flash of challenge, intelligence, firmness of tone. Nothing quite explained it.

She glanced at the envelope and tucked it into her pocket. The baby, furious now, was arching her back, having moved on to healthy screams. "Can you endure us?" Harriet asked.

"I certainly can try," Anna said.

"Splendid, that's kind of you. There's another one. Twins."

The gazes they exchanged hovered somewhere between that shred of humor and serious intent, and Anna stepped forward, reaching out both arms for the baby. Harriet handed the child over, thinking, perhaps this girl will work out after all.

How strange to remember those mutually skeptical beginnings. Anna's presence had brought an order to their lives that freed Harriet to retreat to her bedroom and scribble away without guilt or reproof. Anna was the one who scrubbed the floors, cleaned up the trash, rolled out the pie dough, and fed the babies (a new one conceived each time Calvin returned home, it seemed).

"Am I a difficult person to work for?" Harriet asked one afternoon as Anna was changing one baby's napkins while the other banged for her supper with a spoon. She had just emerged from her study after a day of writing. Her hand ached and her eyes burned, but she had produced enough pages to calm her anxieties for the moment. And here was this young girl, doing everything that made the household work.

"No, ma'am. My feeling is, we're working together." Anna barely looked up as she said it. "Don't you think so too?"

"You work harder," Harriet said. "But I'll try to believe it."

And then came the summer of 1849. Each morning began with a shimmering band of heat spreading up from the horizon to a level of suffocation by midday. Calvin was away on another lecturing trip, and she and Anna were alone.

There was no writing. Together they doused the children with ladles of water at midday to cool them, but there was no relief, even at night. The heat could be endured, they told each other. It was the cholera that crept up with the sun that frightened them. People were dying in town, dozens each day. Harriet ordered the children to stay indoors and would stand in the doorway like a sentinel, arms crossed, as if to ward off disease with her will. She came back from market on the Fourth of July more frightened than she had ever been before.

"Anna, people are dancing and drinking in the streets," she whispered. "Some of them are lying by the side of the road, vomiting and laughing. It's like Poe's story, 'The Masque of the Red Death.'"

With no further words, they put their arms around each other.

Anna was first to hear the laundress coughing. She walked outside just in time to see the poor woman fainting over her scrubbing board. A wet shirt fell from her hands as her dark hair loosened, floating amidst the suds, a sight that Harriet could never erase from memory.

She was hurried off by her family to die, but it was too late. No amount of vigilance by Harriet would suffice now. They were not to be spared.

But why did it have to be Charley? Harriet spotted the bright, rosy flush of fever as she bundled him into his nightclothes that very evening. By morning the lively eighteen-month-old was drained of all bounce and verve, his small form limp.

For three days he lay there as she and Anna held vigil, his fingers curled around a favorite painted wood horse, until his eyes turned opaque and he released his grip.

"No." The word was torn from Harriet, cutting through the air with a sound as ragged and piercing as a saw drawn against metal.

"God has taken him, Mrs. Stowe," Anna said, choking on the words.

"No. He can't have him." Crying, Harriet leaned into the cradle to lift her son's small form into her arms. It took all of Anna's strength to gently release the grasp of the living from the dead.

Harriet searches in her memories for this lost child. It is hard to remember the arch of his chin or the liveliness of his eyes when he laughed. What color were Charley's eyes? Were they blue? Surely they were, but she feels doubt. Hazel, perhaps. Anna might know. He was but a tiny hiccup of life, gone so fast, but loved no less than those who endured. Perhaps more. She has never confessed this to anyone but Anna.

Together the two women had lined a small coffin in brown felt. It was Anna who persuaded a photographer to take a picture of Charley before the lid was closed, a picture wept over many times in the intervening years. And only Anna understood why Harriet was able to write so eloquently of a slave mother's loss when a baby was taken away; only she knew how Harriet wept as she wrote those pages of *Uncle Tom's Cabin*. After that, Anna continued to call her Mrs. Stowe in public. But somewhere during the days of Charley's dying, when they held each other and cried, she, Anna's employer, became Harriet. She assumed it would be that way for the rest of their lives.

*   *   *

Mary smiles vaguely at Anna's retreating back. "So nice that she still helps you out, Hattie," she murmurs. "Now tell me what else is going on in this sad house."

"I had an unexpected visitor shortly before you came. Frank Moulton. Do you remember him?"

"I certainly do. What could he possibly want with us?"

"He said he wanted my help getting Elizabeth Tilton reinstated as a member of the church. Can you believe such audacity? I think he *really* wanted to force some kind of admission from me that Henry was indeed guilty."

"He's talking about the trial? Oh, for heaven's sake. A good man is dying, and bringing that up is despicable. I hope you sent him packing fast."

"Yes, of course."

"I pity Bella," Mary says unexpectedly.

"Pity? You're not serious, surely."

"Have some sympathy, Hattie. She's suffered too."

"She caused her own problems, and I won't ever forget what she did to Henry. Betrayal is betrayal. It's quite simple."

"You're a smart woman, dear, you should realize it's never simple."

Picking up a fork, Harriet takes a careful bite out of the cake on her plate. "Mary, I'm not a harsh person, you know that. And I might remind you, you were angry too."

"Yes, indeed," Mary answers. "But the older I grow, the more I see."

"I don't understand."

"Think about the fact that Bella never had the education she wanted. Now I never cared much for studying books, but she was as thirsty for learning as you and Catharine, and she didn't get her fair share."

That truth had caused considerable consternation in the family. When money grew tight and Isabella was pulled from school, she didn't stay quiet about it. She had sobbed bitterly at the dinner table, begging Lyman—who sat smoldering with ill-concealed impatience—to change his mind. "There's money to educate the boys, why not me?" she wailed. It made them all uncomfortable, but it confirmed the family story about this charming, maddening, flighty young girl whose feelings frequently bubbled over into protest. Where was her stoicism? Her Beecher grit? And then her mother died, and Lyman decided he was too exhausted to deal anymore with a volatile child. He sent her off to to live with Mary and her husband, where she received a final, well-meant patchwork job of mothering. Lyman rarely saw her again. Could there be a hunger, a sense of deprivation that pulled her to passionate causes? Mary seems quite willing to entertain the possibility.

"I know the list of deprivations, and I understand the pain they brought her," Harriet says. "But I also feel we've suffered because of her excitability and rash judgment, and I don't feel sorry for her. Especially now that she's here. She's going to cause some problem, you wait and see."

"Perhaps, I don't know. Just remember, we fear the loss of our brother, but so does she."

A silence falls. For a moment the two sisters sip tea, not speaking.

"Are the two of you talking again?" Mary finally says.

"A few words every now and then, if I run into her somewhere. Enough to be civil." Harriet looks into her sister's eyes and holds her gaze. "I wonder sometimes if the Bella we knew was always false, and the true one only showed her colors when Henry was besieged. Could her nature be different from ours? Because of our different mothers?"

Mary sets her cup down with care. "Who is to say? She wasn't like her mother."

They sit again in silence, remembering Harriet Porter, the ethereally remote second wife Lyman Beecher brought home to a houseful of lonely children. Harriet remembers being taken up in her stepmother's lap, playing with her lovely hands ornamented with elaborate rings, and thinking of her as a strange princess rather than as a new mama. But Lyman's new wife's remoteness turned to coldness as she began bearing her own children, with little affection shown for the ones she had inherited.

"Poor woman," Mary says. "It must have been hard taking us all on."

Mary is in all too forgiving a mood. "I can't excuse her, and I certainly can't excuse Isabella," Harriet says. "She's without a shred of good judgment."

"She is hasty, but she has a good brain, though it's not always readily apparent. Remember, I raised her for a few years after that woman died. She has a true heart, regardless of her faults."

"Mary, you saw all those reporters outside on the sidewalk. They will sniff her out fast. They would love to see Isabella do something dramatic and reckless, I can assure you. And she has never failed them."

"They took her down too."

Harriet tries to hide her irritation. This business of scraping away at the scabs of the past is self-indulgent, and if it were anyone but Mary, she would be saying so.

But Mary, always tactful, changes the subject. "I was thinking the other day of our trip to England in 'fifty-three. Now wasn't that a triumph? All those counts and countesses praising your book to the skies. I look back on it now and can hardly believe it all happened. It was a happy time, Hattie."

"Yes, it was."

"That last night—"

"Calvin amazed me."

"Dear, he was superb."

Harriet is catapulted back in memory to the final night of her visit to London in the aftermath of the excitement over *Uncle Tom's Cabin*. She and Calvin and Mary were feted at Exeter Hall in London, culminating a giddy tour, and thousands of people showed up to meet her and listen to speeches praising her work. At first she had felt quite dazzled, amazed at being lionized for an American story. But the politics became clear as Lord Shaftesbury railed on, in a long, rather pompous speech, about the craven nature of President Pierce. He has pledged to enforce the Fugitive Slave Act, Shaftesbury thundered. Is there a better example of cowardice? The place exploded in sympathetic hisses and boos. America pretends to be a free country, he said; here is evidence that it is not.

Calvin, usually so quiet at these events, became restive. "This isn't good," he muttered. "They like you, Hattie, but not our government."

Harriet glanced over at their hostess, the Duchess of Sutherland. Her pale skin had faded to alabaster, and her patrician lips were drawn so tight they almost disappeared. But her regal good manners were keeping her from objecting to the seizure of her evening.

"We can't just walk out," Harriet whispered.

Calvin said nothing. Instead he tugged at his waistcoat, cleared his throat, and stood, raising his hand for silence. Somehow his reed-thin voice, a challenge to project even in classrooms, managed to carry through the hall. "May I point out, you buy American cotton, almost all of what we produce," he said. "If you want slavery to die in America, then stop buying our cotton." Abruptly, he sat down.

There were some mutterings and throat-clearings, but for the most part, the crowd went silent. Harriet glanced at her husband's flushed face. No matter how many years one was married, a spouse could still surprise.

"You astonish me," she whispered.

He flushed a deeper red. "They were taking advantage of you."

She had loved him for that.

With order restored in the hall, the duchess stood and faced Harriet, obviously relieved to have her event back on course. She held a red velvet drawstring bag in her hand.

"Mrs. Stowe, I hope you will accept this as a gift of faith in the future. Would you kindly hold out your hand?" Smiling, she took an overscale bracelet of ten large gold links out of the velvet bag and slipped it onto Harriet's wrist. Harriet's first thought was that the bracelet was far too large for her, and she feared it falling off. She lifted her hand to keep that from happening, watching how the light from the chandeliers in the hall caught, sparkled, and broke in shards across the golden links.

"I know you recognize this," the duchess said.

And then Harriet understood. "Slave fetters," she said.

"The fetters that hold America's slaves in bondage," the duchess said. "I've had three of the links inscribed with the dates that mark England's fight against slavery. Now it's up to your country to break the chains. You've started the process, Mrs. Stowe. And you are the one to write that history—on the links of this bracelet. And," she added, "if our politicians have your husband's common sense, we'll stop buying your cotton."

No honor, aside from her meeting with Mr. Lincoln, ever quite equaled that moment.

When the president signed a bill abolishing slavery in the District of Columbia in April 1862, Harriet felt weighted with a solemn responsibility. With Isabella by her side, she removed the duchess's gift from its velvet pouch and laid it on the sideboard in her dining room. The bracelet immediately caught the light—not from glittering chandeliers this time, but from the glow of a small gaslight, which gave the gold a more mellow, exotic cast.

"I should have today's date inscribed," Harriet said. "Do you agree? I know it's just a first step, but—"

"Oh, absolutely. You've already written history, and now you must record it." Bella said it quite matter-of-factly, as if it were the most natural choice in the world. It was this curious thing about her—the flighty girl unable to remember where she put her pocketbook could cut through hesitation with swift clarity. Not common sense, of course. Clarity.

Harriet was still indecisive. "I don't want to be premature," she said. Everything she did these days seemed to have ramifications that left her scrambling. The fact that her name triggered instant anger as well as admiration and respect meant that center stage, at times, burned too hot.

"If you were worried about being premature, you wouldn't have written *Uncle Tom's Cabin,*" Bella replied. "Can I come with you when you take the bracelet to the engraver? Oh, please, Hattie, it would be such a privilege."

Her eyes were shining. Sometimes Harriet felt Bella's exuberance boiled too high, but not tonight. "Of course you can," she replied. And then, on impulse, she picked up the bracelet and held it out to her sister. "Would you like to try it on?"

Harriet could still see Bella slipping the bracelet over her slender wrist. What a beauty her sister had become, she thought. How graceful and luminous she was, even though she had taken to ranting on about women's suffrage.

"Hattie, you started all this," Isabella said, stroking each link. "You're the one. You woke the country up, you did, you know."

Harriet remembered feeling both her usual pride and its counter-emotion: the desire to pull back, away from all the uproar and anger, back to the domestic life where no one could hurt her. "We have a long way to go," she managed.

"I know. But it wouldn't be happening without you. Remember what Mr. Lincoln said."

How could she forget? Standing there in the White House a few months after the war began, shocked at her first sight of the rough, scrubby, hollow-eyed man who held the presidency, she had not at first known what to talk about. He seemed so raw and rustic. She could remember little of the conversation, but one comment of his she would not forget: "So this is the little lady who made this big war." It had cost her some sleepless nights, if truth be told. She told no one, for all saw his remark as admiring, but she felt Lincoln had not so much complimented her as burdened her with heavy responsibility.

Isabella slipped the bracelet off and gently put it over her sister's wrist. "Think of this as another talisman, Hattie. What a thrill, to be able to mark the milestones on it. Don't be afraid."

Afraid? Harriet stared at the bracelet, her heart quickening. Did she seem afraid lately? Maybe she was pulling into something of a cocoon. If so, it was partly because Calvin was traveling all the time again, back to the old pattern, and writing home very little. She wasn't actually afraid. She was conserving her energy, staying close to home, finding comfort with pen and paper. It helped her through lonely times. Bella, by contrast, could use a little more caution in her life, a little less rushing to embrace the world.

"I wonder if we'll live to see them all inscribed?" Isabella said, interrupting her thoughts.

Ashamed of the negative track of her thinking, Harriet spoke quickly, assuring her sister that the dam had broken; slavery could not survive. Every state would follow, Mr. Lincoln would make sure of it.

"I'll tell you what," she said on impulse. "You and I will take this bracelet to the engraver every time there is a victory. Together. Our ritual, because it *will* happen in our lifetimes. What do you say?"

Isabella jumped up, her chair clattering to the floor. She reached across the table to hug her sister. "I would love that," she said.

And so they had. They made their second trek the day after Lincoln's Emancipation Proclamation abolished slavery in the rebel states. Holding hands, they had watched the engraver carefully etch the date on the second gold link: January 1, 1863. A third trip came only weeks later, marking Congress's all-important endorsement of Lincoln's bold move. Twice more—once in 'sixty-four when Maryland became a free state, and then again in 'sixty-five, when Missouri followed suit.

Missouri's emancipation of the slaves was their last trip to the engraver. Two of the bracelet's links remain blank. Harriet stares at the cake on her plate, hardly seeing it. Those trips had taken on almost religious significance to them both, uniting them in heart and mind. No one but Bella shares the memory of the engraver's tool burning history into the soft gold; no one else understands the emotion of those moments. Harriet feels suddenly cheated. The sister who was there with her should be here now to share the memory; instead she has willfully made herself a traitorous outcast.

"There is no forgiving—" she begins.

The sudden noise of a door slamming makes Harriet and Mary jump. Eunice is home, and from the sound of her voice, she is not happy.

✢   CHAPTER FIVE   ✢

March 7, 1887, Noon

ISABELLA WALKS ON trembling legs to the corner of Hicks and Montague and pauses in front of William Harvey's curio shop. She stares through the glass window at a jumble of Egyptian scarabs, seal rings, and snuffboxes, not really seeing them. She has made a mistake, caught up in the fear that a fortuitous moment would be lost if she didn't grab it. She leans against the window, welcoming the cold surface of the glass against her brow, praying for invisibility. A few carriages have rattled by, and a street sweeper is briskly wielding a broom, but he hasn't looked up. Behind her, she sees the reflection of two young women in velvet berets and flounced skirts staring, round-eyed, whispering. One of them giggles, a high-pitched sound that tells Isabella exactly how much entertainment she has just provided. Quickly they scuttle away.

John would be railing at her if he were here right now, scolding her for being so impetuous. The last person to approach was Eunice. The very last. What had possessed her?

"Well, that can't have been much fun," a voice says. She turns to see Brady Puckett standing directly behind her, hands in pockets, a wry smile on his face.

"I'm sorry you witnessed it," she says, flushing with embarrassment.

"Better me than most of the other reporters roaming these streets," he says with a shrug. "It must have taken some nerve to confront that woman. She's one formidable lady."

"It was a terrible mistake, and now you're going to write something about it, aren't you? I'm going to be laughed at and—"

His smile vanishes. "Mrs. Hooker, I'm not going to write about it; it's over. Look, I just wanted to see you again. I don't remember you being so suspicious the last time we talked to each other."

Isabella fumbles with her pocketbook, wanting to draw out a handkerchief but not wanting him to see her crying. The wind is blowing off the harbor now, cold enough to turn the many puddles along Montague into ice. She shivers. There seems to be no hint of spring anywhere.

"May I please buy you tea or something? You look like you need to sit down."

She looks directly at him now, deciding to forgo the handkerchief. There are deep lines in his forehead that weren't there sixteen years ago, but he seems surprisingly unaged. She wonders fleetingly what he sees, looking at her. "That's kind of you," she says. "But we need to understand each other first. I'm not going to give you a story about my brother."

"If you say so."

"Or Victoria Woodhull."

A lifted eyebrow is his only comment, but she feels stronger.

The tea shop is almost deserted. They seat themselves at a small, round table away from the window that fronts on Montague, and Isabella takes extra time removing her gloves, alternately relieved to have somewhere to sit and nervous that she will be seen and recognized.

"I don't have to ask why you're here. That was pretty easy to figure out after hearing your exchange with Mrs. Beecher," Puckett says.

"I made a mistake," Isabella repeats.

"I disagree. If you hadn't asked her, you wouldn't have known that it's a waste of time trying to get her permission to get in the house—but then, as I recall, you're an optimist." Again, a wry smile. "Although anyone living here could have told you Eunice Beecher never forgives. She's still back in the courthouse, living that trial."

"You must have covered it."

"What reporter didn't? I covered a lot of stories about the scandal. My favorite was the one about Susan B. Anthony and Mrs. Tilton barricading themselves behind the bedroom door to escape Elizabeth's crazy husband. Remember that? Theodore, hammering away, demanding to be let in? A little dignity lost there."

She remembers a mocking story under his byline. "They didn't have much choice," she says with annoyance.

"No, they didn't. Tilton was a lunatic." He laughs, stretching out his legs. "So how are things up at Nook Farm? Quite a fancy neighborhood of literary people, as I recall. Is Sam Clemens still living next to your sister? I hear his house was built to look like a river steamer."

"He is, and it doesn't, actually. That's just a story."

"Are any of them speaking to you yet?"

"Yes, of course." She keeps her voice light, for it has become second nature to pretend nothing is wrong when smiles still seem cool at a Nook Farm Sunday sociable or she is passed over to tend a booth at a charity bazaar. In truth—except for Harriet, who nods hello only when she has to—most of Isabella's neighbors have long forgotten they ostracized her in the first place, so it is up to her to forget how much indifference can still hurt. When she needs it, John reminds her gently that no one stays the center of attention for long. "They don't care anymore, Bella. There are newer scandals for those who thrive on them."

"So if everything is rosy, I suppose you and your sister are playing croquet together again. Seems I heard once that the two of you liked the game."

"I'm sorry, but I don't want to talk about Harriet or any of my brothers and sisters."

Puckett again raises an eyebrow. "I see. So we're not talking about the Reverend Beecher, Victoria Woodhull, or Mrs. Stowe or anyone else—so just why did you decide to come down here and meet me, Mrs. Hooker?"

She concentrates on folding her gloves and tucking them in her pocketbook, taking as long as she can. "I don't quite know," she finally says.

"Could it be just to renew the acquaintanceship we struck up at the hotel—to say hello, how are you, what a helluva convention that was—"

"I don't like profanity." She bites her lip; she must sound terribly prudish.

Puckett seems unperturbed. A waiter hovers, and he orders tea and sandwiches, which are promptly brought to the table. She is grateful to have a warm cup to hold in her hands so quickly.

"I come across pretty rough, I suppose," he says. "It's the sense of humor I've developed roaming the streets for stories. I've been doing this for too many years, and I don't have much faith in human nature anymore. So I laugh." He shrugs. "It does the job."

"I *was* curious to talk to you again," she says slowly. "You did me a great favor."

"I've not forgotten the look on your face when you opened your hotel room door that night."

She flushes. She can only imagine what she must have looked like. She had just finished tearing her room apart in a search for her speech and half-expected to see Miss Anthony standing there, demanding to know why she wasn't in the convention hall. She had braced herself to confess to incompetence. And there stood this reporter, doffing his hat, holding out her manuscript.

"You left this on a chair in the conference room," he had said. "I gave it a quick scan, and I think it reads very well. Could be better than Victoria Woodhull's."

"Oh my goodness, you *found* it? Please come in!"

He handed her the speech as he stepped inside, stopping as he took in the disorder of the room—the open drawers, dismantled bedding, and clothing scattered on the floor.

"Well, you can stop tearing the place up looking for it," he said with mild amusement.

"Indeed I can, and I thank you. Who are you? What is your name?"

"Brady Puckett, *Brooklyn Eagle,*" he said. "Remember me? I'm the one you threw out this afternoon."

She colored, then felt an overflowing of gratitude. "I'm sure I've read your stories," she added, trying to remember what he had written.

"If you have, you know I'm no foe of suffrage," he said. "As long as the people I'm writing about are intelligent. Can't stand the fools—but then, neither can you, right?"

"Right." She was flustered now. "Thank you," she said again.

He hesitated, a shadow passing across his eyes. Then he tipped his hat and bowed, a small, mocking bow. "I'll be in the audience," he said. "Good luck, Mrs. Hooker."

Sixteen years ago. No one had been more important to her that night than this stranger now sitting across from her in this tea shop.

"You look the same," he says, breaking into her thoughts. "Not much different from sixteen years ago, if you don't mind my saying so."

"Thank you." The words come out too crisply. She hates the false courtesies men bestow on middle-aged women but feels a bit churlish. He obviously meant it as a compliment.

He bites into his sandwich, talking with his mouth open as he chews. He asks her, quite soberly, about her work. Is she still as committed to women's rights as she was in the seventies? Oh yes, she assures him. Any successes? She detects a slight twitch to his mouth. She quickly mentions a bill granting property rights to married women passed in 1877 in Connecticut. He has the grace not to note that was ten years ago, but she feels a familiar churning in her stomach. It's a sorry record indeed for women's rights. John thinks she argues too bitterly about it, which sometimes makes her frustrated enough to pick quarrels with him, but she doesn't tell Puckett that.

"I'm not going to deny that it hurts to see all our hard work treated like a joke," she says. "Or that suffrage is stalled."

"So what went wrong?"

He eases in the question as gently as an egg into boiling water, but she knows what this is about. He must be hoping she will join the chorus that blames Victoria for single-handedly killing the movement. It's quite clever, really—an invitation to declare herself fooled into believing in the woman's intuitive brilliance, the route many have taken. Well, she won't do it.

"Many things," she says neutrally.

"Are you still in touch with Mrs. Stanton?"

"Not in quite a while." She hasn't seen Elizabeth in several years and wonders, not for the first time, how people as fused by commitment to a cause as they were could fade from each other's lives. Elizabeth was the one who managed to cut through all the arguments and disagreements, keeping the suffragists on course—at least until the debacle over Henry. Nothing was the same afterward.

"I liked her stubbornness. Is it true she wouldn't get married until the word *obey* was taken out of the marriage ceremony?"

"Yes, it's true. Go ahead and cluck."

"I'm not clucking at *that*. But I hear she's doing endorsements for that underwear company, Lewis Knitting. What do you think of that?"

"She's obviously free to do what she wants, Mr. Puckett."

Puckett laughs again. "I'm sorry, but Mrs. Stanton advertising union suits tickles my funnybone." He leans forward. "I can laugh at her and still admire her, Mrs. Hooker. Mark my words, you'll win over enough pompous, fat congressmen one of these days to get the vote; then you can vote them out of office. That'll be a great story."

Isabella is relaxing now, at least enough to stop looking at the door every moment in fear of seeing a familiar face. She sips her tea, feeling warmer inside.

"You know, we came close to meeting again," Puckett says. "You probably don't remember."

"Oh, yes, I do." The day she visited Victoria at the Tombs. She had recognized Puckett's voice shouting to the other reporters to back off and give her air. "It was at the prison, wasn't it? You were the only one that day who didn't treat me like prey."

"Well, you were, you know. You chose to go there, and that was news. But I'm talking about the day Woodhull testified before Congress."

"You were there?"

"I wouldn't have missed it. A woman making a presentation to both House and Senate Judiciary Committees? For the first time, in a room crammed with suffragists?" He slaps his hand against the table, a sharp sound that makes Isabella jump. "Any reporter who could get a seat wanted to hear Mrs. Woodhull."

"We all did."

She is somewhere else now, drawn back to that January day in 1871. In a crowded, overheated room, hunched forward with other earnest convention organizers, all of them sweating through their tight, proper shirtwaists of serge and silk, bent on putting the final touches on their plans for the convention. An aide of Susan Anthony's had suddenly burst into the room with shocking news.

A woman, some strange woman, was about to testify before the Judiciary Committees of *both houses* of Congress; yes, it was unbelievable.

Who was this woman? Was she trying to upstage the convention?

And that was the moment Isabella first heard the name of Victoria Woodhull. No, that wasn't quite true. She had listened vaguely to stories about a woman who called herself a stockbroker who had somehow managed to wrap Commodore Vanderbilt around her little finger. A woman who had been married twice and, rumor had it, lived in a bizarre arrangement with both husbands, which added a new twist to free love. The name had never quite caught in her memory—until now.

"What is she testifying about?"

"Women deserving the vote—no, women *having a right* to the vote!"

The women stared at one another, perplexed. How could that be? If Congress was serious, wouldn't it be Mrs. Stanton or Miss Anthony who was invited to testify? Who was this stranger invited so easily into the most powerful male bastion in the country? Would their convention become a sideshow?

The indignation in the room was spiraling, and Isabella's head began to ache. What good did it do to deplore the absurdity of some strange woman with a shady reputation being the first to get an invitation to testify before Congress about women's rights? It was ridiculous to sit here and plan a convention schedule if a woman— any woman—was performing in such a historic role. Whoever Victoria Woodhull was, and however she had managed to finagle an appearance before a joint congressional committee, attention must be paid.

"Enough talk, I'm going to the hearing," she said. "We'll convene the convention later, that's all." She jumped to her feet and grabbed her coat.

Within seconds, every woman in the room was pulling her coat from one of the heavy wood hangers in the cloakroom, turning up her collar, buttoning, grabbing pencil and paper. The question now was not what they should do but how fast could they traverse the streets of Washington to reach the hearing room on Capitol Hill.

Not quite fast enough. The room was jammed when Isabella, along with Susan Anthony and the others, elbowed her way in, trying vainly to find a seat. Susan, her thick, gray hair pulled straight back, her round, gold-rimmed spectacles slipping down her nose, glared imperiously around the room, causing more than a few to squirm, but no one was giving up a seat. People were whispering about the featured speaker, telling stories of her escapades. A barely restrained excitement filled the air.

"I'll get more chairs," Isabella said. She hurried back to the hall, pushing her way through the crowd.

In the anteroom, standing with her back against the wall, was a beautiful young woman wearing a large felt hat and a black velvet dress. She seemed quite tiny, with huge, dark blue eyes. At her throat was a single white rose. She didn't look sinful or daring; she looked frightened out of her wits.

So this was the mysterious Victoria Woodhull. Isabella was debating whether to walk up and introduce herself when a young, officious Senate aide, obviously excited, brushed past her and took the young woman by the hand. "It's time," he said, his cheeks turning pink as he touched her fingers. "Now I want to warn you, you've got suffragists in there, and some of them are wary because they've heard you defend free love."

"Who?" the young woman asked in a low, barely audible voice.

"Anthony, for one. There's a Beecher in there, too—Isabella Hooker. Watch out for her."

Isabella stepped forward, ready to object. But a second Senate aide, more pompous than the first, had strolled up, clearly intent on ingratiating himself with the vulnerable-looking woman with the large, frightened eyes. "Don't you worry your pretty little head, Mrs. Woodhull." He chuckled. "No Beecher shall take *you* to task. I am reliably assured that Henry Ward Beecher preaches to at least twenty of his mistresses every Sunday."

Something flashed across Victoria's face, animating it instantly. Her small red tongue flicked quickly over her upper lip; she looked like a cat offered a bowl of cream.

At that moment she and Isabella locked eyes, and the cat disappeared. Now she was drawing Isabella into cheery complicity, conveying with a quick wink their shared knowledge of vain, strutting males who think they are protectors but in truth are not. Isabella couldn't look away. The demure demeanor of this strange woman was a façade, and she was being invited to share the joke.

They broke eye contact only when Representative Benjamin Butler appeared to escort Victoria into the hearing room. Isabella, carrying chairs, hurried in ahead of them and took a front row seat with Susan next to her.

"Look at that woman," Susan muttered.

Victoria had entered the hearing room with a light step, swinging her hips like a dancer while holding tightly to Butler's hand. Her skin had taken on a luminous glow. She offered a tremulous smile to the crowd, as if inviting them to protect her.

Isabella glanced at the committee members gathered around a large mahogany table. They looked slightly stunned.

Butler escorted her to her seat at the center of the room and cleared his throat. "Gentlemen, it is my pleasure to introduce Mrs. Victoria Woodhull, who is here to acquaint us with her views on the rights of women." A few more words, and then Butler nodded in Victoria's direction. "The floor is yours, Mrs. Woodhull," he said grandly.

Victoria stood, a document in her hand, and began to speak in an almost inaudible whisper. Isabella glanced at Susan. Was this going to be another embarrassment for women?

But Victoria's voice grew stronger, and by some theatrical magic, her presence swelled, filling the room. She held her document aloft. "Senators and Members of Congress, I am here, not to plead a weak cause, but to prove to you that the right to vote is the birthright of all women who are citizens of the United States." Her eyes flashed with amusement. "I see your skepticism, gentlemen. But I believe you are men of logic, and *I will prove my case.*"

Without apology or hesitation, she outlined her argument, with the ease of a trained lawyer and the fire of an actress comfortable with center stage.

"Look at the Constitution *as it is,*" she declared. "The basis of equality is constructed *by all* and *for all* and from which all partake of *equal* rights, privileges, and immunities. Surely no man of intelligence can deny *that!*" She paced the room as she spoke, the gentle folds of her velvet dress swirling sensuously around her body. The men at the table stared, agape. It was a masterful performance.

"We need her," Susan whispered.

Isabella nodded. She was forming a plan.

Victoria spoke for half an hour. Afterward, dozens of women crowded around in the corridor outside to congratulate her for presenting an argument for the vote that members of Congress *had actually listened to,* which surely was unprecedented. Isabella held back until the crowd thinned and then moved forward.

"Mrs. Woodhull, I am a Beecher. Will you talk to me anyway?" she said.

A sharp, amused intelligence flashed from those large, extraordinary eyes. "I knew who you were from the moment I saw you," Victoria said in a soft voice. "And there's no one I would rather talk with today."

By that afternoon, Victoria Woodhull was speaking from the platform as a spokeswoman for the National Woman Suffrage Association, with Isabella leading the applause.

"Please notice I'm not *asking* you anything about Woodhull," Puckett says, interrupting her thoughts. "But if it isn't breaking our ground rules, I'll just say she was impressive that morning, that's for sure. Even if it was futile. We laid bets on how long it would take for them to turn her down."

"She was amazing," Isabella says softly, forgetting her resistance.

She looks around for the first time at her surroundings, noting the scrupulously clean wood floor and the yellow twill curtains that give this little place its cheery atmosphere. These new tea shops are quite popular, but this one is almost empty. Only one man is here, reading his newspaper, repeatedly sniffling and blowing his nose into a large linen handkerchief. The waiter keeps watching the door, obviously hoping for more business as he polishes the bar's mahogany countertop. She hopes the opposite. But she feels lifted above the worrisome details of her presence in the Heights, somehow calmer. More herself. To sit here and talk now seems a reasonable thing to do, not a desperate way of getting off the street.

"What do you want here, Mrs. Hooker?" Puckett asks in an entirely new tone.

"You already know. I want to see my brother," she replies. "That's why I'm here."

He sighs. "I don't know why, to tell you the truth."

"You don't have to know. I do."

"Is it worth it?"

That thought has occurred to her more than once, but she

needn't acknowledge it now. "Of course it is, how can you ask me that?"

"After he's ruined a few lives, including, may I say, yours?"

"He hasn't ruined my life."

"He's a hypocrite and a liar, and you've said so all along. Why the change of heart now?" His voice becomes ruminative, as if she weren't there. "There was always a softness to the man. Something emotionally corpulent. A softness turned to rot, like a peach left in the sun too long."

Isabella stands up. What is she doing here, with this man? "I'd like to remind you, you're talking about my brother," she protests.

He stands up too, leaning across the table. "Who survived, Mrs. Hooker?" he says quietly. "You Beechers tend to cannibalize yourselves as well as others. Henry never stopped looking foolish, never stopped trying to be the same rakish saint he had created. And how about Elizabeth Tilton? She lost every shred of dignity and reputation. Every—"

"What is this attack about? Why does this involve you?" she says, angry to the verge of tears.

Puckett stops, his face darkening. He is breathing hard. Then he slumps back into his chair. "I'm sorry," he says. "I understand if you walk out of here right now. Look, maybe I can help you. But I'm going to ask you something first—will you come somewhere with me?"

"Where?" she asks. "And why?"

He doesn't answer immediately. Then he says, "To see Elizabeth Tilton. She lives with her daughter."

"What an absurd request," Isabella says, taken aback. "Why would I want to do that?"

"Maybe to get the focus off yourself and your family? Just a thought."

She hesitates, poised to flee. But she is stung by the challenge in his words; the barely concealed edge of disdain. He will find she is no coward.

Slowly, with some apprehension, she nods.

*   *   *

The house on Livingston Street looks like a worn shoe, scuffed and faded, its exterior far shabbier than its neighbors' on this tree-lined street in the Heights. Isabella slows her step as they approach. Twelve years ago people used to do the same as they walked by, whispering to one another the latest delectable tidbits about the glamorous Tiltons. This is where it happened, they would say. How scandalous. Such an accomplished man, that handsome Theodore Tilton, an editor of national renown. And his wife, Elizabeth, so lovely with her dark eyes and musical laugh. A striking couple, so in love, so glittering and charming, dancing through the social whirl of mid-century, delighting all they met. It was a provocative friendship they forged with the Reverend Beecher. The three of them shared passions for everything from religion to politics, but there were more corporeal passions being enjoyed, right here on Livingston Street, no doubt about it. Some claimed all Beecher wanted was a warm haven with good friends where he could ease the loneliness he felt in his own home, a loneliness that no number of layered Oriental carpets could assuage. But motivations change.

And some said they remembered seeing Henry walking down this street in the evenings, full of cheer and goodwill for all he passed—anticipating his welcome at the Tilton home, perhaps? Some said they saw the door flying open when he knocked; they claimed glimpses of Elizabeth greeting him with shy delight. Imagination filled in the rest: Theodore jumping up and embracing his friend and mentor, the evening beginning. Good talk, warm laughter. Conversations about God, about love and friendship. Their shared belief that men and women did not have to be married to have the kind of emotional intimacy they enjoyed. The giddy reality of being freed from sanctimonious cant. Elizabeth, fluttering from one man to the other, touching Henry's cheek, laughing, running her hands through her husband's hair, then back again to Henry, swept away by them both, leaving both awash in warm waves of male power. Was that how it happened?

It was when Theodore began to increase his restless, frequent travels that things soured. There were rumors of his affairs. This man, who never traveled without copies of the New Testament and *The North American Review,* his writing portfolio, a roll of letter stamps, and always, a brand-new English toothbrush dutifully purchased by Elizabeth—anyone so precise had to be controlling. Maybe he wasn't such a kind, jovial man. Some insisted they always saw a certain coldness in his manner. They claimed he could easily bully his soft wife into feeling guilty about everything, which could ease a man's mind when he was irritable. But if all this was true, to whom would she turn? To Henry, of course. For he was not just a friend, not just a man, he was her spiritual mentor. When she was sad, she could talk to him as a confessor. When she cried, he could embrace her to give spiritual consolation.

So the warm evenings on Livingston Street continued without Theodore, the curtains tightly closed.

They have reached the steps. The mortar between the bricks is crumbling, and a piece of brownstone from the bottom step has broken away, ready to trip the unwary. All the curtains are again drawn tight, as if anyone out on the street still fantasizes about what went on behind them anymore. And then again, maybe they do. Even tarnished glamour retains a certain sheen.

Puckett rings the doorbell once. The door opens. A thin, worn-looking woman who appears to be in her thirties answers, leaving the chain on, peering out.

"Hello, Florence," he says.

"Oh, Mr. Puckett, it's you," she says, sliding the chain off, opening the door. Puckett walks in first, and the woman embraces him with easy familiarity.

Isabella tries to rid her mind of imagined scenes as she looks around her surroundings. She has been here only once, back when everyone was still friends. But the sofas and ottomans look familiar, although more threadbare than luxurious now. They are still solid and sturdy, bought in a calmer time, when society seemed stable and furnishings were expected, like marriages, to last forever. The fire screen has been painstakingly worked in petit point, and a faded bouquet of orange wax flowers sits under a glass dome on the side-board. Elizabeth used to hang baskets of fresh flowers in the hall-way, a charming habit that Henry once suggested to Eunice, and learned never to mention again. They are no more. But the oil paint-ing of Shakespeare, the one by William Page showing the scar over his left eye, still hangs in the parlor. Isabella marvels at this, wonder-ing what stopped Theodore Tilton from making off with it when the marriage ended.

"How is she?" he asks.

"Not well," the woman replies. "She knows he's dying, I can't hide it from her. It's making things difficult."

"Her sight?"

"Worse than when you were here last. I have to hold her by the hand now to come down the stairs. I don't know what we would do without—" Only then does the woman look inquiringly at Isabella.

Puckett clears his throat. "This is Mrs. Hooker," he said. "Mrs. Isabella Hooker."

The younger woman stares. "Mrs. Isabella *Beecher* Hooker, am I right?"

"Yes," Isabella says, wondering if she is to be shown the door.

"Can we see your mother?" Puckett asks gently.

Saying nothing, and still staring at Isabella, the woman nods. She turns and starts up the stairs, Puckett and Isabella following.

Elizabeth Tilton sits in front of a window, the pocket doors opened wide, staring out onto the street. She is wearing a worn wrapper, and her hair is still dark and curled to her shoulders. Is-abella tries to remember what she looked like twelve years before, recalling only that there were but two existing photographs of her, one of which had been in the possession of her husband. She had as a result been drawn often fancifully by artists at the trial. They wanted images of a beautiful, mysterious woman tinged with hints of vulnerability. The vulnerability is there, but there is nothing mys-terious about the woman seated by the window. She seems like an afterthought in the room, almost vaporous. Was she always that way? Was that why she floated between Theodore and Henry, denying adultery to please one, admitting to it to please the other? And then shifting again, so all despaired of ever hearing the truth? She sits with her hands—skin like translucent parchment, criss-crossed with blue veins—folded in her lap.

"I've brought someone to see you," Puckett says. His voice has lost its professional mix of mockery and toughness.

"Hello, Mrs. Tilton," Isabella says. She would not presume to call her Elizabeth.

"Who are you?" Elizabeth says in a faint voice. "I'm sorry, I don't see very well."

"I'm Isabella Hooker."

A smile plays across the seated woman's lips. "Truly?" she asks.
"Yes."

"Mr. Puckett?" Elizabeth reaches out a hand, groping through the air in Puckett's general direction. "I'm not being mocked, am I?"

"I wouldn't have brought her here for such a purpose," he says. "I think she has something to say to you."

Isabella casts him a swift, alarmed glance. Something to say? She has nothing to say, only pity to offer.

Elizabeth speaks first. "Mrs. Hooker, my condolences. I know Henry is dying, and I have been sitting here all morning, thinking about him. Remembering. Now he must meet his God, and I pray he is ready."

"So do I," Isabella says.

"We all have regrets, don't we? They haunt us, but we need to acknowledge our mistakes. To do otherwise is to die falsely justified." She seems to be talking as much to herself as to her visitor.

"Yes, I agree," Isabella says weakly. The questions she wants to ask refuse to emerge.

Elizabeth shivers. Puckett immediately walks to a chair, retrieves a shawl, and tucks it across her shoulders with almost tender famil-iarity. The daughter, hovering behind Isabella, murmurs, "The heating bill was so high this month . . ."

"I'll take care of it, don't worry," he says. "Just turn the furnace up."

She nods and vanishes from the doorway.

"I'm not a particularly strong-minded woman, Mrs. Hooker, but you know that. My mistake was trying to please everybody. What was yours?"

"Stubbornness, perhaps," Isabella says after a moment of hesitation. She still isn't sure.

"I could have used more of that trait." Elizabeth smiles again, clearly with effort. "I know what you want to ask. Which of my stories was true? I waited too long to be believed. I could only do it when no one was pulling at me anymore—not Henry, not Theodore. And I found then to my sadness that either no one believed me or, worse, they didn't care anymore. I think the latter is the worst, but it comes to all of us eventually."

Isabella can hear the faint hissing of the radiator coming to life. Puckett is leaning against the door, hands shoved in his pockets, listening to their exchange. She steps forward, taking one of Elizabeth's hands in her own.

"Mrs. Tilton," she says. "I'm sorry."

Elizabeth's almost opaque eyes are barely focused, and a tear slowly trickles down her cheek. "Thank you," she says.

"So you found you had something to say after all," Puckett says as they emerge onto the street and walk down to the harbor, the wind whipping at their coats. "Must be a first for a Beecher. Too bad you aren't the official spokeswoman for your family."

"You obviously take care of her." Isabella understands his challenging style better now. "Why?"

Leaning into the wind, he tells her in quick, terse fashion. His mother died when he was small, and his father deserted the family, leaving Brady and his brothers and sisters in the care of a neighbor. That neighbor had children of her own, including a shy little girl named Elizabeth, who grew up to marry the dashing, famous Theodore Tilton.

"So the two of you share the bond of brother and sister," she says.

"Well, not quite," he says. "I'm just paying back her mother's kindness."

"That's not what I saw back there." She wonders why he feels he has to be so brusque.

"So—do you *still* want to see that brother of yours?"

"More than ever."

Puckett sighs as they turn from the harbor with its frothy waves and leaden skies and walk back toward the center of town. He doesn't respond immediately. "Well," he says, "in for a dime, in for a dollar. Maybe I can help you."

"How?"

"Who's in that house?"

"Eunice, of course. My sister Harriet, and a woman who used to be a nursemaid for her children, Anna Smith. She's devoted to Harriet."

"Mrs. Perkins showed up this morning, though few recognized her," he says. "The Beecher children are coming, and some of your brothers, I hear. Getting crowded at old 124 Hicks Street."

So Mary was there too. It was as if each loved person invited to climb those stairs and disappear within Henry's house was somehow lost to her.

"You need an advocate in there who can work around Mrs. Beecher. Why don't you write a note? I can get it into that house, guaranteed."

She considers his offer; it sounds so simple. She could explain her feelings, pour out her hope for reconciliation, ask for a last, precious meeting with Henry. But to whom would she send it? And what would happen if she wrote a note and gave it to this man and saw it tomorrow on the front page of the *Eagle*?

"No, I don't think so," she says.

"You still don't trust me. Well, I understand, why should you? But I've got some contacts on Mrs. Beecher's staff of happy servants, and I can get a note in there. You can't." He pauses, then adds almost indifferently, "It's probably your only chance."

Isabella tries to think. She could write a note to Mary. Harriet would spurn her, she is sure of it. But Mary is fair-minded and never needs to thrust herself forward for credit. Mary knows how to change minds quietly. Yes, Mary.

"What do you want from this?" she asks.

"You were treated badly. Just because I'm a reporter doesn't mean I'm here to pick over your bones again. If you get in, that's a good story, and I want to write it. That's what I want."

What does she have to lose, after all? For a long moment, Isabella walks in silence, glancing at Puckett's face, looking for something to warn her off this one chance to see Henry again. His expression does not waver.

"All right, I'll do it."

He breaks into a smile and points to a small shop just ahead of them. "Good. There's a stationery shop. I'll run in and get some writing paper."

CHAPTER SIX

March 7, 1887, 2:00 p.m.

"DID YOU KNOW she was here?" Eunice strides into the parlor, flings her muff down on a chair, and addresses Harriet without so much as a glance at Mary. "You did, didn't you? I can tell it in your face. How could you not warn me? She was waiting to accost me on the street! I can't believe you left me vulnerable like that!"

"I'm sorry, I didn't want to upset you," Harriet says. "I had no idea she would attempt to approach you on the street."

"Upset me? Do you Beechers have any idea how much I loathe that sister of yours? Do you have any idea what she did to our lives?" Eunice is crying now, fumbling for a handkerchief, her plain features contorted.

"Please, dear, pull yourself together." Mary jumps up and puts a comforting arm around Eunice's shoulders. "Hattie wasn't trying to hurt you. We all need each other right now, we mustn't quarrel. Henry needs us."

That seems to calm her. But as Harriet and Mary acknowledge in a quickly exchanged glance, it won't be for long.

"Mother?"

A tall, reed-thin man in a wool plaid cap appears in the open doorway, staring at them, frowning. Standing behind him, peeking past his legs, are two wide-eyed children. It is Harry Beecher, Henry and Eunice's eldest son.

"Harry, you've come." Eunice rushes forward to embrace her son fervently, then bends down to brush the cheek of each grandchild with a kiss.

Harry nods warily when Harriet steps forward to greet him, clearly wondering what kind of dispute he has interrupted. But he asks nothing, just puts a protective arm around his mother's shoulder. Harriet hasn't seen this son in years. Is he still in the army?

There are more people filling the open doorway now: another son, Willie, walks in, his nose red with the cold. And behind him Thomas Beecher, looking very grave, holding his fair-haired wife's arm. Harriet exchanges more greetings, warmly with her brother, more diffidently with the newly arrived Beecher children. Willie is eyeing her somewhat distrustfully, taking the cue from his brother.

Harriet busies herself collecting coats, fighting exhaustion. The odor of damp wool begins to permeate the crowded parlor. It will be as it always is at these increasingly mournful family gatherings—a mixture of awkward conversation, feelings of impending loss held back or shared only with whispers and hugs, children trying not to forget that a family member is dying and they aren't supposed to be playing and enjoying themselves. Her thoughts fly back to the days before Calvin's death. Too soon, too soon again.

"Mrs. Beecher?"

It is the nurse, standing at the parlor door. She is breathless from running down the stairs. "Ma'am, I think your husband is waking."

Eunice's face pales as she raises one still-gloved hand to her mouth. She hurries from the room, running up the stairs, skirt hiked high, with her two sons and Harriet and Mary right behind her. Upstairs, she kneels next to Henry's bed, tears off her gloves, and fumbles for his hand.

"Henry?" she whispers.

Harriet clutches her sister's hand at the foot of the bed, straining to see a sign of recognition on Henry's still face, realizing his eyelids are fluttering. Can he indeed come out of this coma? Is there hope after all?

Eunice speaks again. "Henry, can you speak to me? Can you hear me?"

His eyelids lift, then close.

"I think you can," she says. She has forgotten, for just one brief moment, anyone else in the room. Her voice quickens, the words tumbling one into another. Her voice prods. "Henry, remember when you asked me to marry you? And you got me this engagement ring?" She lifts her left hand and holds it before his face. "See? I'm wearing it again. I don't care anymore that it cost eighty-five cents, we were happy then. I don't want the fancy one. Can you hear me? Please hear me."

Hardly a breath is drawn by anyone in the room; they are pitying witnesses to this weeping woman's regrets. Harriet wills her brother to open his eyes, hoping this for Eunice. Let something pass between them, she thinks, remembering Calvin's last hours. It will help, it will help. From somewhere she hears the fretful whine of a child questioning why he can't go into his grandfather's sickroom. Are Henry's lips moving? Harriet leans forward, hoping it is so, but she sees no change in his face. As she straightens, she sees the cook slip into the room, hover uncertainly by the doorway, and then move toward Mary.

"I think you can hear me, I do. I've not been always what you wanted me to be, but I've tried. Henry, I've tried." Eunice's voice quivers.

Harry steps forward, eyes filled with sympathy for his mother's pain. "Mother," he whispers. "It's no good."

The room falls silent. Henry's chest continues to rise and then fall with a rasping exhalation of air, but his eyes do not open. Harriet and Mary stand still, barely breathing themselves. Eunice stares at her husband's face and squeezes his hand. No one else moves.

"I'm sorry, I must have misconstrued what I was seeing, Mrs. Beecher," the nurse finally says in a faltering voice.

"Apparently." Eunice rises, turns from her husband's bed, walks past them all and out of the room. She pauses only to speak to the cook, who then exits the room with her.

Only later does Harriet remember that the cook, looking flustered, had held in her hand what appeared to be a white envelope.

"Well, the letter's in the house." Puckett slides into a seat next to Isabella at the tea shop where she awaited him. "Hope it does something for you."

"Thank you." She is anxious to leave now. Writing her imploring note has left her exhausted. She doesn't ask Puckett to whom he delivered it; what's the use? She has to trust him. "I asked Mary to send a message to me at the boardinghouse if there was a way."

"You do know this is a long chance," Puckett says, looking a little uneasy.

Harriet pieces it all together only later. She remembers walking down the stairs, seeing Eunice and the cook in agitated conversation, then seeing Eunice snatch the white envelope from the cook's hand. And yes, Eunice had an oddly grim smile on her face as she marched into the library and settled herself at the writing desk. Harriet had walked by, hesitating. The cook was standing as if at attention, hands clasped in front of her. Her eyes darted to Harriet, then away. She seemed desperate.

"Is something the matter?"

The cook glanced at the open library door. "No, ma'am," she said.

Eunice emerged at that moment with a different envelope. Wordlessly, she gave it to the cook, who bobbed her head and immediately vanished in the direction of the kitchen.

"Those coats are smelling up the house," Eunice said to Harriet, glancing toward the overloaded coat tree. "Will you help me carry them to the third floor?"

*   *   *

March 7, 1887, 5:00 p.m.

The note is brought to Isabella by the landlady's son. "Some woman said you should have this right away," he says with an indifferent, why-did-they-ask-me tone.

Isabella thanks him, closes the door, and sits on the bed, breathing slowly to calm her nerves. She must expect disappointment. If she expects it, failure will not be as painful. She opens the envelope and scans its contents.

"Come at six o'clock," it says.

Nothing else. No signature. No warnings. Just a simple statement of the time when she should come.

She wants to jump up and dance around the room. She *is* welcome after all. She *can* see her brother one last time. Mary is wonderfully artful; how did she persuade Eunice to agree? Somehow she managed it. And whether Henry is conscious or not, she will reach him and apologize for her own stubbornness; she will reconnect with the brother she has always loved. They will find each other with this last reunion, and both will have a chance to be whole again. God must intend it to be so, or this chance would not have come her way.

She rocks back and forth on the bed, weak with relief. A quick glance at the clock tells her it is already after five. She will bring a gift for Eunice. Yes, some cakes. But she must hurry, the bakery will close soon. She will walk up those steps, the very ones where she and Henry stood together, covered with flowers, sharing the joy of his twenty-fifth anniversary as pastor of Plymouth Church, oh, so long ago. She will walk up those steps again, with her head high.

She leaves and hurries away just as the stocky figure of Anna Smith, her face red with anger after wringing the truth from Eunice's distraught cook, starts toward the boardinghouse at an awkward trot. But Isabella has disappeared.

*   *   *

March 7, 1887, 6:00 p.m.

Isabella wraps her coat tightly, hugging the collar close to her neck with one hand so it will not whip open in the wind, clutching a loaf of fresh-baked pumpkin bread in the other. She hesitates at the sight of the throng of reporters in front of Henry's house. But it is all right, she can endure their scrutiny now. Slowly she makes her way through the crowd, raising her head only to see if she can spot someone at the parlor window. Surely Mary will be watching for her. She doesn't see Puckett rounding the corner at a run, wildly looking left and right.

"Well, look who's here! Mrs. Hooker!" The reporters part in astonishment, then press in again. Isabella pushes her shoulders straight, determined not to act like a scuttling bug before their onslaught. If she has learned anything from those days when she cringed at seeing her picture in every paper, it is to stand proud. Will there be some sign of welcome? She looks up again and this time sees a figure standing in the window.

She is at the bottom of the steps. Taking a deep breath, she starts up, buoyed by the murmurs and shouts of the crowd around her. I am going to see Henry, she tells herself. Together, we will mend it all. My family is in this house. If Henry is to go to God, he will go with an eased heart. Two steps up, now three. The person at the window is gesticulating. Who is it? Only a few more steps. She looks again.

It isn't Mary. It is Harriet, waving her arms. What is she saying? Something. But Isabella is on the top step now, and there is no retreat. She lifts her hand and pulls back the knocker just as Puckett yells from the bottom of the stairs.

"It's a trick! Come down!"

The door flies open, whipping the knocker from her hand. Standing in front of her is Eunice, her face flushed deep red and her eyes lit with triumphant malice.

"You contemptuous woman," she screams. "Get off my steps!" She slams the door shut with such force that Isabella teeters backward, catching her balance at the last second.

The crowd below sways and titters as Isabella turns around to descend the steps. They are laughing. What has she done? She thinks for a moment that she will faint, but with a great effort of will, she steadies herself. She glances back at the window. Her sister has vanished; her entire family has vanished, and it happened a long time ago, and how could she have dreamed she would be allowed to enter this house? With great effort she descends one step and pauses, holding tight to the railing for support, knowing full well what she has done. The wound is ripped open. She has given public permission to turn Henry's final illness into a circus, throwing the Beechers once again into the world of gossip and titillation. Down one more step, still holding on to the iron railing. And what does she see, past the clamoring crowd, down the block, prancing under the street-lamp? That strange figure of this morning, singing again, the words faint but recognizable.

> Beecher, Beecher is my name—
> Beecher till I die!
> I never kissed Mis' Tilton—
> I never told a lie!

It is as if a curtain has parted, and she is hurtling back into the past.

PART TWO

CHAPTER SEVEN

Nook Farm, Hartford, Connecticut
September 16, 1872

T HE WIND IS PICKING UP; Isabella, shivering, quickens her pace to reach the thickly entwined blackberry bushes, anxious to feel the warmth of the sun. She loves this isolated spot behind Nook Farm, grateful that all the fashionable people of her neighborhood seem indifferent to its charms, leaving it, for the most part, to her and the dragonflies.

She reaches the shelter of the bushes and draws a sigh of relief. She needs a respite. There is trouble coming today, which is probably why Catharine is acting more impossible than usual. How else to explain her switching suddenly this afternoon from railing about young girls dancing on the stage of the Grand Opera House to attacking the suffragists? She's done it before, but this time it feels uncomfortably personal.

"Respectable women do not fight for the vote, and yet on you go, aligning yourself with people I would not allow in my home," Catharine had said as she brushed a speck of dust off the velvet sofa in Harriet's parlor.

"Oh dear, do I have to leave?" Isabella knew from experience to try for levity with her opinionated eldest sister.

Catharine didn't seem to hear. "Agitating for the vote is bad enough, but your group is losing all credibility with this business of making divorce easy for women."

"It isn't making it 'easy,'" Isabella retorted. "We're trying to make it possible for women to escape abusive husbands."

"All very fine sounding. It will destroy the family, that's what it will do."

"It will not destroy the family, it will save the families being destroyed now," Isabella said as calmly as she could. She'd said it all before.

But Catharine was not backing off.

"I don't know what stubbornness keeps you from seeing the damage these women are doing. I have no respect for any of them, but Victoria Woodhull is in a class by herself. I can't abide that woman. She's little better than a common prostitute. I can't understand how my *own sister* continues to be involved with such a person. She is out to cause mischief, and she will find a way to—"

"Catharine, not now." Harriet's voice cut in firmly, edged with warning. She had been sitting silently in front of her easel, mixing colors from her battered metal paint box. She did it absentmindedly, a habit that left as many daubings of color on her gray smock as on her canvas, a joke they usually all enjoyed.

"That's all very well for you to say, Hattie. You manage sometimes such glacial calm, I'm astonished. But that's not my nature. And you're as disturbed by that woman as I am."

"Indeed I am," Harriet replied, sending her a conciliatory smile. "But picking a quarrel with Bella this afternoon doesn't help anything."

"Oh, for heaven's sake, why are we pretending? Edward wouldn't have insisted on all of us coming up here tonight if there wasn't trouble in the air. I'm sorry, Bella, but trouble tends to be associated with your suffragist friends, and that's the fact of it." Catharine drew a handkerchief from her apron pocket and dabbed at her nose.

Isabella bit down on the end of her tongue to avoid replying. It was a method she used to keep herself from speaking too quickly, but it didn't often work.

"We'll know soon enough. Right now, I'd like the peace to finish this painting." Harriet nodded toward the delicate yellow blossom on her canvas and lifted her brush, holding it poised.

"Of course, we don't want to disturb you, do we?" Isabella glanced at Catharine, then continued without waiting for an answer, as if the thought had just occurred to her. "I think I'll go for a short walk."

She opened the door and made her escape to the blackberry bushes. She could think a little more about what was coming if she could be alone and breathe some fresh air.

This has to be about Henry, she tells herself. Edward had cast himself as his younger brother's protector ever since Henry, in an act of kindness, made Edward his "adviser" at Plymouth Church after he lost his job at the *Christian Union*. Everyone saw it coming, of course, except Edward. He could not grasp modern needs, and no one wanted to read his backward-looking articles on preexistence and eternal damnation anymore. It was quite in character for him to sweep into Hartford with great certitude on anything that affected Henry, as an act of gratitude if nothing else.

Mary is coming, and so are Thomas and William. That makes seven, including herself, of the surviving ten Beecher children. Poor Charles, so idealistic, worn down by struggles with his ministry and the deaths of his three children, is happy now as superintendent of education in Florida. Nothing can move him from there. And Jim? Her baby brother, the youngest; always restless, always on the edge of disaster, and now a respected minister in the Catskills—nothing will budge him either.

Regardless, this is to be the largest family gathering in some time. The whole community seems to suspect something big is happening. Neighbors have been peeking at them from behind their bedroom curtains all morning, curious and wary.

Usually she and her brothers and sisters communicate with their round-robin letters, those wonderful gossipy missives sent back and forth that Isabella has looked forward to for years. They all exhaust one another when they dwell too long in the same firmament, which isn't surprising, given their early competition for Father's approval and attention. The privilege of being Beechers has opened many doors for them, but the burden of finding common ground for public positions has rubbed nerves raw more than once. Thank goodness for the letters.

Isabella surveys the berries. Why leave them to rot? She reaches into the bushes, remembering how she had once reached too far and fallen into the prickly center of a blackberry bush, only to be scolded severely when she ran home, crying, her face and hands scratched and bleeding. How old had she been? Perhaps ten. Scolded, of course, for not being more careful, but also for being greedy, which had puzzled her at the time.

With her hands full, she pulls up the edges of her apron to form a bag and tosses in more berries. She will surprise her sisters, who have little regard for her domestic skills. Maybe she will shock them totally and make a pie. The thought pleases her. Yes, she will make a pie. It isn't long before the outer branches are bare, making the clusters deep inside increasingly tempting . . . just as they were so long ago.

Henry was there the day she fell into the bush.

He had reached in first, teasing her to do the same. How could she resist? Henry made everything a happy game, and she loved that. It suited her nature. And so she reached in with abandon, reckless of safety.

"I didn't want you to dive in face-first," he said later, sitting by her bed, holding a wet cloth to the scratches on her face. "You have to protect yourself, Bella."

"You didn't."

"Yes, I did."

"How?"

"I was bigger than you."

Isabella took his hand and held it to her face. How was she to puzzle out boundaries when presented with joyful challenges? It was much too hard a question, so she asked an easier one.

"Henry, why is it greedy to pick berries that God meant us to eat?"

The flash in his eyes was immediate. "Keep asking that question," he said.

"What's the answer?"

"The puzzle, little Bella, is in the question."

She spent years not understanding, and now that she does, she is afraid, afraid for Henry. She hears the voices of those who dismiss him for what they call his "religion of gush." Anyone as famous as Henry is sure to draw detractors. Anyone who speaks openly of love as a virtue and not as something to be hidden beneath the dead weight of respectability is going to be criticized. But oh, how vulnerable he is! The whispers and stories about his behavior with women are multiplying, and she is convinced Henry doesn't know how to protect himself any better than she did as a child diving into the blackberry bush. Why has he wavered so between excessive caution and recklessness? Taking too conservative a stance on the reforms women wanted was one thing, but mocking Victoria's run for the presidency was another. I can understand his position on that, Isabella tells herself. Victoria was veering toward theater, and few suffragists thought her candidacy was a wise choice. But Henry, Henry, why did you publicly make fun of her? I fear you have made a formidible enemy, and nothing I have said has made you realize this.

How quickly the ground has shifted! Can it be only one year since Victoria burst out of nowhere to join the movement? So brave and fearless, she hadn't cared what people thought of her, she cared only about getting results, and the more outrageous her tactics, the more attention was paid. It was when her demands for sexual freedom for women became too persistent that male supporters balked. Yes, they were cowards, but it was no secret that men wanted exclusive claim to marital dalliances. Both sexes lived with the assumption that respectable women must be pure and above reproach. Isabella didn't like this hypocrisy any better than Victoria, but most women knew when to keep their hands off a dangerously hot stove.

Not Victoria. "Free love" has become her rallying cry, making it harder to change the subject back to giving women the vote.

"Don't shrink from this," Victoria had exhorted them just last week. "You can't be for women's rights without sexual freedom. Separate the hypocrites out and expose them!" She had glanced at Isabella—how? Pityingly?

Henry's name didn't have to be mentioned for everyone to know he was one of her targets. Isabella had not been able to untie the knot in her stomach as she listened to Victoria's veiled threats. But surely Victoria wouldn't put Henry's reputation in jeopardy—not the reputation of a man who had done so much for so many people. Victoria knew he was a good man and a friend to the cause.

"We must face the fact that she is willing to stake her future on the banner of free love," Susan Anthony had said worriedly. "And she doesn't care if she takes all of us with her."

Isabella had argued that Victoria was being made a scapegoat by those out to divide women against one another, one of Susan's own earlier arguments. Isabella had spoken with great passion, trying to fight her own uncertainty. Wasn't it cowardly to pull away from someone so committed to suffrage? Victoria's very nature was to challenge and provoke, that was what had ignited them all and given them energy. We are all at risk when someone like Thomas Nast feels free to caricature her as Mrs. Satan, she had said. Victoria pulled us out of our timidity; how can we desert her? Yes, we must talk sense to her, but we also must fight against the fear of new ideas; resist those who would pull us down. Her own sisters felt threatened, but that—

"You are caught in something of a pickle, Bella," Susan had said quietly.

The light is shifting, the sun lower in the sky. Clutching her apron carefully with one hand, she grabs deep into the bush with the other, closing her fingers tight over a crust of thorns. She wipes the blood onto her apron, impatient with herself. Holding tight now with both hands to her laden apron, she begins making her way down the hill and west toward Harriet's house on Forest Street in the family compound of Nook Farm.

"Bella, have you been daydreaming again? We've been waiting for you." Harriet is at the kitchen door, looking tense, glancing back and forth from her sister to the window of a neighbor's house across the path. Such a tiny woman, and yet always fired with energy; Isabella feels a rush of love. Hattie's gray smock has vanished, and her plain black serge makes her look unusually severe—or perhaps it is the lines of worry across her brow. "Everyone is in the parlor, and Edward wants you there, now. And if Margaret Hastings across the way doesn't pull her nose back in soon, I'm going to send the dog over to bite it off."

Isabella hurries in, still clutching her apron of berries, murmuring apologies.

"Edward has brought very bad news, and you need to brace yourself. Victoria Woodhull has done something outrageous and damaging."

Isabella follows her sister to the parlor, all voices stopping as she enters the room. She faces a strange tableau.

Catharine has the formidable, no-nonsense look of the schoolteacher she is, and she is obviously prepared to declare her expert position on the topic at hand. She is used to being an expert; she was once the most famous of all the Beechers for her work establishing respected schools for girls. Her books on the right way to till a garden, carve a roast, or clean a house are bibles for America's women, and no one treads on her turf, be it academic or domestic. Yet she is holding her hands unnaturally still in her lap, which makes Isabella uneasy. Mary wears her usual calm, motherly expression, while William sits slightly separated, averting his dark, gaunt face from the group, staring gloomily into the hearth. Why is it this one brother always seems to fade into the background? Thomas, clean-shaven with large, gray eyes, his bearing as straight and uncompromising as when he served as a chaplain during the war, sends a warm smile in her direction. Dear Tom, always passionate about working rights and scornful of religious prejudice. He is prone to cynicism when it comes to grand gestures, which sometimes puts him at odds with Henry.

Harriet's Calvin is standing straight as a stovepipe, hovering by the doorway, clearing his throat continuously. A wool muffler is wound about his neck; another cold, probably. Calvin, an amiable, scholarly man, is always catching colds. And Edward, clearly in charge, stands by the fireplace, glaring at her like a schoolmaster as she enters the room. His hair is thinning, but his beard remains full, almost obscuring the fact that his shirt is too tight around the neck, inflaming an unfortunate boil.

"The news was all over Boston two days ago," he says in an accusing tone. "No one is talking about anything else."

"What news?" Isabella asks calmly. Edward is not *her* schoolmaster, she reminds herself.

"Victoria Woodhull." Edward turns to face his young half sister, pronouncing each syllable of the name with distaste. "She has denounced Henry in a speech before the American Association of Spiritualists. Bella, do you hear? She has called him an adulterer."

"In a speech? She accused Henry in a speech?"

"Yes," Edward says. "Her charges are obviously lurid products of an inflamed mind. Fortunately, no newspaper will touch this; it's far too sordid and false. But she is capable of anything."

Isabella cannot utter the words at the tip of her tongue. What are the details? Her fears have shape now; they are real.

"I've said it time and time again, that woman is dangerous," Catharine says.

"Did she name anyone?" Isabella manages to ask.

"Who do you think?"

Isabella waits.

"Elizabeth Tilton, of course," Edward says. "Woodhull claims Theodore has wrung from his wife a confession. He's a lying blackguard if that's true."

His words hang in the air, oddly harsh when spoken aloud. Elizabeth Tilton's name has been bandied about for months as Henry's love interest, but only in whispers. It's true, people are saying; everyone knows it. He's had other affairs; have you heard about the deathbed confession of the wife of Henry Bowen, owner of *The Independent*? Unbelievable! But would the pastor of Plymouth Church—think about it!—engage in a relationship with the wife of his best friend? Consider the woman in question, the supposedly "scarlet" woman named Elizabeth. Anyone seeing this tiny, shy woman with black hair (she looks like a small, pecking bird) would never believe she was having an affair. She does not appear capable of such deception. Could it be but idle gossip?

Nobody will wonder that now, Isabella realizes. Victoria has given the gossip public voice. Henry's jokes about her audacious campaign for the presidency must have scared off too many potential contributors and made her very unhappy. Isabella's heart begins to race. But to do *this*? Is her passionate friend capable of such petty revenge? What—

Edward's flat voice interrupts her thoughts. "Had you no inkling of this attack, Bella?"

All eyes are on her. She has a fleeting memory of clutching her fork at the family dinner table when Father unexpectedly asked her to recite her multiplication tables. Everyone turning in her direction, waiting for her to perform. A memory of panic.

"You mean, did I know what she was going to do?" An astonishing question, from her own brother.

"Of course you didn't, " Harriet breaks in impatiently. "Edward, really. We all know Bella would never leave us vulnerable to a defamatory attack."

"No, of course she wouldn't," Catharine echoes loyally, leaning forward to pat Isabella's hand. "You've been misled by this woman, dear."

The tension in the air eases. Even William looks toward her now, although with a certain caution in his eyes. William, so sweet and affable, always searching for the noncontroversial center. When he finds it, he will root himself, making sure never to adopt any view too strongly, never committing to one side or another. It gives her a pang to realize he is doing that tonight.

"I'm sure we all agree that you must immediately disassociate yourself from that crowd," Mary says, sounding like the surrogate mother she once was. "Do you understand, Bella?"

"I understand that something dreadful has been done to my brother, and I need to find out more." She doesn't want to slip back into being the baby, subject to direction from her older brothers and sisters. Nor is there any use in protesting the depth of her commitment to suffrage, which none of them seemed to understand under the best of circumstances. She must talk to Victoria.

"I don't see how there can be any question here," Edward says.

Thomas lets out a snort. "Except for the possibility that Henry is guilty."

Harriet's voice cuts in sharply. "He is not guilty."

Again a silence descends on the room.

"We must present a united front," Edward says. "An attack on Henry is an attack on the Beecher name, and we all know it. And we can't let this crazy woman jeopardize our family's reputation. I'm sorry, Isabella, but I must say what I believe, even if she is a friend of yours. We will not allow her to taint us with scandal."

Isabella sees the pain in his eyes, and for once she does not have to bite her tongue to stop from saying the wrong thing. "I understand," she says. "I intend to talk to her, and I will defend Henry to the utmost."

"Thank God Father is not alive to see this," Catharine bursts out.

They all pause for a moment, remembering the stern, righteous father who prayed unceasingly for their souls when they were children. That he might be in this room, hearing this news, is unthinkable.

"The important thing now is that we stand together. There is an onslaught coming, I assure you, and we *must* stand together," Edward says.

Isabella starts to reply and is stopped by Catharine's startled voice. "Bella, what in heaven's name is in your apron? I believe it is leaking on Harriet's carpet!"

Isabella looks down and realizes she is still clutching the sides of her apron. A few drops of juice have indeed oozed through the fabric onto Hattie's blue-patterned Brussels carpet. "Blackberries," she says. "I'm going to make a pie for dinner."

"And what have you done to your hand?" This from Mary.

"Nothing, I just nicked myself on a thorn, that's all."

"Bella, you are so clumsy," Catharine says. "And when did you last make a pie, dear?" She looks doubtfully at the contents of Isabella's apron. "They'll need a good washing. There may be blood on them. Go get a damp cloth and a little baking soda for the carpet; I'll make the pie."

Without a word, Isabella turns and marches out of the parlor, through the dining room, and to the kitchen door. She opens the door and gives her apron a single vigorous shake, heaving all the berries into the dirt by the back stoop. She walks back inside, rips off her apron, wads it tight, and tosses it into the corner.

Harriet is standing in the doorway, gazing at her with exasperation.

"Catharine didn't mean to hurt your feelings. You didn't have to throw the berries away," she says.

"It was to be my pie," Isabella replies. Her flare of anger has subsided; she already regrets the move. Must she constantly confirm the family view of her as impulsive?

It is as if Harriet is reading her thoughts. "When you do something like that, you only make the others question your judgment more."

"I don't want Henry to be hurt, or any of us to be damaged," Isabella says. "But the rumors about him have been around for a long time. I know Henry ignores them. But do we really know the truth? Whatever it is, it doesn't excuse Victoria's actions, but— Hattie, I have to be able to talk to you about this."

Harriet clasps her hands tightly behind her back and frowns. "I don't believe a word from Victoria Woodhull's lips," she says. "She tries to destroy everything she touches. I tried to warn you months ago, but you've been mesmerized by her. She's been putting out poisonous rumors about Henry all year, but that doesn't make them true."

"They aren't just coming from her. The whole town—"

"Don't entertain these thoughts, Bella. He needs us."

"You know how much I adore him. Why isn't he here? Why isn't he here to tell us directly if the story isn't true? Hattie, I think it is."

Harriet stares at her with those deep, grave eyes that have been an anchor for Isabella over many years, giving her not only a sight line into a confusing world, but a way to laugh at it when necessary. Now, they seem opaque.

"He has publicly denied it. That's enough for me—and should be for you."

It will be a moment Isabella will long remember. But not how she answered; that had been with some mush of words that came out sounding all right, at least acceptable enough for her to go back to the parlor with Hattie and join the others, to hear Catharine murmuring regrets for her bossiness, to listen to Edward declaim about family unity and responsibility; to watch William pace about, mumbling innocuously about the weather; to hear a few sympathetic words from Thomas. Everyone seemed eager to reduce the tension.

She had even helped Catharine fix dinner by peeling the potatoes and tying the roast, and sat through dinner, munching stalks from the celery goblet, eating off Hattie's blue and violet Minton china, drinking from the teacups with the delicate green handles that she had always loved. By the time they reached dessert, everyone was relaxing. They were a family, they could be a family. They could put their worries about Henry aside for the evening.

Someone asked who held the latest family round-robin letter and when was it going to be sent on?

"Catharine, I'll wager it's you—you hold the letters too long," Mary complained.

Thomas smiled and said teasingly, "That's because she's figuring out how to lecture us once more on the virtues of unbolted flour."

"My point has to do with the dangers of sluggish bowels," Catharine replied earnestly. "I don't want any of my family to suffer those horrors. If I told you the stories—"

Isabella raised her hands in mock surrender. "You have, and I promise never to bake with bolted wheat again."

"I welcome all the advice we send back and forth to each other," said Mary. "Though I wish you would stop writing along the letter margins, Hattie. I couldn't read your scribbles last time."

"Hattie has the worst handwriting of any of us, doesn't everyone agree?" Tom said slyly.

William began to nod but thought better of it when he saw his sister frown.

"Well, I could read it well enough to get Hattie's tips for redecorating my parlor," Mary retorted.

"Your parlor looks very nice, dear, but you could have used the glazed English print for the sofa instead of the French twill." Catharine was not about to give up her superior knowledge of home décor. "Much more economical. Why you spent eighty cents a yard is beyond me. By the way, does anybody know how Brother Jim is doing? He's been sounding restless again, dissatisfied—"

"Oh, Jim is always dissatisfied about something." Harriet sighed. "He's probably taken a dislike to mountains."

"Here we go, the Beecher buzz again." Calvin chortled, clearly pleased the earlier tension had dissipated. "What a gossipy group you are."

"Edward, I've been waiting to ask you this since the last time we were together—do you have time this evening to help me with my chess game?" William suddenly asked, turning to his younger brother.

Edward flushed and nodded, clearly pleased. He launched into a description of the opening moves that William must master immediately. "We'll play after dinner," he said.

Near the end of the evening, Harriet impulsively raised her glass. "A toast to the family," she said. "As long as we have each other, we can embrace the world or hold it at bay—our choice."

Isabella lifted her glass high, feeling the warmth of inclusion and belonging reflected in the expressions of her brothers and sisters. Her senses were sharpened by her hunger for them all that evening, giving her every detail: the sound of laughter, the comic way Edward twitched his nose when he was holding forth, the relaxed grin on Tom's face, the fragrance of the bluebells Harriet had placed in the center of the table. She felt a surge of fierce love for them all. She would remember everything about that evening, for it was destined not to be duplicated again.

New York City
September 18, 1872

Isabella draws a quick breath as Victoria opens the door of her dilapidated rooming house, startled at the almost maniacal look on her friend's face. She is wearing a wrapper at midday, and her dark hair tumbles loose about her face, giving her an unsettled, childlike look. Her small, delicate chin is thrust forward, as if to ward off an expected blow.

"Well, it took you long enough to come." Victoria's voice seems barely under control, starting throaty and deep, then spiraling. "Too afraid to visit, I suppose? After all, I'm not the heroine of the movement anymore. Let's see, what are they calling me now? Ah, yes, the prostitute who wanted to become president. The tainted, crazy woman to be discarded like a dirty handkerchief! So what are you here for? To join the chorus of denunciation?"

"You know better," Isabella says in as calm a voice as she can manage. "But you've been denouncing my brother, and you are damaging my whole family."

"Damaging the *Beechers*? Wonderful! I'm sure they're all hopping mad at me, especially those witchlike sisters of yours. They hate me. How does it feel to try to straddle this divide, Bella? How uncomfortable is it to hear the truth about Henry?"

"Don't start by challenging me," Isabella says. Victoria is even more volatile than usual, and she must stay a steady course. "Why did you do it? What did you gain?"

"Why did I do it? Because he's a hypocrite. When will you face it? And what I got out of it was attention." Victoria laughs, beckoning her in.

Isabella steps inside. Susan Anthony had warned her not to come, telling her that walking into Victoria's territory now would be like walking into a spider's web. If Victoria turned suffragists into figures of mockery, she would destroy everything.

But she had to defend her brother, Isabella argued back. And she had to wake Victoria up to the damage she was doing and get her to change course. Remember, she told Susan, she's politically the boldest of us all. Who else could have gotten Congress to consider seriously the right of women citizens to vote? We need her, she said, carried away again by her own argument. We just need to figure out a way to calm her down. Besides, could women have come this far without her?

"It doesn't matter," Susan said flatly. "We can't go on *with* her."

With Susan's voice ringing in her ears, Isabella faces Victoria squarely. "I'm here to protest what you did to my brother," she says. "And I won't stay if you insist on putting on a performance."

Victoria's expression softens. She drops her challenging stance and takes Isabella's hand. "I must remember, you are different from the others. Come in, dear friend, sit down, and let me share some things with you."

Isabella follows her into a tiny, cluttered room stacked with papers—papers on the floor, on the chairs, on an ancient sofa that sags under the weight. All this clutter, this energy, this pursuing of ideas and causes is what has made Victoria exciting to be around, and now all Isabella can think of is, there is nowhere to sit.

"Oh, just shove it all on the floor," Victoria says impatiently. She sweeps a stack off one chair and sinks into it; Isabella hesitates, then does the same.

"I have a wonderful speech ready for the next convention," Victoria says. "You led the last one superbly, and I must say, giving me a platform was one of the best things you did. Wait until you hear it! There's more than suffrage at stake this time."

Isabella knows Victoria stands little chance of being invited to speak again, but she says nothing.

"Why aren't you answering, Bella? Are you holding something back?"

"You are making many enemies, and you must stop, or you will defeat the very goals we all hold dear." Isabella looks her straight in the eye and will not look away. Surely Victoria can be brought around.

"I hold dear much more than suffrage. *Oppressive men* are at the core of every problem, and you know it. I have to fight them."

"What I know right now is that we are losing both women and good men who think all we want is free love without responsibility, and we can't let that destroy our movement. It's a trap. It's empowering our enemies—"

"Those enemies include your righteously moral sisters, don't they?" Victoria says with a sly smile. "Are they forcing this compromise talk on you? I've always thought you *support* equal rights for women. Is that what you're here for, to try to dissuade me from speaking the truth?"

"I—"

"Listen to me, Bella. Your brother *denounces* free love and then goes right out and *practices* it. And why is he skittering away from me? Why is he drying up the contributions I need to survive? Why is he impoverishing me? Because he's afraid of being exposed, that's why! I've known him as a man of worth, a man who understands that God did not intend for either men or women to deny their sexual selves, but he will not step forward and tell the truth. I will flush him out yet!"

"You can't force him to ruin himself," Isabella bursts out.

Victoria leans forward, lowering her voice to a theatrical whisper. "It's hypocrisy that I'm fighting. My erstwhile supporters were two-faced hypocrites. They run from all the stories about me— Oh, I know you've heard them. I even know your esteemed sister Harriet passed around the one about me inviting a United States senator to spend the night in my room!" She leans back and laughs. "So what if I did?"

"I don't care about that," Isabella says. She will not let Victoria turn this into a diatribe against Harriet and Catharine. "If you force a scandal, you destroy people. You destroy Henry. You destroy Lib Tilton." She takes a deep breath. "You destroy me, your friend. Is that what you want to do?"

"Destroy? What about the efforts to destroy *me*? Do you know what Julia Ward Howe called me after my speech? A self-aggrandizing harlot! And what about your brother's destruction of Theodore Tilton? Do you want to know more about that?"

"That's beside the point. I—"

"When the very precious Mrs. Stanton first told me the rumors about your brother, I decided to see for myself. I spent two nights last winter watching the Tilton home. I saw Theodore the second night, his coat collar up, hunched over, trying to stay in the shadows across the street. And I knew he was there for the same reason. Imagine the expression on that poor man's face when Henry climbed the stairs to his front door as if he owned them, there to be greeted with an embrace from Theodore's wife. You can't imagine that, I know. Listen! I will tell you more."

Her voice is now rising from deep in her throat. "It was a rainy night. Tilton was there . . . for what—who knows how many times? He waits. He sees your brother striding up the street, all muscle and certitude. What does he think? Perhaps it isn't what he suspects . . . perhaps this is a visit from a man of God . . . But then his wife answers the door . . . framed in the light. What is she wearing? Something diaphanous . . . floating . . . revealing. Her arms are out, and he sees them lace delicately around the back of this intruder who crosses his family threshold desecrating the name of God! Now, my dear Bella, *who* is destroying *whom*?"

Her performance is flawless.

Isabella wonders about Victoria standing outside the Tilton home for two nights running. She knows the rumors, spread with knowing winks, that Victoria often visited Theodore there when Elizabeth was away, rumors fed by his enthusiastic editorial endorsement in *Golden Age* of her view that marriage is of the heart and not of the law.

Can't Victoria see how her behavior feeds such rumors, especially among those who now dismiss her as a coarse opportunist? These include many of the very same people who once believed in her because of her amazing ability to scratch into their private dreams and fire them with passionate commitment. Such a waste! How can she, Isabella, abandon this woman, even when, in her heart, she knows the Woodhull star is descending?

"You are being very melodramatic," she says after a slight hesitation. "What do you want?"

"Acknowledgment that I am not a liar. And an apology for mocking my goals. How can he criticize me even as he secretly lives my values—"

"Let me ask you something. If Henry steps forward, if he does bring his own views into—into harmony with his actions, will you leave him alone?"

Victoria considers this silently for a moment. "I would welcome his honesty," she says finally. "And I would champion his leadership if he steps forward and speaks with that level of clarity."

"He pulled back from scandal, not from his beliefs."

"Then let him say so," whispers Victoria. Her eyes turn distant, as if she is listening to something far away, then immediately refocus. "Enough of this, Bella. Let's put our minds together and work on fashioning our next convention. I think you should start speaking publicly more. You're good, and very persuasive. I have some ideas. You can take them back to Susan and Elizabeth, if they'll listen."

"Another time."

"No, right now."

Isabella sinks back into her chair.

The sky is darkening when Isabella finally leaves, half drunk on talk and strategizing. Any visit with Victoria is like a swim in a turbulent sea. But she still makes Isabella believe that women can dance on the crests of waves, that all things are possible. Society will change, women will have rights and be able to fight for them at the ballot box. It will happen, the suffragists will win and the world will be better.

She takes long steps as she walks down the street, thinking of Victoria's daring ankle-length skirts, lifting her own slightly to see if she can replicate Victoria's casual stride, looking right and left to make sure no one is watching. The movement of air around her legs is invigorating. It is absurd, really, the clothes women continue to wear. Whalebone corsets, long, scratchy drawers, silk stockings, layers of starched cotton petticoats covered with tightly laced dresses that make it hard to digest food. Putting up with it makes women as cramped in their minds as they are in their corsets, she's convinced of it. What if women could wear trousers without being laughed at? Her one attempt at wearing bloomers in the 1850s produced such ridicule she quickly abandoned them. Oh, the women who pretended to be men and fought in the war got away with it. But wouldn't ordinary women find the elemental movements of sitting and walking to be much easier and freer? Of course. We aren't allowed honesty, she thinks. Or freedom. Men still can do what they want and call it whatever they want, but if they allow themselves free sexuality and deny it to women, they are truly hypocrites.

Isabella barely notices her mental segue from trousers to free love, because it is all of a piece. Not that she has any intention of damaging her marriage to John Hooker with radical behavior. He has been a good husband; indeed, waiting patiently for two years before she was willing to let herself be swallowed into marriage. But since that night she was shocked into facing the truth, the night she and Anna Dickinson talked until dawn, her radical soul has grown. It has taken her from her first forays into suffrage to women like Elizabeth and Susan—and Victoria. It still makes her laugh to remember how a friend objecting to her joining Susan Anthony called Susan "the one really hoofed and horned demon of this movement." There would always be a demonization of the radical, that she has learned. So perhaps there might yet be acceptance of Victoria—the latest woman to be demonized.

What a long road she has traveled since those evenings as a young woman spent with John amidst the lovely, musty smelling old books of his library, where she mended socks for the children while he read from Blackstone's *Commentaries*. She smiles at the memory of his patient silence as she denounced the laws that left women without equal rights. More than once, she had declared she wished she had been born a man. Or at least was as talented as her sisters.

One evening, the mending put away, she had walked out in the fields under the stars, thinking wistfully of the achievements of her family. Her sisters and brothers were eagles with splendid wingspans that kept them soaring ever higher as she tried to keep up with them. She was nothing more than a sparrow, and she must learn to accept her place. She could accept her lack of importance in the world, she had told herself. She could accept living in the after-glow of Beecher fame. But she felt a yearning that night as she looked up at the full moon. And although her true life would eventually ease those yearnings, she has not forgotten how she felt.

Isabella trudges on down the street in a glow of renewed determination. She must talk to Henry. He must step forward and take charge of this. If she can make him understand what is at stake, perhaps all can be resolved.

✢ CHAPTER EIGHT ✣

Brooklyn Heights
October 8, 1872

THE SOUND OF the pounding drums comes first, followed by so vigorous a tootling of horns that heads begin popping from upstairs windows. The Navy Yard band can't be seen yet, but it is coming. Isabella hurries as quickly as she can toward Columbia Street, angry with herself for being late for Henry's anniversary celebration. How can it be twenty-five years since her brother became pastor of Plymouth Church? Where have the years gone? She rounds the corner at Pierrepont and sees ahead of her an extraordinary sight: a sea of men, women, and children marching in the street behind the band, holding aloft banners suspended on spears with gilt points that glitter in the afternoon sun.

"They're headed for Reverend Beecher's house!" yells a woman leaning from an upstairs window. She is waving a flag, calling and laughing to neighbors leaning from their windows across the street.

Isabella is running now. She will get to Henry's house before the procession if she does anything again in her entire life, and no one is going to notice her hat is askew and her jacket unbuttoned, and even if they do, she doesn't care. Breathless, she rounds the next corner and is in sight of the house when she hears someone calling her name.

"Bella! You're here, you made it, come join me!" Henry stands on the top step of a stoop jammed with people, a large grin on his face as he spreads his arms to force a path for Isabella through the crowd. He is not wearing his signature floppy hat. His long hair is whipping back and forth in the wind, giving him a carefree, young look she hasn't seen in some time. Isabella clambers up, waving to some and stopping to hug her nephews and nieces as Henry's family and friends shout their hellos over the noise of the approaching band. Henry scoops her up into one of his most exuberant bear hugs. Behind him stands Eunice, a flush of color on her cheeks, excited enough herself to actually smile and wave at her sister-in-law.

"You looked like you were parting the Red Sea!" Isabella says with a laugh as he releases her.

"For you, I could do it. I'm glad you came, little sister," he says in a voice vibrating with emotion. For an instant, it is just the two of them on that stoop, sharing a moment of precious closeness.

The band grows louder. The steps are even more crowded now, as friends and neighbors climb up, reaching to shake Henry's hand and shout their congratulations. Suddenly the parade bursts around the corner in full color. The Navy Yard band is playing something brassy and gay, and hundreds of people pour into the street, singing and cheering as they march under the banners. Men in the crowd below doff their hats to Henry, while the women wave handkerchiefs.

Now there are a thousand children from the Sunday schools marching in front of Henry's house, many of them carrying baskets of blossoms. One young girl in white breaks ranks and tosses some blooms up to Henry. He catches a rose, makes an elaborate bow of thanks, and tucks it behind his ear to the laughter of all on the stoop. Another flower is tossed, and then another. Soon dozens of children are tossing flowers, producing a snowstorm of blossoms that leave normally staid men and women laughing and ducking as the flowers land on their hats and shoulders and quickly cover their shoes. The stoop is now a fragrant bower, and Eunice seems overcome. She raises her arms, cupping handfuls of flowers and gathering them to her bosom, her smile shy, her eyes watering.

Isabella tucks a flower in her hat, feeling giddy. What if she had been late? She would have missed this triumphantly happy moment. What a display of love and appreciation! Henry's parishioners have given him the crowning achievement of his career.

"I cannot believe this day. I've known none like it."

Henry has collapsed into what he likes to refer to as one of Eunice's "matchstick" chairs in the front parlor. His large frame causes it to creak alarmingly, but he takes no notice. His face is flushed, and his voice is hoarse from preaching to the crowd of thousands that gathered after the parade to honor him in Plymouth Church.

"Well, Henry, how many men have?" Isabella says. She sits opposite him on an equally delicate chair, trying to find a comfortable position. The two of them, brother and sister, are alone. The excitement of the day is over, dinner finished, and Eunice and all the visiting family members have headed finally for bed. "I wish Harriet could have been here—she wanted to be, but this speaking tour—"

Henry waves his hand casually. "I know, I know; my famous sister is always in demand somewhere or another. Some things can't be helped. But I'm delighted I've had the company of the little prodigal of the family."

"Prodigal?"

"Well, you do stray from the fold now and then," Henry teases.

"I learned independence from my big brother," she says with a smile.

Henry is already thinking of something else. "I can sit here right now and tell you, thank God I became a preacher. Father didn't hold out much hope for me, but for all his debating and swelling and floating here and there, he was wrong. Living with his harsh rule was like being a prisoner in a Puritan penitentiary. I can say it, now! I've done what I was meant to do. I wonder sometimes how I made it through the colic and anguish of hyper-Calvinism to preach the wonders of love."

"It is lucky for us all that you did."

"Happily my constitution was strong. I survived and flourished on my own terms. Do you understand, dear sister? After today, I know my work of the last twenty-five years has meant something." He suddenly laughs, slapping himself on the thigh. "Could you believe Storrs, that old reactionary? He hates my liberal doctrine, the old coot, but he swallowed his disapproval well. You would've thought we were the closest of friends. So laudatory about me, and from *my* pulpit! He knows how to bow to success, I'll say that for him."

She nods, looking for an opening.

"Did you see the story on our family in the *Eagle*? They nattered on about how hapless I was as a young boy, but I suppose that kind of thing warms people's hearts. On the whole, I thought the reporter did a good job." Henry pauses, then adds, "Although I'm sorry he didn't mention you and your brothers."

"It isn't important," she says, grateful that Henry has noticed. Some sloppy reporter hadn't bothered to learn Lyman had married a second time, let alone a third, but old childhood feelings of separateness had been stirred. "Everything was splendid today. You are clearly loved and respected, and I'm very proud of you. It should give you confidence in what you believe, what you are. People can't hurt you if you remain true to yourself."

Henry raises an eyebrow in the old comical way that used to make her laugh as a child. "How serious you are. This isn't a preamble to a lecture, is it?"

"I've been to see Victoria—" Isabella begins. But Henry's face darkens so quickly, she falters.

"I don't want to hear a word about that woman," he says softly.

"I think we should talk about this, Henry."

"Why are you still seeing her? She's trying to destroy me."

"I want to stop the rumors, that's why. And I can assure you, if you acknowledge your intimacy with Lib Tilton, she will not attack you again." She hurries on as he starts to interrupt. "Please listen, I'm not being naïve. This won't go away, I'm sure of it now. The story is already spreading, and if you speak up quickly, you can frame it. *You* will be in charge. Henry, oh, my dear brother, you've opened all our eyes to the hypocrisy of social pretense, that's why you are adored by your congregation. You want to free human experience, all human experience, it is clear in your sermons. This would be brave."

"My dear little sister, I want to tell you what this is all about," he says. "Do you know when Elizabeth first came to me?"

Isabella shakes her head.

"When her baby died. Doesn't it make sense to search for solace from her pastor? You've known that loss."

There is silence for a moment, as Isabella struggles to close the door Henry has cracked open. Babies died. It happened all the time, and women were supposed to heal and move on. They didn't; she hadn't. Not right away. But at least that small wisp of a life—her firstborn son—was taken quickly. Thank God she was given three more children who survived. She hasn't suffered as much as others, for her baby had been a stranger. When Hattie's bouncy little Charley died in the Cincinnati cholera epidemic, it was a harder, deeper loss.

"And so have you," she replies.

Henry's face creases with pain. "That changed Eunice," he says, half to himself. "Embittered her. I know, I've not spoken these words before, but it's the truth, I believe."

For a moment they sit in silence.

"Why did Elizabeth come to you alone?" Isabella ventures. "What about her husband, wasn't he mourning with her? Couldn't Theodore comfort his wife?"

Henry lets out a deep sigh. "Theodore is a remarkable, talented man, whom I've known a long time. I married them, you might remember. But he's not an easy man when it comes to emotions. That was what Elizabeth told me, and I have reason to believe it. She was consumed with guilt and needed a friend, and I was able to meet that need. You know something about irrational guilt, little sister."

Bella nods. She had been terrified when she found herself pregnant a second time. Hating it, fearing death, fearing childbirth; wanting to run from John, not wanting any more babies. And she had turned to Henry for spiritual help.

Henry reaches for her hands and holds them tight. "You were in torment," he said. "You were sure God would punish you with pain and death, terrible fears that were unwarranted. And I told you God would not punish you for having human feelings."

"I felt I was disappearing," she murmurs. Henry had virtually pulled her from a pit of despair. She would never forget that.

"Do you understand, then? Do you understand?"

She blinks, clearing her brain.

"Henry, wasn't there much more between you and Elizabeth?"

"If you mean the times I spent at the Tilton home, that's easily explained. Elizabeth helped edit my book manuscript, and it was easier to work over there."

"Why?"

"I could ask why you keep pressing me, but I'll tell you. Her home was a place of peace." He pauses, his voice taking on a slightly theatrical tremble. "Unlike my own."

"And Theodore?"

"He traveled constantly. I'm asking again, do you understand?"

Yes, she understands. Henry was miserable in his marriage for a long time. Who in town had not caught glimpses of him and Elizabeth over the past few years on the street, riding in a carriage, walking in the park, talking on the green outside Plymouth Church? It is easy to see why a need for human comfort could have drawn them together.

"Yes, I do," she says. "I understand that a compassionate God will not punish you either, Henry. You've shown me that. You and Elizabeth reached out to each other in mutual need, and those emotions you shared were no more sinful than mine. And if the actual commitment of adultery is a sin, it is a sin of the heart, and many have fallen."

"I didn't say—"

"If reaching out to a needful human being makes you a sinner, then the world will understand. Just don't let *other people accuse you first*. It could destroy your ministry. When you admit it, you open yourself to the forgiveness of a loving God. And—"

She stops again. Is she babbling? Henry is staring at her with something akin to horror.

"Are you mad?"

Those three words will come back to her in her sleep, night after night, in the weeks to come. At the moment of hearing them, she sees only his shock.

"I love you and am your loyal supporter," she says, forcing herself to speak calmly.

Henry leans forward, the chair creaking ominously, and places his hand gently over his sister's lips. "For your love and sympathy, I am deeply grateful," he says. His brown eyes, so full of dance only a moment ago, have gone flat. He moistens his full lips with a flick of his tongue, a nervous habit from childhood. "The way you can help me is with your silence. Love me, and do not talk about me."

"But it's true, isn't it?"

"You ask me that?"

"Henry, Lib Tilton has confessed."

"She's a spineless little creature, without morals. I deny it—to you, and to the world. That's the truth."

She hears first not his words but the contempt in his voice. It stops her breath. She feels a shiver of fear for no discernible reason, and then focuses on his denial. It feels strange enough to have finally asked for the truth, but it is surreal to hear an answer she knows in her heart is false. No one in the family has ever asked Henry directly about his guilt or innocence. All the long months of hearing and worrying about the whisperings and rumors surrounding this beloved brother have been spent in hoping the stories would fade and leave him unharmed, not in believing they were lies. Until this moment she had somehow expected he would admit the truth to her if she asked directly. Was that naïve? How many times over the years has he shared confidences with her, the sister who did not scold or implore but who accepted him as who he was? That was their bond. He counted on Harriet for discipline and strength but on her for simple adoration, and now she sees how fragile a base that was. John always chastised her for being too literal, too enveloped in her beliefs about people, to accept contradictions of character. She is facing one now, and she isn't prepared. John was right. Is she simpleminded, as well?

"I'm your sister. We've always been honest with each other."

"And I am being honest now." His voice is steady.

"That is your last word on this?"

"Absolutely. And yours too, little sister."

Isabella stays silent, absorbing this warning.

Nook Farm, Hartford
October 28, 1872

Isabella vaguely registers an unusually large stack of newspapers in front of the Hartford train station as she and John stroll by. They are out for their usual morning walk, but her mind is on the letter delivered the night before, which at that moment, is in her pocket. She fingers it, worrying, thinking how brittle the paper feels as she touches it. It is from Victoria.

"Henry had a grand celebration," the note reads. "Now I will have mine."

"She's angry," Isabella tells her husband. "Henry underestimates her. Everyone underestimates her."

The sharpening wind whips at her coat, and John, in an impulsive gesture, encircles her with his arm as they walk. "I think you worry too much," he says. "And I wish you would step clear of the whole mess. We don't have to be involved."

She squeezes his hand, feeling both frustrated and touched by his cautious protectiveness. John never quite understands that, in as large and important a family as hers, disengagement is a dangerous option. It is only one of the many disagreements of their marriage, but no marriage, from what she can see, is easy. This has proved to be better than most. She starts to reply, but he interrupts.

"What newspaper is that?" John asks. "There must be hundreds of copies here." They stop at the newsstand and pick one off the top of the pile, Isabella wondering why the usually chatty vendor keeps his face averted as they pay their money. John holds the edges firmly against the wind, and that is when he and Isabella first see the front-page story of *Woodhull & Claflin's Weekly*.

Isabella needs John's support to get back home. "Hurry," she whispers. "Hurry before the neighbors see us."

"The woman is insane," John mutters, alarmed at the shakiness of his wife's balance. "She's as much as accused Henry of indulging in orgies in front of Elizabeth Tilton's children."

Isabella tries not to listen. Reading Victoria's charges in print somehow makes all the gossip and whispers true. It is done; there is no looking away anymore. Victoria has stuffed her story with lurid, specific details about Henry's amorous encounters, and most readers will believe every word. It reads as if Victoria had been hiding behind a curtain and watching it all. First comes a declaration that marriage is as injurious to society as slavery—then the sweeping claim that Henry not only believes this but practices free love.

"The immense physical potency of Mr. Beecher, and the indomitable urgency of his great nature for the intimacy and embraces of the noble and cultured women about him, instead of being a bad thing, as the world thinks, or thinks it thinks, or professes to think it thinks, is one of the noblest and grandest endowments of this truly great and representative man. . . . Every great man of Mr. Beecher's type, has had in the past and will ever have, the need for and the right to the loving manifestations of many women."

But even though *"he entertains, on conviction, substantially the same views which I entertain on the social question, he is pretentiously the upholder of the old social slavery, and therefore does what he can to crush and oppose me. . . . I intend that this article shall burst like a bombshell into the ranks of the moralistic social camp!"*

It will, Isabella realizes. Vengeance is yours, Victoria. She feels sick, anxious to reach the haven of home and lock the doors behind her, already knowing that no lock will keep this storm at bay. Victoria has named her, along with Elizabeth Cady Stanton, in the article as her source. She is now the "traitorous" sister.

The newspaper is sold out by midmorning—150,000 copies. Rumors fly that people are paying forty dollars a copy in New York and Boston. Henry Ward Beecher, a hypocrite? Every newspaper in America is scrambling for the story. A local clergyman immediately denounces Henry from his pulpit, saying a scandal this shocking can destroy the foundations of morality. A fault line is opening, a strange, jagged crack between what people fear is true and what they want to believe. What? Henry Ward Beecher, the man of God who had fought so bravely from the pulpit against slavery? Guilty of indulging in illicit love and denying it? Perhaps he is indeed a hero with feet of clay.

It is a nervous time. Those who cheer on Henry's kinder version of God, which spurns hellfire, must now face a new question. Without the constraints of damnation, what holds human passions in check? Beneath the anxious gossip is still the clinging hope that chaste women and discreet men will continue to hold the fabric of society together. But Victoria's charges have sent shivers through the neighborhoods of Brooklyn and New York and Boston. Wives tighten their lips as they watch their husbands reading about Henry's travails, waiting and hoping for strong, male indignation. What if they stay silent? *Hypocrisy* is a vile word, and no one wants to hear it; the finest of collars on the most proper of men become uncomfortable.

. . . And Victoria Woodhull dances gleefully on the widening crack.

Isabella waits by the kitchen window, watching the path. She does not budge from her vigil until evening descends and she finally sees her sister's figure coming slowly up the path. Harriet has a shawl pulled tightly around her shoulders, and her face is drawn and pale. Isabella opens the door and holds out her hand as Harriet comes close, but Harriet draws back.

"I'm not coming in," she says.

"Please, let us talk."

But Harriet shakes her head. "I've been sitting for hours thinking about this. Bella, I have to hear it from you. Is it true that you were Victoria Woodhull's source for that scurrilous story about Henry?"

Isabella leans on the doorknob to hold herself steady. "I did not bring that story to her. I was not her source."

"Why did she name you?"

"I don't know." Isabella is struggling to answer that question herself. She knows Victoria is capable of saying anything to make a point, but to alienate one of her few friends left in the women's movement? Why would she do that? "It's been common gossip for such a long time, she may have thought she heard it from me first. She didn't."

"I notice you don't accuse her of lying. Nor have you denied talking to her about these outrageous charges against your own brother." Harriet's voice is shaking.

"I can't deny that," Isabella answers and sees her sister physically recoil. "Hattie, please— Yes, we talked about it, because everyone was talking about it. You know I was worried about him, we all were. That's why I went to see her after we all met at your house."

"Did you presume his guilt in those conversations?"

Yes, she had. Had she said so to Victoria? No, she'd been careful. Had she said so to Mrs. Stanton? What had she conveyed to these friends of hers in the movement? For a moment, she is shaken with doubt.

"I know the answer, Bella. You undercut your brother while claiming loyalty. I cannot believe this."

"No, that isn't true. I was not disloyal."

"Of course you were. How can you deny it?"

"Think, Hattie," Isabella implores. "I have never been disloyal to Henry, to you—to any of my brothers and sisters, even though we feel differently about many things. I never spoke against any of you when I was the only abolitionist in the family, and I have never voiced a word of criticism about your scorn for my friends. I love you, you and Henry especially. But Hattie, Hattie, I can't lie. I can't pretend to believe something I don't believe." It is no use. She can see the distrust in her sister's eyes, and tears begin to fill her own.

"You've chosen, Bella. Your loyalties are with your suffragist friends, not your family. It doesn't matter if you didn't declare Henry guilty to that Woodhull woman—the fact that you *believe* he's guilty must be known to all of them. And that's enough for me."

Isabella cannot parse out an answer. Yes, it must be. Her very presence in Victoria's home so short a time ago was enough of an affirmation. She will not pretend or protest otherwise; not to Hattie, not to anyone. She will not try to justify herself, try to convince her sister that, egregious as Victoria's action has been, Henry is the one who lied.

"Yes, it probably is," she says, her voice breaking.

Harriet turns on her heel and walks away without a backward glance. She holds her head high, looking small but about as frail as a bolt of iron. She is sixty-one. She has spent her life as a Beecher achieving great celebrity, enduring attacks from her enemies, raising her children, taking pride in family bonds. She does not do well giving small bits of herself to different endeavors or beliefs; to each project, each person, each crisis, she gives her whole soul. She has learned the virtue of decisiveness from fighting for her place within the Beecher brood and prides herself on judging quickly and cleanly. Regrets weaken the spirit. It is very simple—loyalty is all. And so Harriet marches back to her home, having done her flinty Calvinist heritage proud.

Isabella stands watching Harriet head up Forest Street, unable to close the door. There is an early frost on the fields; she will remember that later. She will even remember hoping Hattie would walk more slowly so she wouldn't slip. She watches until her older sister disappears from sight, resisting the need to face what has just happened, what is irrevocable. If she stands here long enough, Hattie will turn around and come back. They will embrace; they will find common ground on this, as they have throughout their lives on everything else.

It is John who finally moves her gently inside and closes the door. Isabella stares at it, thinking, I never want to go outside again.

*   *   *

The lock is back on, but the news of the next week seeps through. Victoria and her sister, Tennie, are hauled into court and charged with sending obscene material through the mail, then thrown into Ludlow Street Jail. Much is made of the fact that those stalwarts of the women's movement, Susan B. Anthony and Elizabeth Cady Stanton, have washed their hands of her.

Isabella weeps on John's shoulder that night—for Henry, for Harriet, for her family, for herself. Even for Victoria.

The next morning, in the batch of angry family letters slipped under the door, she finds one scrawled in Victoria's hand.

"Don't desert me, friend," it reads. "I am in jail for having used my right to say freely what I know to be true. I have broken no law, having printed nothing libelous and nothing obscene. All women should be wary, because if this can happen to me, it can happen to any woman who stands up and speaks the truth. Without honesty, what do we have? Hypocrisy. And that is what keeps women enslaved. Would that your own sisters could understand that!"

Isabella kneels before the fire and drops the letter in the flames, its words already memorized. She can't stay here, cowering. She has to do something.

She will write Henry, try to convince him to do the only moral thing possible at this point. Will he really do nothing to convince the authorities to release these two women in jail, knowing they are innocent of the charges?

"Of course he won't," John says when she poses the question to him at breakfast. She has asked him to refrain from smoking his pipe at the table, and he is especially testy. "The prosecuting attorney is one of his most loyal parishioners."

"I need to write him," she says.

"It's a waste of time. If Harriet thinks you got this cauldron boiling, you can be sure Henry thinks the same. Tom gave you the best advice, Bella."

Tom. The gentlest of her brothers. He had come by that very afternoon, big, shaggy, and diffident, to hug her and sit with her, listening silently as she shared with him the whole muddled mess of misunderstanding and deceit.

"Do you want advice?" he finally asked.

"Yes, I do."

"Do nothing. Speak to no one. Wait this out."

She had gazed at him, seeing the quiet earnestness in his eyes. Tom was never one to charge ahead, never one to initiate change or challenge, and those traits had given him a more stable life than most of the Beechers.

"Do you think Henry is guilty?" she asked him directly.

Tom's eyes had followed the rainbow shards of light from the leaded-glass window of the parlor to the mirror behind his sister's chair. "Lib Tilton says one thing, and then another, but I've felt for a long time that Henry has slippery doctrines of expediency," he'd said quietly.

"I had no idea you felt so strongly."

"I do."

"Then stand with me, Tom. I think Henry is tormented. He gives himself no way out."

Tom had shaken his head, folding his fingers into a clumsy knot. "I can't do that, Bella. When I've had trouble, Henry has helped me out—got me work, given me money. I see the contradiction, but I don't want to be involved. I can't stand on principle alone."

"You can't avoid it. We're a public family, and we're all going to be forced to take sides. Did you hear the talk that they might take Victoria and her sister to the Tombs? People starve in there. They're beaten, abused—"

"Don't try to draw me in. I'm tired of causes and passions. It's hard enough being in this family and being judged for good or ill on what Henry or Harriet does. Maybe you have now the freedom you want."

"Freedom?"

"You've challenged the family. But that means no more family responsibilities. You don't have to show up when Edward calls a family meeting. You don't have to agree with everything Harriet says, just because she is the moral force that sets the rules for the rest of us. And if you miss a birthday gathering, so what?" He smiled faintly. "Bella, you've slipped the family shackles."

"You are joking, aren't you, Tom?"

"Somewhat," Tom said with a sigh. "Not entirely."

"I love my family."

"So do I, but sometimes I think we are a family of strangers."

She rose, leaned forward, and wrapped him in her arms. "Not me, at least I hope not," she'd said.

"No, you less than the others. You're the impulsive one who says what she believes, and that's why you're in trouble." He had smiled once more. "I'll say it again—keep your head down, say nothing, do nothing. Sorry." He stood then and embraced her warmly, giving her a clumsy pat on the back as he left.

She awakes in the middle of the night with an inspired idea. There is a way she can help Henry. Shivering in her thin nightdress, she makes her way to the library, lights a candle, and picks up a pen, feeling tired and feverish.

"My dear brother, I can endure no longer," she writes. If he finds coming forward with a statement acknowledging the truth too shaming, she will help. If he writes out his thoughts, makes clear his frailty but reaffirms his values, she can deliver that message for him. She scribbles faster, excited. She can read it from the pulpit of Plymouth Church if he wants. She will muster all the brothers and sisters, so everyone in the family will be there to show solidarity, refusing to be shamed. His written statement will be a ringing endorsement of his preaching of a God of love, not of wrath. It will reaffirm values, not tear them down. It will acknowledge the truth. It will not let the full weight of the law come down on a misguided but truthful woman and make her suffer.

She stops finally, dizzy with the effort. She does not feel well. Is this a wise thing to do? Does it make sense? Should she think this over tomorrow?

No. True to her nature, she presses on.

"You posted that?" John says in disbelief the next day. "Without telling me? Dear God in heaven, Bella. You don't understand your brother." He slumps in his chair, head in his hands.

Only much later will she learn that, upon reading her letter, Henry erupted in a rage and called her a "dribbling fool." She will hear this delivered in the dry language of a court proceeding and repeat the words, moving her lips, letting herself whisper them. Dribbling fool. Henry called her a dribbling fool. And only much later will she learn he took steps to have her institutionalized because she had fallen under the "satanic influence" of Victoria Woodhull. Only when calmer voices prevailed did he back off, leaving the damaging question of her "mental condition" as a morsel for public gossip.

And only much later will she learn that Harriet called her insane.

All that comes later.

It is a gray, wet Saturday when she responds to a knock on her front door and opens it to a tall man holding a black umbrella. His hair is blond and damp from the rain, pulled straight back from a wide forehead. He is strikingly handsome, almost as handsome as he was years ago when editor of *The Independent*.

"Theodore," she says with astonishment.

"Mrs. Hooker." Tilton gives a jerking nod of his head. "May I talk with you?"

She steps aside, too stunned to answer.

"I'm here as an emissary for your brother," he says. His umbrella is dripping water on the floor, but he seems to have forgotten it. His manner is impatient, as if he has only a few precious moments to waste on a minor errand.

"*You?* Speaking for Henry?"

"Absolutely. You forget, Henry and I still share one thing in common. We want this outrageous story to go away."

"What—"

"Your letter has made the rounds, Mrs. Hooker. Not a very smart move."

"But an honest one."

He shakes his head, making no further move into the house. Isabella is reminded of how little she liked the man, even before the scandal. Tilton had always fawned too much over Henry, had always seemed coldly ambitious even as he ignored the shy, soft-spoken Elizabeth. She tries to imagine him weeping under a lamppost outside his home, yearning for his wife, even as she and Henry embraced inside. It is difficult.

"You won't want me as a guest, I can assure you. I'm here to give you a warning. Is your husband at home?"

"He's upstairs, working."

"That's just as well. You probably wouldn't want him to hear what I have to say."

Isabella finds herself counting the drops of water that fall from the umbrella.

"You ran the National Woman Suffrage Association convention last year, didn't you?"

"Yes, I did."

"I understand you did a marvelous job, or so all the women there seemed to think."

Isabella tries to remember whether Elizabeth Tilton had been at the meeting in Washington. Is this what he is alluding to? She waits.

"And you had a good time, I hear." He flashes a hard smile.

"What are you saying?"

"I'll come right to the point, Mrs. Hooker, for my message isn't pleasant. I have strong evidence that you entertained a man in your hotel room the second night of the convention, a room I understand was not shared with your husband. What went on behind closed doors, of course, is not known, but I have witnesses who will swear to the fact that this . . . gentleman . . . left in the early morning hours after all respectable people were home and in bed."

"That is not true!" she says furiously. Then she remembers the reporter from the *Eagle*— the man called Brady Puckett—who came to her room with her speech. Is this what Tilton is talking about? Has some malevolent source fed him a twisted story? Puckett wasn't there for more than five minutes. What terrible distortion has come from that?

Tilton seems to be enjoying her reaction as he elaborately raises a finger to his lips. "Be careful, Mrs. Hooker. Your husband might overhear."

She is being played with. "Get out of my home," she says. "How dare you spread such lies—"

"Who is the hypocrite now, Mrs. Hooker? If your brother should step forward and admit his guilt, keeping all of us on front pages all over this country, what about you?"

"What about *me*? I'm not a hypocrite, and you know it. This is a manufactured slur. How can you do this, you, of all people? You, the—" She cannot say the word.

He gives his umbrella an indifferent shake and turns toward the door. "Go ahead, say it—the cuckold. Make no mistake, your brother is no friend of mine anymore, I assure you. And I heartily wish we had heeded Frank Moulton's warnings about that Woodhull woman when he said she was not to be ignored. But your idea of feeding this scandal with further revelation—from Henry's pulpit, of all places—is insane. You're a beautiful woman, Mrs. Hooker; you're a radical suffragist, and you're a friend of Woodhull. That's all people need to know to believe that you have enjoyed sexual dalliances yourself. Think about it."

"This is a desperate lie."

"But believable. Henry and I are willing to take it all the way. Good day. Hope the weather is in for a change." He tips his hat, opens the door, steps out, opening his umbrella, and stalks off. He has a spindly look as he strides away.

Can a man who was once one of the most famous editors in the country be so desperate as to take on the role of blackmailer? Perhaps it isn't as much of a leap as it appears when the stakes have been raised so high. What is the reputation of one more woman when that of a proud man is rapidly shriveling? Nothing surely is more humiliating than the laughter, the jokes that destroy. In the face of such humiliation, can malice be pardoned? Isabella cannot form these thoughts right now; it will take others to puzzle through Tilton's motives. But what she knows now, without framing the words, is that mutual destruction has become a casual affair, and moral reflection is no longer part of the unfolding drama.

She slams the door and turns around. John stands in the doorway, hands dangling at his sides. He looks stooped, caved in.

"It's not true," she whispers.

"Oh, Bella."

Does he believe her? Her heart begins a painful thumping, and the palms of her hands grow damp. There have been times, there have been opportunities. On various occasions she still feels a special pleasure when men look her way with interest in their eyes. John has joked about it in the past. Is he thinking of that right now? And how often has she held forth at dinner and in the parlor about the right of women to sexual liberation? John has always treated her views with respect, even when he was annoyed at her many absences at conferences and her haphazard approach to domestic responsibilities. He has always been her supporter, a staunch believer in equal rights. Does he trust her?

For a long moment they stand facing each other, neither seemingly able to move or say anything more.

John breaks the spell first. He steps toward his wife, leans close, and kisses her on the lips. "Tilton is deplorable," he says. "I hope he drowns out there."

She smiles, close to tears.

John takes her hand, holding it gently. "Shall we have dinner?"

✣ CHAPTER NINE ✣

November 1872

THE DAYS THAT FOLLOW are dull and dark with approaching winter. When the wind blows through the naked blackberry bushes behind Nook Farm, their limbs rattle like old bones. Isabella walks along the path between them, hating that lonely sound.

She cannot get warm. Not here, not in the house, even with a full, blazing fire. John worries that she is ill and wants her to see the doctor, but there will be nothing for him to do, she knows that. So she tries not to hunch over in the house, tries not to let her husband see her don extra shawls and rub her cold feet.

Time has gone flat. Livy Clemens's husband has ordered her not to talk to Isabella, and this mandate is spreading to the other good matrons of Nook Farm. People turn their backs on her when she walks to the dry goods store, pretending she isn't there. The bakery clerk refuses to wait on her, and she is forced to return home without John's favorite biscuits.

She watches for Harriet. Sometimes she catches a glimpse of her preparing the garden for winter, still in her floppy sun hat, tying up vines against the coming frost. Harriet loves her grand garden with its eight different kinds of geraniums, Isabella thinks fondly. She was always moving rosebushes and hedges, fussing with where they should go, asking, "Bella, what do you think? Should the roses go by the pathway or under the parlor window?" And they would chat to-gether, standing in the sun, their feet sprinkled with some of the ma-nure from the truckloads Harriet always had on hand. You can't grow anything without plenty of manure, she would say. Isabella never sees her sister deliberately avoiding her, but the exclusion is in the slope of her shoulders and the aversion of her gaze. Isabella tries on one occasion to walk by Harriet's home slowly, turn at the corner, and walk back, but it is a futile exercise. Harriet never lifts her head.

Isabella follows the news from Brooklyn, reading the papers that John leaves silently on the dining room table, making no comment. Victoria's attack on Henry has not brought scandal down on his head. It has only made him more popular than ever. Hundreds of people are taking the Fulton Ferry to Brooklyn Heights, pulling their coats together against the cold, laughing and joking and climbing the hill to Plymouth Church, in hopes of catching a glimpse of the genial, thick-jowled man who manages to blend a rakish manner with true devotion to God, all the while seeming to think he is much younger than his sixty-odd years.

If they don't understand the mix, it doesn't matter. It is entertain-ing, and Henry seems happy to oblige, meeting them at the door of the church with handshakes and hugs, seemingly impervious to harm.

Things are not going so well for Victoria. In those same silently stacked newspapers, Isabella learns that Victoria and her sister have been transferred to the notorious prison known as the Tombs. A wretched, dank prison used primarily for murderers, where inmates sleep on cement floors and eat scraps of bread shoved through the bars of their cells on a schedule indifferent to hunger.

Isabella cries the morning she reads this news, puts her head down on the papers and cries, ink from the newsprint transferring to her forehead. John comes into the dining room and strokes her hair but knows better than to say anything.

No word from Susan Anthony, and no word from Mrs. Stanton. They have backed off, taking themselves to the sidelines, trying for invisibility. To be sympathetic to Victoria is to court disaster, for she has broken not only the rules of civility but those of common sense. She is on her own.

"I don't care if I'm considered respectable anymore," Isabella says to John one night as they lie next to each other in bed.

"Tell me that, no one else," he replies, softening the message with a kiss.

Even saying it is freeing. She kisses him back, filled with silent rebellion.

The next morning John leaves early on a business trip to Boston. Shortly after, Isabella puts on her heavy coat and gloves and takes the train to New York, leaving a note for her husband.

"Dearest John," it reads. "I am going to try to visit Victoria. Please don't be angry with me. I will take the late train home tonight."

She steps from the carriage at Centre Street and gazes at the fearsome structure known as the Tombs. It is deliberately modeled after an Egyptian mausoleum as a way of frightening criminals, or so she has heard. She isn't surprised by the buzzing from the guards as she makes her way to the warden's office; the presence of a woman in these narrow, dimly lit corridors must be a rarity. She does not respond to the stares of those taking in her crisp shirtwaist, the silver web belt around her slim waist; all the signs of privilege. She looks straight ahead.

A flustered clerk offers her a seat and disappears into an adjoining office. A few moments later a rotund man with flushed cheeks and what appear to be bits of his lunch on his vest emerges.

"You want to see the Woodhull?" he asks incredulously.

"Victoria Woodhull. If that is permissible."

"And you are—"

"Mrs. John Hooker, of Hartford, Connecticut."

"Why, may I ask, does a lady like you want to see the likes of that one?"

Isabella draws a deep breath. "Because we—are colleagues."

She hears more buzzing of voices through the door to the hallway, which the clerk has left ajar. Then laughter. The warden paces up and down, as if in deep thought, periodically glancing at her in wonder. He excuses himself, disappearing back into his office. Five minutes pass, and Isabella grows nervous. She pulls on her gloves and stands to go.

He reemerges. "Okay, Mrs. Hooker. I'll give you a couple of minutes. I'll stay with you in case she acts up."

Isabella follows him wordlessly as he leads the way out the door, down a set of stairs, and through a barely lit walkway that stinks of damp and sewage. On each side of her, she sees cells with iron bars. Someone shouts. Immediately faces appear pressed against the bars, faces of wild-looking men with glittering eyes. Her heart pounding, Isabella stares straight ahead.

"Here we are," the warden finally says, pointing to one of the cells. He pounds on the bars. "Woodhull! You got a visitor!"

Isabella steps forward and peers into a tiny space, a cavern dug from the stone. A figure crouches on the floor. Isabella can make nothing out in the gloom except a bucket shoved against the far corner of the cell.

"Victoria?" she says.

The figure unfolds itself and stands, moving toward the bars. She blinks twice, wondering if there has been a mistake. This woman looks like a feral creature, with dirty face and haunted eyes.

"Isabella?"

"Yes." Isabella holds out her hand, and Victoria grabs it, squeezing so hard Isabella winces.

"Are you all right?" she asks. "Are they feeding you?"

"I get swill," Victoria mutters. "They want me to die here."

"No, that can't happen," Isabella says with alarm.

"I didn't say I *would,* I said that's what they want. Everyone has deserted me. What are *you* here for, to gloat?"

"If I wanted to gloat, I'd do it up in the fresh air, not down here," Isabella says. "I'm here because you're my friend, and I don't desert a friend."

But Victoria seems past such niceties. "Ah, so you're here because you feel sorry for me? Be careful, they might decide to put you in here too. Oh, that would be a story, wouldn't it? Do you think your brothers and sisters would brave the Tombs to see you? And don't talk to me about being my friend; I have no friends."

"Stop."

"Afraid I'll start ranting on about Henry again?"

"You waste your time trying to taunt me," Isabella says, frustrated. "Why did you name me as your source? You know I didn't tell you about Henry."

"What's true? I saw it in your face, dear *friend*. Don't deny it; if you do, you're a hypocrite too. Are you angry about that?"

It was a skill of Victoria's, this collecting of bits and shards of truth and twirling them in a kaleidoscope. "Of course I am; you lied. And you set out to hurt my brother. How could I not be?" retorts Isabella.

"For a second time—why are you here?" Victoria is the cat again, purring, licking cream.

Why? Outrage that a woman could be thrown into jail for saying in print what the whole town whispered about; fear that if the police could throw Victoria into jail on trumped-up charges, they could do the same with any suffragist.

"You didn't commit a crime, that's why. And putting you in here is wrong," Isabella says.

Victoria studies her face before answering. "I can't make up my mind sometimes whether you are really a Beecher or not. If that's what you think, then find a way to get me out of here."

The hallway is growing noisier with the raucous jeers of the other inmates as they rattle the bars of their cells. The warden steps forward, touching Isabella's arm.

"That's enough," he says. "Let's go."

"She doesn't belong here, she's innocent. When will she be released?" Isabella asks as she reluctantly pulls her hand from Victoria's grasp.

"Search me, ma'am. Now let's go, right now. These pigs don't know how to react to seeing a respectable woman down here."

"Are you a respectable woman?" yells Victoria as Isabella turns and follows the warden. "Is that what you are? Is that *all* you are?"

"She may be your friend, but she's crazy," the warden mumbles.

The crowd on the main floor seems to have grown. Isabella thanks the warden and begins to make her way back down the corridor to the front of the building. As she steps out the door, a surge of shouting reporters almost pushes her back inside.

"Why'd you come, Mrs. Hooker? What'd she tell you? Is your brother guilty?" The shouted questions are coming from every side as Isabella tries to push her way through to her waiting carriage. She hasn't anticipated this.

"Talk to us, Mrs. Hooker," yells one. "You came here, now tell us why!"

"I have nothing to say," she manages.

"Don't go yet, give us a story." Someone pushes her, then someone shoves back. "For Christ's sake, give the woman some air!" Isabella turns in the direction of this voice and sees Brady Puckett, the man who helped her at the convention, looking angry and clutching a notebook. He is trying to clear her a path, but another man elbows him away.

"What's the matter, Puckett, you looking for an exclusive?" he yells. "Is your brother guilty, Mrs. Hooker?"

"I—"

"Once and for all, is he?"

"He is a good man and a—"

"Is he guilty?"

Afterward she couldn't quite say how it happened. Perhaps she tripped before she was punched. But suddenly she felt a searing pain in her left eye. The papers the next day would say it was a policeman who hit her accidentally with his billy stick, but she never knew or cared. All she remembered was her panic.

"Yes! Now let me go," she screamed. "Let me go!"

John is angry, angrier than she has ever seen him. At breakfast he slams the newspaper down in front of her and begins to pace the room, hands clasped behind his back. Her trip to the Tombs was close to treachery, he declares. She is the center of this scandal now. What is she trying to do, convince him—her truest supporter—that she is indeed unbalanced? Has she no understanding at all of the need to tamp down this volatile situation? How can she have thought her visit would go unnoticed? Let alone declaring to the world that indeed Henry is guilty?

She raises her eyes and looks at him.

He stops, aghast. "God, Bella, your eye. You really were hit."

"It's just swollen," she says.

John pulls up the chair next to her and takes both her hands in his. "My beautiful wife," he says, shaking his head slowly. "I don't know what propels you, Bella. After all these years, I thought I knew, but here you've gone and tightened the link between you and Victoria. I will defend you to the death, but you baffle me."

She can't explain her actions adequately, even to herself. How can she tell John that, watching Victoria behind those bars, she felt herself in that cell? She doesn't understand the source of her impulsiveness: she only knows she is ruled by an instant surge of connection with someone hurt or wronged. When she was a child, if a playmate fell and skinned her knee, it would be Isabella who would feel the pain and burst into tears. She has indeed stumbled into a pit, but even now she can't see how she could have avoided it. There is something crazed about Victoria, but what she saw at the Tombs was dismaying. No one deserves that. And injustice has made her tremble since she was a child banging on the family dinner table with her spoon to get attention. Only last year, Victoria was the heroine of the suffragist movement, giving it much-needed vitality and focus; doesn't she deserve *some* loyalty?

Isabella looks at John's face and knows his answer: not if that vitality is used to destroy. But to be imprisoned for writing what she knew to be true? What everyone knew, or should know, to be true? How could Henry be part of this travesty? That's what twists her stomach, causing her at times to double over. Her bruised eye is nothing.

"I can't get out of my head the fact that she broke no law and was sent to the Tombs," she says. "I kept thinking of how frightened she must be, and that's why I went. To let her know she wasn't alone."

"Will you stop fixating on *Victoria*? You should not have gone there, Bella. Damn it, do you hear me?"

Perhaps it is John's cursing. But suddenly she has to defend herself.

"I'm standing up for honesty," she flares back. "I'm sick of all the hypocrisy. It's everywhere, and it's wrong."

"Oh, so you are trying to punish Henry?"

"No!" She is furious now. "I'm standing up for *truth*. That's what being a Beecher is supposed to be about!"

"You are being self-righteous! How can you stand here and make moral decisions for others? Especially *a member of your own family*?"

They stare at each other. The very ground under her feels as if it is crumbling away. If John is not with her, what can she do?

John recovers first. "I know what you're trying to say, and I'm not saying you're wrong. But you're not necessarily right either."

"I must take a stand," she says.

"We live under siege now, Bella," he says quietly. "The one thing I know is, this won't be over for a long time. We all must live with the consequences of our actions, and you are no exception." He says no more, simply rises and leaves the room, looking older and more worn than ever before. He knows what his wife has unleashed. He knows how savagely a monolithic enterprise will respond when attacked, and the Beecher family, proud, wary, internally fractious but united against enemies, is perfectly capable of turning on its own.

The months that follow are, if anything, more lonely than before. The neighborhood remains silent; all backs are turned on Isabella on her infrequent forays into town. Once she runs into Samuel Clemens at the shoemaker's. How dapper he looks, with his splendid, imposing head of white hair, the erectness of his carriage. The man many refer to only as Mark Twain always dresses elegantly for his trips to town, carrying a walking stick, with which he likes to tap out a tune on the brick walks for the enjoyment of the children who follow him around. There is no smile on his face when he sees Isabella; he actually appears not to see her at all as he picks up his boots, walks past her, and leaves the shoemaker's shop.

She hears through John that Harriet has asked about her after the encounter with the billy club on the steps of the Tombs.

"She wanted to know if you were all right," he reports. "I told her yes. Your eye was swollen and black and blue, but your vision was unimpaired."

"Did she say anything else?" Isabella prompts. "Anything at all?"

John shakes his head in the negative.

"How did she look?"

"She looked worn."

"Worried, perhaps? Wanting to see me? Could I send over something, perhaps a tumbler of candytuft seed?"

John throws up his hands. "Stop, dear. She had nothing more to say. I can tell you nothing more."

On this small morsel, Isabella feeds for months. Her sister still cares, she is sure of it.

Another time she hears through her daughter that Calvin Stowe is ill. He collapsed at the house, temporarily paralyzed, while Harriet was away on a trip.

"I must go over there," she insists to John.

"I spotted him riding a horse this morning," John says. "He's always imagining an illness. Whatever was wrong, he's fine."

It was malaria, they learn. It will come and go. Harriet is gone frequently. Will he remember to take his quinine? Isabella worries.

"She'll watch out for him," says her patient husband, lowering his newspaper. "He's a lot better off than the economy right now. I'm more worried about iron production than I am about Calvin."

"The economy?"

"We're building railroads too fast," John grumbles. He turns back to his newspaper with a frown.

Sometimes during the long evenings at home, Isabella broods

over what she could have done differently. She should not have gone to the Tombs. She should not have written to Henry. Or, perhaps, she could have phrased her letter in a different way. She still believes if Henry had taken charge of the scandal before Victoria's attack, he could have found a sympathetic press; he could have been spared the rancid charge of hypocrisy. But she should have been more sensitive to his fears. And what about Eunice? Never once had she thought what an admission of guilt would have meant to Eunice, which saddens her now.

But then, no one in the family thinks a great deal about Eunice.

At night, she tosses about, dreaming different scenarios. The most haunting, the one hardest to wake up from to face the day: Harriet has not deserted her, has stood with her. If only it were true.

During the days, she lives with reality. She is grateful for the few friends who write, particularly Hannah Comstock, who points out that Harriet, of all people, should understand the price of truth. After years of acclaim, she took a dreadful drubbing for writing her book detailing Lady Byron's charges of incest against her husband. Didn't she remember that Isabella stood loyally by her side through it all? "If your sister Harriet would come to your aid in this your day of trial, as you went to her with your great heart and willing hands—how much she could do for you and your brother," she wrote.

Hannah's kindness in bringing this up touches Isabella. She puts down the letter and stares out the window, remembering that chaotic time in 1869.

Harriet had wanted to defend a dear friend against charges that her cold nature had driven her husband into exile and early death. And she had seen so clearly the cost of sexual hypocrisy. Was it the storm of protest that descended on her for attacking a revered poet that made it impossible for her to face Henry's hypocrisy now? Lord Byron had carried on a sexual liaison with his stepsister, which devastated his wife. Writing about it had been a terrible mistake, and that first step into the new world of feminist writing was also the last time Harriet wrote passionately to right a wrong.

There is more than enough time these days for Isabella to mull over such things. To think about the costs of fame: about how it begins, arcs, and fades; about how, at first, it is a bit unnerving and rather delicious. That first year after *Uncle Tom's Cabin* was published, Harriet used to redden with both embarrassment and pleasure when people at the market would turn and stare as she passed by. After a while she seemed not to notice, but because she expected recognition, there would be a slight edge of annoyance in her voice if someone did not quite place her immediately. After *Lady Byron Vindicated* came out, adulation dribbled away. Then indifference set in. One day a new produce man at the market who had never heard of Harriet told her to wait her turn, he was busy. He was quite brusque, with not an ounce of deference. A small episode, but Isabella saw her sister's cheeks redden again and knew a Beecher prerogative had just died. Something vanished in herself that day. A residual jealousy? Perhaps. She tucks Hannah's letter back deep into a drawer of her desk, one small comfort to re-savor when all calms down.

Which won't be soon. John is right, the scandal is not going away. The papers are filled with it, every day.

Victoria and her sister are released from prison, but still no one in the women's movement steps forward to say a good word for their former heroine. Susan Anthony and Elizabeth Cady Stanton decline, saying they don't want to hurt Lib Tilton. Victoria has forced them all to tiptoe over hot coals. Nothing is clear.

"They should speak up," John says angrily. "These are your friends? Forget Victoria. They need to support *you*. You've told the truth about Henry, and they know it's true. Bella, people want to know why you stayed friends with that woman when she was so clearly out to get Henry—and anyone else who crossed her. You *have* a defense." He watches her carefully now. "All you have to do is say you stayed friends because you were trying to talk her out of publishing her charges."

"But that's not true," Isabella says. She sits at the dining table, staring down at a cold plate of eggs and ham. She has no appetite. "I didn't know she would go that far. I stayed with her because of her courage. She's simply without fear, and that takes my breath away. There's very little of that in women. Not in me, certainly. And you can't change the way society works if you're afraid."

"Well, I'm scared to death, and I don't believe a damn thing is going to change," he says. "Susan and Elizabeth think they can keep this from coming down on the heads of women? They're wrong. It will anyway. And I don't give a damn about any of them except you."

Isabella stands and reaches forward over the dining table to kiss him, heedless of almost knocking her plate to the floor.

In December, unchastened, Victoria publishes her charges again. Lib Tilton confesses all in a letter to Reverend Storrs, Henry's conservative rival at the Church of the Pilgrims, setting off a renewed clamor in the press. Anthony Comstock, the self-appointed antivice crusader, goes after Victoria as she and her sister are distributing copies of their weekly paper—which causes the authorities to jail them again, charging them with obscenity. Some of Henry's parishioners begin talking about trying Theodore Tilton for slander, but nothing comes of it.

"I think it's dying down," Isabella says to John in March.

"I wish we could go away for a while," he replies.

Fall 1873

But somehow they don't. Isabella realizes later that John was worrying more and more about money. He debates about cashing in his holdings with the banking house of Jay Cooke & Co. but decides he is fretting too much.

Other things distract her. Susan Anthony is charged in June with the crime of registering to vote in Rochester, New York. She faces an all-male jury, ready to argue that the Fourteenth Amendment, which declares no legal privileges can be denied to any citizen, means that women should have the right to vote. But just before the trial begins, the judge pulls a piece of paper from the pocket of his robe.

It is his verdict. Guilty as charged. The fine is one hundred dollars.

"She won't pay it," Isabella declares.

"I know you wouldn't," John says with a smile.

On September 18, the Cooke banking house declares bankruptcy. That means the collapse of financing for the new Northern Pacific Railway. Within hours investors are pounding on the doors of their brokerage houses with orders to sell. The market plummets. When European investors begin calling in American loans, the New York Stock Exchange shuts down, staying closed for ten days.

"John, are we all right?" Isabella asks.

He looks at her, his face gray. "I think I can save the house," he says.

The months that follow are filled with tension, as John tries to ride through the worst of what the papers are soon to call the Panic of 1873. Isabella sets out to cut costs to the bone, trying not to spend a dollar more than she needs to. John takes on as many new clients as he can. Isabella watches him bent over the constant stack of household bills, feeling helpless. Why can't she do anything? Why has she not a single talent that can be translated into money? Thoughts like these push out—for the moment—the heartache of Harriet's abandonment.

John's efforts result in a brighter financial picture for the Hookers by the time winter settles in. Much of their savings has disappeared, but they are able to pay their debts—and keep their home. The crisis eases.

Only then can Isabella focus on what the repercussions of the scandal are doing to the suffragist cause. Susan writes her an agonized letter early in 1874, telling her women are abandoning the movement, and there seems to be nothing that will stop the exodus.

"Women are afraid of being tainted with the 'free love' stigma," she writes. "Victoria has taken down what she helped to build. Isabella, so much is lost." Isabella cannot sleep that night. All she can do is stare at the ceiling and wonder what might have been if Victoria could have freed them all with her ideas instead of shackling them to a fruitless cause.

May 1874

John and Isabella finally sail to Europe. Isabella worries about spending the money, but John is set on getting his wife out of the country and away from the constant seething scandal. Each day of the voyage Isabella stands at the rail, staring out across the sea, feeling a great tug in her heart back to home. John thinks this trip will ease her mind, but it isn't happening.

They bump into a relative of John's one sunny afternoon near the fountain at the Piazza Navona in Rome. "Did you hear the news?" he says, clearly filled to bursting with how much he has to convey. "Elizabeth has left Theodore and now denies she and Henry ever had an affair. But it doesn't matter—Theodore has forced Henry's church to hold a hearing by presenting them with plenty of evidence of the affair. They can't avoid it now, and the city is in an uproar. There's going to be a full church trial, I'm told, sometime soon. And Isabella, we hear your brother-in-law is ill again. Malaria, I think."

Against all entreaties from her husband, Isabella insists they return home.

"You take one deep breath there and reporters will be besieging you," John says. "If Harriet needs you, she knows how to reach you."

"I won't do anything rash," Isabella replies. "I just want to be there. If she needs me." And all the way home, standing again at the rail, looking out on the dark Atlantic waters, Isabella prays that Harriet will.

They dock in New York Harbor on July 28, just in time to have thrust in their hands several copies of that day's newspapers. John scans them first as Isabella tells the porters where to stack their bags for the rail trip home to Hartford. It is not until they board their train a few hours later that John places one newspaper on an exhausted Isabella's lap.

"Well, here's the latest story," he says. "Apparently Mrs. Stanton and Miss Anthony were the first to hear confessions from both the Tiltons on a rather extraordinary night." He leans back in his seat and stares out the window. "It's a gleeful piece. Whoever the reporter is, he got to Mrs. Stanton. And once reporters start to laugh, the whole house of cards comes down."

Isabella scans the story, registering the byline. Brady Puckett. Remembering his sardonic humor, she can imagine how much he relished writing it.

In the midst of a dinner with Mrs. Stanton and a friend of hers one evening, writes Puckett, Theodore Tilton impulsively poured out the whole story of his wife's faithlessness. His suffering, his sense of betrayal. When asked about this heart-wrenching confession of marital pain by the *Brooklyn Eagle,* Mrs. Stanton readily confirmed the account. And *why,* she was asked, did the heartbroken Tilton take his story to one of the most prominent suffragists in the country?

"We were reformers," Mrs. Stanton told Puckett. "Theodore gave us the story as a phase of social life."

A phase of social life? "There's richness for you," Puckett chortles in print. The story gets better, he tells his readers. That same night Miss Anthony was dining with Elizabeth Tilton, who confessed all. And later that evening, when Theodore Tilton rushed home to confront his wife, the two women barricaded themselves behind a locked door with Theodore on the other side, pounding and hollering and demanding to be let in. A ludicrous scene indeed.

It would spoil the story of course to point out that Miss Anthony and Mrs. Stanton, longtime friends of the Tiltons, were probably doing their best to calm them down and ward off a greater public scandal. Even if they were not speaking up for Isabella or for Victoria, they shouldn't be described as participants in some prancing comedy of errors. Isabella is frustrated. Does it have to be the only reporter she respects who would expose good people to public mockery?

Her eye wanders down the page and stops at another byline. This is a story defending Henry, calling him "an honorable man" and declaring that those who claim he isn't telling the truth are a pack of "half-crazy women."

Her eye wanders back to the byline, and she lets out a sharp cry.

"What is it?" demands John. She hands him the paper and covers her eyes. The story is written by Catharine Beecher.

The church hearing begins in an atmosphere of public skepticism. It doesn't help that Henry has himself appointed the six members of the committee charged to investigate his behavior. Within days, facing overwhelming news coverage, it seems to Isabella that the entire region is dividing into Beecherites and anti-Beecherites. Henry takes the stand before the committee—packed with his friends, according to the newspapers—and rips Tilton apart, accusing him of "loose notions of marriage and divorce" and saying he wants nothing more than to sow the evil seeds of free love. Henry charges blackmail. Some murmur this is strange—how can an innocent man be blackmailed?

Tilton counterattacks, charging Henry with preaching and practicing free love his entire adult life. And who is his source on this? "His half sister," declares Tilton before the committee, his handsome face pinched and resolute. "Mrs. Isabella Hooker, who has shown herself to be a bosom friend of Victoria Woodhull."

Isabella is sick to her stomach the morning she reads that.

There is more. Tilton declares that Henry lives in a loveless marriage and so seeks out the wives of other men. He has "a wife who is not a mate," he says, adding, "Many of his relatives stand in fear of this woman, and some of them have not entered her house for years. I know that my allusion to Mr. Beecher's homelife is rough and harsh, but I know also that it is true."

And yet more. One defender of Henry's testifies that Isabella is "insane." He hints darkly that she harbors an "unnatural" affection for Victoria Woodhull.

John hides the paper the morning it reports that her brother

William has said, all things considered, now that he thinks about it, this charge is probably true.

On August 22, 1874, the final report of the committee is read in church. The Reverend Henry Beecher is declared not guilty, a verdict instantly met with torrents of applause from the congregation. The mayor of Philadelphia sends his congratulations. The head of the Episcopal Church conveys a message of approval. Three Republican members of Congress denounce Henry's accuser on the floor and enter their stirring speeches into the *Congressional Record.* The cluster of politicians ushered into membership at the church, known as "Beecher's boys," are ecstatic. Loyalty has been rewarded; honor is intact. Plymouth Church has avoided a scandal.

It is the usually level Frank Moulton, the man who swore Henry had confessed to him, who provides counterpoint. "You are a liar, sir!" he bellows, rising in protest after the report is read. His wife pulls him down to his seat, but the damage is done.

"You are the liar, Moulton!" yells a usually staid member of Henry's congregation, a man with long white sideburns and a distinguished mustache. He draws a gun from his pocket and waves it in the air, causing church members to dive for the floor as he screams threats against Moulton. The police are quickly called, and within ten minutes the man is escorted from the church and sent home. The next day, Emma Moulton emerges from her home to find a small black coffin on the doorstep. Scrawled on it in blood is the name "Francis D. P. Moulton."

A messy affair, at the end. But Henry has won.

The next month, the U.S. Supreme Court decides unanimously that Victoria's argument for suffrage is spurious. The fact that women are American citizens, the court declares, does not mean they have the right to vote.

That's a relief, clusters of men tell one another in the country's shops and drawing rooms. It was a ridiculous notion in the first place, something only a woman like Victoria Woodhull could promote. How did it ever get taken seriously?

CHAPTER TEN

Winter 1874

THE CLOCK IN THE PARLOR seems to be ticking louder than usual. Isabella decides it must need oiling. She will call the clockmaker and have it checked out; it is, after all, very old. Clocks need tending, just like people.

John smiles when she informs him. "This couldn't have anything to do with your sealing yourself off here from the clamor of your family?" he asks.

Isabella puts down the knitting in her hands. Since Henry's exoneration, the angry letters from her brothers and sisters are piling up on the library table. She no longer sees any reason to read them. The message is always the same: break all ties with "Mrs. Stanton and Miss Anthony and all that set," as Mary put it, or none of them will speak to her again. Henry is now officially proved innocent. She must join them in denying his guilt. This, they inform her, is her last chance for redemption.

"It doesn't seem to be enough that I've promised I'll say nothing about the matter for the rest of my life," she tells her husband.

"And that you've made a monastic vow to stay entombed here for the same amount of time?"

"I doubt if any of them care."

"I don't want my Bella turning bitter," John says gently.

Unthinking, Isabella raises the half-knit sweater to her eyes and wipes the tears. "What I wish for now is an end to this constant barrage of scolding letters."

"Ah, the plague of being from a literary family."

She tries to smile. She is thinking of the "last chance" her family is offering her: redemption for a lie that proves her loyalty. How can that be a moral choice? She gropes for a way to break the impasse. All families find themselves thrown from time to time into different warring camps, but sheer survival of loving bonds depends on learning when to hold one's tongue, when to back away. Certain topics surely are avoided at every dinner table, with words parsed carefully to keep the peace. She knows this as a sister, as a wife, and definitely as a mother. She's managed the careful balance, perhaps less deftly than Hattie, but certainly with less clumsiness than Catharine.

This is different. Do her brothers and sisters know what they are asking? How can they expect her to tell a blatant lie that no one will believe at this point anyway? They are telling her that loyalty is more important than truth. She feels pressure building in her head. If she accepts that Beecher mandate, she is denying the core of what her family is supposed to be all about. Truth is supposed to win out over all. Do Hattie and the rest of them not see the contradiction here? She covers her face with her hands, her head throbbing now. She is caught. Decency requires the truth, and love requires a lie. She cannot settle for ambiguity; surely God frowns on moral ambiguity. But He gives no guidelines.

John walks over to the table and picks one letter off the top of the pile. He opens it and reads, standing so still Isabella becomes anxious. Then he walks back and hands it to her.

"I think you will want to read this one," he says. "But before you do, a piece of news: Tilton has filed suit in the Brooklyn city court. He's charging alienation of affections, and he wants one hundred thousand dollars in damages."

Isabella jumps to her feet, the yarn in her lap tumbling to the floor. "There is going to be another trial?" she asks.

"Without question," John says, shaking his head.

"Then it is not over."

"My dear, it has barely begun. Prepare yourself; it will be a circus."

Isabella sinks back into her chair.

"But not everything is gloomy." John points to the letter in her hand. "Open that," he says.

She holds it gingerly between two fingers, as if she expects it to burst into flames. "Who is it from?"

This time it is John's turn to smile. "Catharine. She wants to see you, and not for a lecture."

Isabella reaches her sister's home by the afternoon of the next day, feeling nervous, less buoyed by John's urging to consider the fact that the tone of Catharine's note, if not exactly conciliatory, is somewhat inviting.

"Our family is imperiled," Catharine had written. "But don't lose heart, Bella. Come see me."

As she lifts her hand to raise the clapper, Isabella prays that John was right, and that she isn't coming for a typical Catharine scolding. After that terrible, dismissive article in the *Eagle,* she has no stomach for an attack and vows to turn on her heel if one is launched.

Catharine opens the door before the clapper descends. She must have been watching from a window. Isabella hasn't seen her sister since the night at Nook Farm when they last congregated as a family, and is astonished at how she has aged. Her solid, robust body has shriveled, and she seems almost as small as Harriet. Instead of the black lace dress and black self-made shoes with velvet uppers that are her trademark, she wears a vaguely Oriental-looking morning dress. Her gray hair, usually plumped in almost coquettish sausage curls, is pulled straight back now. Isabella remembers clearly how those curls used to bob up and down when a vigorous Catharine led student groups in recital. She was taken seriously then; now many think of her as an eccentric, past her time. The fact that the first school she founded, the Hartford Female Seminary, is still a functioning, highly respected institution goes unnoticed.

"Good, I didn't scare you off," Catharine says by way of greeting. "Come in, dear."

"Hello, Catharine," Isabella says carefully. She hesitates. She must get this settled first. "I'm bewildered by your attack on me in the *Eagle*. Why did you do that?"

"Directly to the point, Bella. That's good. I wrote in a heated moment, and I apologize. I didn't aim it at you personally, but I understand why you think so. Now will you come in?"

Pulled by the force of her sister's personality, Isabella follows Catharine into a tiny room cluttered with books and boxes. It is obvious Catharine is only temporarily perched in this rooming house. A perpetual wanderer, she never lives very long in one place. "She's too old to be wandering like a trunk without a label," Harriet once tartly observed. But Isabella wonders if that restlessness isn't part of all of them, part of what drives the family.

She felt that when she was only ten, the year Lyman Beecher decided it was his mission in life to fight for the soul of the West, and the only way to do that was to move the entire family—nine of them at that point—to Cincinnati. Her memories of the trip are vivid. She will never forget bouncing around in the big, old-fashioned stage with four great horses that took them across the Alleghenies; brother George sitting up on the box, leading them all in singing hymns and songs, and Catharine scribbling away inside the stage, refusing to join in because she was drawing up plans for a school. Later she told Isabella she had been worried about Father's feverish dream of founding a seminary in the rough boomtown culture of the West. What if it failed? With Mary's and Harriet's help, she established her school as quickly as she could after reaching Cincinnati. All three sisters taught there. They worked hard, drummed up students from Ohio and Kentucky, and somehow held on, helping with family bills, as Lyman struggled to keep his Lane Seminary afloat.

Catharine was filled with energy and zest during those years, but she wasn't warm and funny, like Henry. And she wasn't a big sister who let Isabella tag along and taught her things, like Harriet. She seemed brittle somehow. Isabella used to imagine that if she reached out and poked Catharine, her older sister might break. Isabella wondered why, but then one afternoon, lying in the grass on a hot summer day, Harriet told her "the story" that no one talked about.

Catharine had loved a young man, a fellow teacher, named Alexander Fisher. They were planning their wedding when he was lost at sea. Worse, he had not yet found redemption at the time of his death. He hadn't found the calling to God that—according to Lyman Beecher—was the only route to heaven. And that meant his soul was damned to hell for eternity, yes, the soul of this fine man who loved God and lived a decent, devout life. "It is God's law, Catharine," her father said sadly. "We can only pity him now."

Harriet told her little sister of standing behind a door and listening to the twenty-two-year-old Catharine weep in her father's study, crying out that this was not possible, and if it were true, this was not a God she wanted. This was a God she would defy and fight to her dying day.

Isabella had not been able to sleep that night.

She looks around the room. Behind a stack of books on the floor, she spots Catharine's guitar. In her mind's eye, she can see Catharine plunking away, singing in a reedy voice old songs that no one knows anymore. Does she still play?

"Yes, I still play," Catharine says with a slight smile, unnerving Isabella with this ability to divine her thoughts.

"I loved listening to you as a child, especially when I was doing my lessons after school," she says.

"You were a good little audience of one, bouncing up and down, clapping your hands," Catharine says. "Not a great student, but a wonderful listener."

"School enthralled me. I only wish I had been given the opportunity to stay longer."

"We ran out of money," Catharine says simply. "Now, sit down."

Isabella obeys.

"We're an argumentative lot, we Beechers. But we've always supported each other when there is trouble. A family practice now discarded."

"Indeed," Isabella murmurs.

Catharine seems not to hear. "You're a hard one. You run with a disreputable group. Still, although I can't say this publicly, you could be right about Henry. Now I'm not saying you *are,* but—"

"You think so?" Isabella is astonished. "And you let me hang out here, reviled and hated? Why?"

"Family must prevail," Catharine says, as if it is the most natural conclusion in the world. She clucks at the sight of Isabella's instant tears, pulling a wrinkled linen handkerchief from her sleeve and offering it to her.

"I don't understand cowardice," Isabella says.

"Don't call me a coward, dear. You know better."

Isabella does know better. "I'm sorry," she manages as she takes the handkerchief and dabs her eyes. "I feel alone, Catharine. Everyone is angry with me, even Harriet. It's as if I've broken some law of God's by telling the truth."

"Not always a virtue," murmurs Catharine.

"Yes, John says the same thing."

"You need to understand some things about Harriet. There is nothing she values more than family. She'll fight for it over everything else. Do you remember Zillah?"

"Their maid in Cincinnati?"

"How she suddenly disappeared, and no one talked about it?"

"Yes, I think I do."

"Hattie kept her good deeds quiet. Oh, everyone knows how John Rankin mesmerized Hattie with that tale of the young slave mother who escaped across the ice with her baby. The one she named Eliza. But it was Zillah she personally helped."

"What did she do?"

"Saved her, in the nick of time. Her owner showed up less than an hour after Zillah confessed to Hattie she was a runaway slave. I don't know how they did it, but Hattie and Calvin bundled the poor thing into the wagon and drove west all night, not sure how to spot the next station on the Underground Railroad. Then Harriet saw a lantern hanging from the window of a house darkened for night.

Rankin had told her that was the signal of a safe house. If she was wrong, Zillah was lost, but she wasn't."

"Why hasn't Harriet told me this?"

"Probably because there was no happy ending. That woman was desperate for her children, but try as she could, Harriet could locate neither of them. When Charley died, all of Zillah's grief just poured back into her mind. Nothing to her is more precious than family, do you understand?" Catharine takes a deep breath. "And you have to know how she struggles with her fears about Calvin."

Isabella, taken aback, doesn't immediately respond.

"Come now, Bella, don't act surprised."

"I've had some sense of it over the years." As a young girl she had been both curious about and enthralled by the passionate intensity she could sense between Hattie and the serious, tall brother-in-law with the skinny nose. It was quite romantic, she thought, until the babies began coming. Calvin traveled frequently, raising money for his school and giving lectures. Harriet had once confided that his frequent absences were the only way they could keep the size of their family down, flushing and giggling in schoolgirl fashion when Isabella pressed her for details. But she wasn't giggling the day she walked into Isabella's room and held out a letter in her hand.

"Bella, would you read this? Just tell me if I'm nattering on too much about my complaints." Hattie looked oddly sad.

"He is still coming home next week, isn't he?" Isabella asked, wondering.

"Yes. Oh, please, just read it."

The letter shocked Isabella. Not sounding at all like herself, Hattie had scribbled an outpouring of hurt and loneliness, going on vaguely for several pages about the specter of temptations when a husband and wife endure long separations. Isabella kept her eyes down as she read, wondering how to respond, rereading some lines a second and third time:

> *You will love me very much at first when you come home, and then will it be as before, all forced off into months of cold indifference. I do not know as this can be helped, but it seems to me as if my mind was like one of those*

plants which can very well bear a long steady winter but is killed by occasional warm spells forcing out all the little blossom buds to be nipped by succeeding frosts. It is thoughts like these that often sadden my anticipation of your return which tho I desire I sometimes also dread.

Finally Isabella looked up. "Hattie, I'm sorry," she said.

Harriet blinked, startled. "What do you mean?"

"I mean—your concerns. Well, I can see what you fear—"

Harriet reached out for the letter, shaking her head vigorously. "No, no, you misunderstand. I'm just concerned about the spiritual effect of long separations. It all works out when he's home, of course. The difficulty is the maintaining of a spiritual life, with all this travel."

"It sounds—"

Harriet's voice sharpened. "No, no. I wish he would write more, of course, but he's much too busy. I just wondered if this was too whiny and long-winded."

"It isn't."

Harriet folded the letter in two, then folded it again, and yet again. "Thank you, Bella." She turned and left the room. They never spoke of the incident again.

"Does she think he's unfaithful?"

"Fact is not the point," Catharine says impatiently, in her best teacher's voice. "It's what she fears."

"Should I try to talk to her?" Isabella asks.

"No, dear, she wouldn't listen. Don't expect her to trace this back to Calvin. Harriet is a stubborn one, always was. She used to sit in the corner, listen to everybody, say nothing—then make pronouncements which brooked no argument. A little like Father, I suppose. When she first started making speeches, she would practice in front of the mirror, pulling her hair back and lifting one finger in the air to make her points." Catharine smiles at the memory. "Just like Father."

"I miss her," Isabella says.

"I used to be jealous of the bond between the two of you." Catharine's face turns pink. "But I was the oldest, and somebody had to be in charge. You and the others just thought I was bossy."

It is Isabella's turn to flush.

"I can't help you through this, Bella. All I can do is tell you, you are loved. Don't judge me too harshly. I'm losing this little garret"— she waves her arms, to take in the small set of rooms—"and moving in with Henry and Eunice. Finances, you understand."

"You'll be there during the trial."

"Yes." Her voice is gentle.

"So therefore inaccessible to me."

"Indeed. That's why I wanted to see you now."

Isabella lowers her head, her shoulders slumping forward. Tom will not stand up with her, and now, Catharine. She looks up again. "Do you remember the slave ship that docked in Cincinnati? With all the slaves chained together?"

Catharine looks puzzled, then her brow clears. "Yes, a shocking introduction to slavery for you. We never saw things like that in New England. Harriet was worried about you, as I recall."

"I used to dream I was on that vessel, that I was chained with the others. I couldn't turn, or raise my hand, or walk. Catharine, I feel chained now."

Her words are met with silence.

"Strange that you say so," Catharine finally responds. "Harriet has said something similar."

"What do you mean?"

"She is unsure what to do about the bracelet."

"The one she was given in England? The slave fetters?"

Catharine nods.

Isabella hasn't thought about Harriet's gold bracelet in years. "What did she say?"

"Oh—" Catharine waves her hand in a vague, distracted gesture. "Something about it holding her down. I don't recall. Now I'll fix our tea." And she vanishes into the tiny kitchen, clattering about, popping her head back through the door to ask if Isabella wants a ginger biscuit, apologizing for not having butter, eventually returning with a small clay teapot in one hand and two cups in the other.

"Have you read my books, Bella?"

Isabella sees the diffidence, almost a shyness, in her sister's expression as she asks this question.

"Some of them," she says awkwardly. She has for years resisted Catharine's voluminous domestic advice, scorning her lack of experience as a married woman. She gave up after reading in *A Treatise on Domestic Economy* that she was supposed to use twenty ingredients to wash clothes properly, deploring to John the myopia of spinsterhood even as, on occasion, she envied it.

Catharine smiles and begins searching through the stacks of books in the room. "I'll give you a copy of *Miss Beecher's Housekeeper and Healthkeeper* if I can find one. You might like some of the recipes. There's gardening and designing advice too. Ah, here we are!" Triumphantly she pulls out a book and offers it to her youngest sister.

"Thank you, Catharine." Isabella closes her hand around the worn spine. "I will read it, I promise."

"Another thing," Catharine says unexpectedly. "As close as the two of you were, you've never quite understood each other."

Isabella grips the book more tightly. "Why do you believe that?" she asks.

"I'm thinking of various missteps. That séance you took her to, for example."

Yes, the séance. Her failed attempt to bring Hattie into the exciting possibilities opened up by communications with the spirits. Isabella bites her tongue to hold back the frustration she still feels at her inability to introduce Hattie to the deep and abiding comforts of spiritualism.

"Are you still a believer?" Catharine asks.

"Yes," Isabella replies. It is her turn to be diffident. "You may laugh, but there are many other believers."

"Oh, I know, dear."

She will not attempt to explain it to Catharine, it would be a waste of time. But spiritualism remains an emotional mainstay in her life. She is convinced it is possible to reach out to lost children and loved ones, and she is proud that spiritualism long ago caught the hope and imagination of many intelligent, respectable people. If she wanted to, she could reel off names, each convert adding more credence to the movement. Horace Greeley? Definitely, a believer. And all those women with eloquent voices who emerged to channel the voices of the great philosophers of the past; she has been there, she has seen it. She is convinced there is a kinder world beyond the grave, and if more people would reach out, they would find themselves freed from rigid beliefs of doom and despair.

Catharine seems oblivious to the intensity of Isabella's feelings. "It certainly wasn't Harriet's cup of tea," she said. "Ah well, there were always things we couldn't accept about each other, perhaps about Henry most of all. We all just have to do the best with what we have. And the trial will not last forever. It will end."

Isabella has a sudden picture in her mind of Catharine, only last year, sitting by the fireside at Tom's house, rereading her love letters from Alexander and then, one by one, feeding them to the fire. Tom and his wife had confided their consternation as they watched this sad, systematic ritual of lost hope and history. They had felt they should not intervene, for Catharine's life was her own.

And she, by contrast, would have probably rushed in and implored her sister not to burn them.

It is time to go. She embraces Catherine wordlessly, feeling a twinge of fear at the frailty of her bones. The trial will indeed end; all things will, and that is scant comfort at the moment.

Isabella stares out the window of the carriage, remembering the séance debacle. She was still trying to convince Catharine and Harriet midway through 1871 that Victoria's keen mind and rhetorical flair made her a dazzling champion for women. Catharine was impossible, but Harriet at least would listen to Isabella's accounts of this uneducated, intelligent woman who lived by her own rules (as she downplayed, of course, the fact that Victoria shared with both her husband and her ex-husband one apartment), stressing that her ability to cajole and convince was drawing men and women alike to the suffragist cause. Harriet at least asked questions.

"Isn't she a spiritualist?" she said.

"She's more than a believer, she is a medium through which spirits reach the living. And she is a healer," Isabella replied eagerly. "It's amazing, Hattie. Women come to her, and she reaches out to them and something magnetic goes between them."

"Have you seen that happen?"

"I've seen the way women respond to her. They are enthralled, invigorated—"

"But not necessarily cured of disease, I imagine." The sides of Harriet's mouth curved up slightly.

Isabella decided quickly on a challenge. "Well, why don't you see for yourself? Will you come with me to one of her séances?"

Harriet's smile did not go away. "I will."

The séance was held in the home of a gentleman friend of Victoria's, a grand place in the Heights Isabella had never been in before. She was relieved to see the invited group included some of Harriet's acquaintances. At least her sister wouldn't decry the event as a gathering of questionable characters. All were dressed in fine clothes, as if preparing for a ball. Two of the women had recently lost children and sat slightly apart, receiving murmured condolences from the others. But there was a restrained excitement as they gathered around the large, oval parlor table. It was so highly polished, Isabella could see her face reflected in the burnished surface.

Victoria glided into the room in a red silk gown that seemed more suited for a ball than a parlor. The neckline was cut well below the swell of her breasts. Her lips were painted and her face powdered. Isabella glanced at her sister, nervous about a negative reaction, but Harriet simply gazed at Victoria with no change of expression.

They took their seats, the gaslight lowered, with Victoria at the head of the table. Two lit candles behind Victoria cast a luminous, flickering halo around her head. She sat in perfect silence for at least three or four minutes. No one coughed, although Isabella could hear the noisy breathing of the man sitting directly opposite her.

A rapping began from underneath the table.

"The spirits have joined us," Victoria said calmly.

More rapping.

"I cannot see Mr. Morley's hands," Harriet suddenly said. "He should put them *on* the table, wouldn't you say, Mrs. Woodhull?"

A murmur of discomfort went around the table as Mr. Morley—the man with the raspy breath—took both hands from his lap and slapped them down in front of him, in plain view of all, glaring at Harriet.

"To please Mrs. Stowe, everybody hold hands *above* the table," Victoria ordered serenely. "We will form a spirit circle that can't be challenged."

Isabella took Harriet's hand and the hand of a somber-looking elderly lawyer, hoping her nervousness wouldn't be betrayed by her sweaty palms.

Again, a short silence. Then more rapping. Isabella looked swiftly around the table; all had their hands in plain view.

"Who am I calling tonight?" Victoria sounded as if she were in a trance.

"Is my baby in heaven?" asked one of the newly bereft mothers in a shaky voice.

"Rap twice if the answer is yes," Victoria intoned. "Once if the answer is no."

At first, nothing. Then one sharp knock and silence. The woman started to cry. Then a second knock. "Thank you," the woman whispered.

"Who is next?" said Victoria. "Mrs. Stowe, with whom do you wish to speak?"

Isabella saw the smile that played over her friend's lips. If there was to be a challenge from Harriet, Victoria planned to co-opt it.

"My mother," Harriet said, after a pause.

"Mrs. Stowe wishes to speak to her mother," Victoria said in a monotone. She paused, listening. "Yes, they say she is there. She will speak to you both."

Isabella began to explain. "We don't—"

Harriet stopped her. "To both of us?" she said to Victoria.

"Yes."

"I think that would be difficult. My mother, of course, never knew Isabella."

Victoria's brow remained smooth, unperturbed. "I am listening for further information," she said.

"Don't bother. Your 'spirits' should have the facts." Harriet pushed back from the table and stood. "I'm sorry, and I apologize to you good people here, but I think this is nonsense."

"You have insulted the spirits, Mrs. Stowe," Victoria said acidly.

"That may be, Mrs. Woodhull, but I suspect they have no knowledge of what is going on at this table, so therefore it would be hard to insult any of them."

"You have insulted me."

Victoria's words brought total silence to the table. Isabella stared straight ahead, berating herself for ever thinking she could bring these two women together. One stitch plucked, and now all was unraveling and she could do nothing about it.

"That would be appropriate," Harriet said. She turned her gaze to the shocked faces around the table, resting finally on Isabella. "I'm afraid I'm leaving you, now. I really can't stay for this."

Isabella settles back into her seat in the carriage, closing her eyes. Harriet spurned spiritualism after that, mocked it really, and Isabella had learned to mute her own fervent beliefs in front of her sister. Harriet always insisted that Victoria had put someone in the basement, positioning the person directly under the table to knock on the floor. She said she had heard of so-called spiritual healers who used this device. Isabella argued there was no evidence of such a ruse, and Victoria was no charlatan.

"Her entire history is as a charlatan," Harriet scoffed.

So there was no way after that of convincing Harriet of Victoria's credibility on anything. No way of arguing that Victoria was only the channel for the spirits and could not have known they had separate mothers. No way of convincing Harriet that Victoria held in her mind the answers to urgent questions about women's lives and futures. Harriet had taken an instant dislike to the woman in the red dress that day, and everything since stemmed from that.

John is already in bed reading the paper when she returns home.

"Listen to this, Bella," he says with a chuckle. "Someone in Detroit bit into a two-cent piece in his pie and complained to high heaven. But the waiter shut him up, saying, 'I'm sorry it isn't fifteen, but the fact is, times are so hard we can't do any better just now.'" John looks up, grinning.

"That's a stupid story, I don't believe it," Isabella says, throwing her hat onto the dresser and removing her coat.

"I see nothing wrong with a little humor when times are as bad as these."

"You're always bemoaning finances, and I'm sick of it."

"In case you haven't noticed, we lost a great deal of money in 'seventy-three. But then, you think of nothing else these days except Harriet and Henry and that infernal trial. I'm sick of *that*." John throws the paper across the room, swings his legs to the floor, and sits up.

Isabella, in the process of unbuttoning her shirtwaist, freezes. "It's the most important thing that's ever happened to the family—" she begins.

"So what?" her husband says. "Are you paying attention to anything else? Do you realize we've been in a depression since Jay Cooke's railroad failed? That we almost lost our home?"

"Yes, of course I know those things. John—"

But John is pacing now. "Are you aware that Mr. Edison is close to perfecting his phonograph or that the Molly Maguires may be tried for murder? Do you know who the Molly Maguires *are*?"

Isabella bursts into tears.

John strides across the room and puts his arms around her. "I'm sorry, Bella. I'm just sick of it all."

"I want to think about those things, I want to know," she sobs. "That's what we've always done together, talk about the world, about the children, about interesting things, even bad jokes, and I'm sick of it too!"

John lets out another chuckle, holding her tighter. Then he gently guides her over to the bed and seats her on his lap. For a long moment they hold each other, saying nothing. He speaks first. "I'm sorry, I haven't asked you about your visit with Catharine."

"She said she was not attacking me in that article and that she actually thinks Henry is guilty—but none of us have a right to say so." Isabella shakes her head wearily. "I love her; I fear we'll lose her soon. But I don't understand her; I never will."

"You missed your share of the Beecher ferocity," John says. "But I don't want you to see yourself as the waif with her nose against the window, peering in. You've always been anxious about your family, and I fear it will consume you."

"Not if I have you."

"Nothing to worry about there, although I may shout a bit now and then."

"And I'll cry."

They smile at each other.

"Remember, Bella, you didn't cause this mess. Henry did. And you can't resolve it."

That night Isabella drifts off to sleep next to John, and into a troubled dream. She is crocheting a lace tablecloth, something she has never attempted in her life. She sits in her chair by the fire, weaving the crochet hook through the delicate strands of linen, trying to work meticulously. But try as she might, she makes no progress. A sweep of lace appears to emerge in her hands and then vanishes, and all she has for her work is a bundle of loose strands falling to the floor. Her hands are aching. Her shoulders are stooped. She can barely see the material in her hands. Why am I doing this, she asks herself in the dream. I don't like to sew. I hate the design. I don't like lace tablecloths.

And then the strands begin to float in the air. She reaches to grab them back and hold them, but they keep floating away, higher, to the ceiling, then out the window, funneling themselves into a strangely intricate pattern as they move up into the sky and disappear. Isabella tries to run to the window, but her legs will not move. She feels suddenly peaceful, as if she is floating too. Indeed her body is curling lazily, funneling through the window, and it feels good. Far away, in the sky beyond, she glimpses the floating strands of linen. Let them go, she says to herself. Let them go.

PART THREE

❧ CHAPTER ELEVEN ❧

Brooklyn
January 11, 1875

WHEN HAS THERE last been so much ice? Not since the East River froze in 1867, when people could walk or skate across the frozen river between New York and Brooklyn. Every branch, every cobblestone leading up to the Brooklyn courthouse is encased in a crystalline shell. Even the ships in the harbor are locked in place, unable to move, creaking within their glittering prisons. All of Brooklyn seems encased.

That hasn't stopped thousands of people from slipping and sliding their way to city court for the first day of the trial of Henry Ward Beecher. Harriet steps from her carriage onto the slippery sidewalk and walks slowly through the crowd, past vendors hawking ham sandwiches and mince pies and people haggling with peddlers who are selling tickets for ten dollars each. Even as she mounts the steps to the courthouse, the city bailiff is turning hundreds of people away, shouting, "No room left!"

For a moment, she fears she won't be let inside. She reaches the doors, which the bailiff is trying now to close.

"Let me in," she demands. "I'm Harriet Beecher Stowe, Reverend Beecher's sister."

The bailiff shakes his head and continues tugging at the doors until someone pokes him on the shoulder and says, "Let her in. That's Mrs. Stowe, the one who wrote that Uncle Tom book." He raises an arm to hold back the crowd and beckons her inside. "Should've spoke up louder," he mumbles.

Harriet gives him a stony look and starts up the iron spiral staircase to the courtroom. It will not do to show anything but strength in this situation. Calvin had laughed at her this morning, saying she had the attitude of a soldier heading into battle, and he was glad she wasn't carrying a rifle in the folds of her skirt. She'd smiled, nonplussed that he could make such a lame joke on a day like this. She *was* going into battle; her brother's reputation and honor were at stake. If all she could do was sit there and stare at that miserable Theodore Tilton and his timorous wife, then she would do so. She would bear silent witness. Nobody in that courtroom would see a sniveling Beecher, and nobody would see one humbled by shame.

She repeats this mantra as she mounts the stairs, giving only a quick glance at a bewildered looking man with muscular arms and a handlebar mustache much too big for his leathery face, standing on the landing. He looks like someone who might work on the docks. He is holding a piece of paper in his hands and glancing right and left.

"Lady, can I ask you a question?" he says, holding up the slip of paper. "I got this, and it says I gotta be a juror. Where do I go? What do I do?"

She stops and stares at him, his query sinking in, realizing suddenly that this could be one of the people deciding Henry's fate. She has a wild desire to tell him he should go home, there can be no trial; the Reverend Henry Ward Beecher is innocent of all charges, and that is that.

"Lady? You hear me?"

He looks so perplexed, so unsure of himself, so small a cog in the machinery of life. She could take his hand, greet him warmly, say good things about her brother, prepare him to be an ally—

"I believe the jury room is to the left, second door past the stairs," she says.

He nods with relief, tips his hat, and hurries off.

Feeling foolish, Harriet enters the courtroom and looks around for the block of seats saved for the Beecher family. The room is jammed, with dozens of people standing along the walls.

The first person she recognizes is a haggard-looking Theodore Tilton, slumped in his seat, chin almost to his chest. Even in so sullen a posture, he projects an air of exasperation. Get on with it, is his demeanor. I'm here to destroy and shame, so let's get on with it.

There might be some who pity the man. Some who might say, Isn't he the victim of this sordid drama? They spread the whispers that Theodore's wife had been impregnated by Henry, and what man should be expected to endure that? But there are also rumors that Theodore carried on adulterous affairs of his own—and there is the nasty story that he forced his wife to have an abortion. The trial has not begun, but many already feel there are no winners here.

Harriet sweeps by him without a glance. She sees Henry just a short distance away. He is standing, surveying the room with an air of studied seriousness, hands clasped in front of him, looking as dignified as he does in church, almost as if he were about to mount the podium and give one of his sermons. He is in a nondescript cloth overcoat, not the usual semimilitary cloak that gives him such verve and swagger.

Eunice sits silently next to him. Her pure white hair is pulled severely taut and topped with a huge black velvet bonnet that dwarfs her features, aging her by twenty years. It is not a charitable thought, but in truth, she looks old enough to be Henry's mother. Why such a choice, Harriet wonders. She slips into her seat behind them, next to the Beecher children and her brothers Edward and Tom. Catharine has stayed home, explaining she will prepare a good meal for the evening and she isn't ready to face the opening day of the carnival.

The bailiff's gavel goes down, calling the court to order. Chief Judge Joseph Neilson strides out in his black robe and mounts the steps to his seat, and the room falls silent.

A slight commotion breaks out in the back. Harriet turns and sees Elizabeth Tilton walking to her seat, accompanied by her step-father and two friends. An appreciative murmur sweeps through the crowd, for she moves with unexpected grace and elegance, projecting the aura of mystery that has made her a favorite in this unfolding drama. Elizabeth wears a loose velvet cloak over a walking dress of crisp black silk. On her head is a small black velvet bonnet, darker, if possible, than her abundant black hair, with a veil caught up to the crown that looks long enough to be lowered over the face. Adulteress or wronged wife? The room seems to tremble with libidinous expectation.

She wants to hide her face, Harriet realizes. That's what Eunice is trying to do too, with that cavernous bonnet.

Judge Neilson bangs his gavel. "Bring the jury pool in," he orders.

A group of people emerges from the recesses of the court chambers and moves in single file into the courtroom, lining up before two rows of yellow chairs. Harriet sees the man with the handlebar mustache. His eyes are darting around, taking in the huge crowd of people. His mouth hangs slightly open.

"You may sit down," the judge says.

The process of choosing a jury has begun.

The evening is almost festive. The family is inside the house again, doors locked against the boorish world that now sees the Beechers as their chief source of entertainment. Catharine has cooked up a huge platter of chicken, which she places in the middle of the dining room table to the approving applause of her brothers and sisters. Chairs are drawn close to the table, and spirits relax under the cheery glow of a gaslight chandelier turned high.

"Could you believe all those people in the gallery, tossing about food wrappings and apple cores?" Edward tucks a large, white napkin between the buttons of his vest before sipping his wine. "And did you see the lady reporter from San Francisco?" He laughs. Edward sometimes has a gratingly sharp laugh.

Henry nods, happily reaching for a chicken leg from the platter in front of him. "Wish there were more of them; my lawyers say women reporters will do a sympathetic turn on Elizabeth at Theodore's expense. Speaking of Elizabeth—" His mouth is full as he turns to his wife. "I want you to go over and talk to her tomorrow, just chat a bit. It looks good; it adds a civil tone."

Eunice barely changes expression, but her eyes widen.

"The lawyers want it, dear," Henry says quickly. "Please—for me. It doesn't hurt to appear sympathetic."

Slowly, Eunice nods assent.

"What did you think of Tilton's lawyer, Sam Morris?" Henry says, turning from Eunice to Edward. "He's supposed to be the best, but he didn't look that sharp, blundering around, dropping his papers. Neilson looked annoyed."

"It's an act, don't be taken in," Edward replies. "He slithers around like a snake, but he can swallow a buffalo. That's why Tilton hired him, so watch out."

"I've got a few like him in my corner too," Henry says, almost proudly.

Harriet is vaguely uneasy about the jovial nature of the exchange. After getting over the feeling of being under the scrutiny of a thousand eyes, she had spent her time today studying the jurors. She is eager to know more about each one.

"What does your Mr. Evarts say about the jury pool?" she asks.

Henry reaches for another piece of chicken. "He likes it fine. A few people to worry about, but most are from respectable backgrounds, which makes for more God-fearing men. Did you see how often they looked over at me? That's a good sign, Evarts says. Plus we hear Tilton's drinking again, which won't win him any friends."

"It could go either way," she murmurs.

"Don't worry so much, Hattie," he says, reaching for her hand and squeezing it tight. "We'll get a good jury. And then we'll go after Moulton."

Hearing the name takes Harriet's appetite away. The only credible person testifying against Henry will be Frank Moulton. The talk is, he has letters in which Henry acknowledged the affair.

"Are you worried?" she asks in a low voice under the table chatter. She hasn't talked specifics with Henry about his defense. Her brother always stops such conversations with a big smile and a hug, then changes the subject.

This time she watches his fork falter slightly as it hovers above his plate. "He misrepresents the nature of my letters to him, if that's what you mean. And no jury will believe otherwise," he says. He looks up at her, his eyes suddenly young and beseeching. "Hattie, you aren't having doubts about me, are you?"

"No, no." Horrified, Harriet reaches out and touches her brother's cheek. How can he ask such a question? Her loyalty is passionate and finely honed. It does not accommodate shifting points of view. At every step in this long and painful saga, no matter what rumors or stories were making the rounds, she has only felt more energized. She has been writing strategy-planning letters every day from Nook Farm, scrawling them out as fast as she can, feeling the agitation in her body pour through her fingers into the pen and onto the paper. The family is complaining more than ever about her handwriting, and no wonder—even she has trouble reading these letters, which she has admitted to Calvin with some sheepishness.

"I couldn't do it without you," Henry says. His voice is so low she almost misses the words.

"Say, some reporter wanted to know if Bella was in the courtroom today," Edward blurts out, drawing their attention. "Anyone see her?"

Henry claps a hand to his forehead. "Dear God, don't let that be," he mutters.

Tom hesitates, then puts down his fork. "She wasn't there," he says.

"How do you know?" asks Harriet.

"She decided not to come."

Out of the silence that follows, Catharine speaks first. "So you have seen her?" she asked.

"We talk once in a while," Tom says evasively. He will not look directly at any of them. "So don't go telling me I'm betraying the family by talking to my *sister*."

"Well, don't go talking to her about Henry's defense," Harriet fires back. "You might keep in mind how all this began, Tom. She's as much an enemy as Victoria Woodhull or Frank Moulton."

Tom pushes his chair back from the table, looking both hurt and angry at his sister's attack. "So am I a family pariah now too?"

"No, no," Harriet says for the second time. "Forgive me, I'm speaking too harshly." What possesses her, sometimes? Tom is a loyal brother, and he has common sense. Calvin says she is snapping at people much too easily lately. She'd sensed a certain relief in his demeanor when she left Nook Farm to come down for the first few days of the trial.

"Will you miss me?" she had asked as she gathered notes, letters, and newspaper clippings, anything she needed to give to Henry, just in case he or his lawyers had overlooked something crucial to the defense.

"Yes, Hattie," he'd said quietly. "And I hope you come home less consumed by it all."

Henry has spent this time staring at his plate. Tears begin rolling down his cheeks. "I've done terrible things to all of you," he says. "I've reached out with love and counseling to a needful woman, and look what it has led to! Nobody should have to go through this. This isn't a war room. No one is going to be tested here."

There is a flurry of comforting assurances from around the table as all realize anew that no one here is under greater strain than Henry. His reputation, his entire life, is at stake. Eunice disappears into the kitchen, returning in a moment with a steaming raisin pie. Smiling tentatively, she places it before him.

"Thank you," he says, looking up at her and beaming. "My favorite."

But the mood of the evening has changed. The excitement and euphoria of getting through the first day have dissipated. The sense of unity and safety inside this house, with the world held at bay, seems transitory, which, Harriet realizes as she looks around at her family members, is the truth.

*   *   *

The second day is a repeat of the first: this time thousands are milling about, trying to snag one or two of the three hundred seats in the courtroom. Reporters everywhere. Harriet no longer allows herself to speak in public without carefully weighing her words, no matter how innocent the subject. She never knows when some reporter is about to pounce with questions, scribbling away. Sitting in the courtroom during the tedious process of jury selection is almost a relief, even though the heat and stench of the place are sometimes unbearable, because at least there the reporters must stay in their own section.

What takes her attention the second day is Eunice's face, which remains almost impossibly still. How does she do it? Harriet is fascinated by and then envious of its total immobility. As an idle game, she concentrates for about fifteen minutes on watching only her sister-in-law's eyebrows as she whispers to Henry, turns to address the children, and listens to the judge. They never move. There is not a line in her forehead, not a ripple of a cheek muscle. Her face is frozen, conveying nothing.

By the time five o'clock comes, Harriet is exhausted with the effort of concentrating on the lawyers' questions to the potential jurors. Evarts seems too lackadaisical, not quite as sharp in his questioning as he should be. She itches to ask questions herself. But Henry seems unperturbed, and by the end of the day, the jury is complete. The man with the drooping mustache—looking more confident today—is the last one chosen. She watches him settle heavily into the twelfth yellow chair, pushing it with a sharp squeak until it rests a few inches back and at an angle from the rest. For some reason, this annoys her. She wants symmetry.

Dinner that night is more subdued. Henry is in a brooding mood, and there is little conversation about the trial. Perhaps finally seeing the faces of the twelve people who will decide his fate has sobered him. Tom and Edward are talking about going home the next day, influenced by Eunice's clear desire to see fewer family faces around her dinner table.

After dinner, Harriet slips out for a walk by herself. The evening is clear, though cold, and the streets of the Heights, still slick with ice, are mostly empty. She sees a cluster of carriages on Garden Place, with men in top hats helping women in fur capes descend to the sidewalk, and stops to listen to their animated laughter. A party, she thinks wistfully. People are having a fine time and not worrying about losing their reputations and livelihoods. When had she and Calvin last been to a party? Not for months. She cannot deny it, all her energy and effort have been bound up in the details of this infernal trial.

She walks past the Rivers Dancing Academy at the corner of State and Court, where all the fashionable dances are taught. She sees light and flitting shadows through the shaded windows and stops for a moment, trying to imagine how young women can present themselves in such a place to dance with strangers. The idea intrigues, tugging at her brain. She turns and trudges back toward the water, listening to her footsteps on the crunching ice. She is *too* needful of symmetry. Once somewhat scattered and slapdash, she now needs to have things lined up and predictable and ordered. But she was brave and daring, wasn't she? She wrote a book that changed America; she was praised and commended by President Lincoln himself. She was known. And now a courthouse bailiff identifies her as "the one who wrote that Uncle Tom book." He probably remembers only the stage shows.

She walks on, still wondering when her courage disappeared. It wasn't when the wrath of angry Southerners descended on her after *Uncle Tom's Cabin,* although that astonished her. Bella helped her survive that. No, it happened after the failure of her book about Lady Byron's husband. At the time it had seemed a good way to dip her toe into writing about women's rights, but no one wanted to hear about the incestuous behavior of a literary hero. Bella had encouraged her, but mainly to coax her into the women's movement with her wild-eyed friends.

Harriet kicks a frozen lump of coal from the sidewalk into the street, feeling a bit ashamed of herself. She isn't being fair. And even though she once called them free-love harpies, women like Susan Anthony and Elizabeth Stanton are too intelligent to dismiss. But they made too much of winning the vote, puffing it up into some kind of mystical talisman that would solve all problems.

Why is her mind wandering so? It is time to go back to the house. Harriet pulls her coat close and trudges up Hicks Street, wearied by her thoughts. She must write Calvin before she goes to bed tonight. She misses him, quite piercingly. At some point she must go home to Nook Farm. But not yet.

The trial begins in earnest the next morning, with Tilton's lawyers calling Frank Moulton to the stand. Moulton sits awkwardly in the witness chair, looking as if he'd give anything to be somewhere else. And well he should, Harriet believes. How the man can still claim to be a friend of Henry's while testifying against him is beyond her. The reporters like him, that is clear from their admiring comments in the morning papers. But of course they do—he gives them the drama they want. She clenches and unclenches her hands, trying to emulate the blank expression Eunice has perfected.

One of Tilton's many lawyers, the sharp-eyed former Confederate, Roger Pryor, walks to the center of the courtroom, seeming to stagger under a load of documents he proceeds to deposit—with an elaborate sigh of relief—onto the conference table. He walks then to his chair, a tiny smile on his face, obviously enjoying the stir in the packed courtroom.

"Good theater," Tom whispers. "They want us to think all those are letters confirming Henry's guilt." He has changed his mind about leaving, and deliberately takes the seat next to Harriet today in a gesture of conciliation for which she is grateful. She wants no quarrel with this gentle brother.

"Isn't there one particular one?" she asks nervously. "Henry says it's a fake."

"Yes, the one in which he supposedly confessed; that's the one. Among others."

William Fullerton, another of Tilton's lawyers, stands and faces Moulton. He is a mild-looking man—bald and somewhat pudgy in his rumpled suit—but he is famous for his examinations. He clears his throat and begins the questioning. How long had Mr. Moulton known Mr. Tilton? Since childhood, came the answer.

"And when, sir, did you become an intimate of Henry Ward Beecher?"

"When my wife became a member of his church," answers Moulton. "I'm not much of a churchman myself, so I went only rarely."

"So when did your connection with Mr. Beecher intensify?"

"The night of December 30, 1870," Moulton replies. "Theodore came to my house and showed me a paper."

The courtroom sways with whispers as the lawyer picks up one document and hands it to Moulton. "Is this it?"

"Yes."

"Will you describe it to the court?"

Moulton identifies the paper as a confession of adultery given by a remorseful Elizabeth Tilton to her husband, wrested from her after a marital scene of tears and recrimination.

"And what did you do with it?"

"I put it into my pocket and went to Mr. Beecher's house. We talked for a long time. I told him Theodore wanted to see him, and together we went to my home, where Theodore was waiting for us."

Henry grew greatly agitated on that short walk. He knew now what he faced, Moulton tells the jury. Henry had begged him to stop Theodore from making a public accusation. The shame, the humiliation—Henry was distraught. Moulton promised to try to smooth the waters. When they reached the house, Henry and Theodore went upstairs to talk privately, while Moulton waited downstairs in his own parlor.

Was there shouting? Was it true, as Tilton had claimed, that Henry confessed his guilt in that meeting? Moulton can answer none of this; he heard nothing.

But the drama of that evening was far from over. The three men then marched over to Tilton's home on Livingston Street to talk to Elizabeth, who was recovering from a miscarriage suffered four days before.

A buzz of delighted whispering sweeps again through the court-room. They've been waiting for hints about the rumors that Eliza-beth Tilton was pregnant with Beecher's baby. Could it be true?

"What happened there?"

"Mr. Beecher was allowed to talk to Mrs. Tilton privately. I left Theodore there and returned home."

"And?"

Half an hour later, Moulton tells the court, Henry bounded up the steps of his home, waving a piece of paper and announcing with great relief that Elizabeth had retracted her confession. Theodore showed up next, enraged.

Ah, for the observers sitting in the stifling upper seats of the courtroom, this is delicious. Harriet can sense their pleasure. They expect now that Fullerton will bring forth the fact that Theodore promptly went home, accosted and got from his poor, muddled wife a retraction of *that* retraction, but Tilton's lawyer has other plans.

"And what did you do?" he asks.

"I realized Mrs. Tilton must have buckled under Henry's pres-sure," Moulton says in a monotone. "Her letter absolving him clearly contradicted his own words."

"Please explain, Mr. Moulton." Fullerton's voice holds a tri-umphant ring.

"Mr. Beecher had already given me *his* confession." Moulton speaks slowly, as if with a weight of sadness on his shoulders.

"He confessed to adultery with Mrs. Tilton?"

"Yes," Moulton replies. "He asked me to give it to Theodore."

"And this is the confession, Mr. Moulton?" Fullerton holds aloft a piece of paper from the pile on the desk.

Moulton takes the paper, sighs. "Yes."

My Dear Friend Moulton:

I ask through you Theodore Tilton's forgiveness, and I humble myself before him as I do before my God. . . . I can ask nothing except that he will remember all the other hearts that would ache. I will not plead for myself. I even wish that I were dead; but others must live and suffer. . . . [Elizabeth]

is guiltless, sinned against, bearing the transgression of another. Her
forgiveness I have. I humbly pray to God that he may put it into the heart of
her husband to forgive me.

"And in the days and months after that?"

"Mr. Beecher came by frequently for advice on what to do about his plight."

"How often?"

Moulton sighs even more deeply. "At least once a day."

Fullerton swerves his bulky shoulders toward the jury box and fixes his gaze on the twelve men sitting there. "Now I ask you," he says, "why did Mr. Beecher, the defendant here, want to go to Moulton's day after day, twice a day sometimes, to see him, to make arrangements to plan, to plot, to conceal something, if it was not adultery?" He pauses, then roars out, *"If it was not adultery, what was it?"*

Harriet is close to tears as she glances at her brother. Their world is crumbling, but Henry's face is impassive. How can he sit still in the face of such blatant lies?

"Calm down, Hattie," Tom whispers, squeezing her hand. "Henry says he never wrote that letter, he just signed it. Remember, this is theater."

How grateful she is to have him sitting next to her. If he were not here, she might have jumped up and humiliated herself before the cross-examination.

That commences after lunch.

"Mr. Moulton," William Evarts begins, looking quite solemn as he hands the "confession letter" to Moulton. "Can you tell us in whose hand this letter is written?"

Moulton hesitates for a fraction of a second. "In mine, sir," he says.

"What? This letter Mr. Beecher gave you was *not* written by him?"

"He was quite agitated and dictated it," Moulton replies, looking resigned.

Harriet waits for the triumphant, withering response this should bring from Evarts, but the lawyer calmly says, "No more questions," and sits down. Harriet clutches at Tom. "They're going to let this amazing admission go by?" she asks.

Tom shrugs his shoulders. "They've got a reason," he says.

Fullerton snatches the initiative back as quickly as he can.

"Oh, indeed, Mr. Beecher's handwriting *is* on this letter," he tells the jury, again waving the document, pointing to a sentence scrawled in Henry's hand at the bottom of the page: "I have entrusted this to Moulton in confidence. H. W. Beecher."

Tom sighs. "That's why," he says.

"Well, I think it was an incredible opportunity lost. Why wasn't Evarts raising doubts? Why—" She stops, realizing people nearby are glancing at her. She calms herself with great effort and glances at the twelfth juror. Her juror. He seems to be dozing.

"I can't quite understand what your lawyers are doing," she says to her brother that night.

"Don't worry," he replies absently, picking up a newspaper, thumbing through the pages.

"They aren't aggressive enough, Henry. They didn't attack when that letter turned out to be written by Moulton, for heaven's sake. And another thing—"

"We have our strategies," he replies. He does not lift his glance from the paper.

There is a loud knock on the door. Harriet jumps up instantly and hurries to confront yet one more reporter. She is getting good at saying nothing in an entertaining way, she tells herself. She can placate these people and send them on their way with empty phrases and sentences, and she is more than a little proud of that. It takes only a moment or two before she returns to the parlor. Henry is still staring at the paper, but he has unbuttoned his vest and jacket, and now lies sprawled out on Eunice's uncomfortable horsehair sofa.

"Henry, dear, I know it's upsetting, but we do need to talk. There was that other letter, the one dated the day before. And aren't there missing papers? I think something should be said about—"

Henry slowly puts down the paper and gazes at her. He doesn't sit up. "I've had enough of the trial today, Hattie."

"How can you be so detached?" she blurts, exasperated. "Your entire future depends on what happens!"

This time he hauls himself up to a sitting position. "I'm as aware of that as you are," he snaps. "Perhaps more so. But you don't seem to understand that this trial is going to go on for a long time. And I'm not going to be devoured by it. Now may I make a suggestion, my dear sister? You're getting too involved."

"Oh!" Harriet's hand flies to her chest.

"You're talking to reporters too much—and enjoying it. And you're obsessed with every detail about this damn thing. I think you should go home for a while."

Harriet's eyes fill with tears. Can Henry really be dismissing her? "Someone has to stand up for you," she whispers.

His eyes soften; he stands and wraps her in a familiar bear hug. "You always have, and I know you always will. I can't tell you how much comfort that brings. But I need you for the long run, Hattie. We've always stood by each other. Don't let me down now."

"I won't," she says, hugging him back. His words are wise, and she feels a little better. Perhaps she is too entwined in this early part of the trial; she is dreaming about it every night.

When she turns away, having assured him she will leave the next morning, she almost feels reconciled. But then she sees Eunice standing in the doorway with a mirthless smile on her face and suddenly wonders: Has Henry done his wife's bidding?

✢ CHAPTER TWELVE ✢

Nook Farm, Hartford
January 15, 1875

IT IS GOOD TO BE HOME, she tells herself repeatedly the first several days. There are things to do. Airing out the bedding, for one. And the silver seems dull; she will polish it. It looks as if some of her plants need repotting too.

Anna Smith stops by the second day, observing with quiet, amused skepticism as Harriet scrubs away at the silver flatware. "I don't quite understand this unnatural domesticity," she says. "Why don't you get out your paints?"

Anna has long since left the employ of the Stowe family. She lives outside Hartford now, a proper married woman with her own husband and home, a home the Stowe children visit as often as they can, still linked to the warmth of the woman who helped raise them. Anna has plumped up in middle age and is not as quick or energetic as she used to be. But each time Harriet hears her knock on the door, her day becomes brighter.

"I'm too restless," she confesses. "I'm sorry. I can't concentrate."

"You need new things to think about."

"Right now, I'm thinking that Henry rushed me out of Brooklyn."

At that moment, Calvin walks into the room and overhears his wife. A broad smile spreads across his face. "Well, this will get your mind off the trial. Sam Clemens is hosting a grand party this weekend."

She drops the polishing cloth. "In the new house?" she says.

"Of course, in the new house, that's where they're living now, or have you been too busy worrying to notice?" Calvin is smiling, enjoying himself.

"I'm eager to see the place," she admits.

"And I'm eager to see you dressing up and looking happy again," he says softly.

Anna picks up the cloth from the floor and deposits it with an expression of distaste on a nearby table. "There's nothing worse than cleaning silver," she says.

"Worse than corralling my children for dinner?" teases Harriet.

"I don't love silver," Anna says simply.

The Clemens house on Farmington Avenue glows on this wintry night with what appears to be the light of a thousand candles, and the effect—an encircling halo on the new-fallen snow—is magical.

"It must have cost Sam a fortune to build that house," Harriet says, peering out her bedroom window at the sight. "It really is a showplace, isn't it?"

"And right next door," Calvin agrees. He picks his razor out of its bath of water and muriatic acid and sets to briskly honing it, glancing at his wife. "Did you see the story in the *Hartford Times*? Quite tongue-in-cheek, in their usual way. They called it one-third riverboat, one-third cathedral, and one-third cuckoo clock."

"Well, it does look a little bit like a riverboat," Harriet murmurs.

"Don't tell me you aren't still excited about finally getting a chance to see the inside," Calvin says as he finishes shaving. He reaches for his shirt.

"Of course I am, but hush, dear, I'm trying to count the gables and the porches. I think they have forty or fifty of each."

Calvin laughs. It is good to hear him laugh. She fingers the black silk of her elegant new gown, hoping the plaiting of white faille covering her bodice is not too low, feeling as pleased with herself as a young girl.

Yes, she is excited they are going to a party. After her anxious days at Henry's trial, she needs a respite. She can forget about the testimony she is missing and spend a little time visiting with friends and neighbors, the way it used to be at Nook Farm. She hadn't realized until tonight how much of a pall had descended over the neighborhood since the scandal blew open. There have been no big parties for months.

"Do you think I should wear my wool muffler?" Calvin asks, a look of concern in his eyes. He gives a slight cough. "I'm still a little poorly from that sore throat, and I don't want to catch a chill."

"We're only walking a few yards," she replies. "If you stretched your hand out this window, you would almost be touching one of Livy's grand gables." She sees the look of hurt in his eyes and hastily adds, "But wear it, by all means. I wouldn't want you to be uncomfortable."

As Calvin contentedly wraps his throat, she puts on her best shawl, loving the swing of her beautiful skirt and the softness of the silk against her shoulders and body. She allows herself to think of her age. She may be in her sixties, but she doesn't feel old. She peers into the glass, smoothing down a loose strand of dark hair, pleased that her skin is still relatively unlined. If Bella were here, she would delight in this self-inspection. Bella was always remonstrating with her, telling her not to be so serious and to stop furrowing her brow all the time. Harriet straightens, taking one last critical peek at her bodice. It is perfectly suitable, she tells herself.

Together they go downstairs. Harriet automatically glances up the street, searching in the gathering darkness for the hurrying figures of her sister and John Hooker. The two couples always went together to neighborhood parties. Isabella was always a little late, breathless and laughing. She would bubble with praise for Harriet's gown, whatever it was, and skip along, chattering about the latest neighborhood gossip, putting them all in a festive, laughing mood.

Harriet glances away, determined not to let anything dampen

her spirits. Livy has assured her that Isabella and John are not on the guest list tonight, which would have been intolerably awkward.

The path between the two houses is indeed only a hundred yards or so, and Calvin has managed not to cough once by the time they reach the front door. The door swings open, bathing the porch in light as they walk up the steps.

Sam Clemens stands in the doorway, dressed in a white suit and vest. His head is splendidly large. His hair is thick and curly enough to make many a woman envious, and his mustache is lavishly full. "Welcome, neighbors," he says exuberantly. "Come in, come in! It's been way too long since we've all celebrated together. How have you been?"

"Fine, Sam," says Calvin, pulling off the muffler. "We've been watching your progress over here. You've got quite a place."

Sam rolls his eyes. "I've been bullyragged all the way by the builder, by his foreman, by the architect, by the tapestry devil who upholstered the furniture, by the idiot who put down the carpet, by the scoundrel who set up the billiard table and left the balls in New York, and by the wildcat who sodded the ground and finished the driveway after the sun went down." He slaps himself on the forehead and groans. "Just think of this thing going on the whole day long, and I am a man who loathes details with all my heart!"

"Well, we love having you finally next door," says Harriet.

Sam pulls her slightly to the side as other guests come up the steps, whispering, "Can you tell us later some of your stories from before the war that brought you to write about slavery? Please say yes."

Flattered, Harriet nods shyly. She knows her fame is on the wane, but Sam's is blazing hot. "If you'll tell us a little about the Tom you're writing about," she says.

"Ah, you've heard," he says with a laugh. "Nothing gets missed here. My Tom is just a boy who doesn't much like whitewashing fences, no big causes. I will, I will."

The two little Clemens girls tumble around in the foyer, peeking excitedly at the crowd of people already filling the house. Harriet smiles at them as Calvin reaches out to shake hands with Sam's friend and collaborator, Charles Dudley Warner. Music is playing, its origin a richly carved music box in the hall. Chandeliers sparkle in every room. Harriet moves into the parlor, admiring the lavish furnishings, tentatively accepting a glass of pale green absinthe from one of the family's many servants. Seven, she has heard. She thinks of the neighborhood story about the butler constantly fighting with Livy's upstairs maid and can't help smiling. There is so much love of life in this house, quarreling servants or not, and it makes her feel good to be here.

"Harriet!" It is Livy Clemens, looking deliciously round and soft in a pale lavender gown. She taps Harriet's glass and winks. "Isn't that a lovely liqueur? See? It's turning an opalescent white. That's because there's a sugar cube in it. It's all the rage in Paris, but be sure to sip, it's very strong. Sam was determined we should have it tonight, so I'm warning all my guests!" Harriet laughs and promises to sip slowly. Soon they are surrounded by other friends and neighbors, chattering away.

After dinner is over, Sam sits down on the piano bench, picks up his banjo, and begins to play and sing in a strikingly beautiful tenor voice. Only then does Calvin whisper the obvious to Harriet. "No one's talking about Henry's trial," he says. "Not a word."

She nods, not sure how she feels about this. At first she was relieved, then a bit self-conscious. She finds herself wanting to bring it up, to say something, wondering if staying completely silent is somehow making it shameful. But she sees no opportunity, particularly after Mrs. Twilling, Isabella's next-door neighbor, greets her coolly and turns away. She chides herself for feeling startled. It is probably inevitable that Bella has some supporters among this crowd, though none would be so impolite as to say so.

Sam finishes a sprightly western ballad that leaves his guests laughing and clapping. He stands, takes a bow, and says, "And now, friends, Mrs. Stowe has promised to share some of her reminiscences of the days before the war, when she lived on the Ohio border. It's no secret to any of you that our neighbor single-handedly woke up this nation to the evils of slavery. We are fortunate to have her with us. Mrs. Stowe?" He reaches out a hand.

Blushing but pleased, Harriet moves forward to sit next to him on the piano bench. She loves speaking to people, although she doesn't go on many speaking tours anymore. She looks out at this gathering of neighbors and friends, and says, "If you will all give me questions, I'll do my best to answer."

Mr. Warner, a genial man with warm eyes, clears his throat. He obviously likes the role of initiating dialogue. "So what first awakened *you*, Mrs. Stowe?" he asks.

"Finding myself living next to a slave state. When we lived in Massachusetts, like so many others, we had no idea what the raw face of slavery looked like." This has been her opening line many times, yet still she wonders about its honesty. No idea? Of course, they had an idea. Slavery existed outside of direct vision, and only when they were forced closer to its gnarled economics had she and her family begun to understand. "That's not quite right," she adds. "We knew it existed, but we averted our eyes. We let ourselves believe that, because it was happening someplace else, it was not our responsibility."

"Until the Fugitive Slave Act," Sam says quietly. "Which was the galvanizing point for many of us."

"Oh, yes." She addresses him directly now. "Wasn't it amazing? Didn't it seem like the end of the world? The government actually passing a *law* allowing slaves to be hauled back from freedom into bondage!" She remembers herself, turning back to the group. "I know some of you, especially my young neighbors, think of that as far in the past, but for Sam and me, it isn't." She searches the eyes of her audience, thinking of how many of them were barely born back in that watershed year.

"Were you part of the Underground Railroad?" a young man lounging by the fireplace asks. His question has the pseudo-respectful tone of someone asked to participate in a not entirely appreciated history lesson.

"Only in a small way." She can do this now; she can separate it from the anguish of lost children. She can tell the story of Zillah without thinking about Charley. She details the night's wild ride, hoping her neighbors and friends can feel the biting cold and the wind in their faces. If they could for one moment understand how frightening it had been for that young woman to be but one step ahead of being sucked back into slavery, it would be deeply satisfying.

"Did you ever see slaves being mistreated?" asks a woman sitting at the back of the room. She asks timidly, almost apologetically, as if anything she might say would be trivial.

The hot, sweaty day on the dock in Cincinnati comes back to Harriet in its full, visual, pungent reality. Everything. Her sister's small hand gone from her grasp; the sight of those poor souls stumbling toward the boat, yanked and pulled by their chains; finding herself pushed to the back of the crowd, trying to reach Bella; ready to scream if she heard a splash from the narrow dock . . .

"Yes," she says. "Down at a boat landing. A group of escaped slaves were being herded onto a ship taking them back to Kentucky—and this was well before the Slave Act."

"Your sister Isabella was there, wasn't she?"

The voice is somewhat shrill and challenging. Harriet turns and finds herself gazing at a determined-looking Mrs. Twilling, a woman of portly appearance with tight curls and a smile that matches.

"Yes, she was."

"She must have been dreadfully upset to see such a sight."

"Indeed she was, as apparently you know."

"Oh, yes, we remain friends. I'm so sorry she's not here tonight, but then, one can't invite everybody. How much did she see? I really want to know."

Harriet senses people stirring. Mrs. Twilling appears to be on a mission to make her neighbors uncomfortable; more to the point, a mission to embarrass Harriet.

"Well, she saw what I saw, of course. The slaves were shackled together—"

Sam interrupts. "Yes, shackles. Terrible things. I've wondered about an artifact people have written about—a slave bracelet you were given in London? I hear it is quite a splendid rendition in gold. Is that right?"

Harriet nods, relieved for the change of subject. "It came from the Duchess of Sutherland, and I value it highly. I've had all the significant dates of freedom—especially of emancipation—inscribed on its links."

"Oh, tell us about the evening this duchess gave you the bracelet," asks a young woman eagerly. "Did you wear a ball gown?"

"I believe so," Harriet says, taken aback.

"Did you wear the bracelet right away? Why don't you wear it now?"

The moment when the duchess first held the bracelet up comes back to Harriet, and she remembers her awe as she stretched out her arm and first felt the touch of the cool metal.

"It is not a piece of jewelry, it is not meant for adornment," she says.

"Oh? A pity," comes the murmur.

"I did put it on," she says. "But it is quite huge. It has ten hollow links, and each one is about an inch and a half wide."

"How did it feel wearing it?" asks Clemens.

She casts a quick glance at her husband, who returns her look with a smile. He remembers how she felt, but it isn't a story she will tell here.

In London that night, after leaving the grand hall and going back to their hotel, she had wrapped the cumbersome bracelet around her ankle, twisting it, trying to imagine being forced to walk as she jerked the chain. Calvin had been dumbfounded when she burst into tears. "You mustn't be so vulnerable to your imagination," he had scolded.

"It was quite light in weight but yet conveyed a psychic burden," she says to her neighbor.

"A sense of being shackled yourself, perhaps?"

It is much too perceptive a question; she wonders if Sam is reading her mind.

"That's fanciful. It wasn't chaining *her* to anything," interjects Mrs. Twilling.

"In a certain way, it gave me that feeling," she says, looking directly at Sam.

His face is serious. "Why?"

"Because it demands something of me I haven't delivered."

She sees Calvin's eyes widen in surprise. She hasn't expressed this thought so bluntly before.

"Oh, come now, Mrs. Stowe, don't be so modest. With all you have accomplished? You delivered the country its conscience," bursts out a robust gentleman chewing on a cigar.

A laugh; the moment passes. Then another question from a genial young stockbroker standing against the back wall: "Mrs. Stowe, what's the true genesis of *Uncle Tom's Cabin*?"

"Daydreaming in church," she promptly replies. She tells them of sitting one morning in her pew when a vision popped into her head: she saw in her mind a cruel slavemaster urging on two muscular slaves as they flogged an old slave with white hair. "It was extraordinarily vivid, and I wrote it out when I returned home," she says, glancing again at her husband. What a moment of affirmation that had been—Calvin had faced her holding the manuscript after reading it, tears streaming down his face. "Hattie, you must go on with it. You must make up a story with this as its climax. The Lord intends it so," he had said.

"Was Uncle Tom based on a real person?" the stockbroker asks.

"Indeed he was, an escaped slave named Josiah Henson, a brave man who risked everything to find freedom," she says. "And yes, because I know you will ask, a young slave mother *did* escape over the frozen Ohio River with her baby, although I didn't see it happen."

"I saw the play as a child," volunteers a young woman. "I was *so* impressed with the fake ice floes onstage! I wonder how they did it. It truly looked real, and I was quite impressed."

"I know it's hard to believe for those of you who were too young then," Harriet says gently, "but people were in *bondage*. They were bought and sold, and families were ripped apart. And still people allowed themselves to think slaves were *better off* with their owners." She searches the faces around her, wondering how many of them ever actually read her book. Has she done anything of lasting value by writing it? She can't resist giving them a jolt.

"Let me tell you about another gift I received," she says. "It wasn't made of gold, it was human flesh. A slave's ear."

She describes opening the box and looking down with horror at its contents and asks them to imagine themselves as that mutilated man or woman.

"You're dragged by the hair, pressed down against a block, and then, wielding a heavy knife, your owner cuts your ear from your body. Think of that! You lie there and bleed. Your owner takes your ear, wraps it in paper, and puts it into a small box. Think of being in dreadful pain, watching him, wondering what he is doing." She pauses for full effect. "And then, with cold viciousness, he addresses that small, innocuous box to Mrs. Harriet Beecher Stowe."

The young woman who remembered the stage ice begins dabbing at her eyes with a handkerchief. Others gasp.

"You've reminded us all of what we mustn't forget, Mrs. Stowe," says the stockbroker, with a bow. "Thank you."

The guests clap. Gracefully, Harriet thanks them and stands. "That's enough history for tonight," she says. "Now, if we're lucky, we can get Sam to play us some songs, because I, for one, would love to dance."

"You're a wonder, madame," her host says gruffly, bussing her on the cheek. He then sits down to play the piano with such infectious glee, soon all are laughing and clapping, and the dancing begins.

Not until shortly after midnight, her face flushed from dancing a final polka, does Harriet concede to Calvin that it is time to head home. They say their goodbyes and step out onto the porch. Snow is falling. The flakes drift slowly across the fields and houses of Nook Farm, softening fences and lampposts, imbuing the scene before her with a soul-easing tranquillity. She inhales deeply. There is a sense of timelessness in the clean, sharp air. It could be yesterday, last year, this moment, or a distant tomorrow. It all floats together, unsullied by strife and bitterness. If she could spread her hands and float with the snow . . .

"An absolutely first-rate party, wasn't it, Hattie?" Calvin says happily, breaking into her thoughts.

"It was magical," she says, taking his arm as they make their way down the steps. "And you, my dear, remain a wonderfully nimble dancer."

The snow is soft and crunchy under their feet, and more than once they slip and slide as they head for the house, giggling at their awkwardness. Calvin suddenly scoops up a handful of snow.

"Watch out, Mrs. Stowe!" he yells and throws it at her.

Sputtering and laughing, Harriet leans over and scoops up her own ammunition, stumbling toward her husband and stuffing it under his cherished muffler. Whooping, he pulls her into a drift and then chases her down the hill, almost to their own kitchen door. Only when they see other departing guests looking in their direction do they remember decorum, managing then to get inside their home, still laughing, their nostrils still filled with the clear, pure air of a snowy winter night.

They make their way upstairs, chatting about the furnishings, about the food—Sam's favorite butter beans and apple puffs were once again on the menu—and about how strange it was to be telling "old" stories that took place before the war, yet feeling they happened yesterday.

It is only after they climb into bed that Calvin raises another subject. Propping up on one elbow, staring down at Harriet, he asks quietly, "What did you mean tonight? What is it you haven't delivered?"

"Oh, I don't know why I said that," she answers quickly. "I haven't the faintest idea. It must have been the absinthe. What did you think of those sharp questions of Mrs. Twilling? I've never much liked her, but she bordered on rude tonight."

"Well, she's Bella's friend. If Sam hadn't switched subjects, she would've been bringing up Henry pretty quick." Calvin sinks into the bed, his voice slightly muffled by the quilt. "That damn trial poisons everything."

"However long it goes on, I'll never understand. How can thinking people believe Henry is guilty?" Harriet turns on her side, seeking the familiar cradle between her husband's arm and body.

Calvin pulls her close. "You've asked that many times, my dear."

"I still don't have a satisfactory answer."

He sighs. "A charismatic man can always be questioned."

"What do you mean?" she says.

"It's in the nature of things."

"I'm afraid I don't understand." It's this annoying habit of his, disappearing behind his words when she most wants to flush him out. She has learned to hold her tongue and remind herself of their different temperaments—he, always cryptic and methodical; she, cursed with the energy to pursue an idea with relentless talk. Perhaps the years of teaching shaped his oblique style of responding, or perhaps it is the product of his anxious soul. She knows that, if pushed too hard, he will retreat further, so she wants to tread carefully. But on this subject it is hard to keep a sharpness out of her voice.

"Think about it, Hattie. A minister, a teacher—a man faces temptation in such roles."

"Not if he is committed to God and to goodness," she retorts.

Calvin slips his arm out from under his wife's head and turns on his side to look at her. With one hand, he strokes her chin. "Use your imagination, then. You can imagine yourself a bound slave; can you reflect a little on this? A man in a position of authority is a counselor to the weak and frail. He sees the tears of women needing solace, needing affection. They come to him, imploring help. They hang on a man's every word. Such emotional outpouring is already an act of intimacy."

"To violate such trust is evil and wrong."

Calvin's voice holds a note of impatience. "My dear, it can happen to any man."

She touches his shoulder gently. "I dreamed once—about you."

"About me, what?"

"Falling." She waits for his reassurance.

A moment passes. He kisses her hand. "Dear Hattie, your fears color even your dreams. Don't obsess on such things, it isn't healthy."

"I'm not obsessing, I'm just telling you about my dream."

"Well, I predict tonight your dreams will be about dancing. Watch out, I may throw a snowball." He kisses her lightly on the forehead. "Now let's get some sleep." He turns away.

Harriet stares at the ceiling, unable to close her eyes. Soon she is listening to her husband's measured breathing and watching the snow fall softly and lazily outside her window. Tomorrow the neighborhood children will be lacing up their boots and rushing out to make snow angels, and she will be listening to their glad shouts. That will feel good. Right now, she feels a dull headache forming. The absinthe, of course. She shouldn't have sipped so freely. Moderation in all things, that is the way. She might as well resign herself to the fact that she will pay a price for that grand party. And it is while she is musing over whether the price was worth it that she finally dozes off.

❧ CHAPTER THIRTEEN ❧

January 17, 1875

THE SNOW KEEPS FALLING. By morning it has swept away all foot-prints of the revelers from the night before. Harriet watches the process of obliteration, standing in her white muslin nightgown at the window as the weak morning sun casts a cold light over the hills and valleys of Nook Farm.

It made no sense to lie in bed, alternately dozing and fighting off anxiety. She tries at first to parse through what she is anxious *about*. Night has a way of intensifying worry; she learned that long ago, but the usual tricks don't work. Even getting up and writing down what she absolutely *must* do today has not lifted the shadows from her mind. She cannot order this in her usual fashion; her anxieties will swell and demand space with no regard for her rigorous deter-mination to take back the reins.

She backs away from the window, reaching for her slippers be-side the bed. Breakfast. The servants will be slow today; fires have to be built; paths have to be shoveled. She will bake the muffins Calvin likes so much, the ones with dried cranberries, if the stove is stoked and ready.

She makes her way down the stairs, treading lightly, remember-ing the time she tried as a child in Litchfield, Connecticut, to float down, thinking, I could be an angel; thus ending up with a bruised nose and scraped hands when she pitched forward and slammed into the floor at the bottom of the staircase. Not an auspicious tumble for a little girl even then intent on being taken seriously, especially by Father—which was hard when one was the least of novelties, a middle child. The first child is pure poetry, Harriet decided long ago. The rest are prose.

She takes out the flour from the pantry and a large mixing bowl from beneath the sink. She does not feel elegant today; she feels about as thin and dry as a pinch of snuff. She has reason still to regret the absinthe, and the sunlight reflecting off the snow and through the window is hurting her eyes. Does she really want to make muffins? The prospect of mixing the dough makes her stomach lurch.

She puts the bowl back in its place and walks slowly through the house toward the front hall, glancing into the back parlor at the large portrait of Eliza, Calvin's first wife. Sometimes she senses visitors wondering why it hangs there, in so prominent a position. But Eliza was a dear friend, and it is fitting that she be remembered in this house. So why does Harriet today feel a twinge of irritation at the sight of her predecessor's face?

The morning newspaper should be at the front door. Calvin was cross yesterday when she rushed to pick it up first, accusing her of "lunging" for it to drink in whatever dreary details were dribbling out from Henry's trial. But he remains asleep, and she will do what she wants. And that now definitely does not include making the muffins.

Harriet opens the door and reaches down for her copy of the *Hartford Courant,* pleased to see the boy has covered it in a piece of oilcloth rather than, as usual, leaving it unprotected from the elements. As she straightens, she sees a figure at the end of the path leading to Forest Street—a woman in a red cape standing still with both hands in a muff. Isabella.

Harriet is not prepared. For a quick second, she thinks her sister is planning to march right up to the open door. She has rehearsed various things to say in an unexpected encounter, but none come to mind now. She feels naked, shivering in her robe.

But Isabella simply stands there, her face grave and meditative, cool as the snow. There seems to be on her lips the faintest hint of a smile, but Harriet can't tell for sure.

Indignation comes to her rescue. She grasps the doorknob and pulls the door shut. What an outrageous intrusion, and it doesn't matter that Bella neither moved forward nor retreated. Had Isabella positioned herself at the end of the path as some kind of dramatic chastisement? How long was she standing in the snow waiting for Harriet to open the door? It is just too much, really. She presses her forehead against the wall, her stomach turbulently reacting now, and vows never to drink a glass of absinthe again.

When Calvin comes down to breakfast, wearing that eccentric yarmulke he favors and holding a handkerchief to his nose, Harriet tells him that she is going back to Brooklyn the next morning.

"For heaven's sake, why?" Calvin pushes back his china eggcup and stares at her. "We've just shared a happy social evening with friends for the first time in months. I would like to have you here, Hattie."

She reaches over and takes his hand in hers. "I won't stay long," she promises. "It's sure to be over soon."

He stares at the egg yolk dripping over the edge of the cup, making no effort to catch it with his spoon. "I saw her too. Your action is not warranted."

Harriet takes a bite of her toast, carefully choosing not to reply.

The train is crowded with men heading back to the city, tall men with loud, cheerful voices holding morning papers they snap open with crisp movements of their wrists, crossing legs that bulge with muscle and strength. This train is popular with commuters. Harriet sits by herself in a window seat, listening to the jokes and conversation. There is something of an exotic element sitting with the husbands of Hartford who routinely rush through breakfast with their families, checking their pocket watches with furrowed brows, depending on vigilant wives to smooth their departures for the mysterious world of commerce.

"So how was the big party over at Sam Clemens's new place?" a man sitting behind Harriet asks. His voice has the relaxed tone of a man comfortable with his place in life.

"Quite entertaining," answers his unseen companion. "Plenty of good whiskey and good food, though Clemens is a little too fond of his Southern dishes. He sang and played the banjo, and Mrs. Stowe held forth for a while."

"Mrs. Stowe? Why?"

"Sam invited her to tell old stories about slavery before the war. He's got some billiard table in that new house of his. All mahogany and brass, with fancy Tiffany lamps hanging everywhere." The man's voice turns wistful. "I'm going to buy me one like that one of these days. I'm going to be as rich as he is, and I won't have to write a book to get there. Say, is your company worried about this new Massachusetts law restricting women to ten-hour workdays?"

The subject shifts to the headache of social reformers cutting into company profits, with speculation that high unemployment will quell their complaints soon enough. The future will depend on the steel-rail rolling mills; nobody can stop a man like Carnegie. A man has to get his money invested fast these days. If not steel, there's always that new tobacco farm in North Carolina.

Harriet keeps staring out the window, listening to them and to the clacking train wheels. For the first time, she feels old. It's been only twenty-three years since she wrote *Uncle Tom's Cabin;* only ten years since the war ended, and now all the men on this train care about is matching Sam Clemens's billiard table. Are they so little interested in the history of their freedoms, or is she just feeling an insult to her vanity? The world is changing, she tells herself. People don't think about slavery, they think about making money from cotton exports. Such evidence of the shortness of memory makes her weary. There is nothing new about people taking the great sacrifices of the past for granted, but how quickly the young wipe their slates clean and start over. She resumes staring out the window, listening to the train wheels turn, and then is jarred back to reality.

"Hear any talk about the Beecher trial?" says the man curious about the party.

"What's there to hear? They might get him off, those Beechers. They're a pretty fierce group. Prussians, marching in lockstep, that's what they are."

"Do you think he's guilty?"

"Sure. Don't you?"

"Of course. But my wife says it's all a plot to destroy values. You know, by tearing down an icon."

The other man laughs. "Twenty dollars he's just another huckster."

"Are you joking? I'm not taking *that* bet."

The courtroom looks tired and smells stale when Harriet takes her seat the next morning, as if a party has been going on within its walls for too long. Crumpled up papers, probably thrown from the upper balcony the day before, litter the floor. A bouquet of roses on the witness desk hangs limp, its blooms as withered as old parchment. The cadre of lawyers drifting about yawn and chat as they wait for the judge to emerge from his chambers.

Henry is recovering from a siege of influenza and still looks deathly pale. Eunice is not here, remaining closeted in her bedroom, apparently still recovering herself from the malady. Tilton sits slumped in his chair, eyes red, looking as if he hasn't slept in a month. Elizabeth floats in with her friends: ethereal, mysterious, beautiful. From the stir that accompanies her arrival, it is clear she remains a favorite of the packed galleries. Only Frank Moulton, dressed elegantly all in black, seems infused with energy as he takes his place in the witness chair.

It is as if nothing has happened since Harriet left. Moulton is still being cross-examined about the stack of letters in his possession: the ones he wrote, the ones Henry wrote to Elizabeth; warnings Henry received from friends; Bella's strange letter offering to convey a confession from the pulpit of Plymouth Church—on and on. Much is still being made of the "confession" letter. By late morning Harriet is half-dozing herself, watching her juror. She knows his name now.

Samuel Flate. He is a journeyman roofer, she has learned that much. He looks pale today. Is he too becoming ill? What—

Her reverie is suddenly broken by a loud noise from the rear of the courtroom. A messenger comes rushing down the aisle with a telegram, which he takes directly to Sam Morris, whispering urgently as Tilton's lawyer rips it open.

"Your Honor," says Morris after a moment. "I would like permission for my witness to leave the witness chair and accompany me out of the courtroom." He hands the telegram to the judge, who scans it quickly and nods. Looking puzzled, Moulton steps down and walks out with Morris.

Fullerton then stands and asks to address the courtroom. "Ladies and gentlemen, we have been informed that Mr. Moulton's mother died unexpectedly this morning. Mr. Moulton is being informed of that fact at this moment." A shocked, sympathetic murmur ripples through the gathered spectators.

"In that case, the questioning for today had best be deferred," says Judge Neilson.

At that moment Frank Moulton steps back into the courtroom; his face is wet with tears as he walks slowly to the witness stand. "No, Your Honor. I am willing to finish this examination."

Harriet clenches her hands and stares at Henry's lawyers, forming the word over and over in her brain: Object, object. Speak up and tell the court it's wrong to keep this suffering man in the witness chair. Otherwise he becomes a total object of pity, an afflicted witness who shows his strength of character by carrying on.

Evarts does nothing. John Porter, Henry's other lawyer, shuffles papers. Only William Beach, Tilton's lawyer, speaks. "The witness is ready to sink his private sorrow in his public duty, Your Honor." The admiration in his face is unmistakable.

The judge nods. The onlookers sigh in sympathy, and the questioning continues.

Harriet is once again consumed with frustration. She glances over at Henry, who looks perfectly serene. Is something wrong with her? Is she falsely seeing opportunities being thrown away?

There is one additional shock when Moulton is questioned in detail about several of the letters in his possession, including the one written by Isabella.

"Did Mr. Beecher fear his sister, Mr. Moulton?"

The question catches Harriet by surprise.

"He did," Moulton replies slowly. "She was not a crazy woman but a bolder Beecher than he, with equal appetite for the world. She has been branded as insane because she advised him to make a clear and full confession in the interest of truth and justice."

"And why did she do that, Mr. Moulton?"

"To rescue a woman from jail who Mrs. Hooker believed was incarcerated for simply telling the truth."

Not the whole story, of course, but spoken so simply, it evokes a murmur from the crowd. Henry's supporters scoff. They see Isabella as either a traitor or a mindless nitwit. But the vast majority of the crowd filling the courtroom doesn't quite know what to make of the rebel of the Beecher family. Everything Moulton says sounds convincing, so could it be that the flighty Isabella Hooker acted from noble purposes after all? The thought can be entertained, can't it? Even if the jailed woman referred to is the notorious, dangerous Victoria Woodhull.

Harriet cannot exhale for a long moment. She senses many eyes on her, and all she can do is stare straight ahead and try not to remember the expression on her sister's face as she stood in the snow two days ago.

That night she silently hands the evening paper to Catharine as they sit alone in the parlor. An admiring account of Moulton's behavior in the courtroom leads the story about the trial. After recounting the "excruciating, noble doggedness of the witness," the report ends thus: "One thing was certain, 'the course of justice,' as it is called, was not to be diverted or stopped by the demise of the mother of the chief witness. Men may come and men may go, but trials go on forever. Especially this one."

"It's getting fashionable to be annoyed," Catharine murmurs.

"Yes, which makes it easier to criticize Henry."

The two sisters sit for a moment in companionable silence. "Shall we go for a walk?" Catharine says. "I'm tired of being constrained in this house."

Harriet is only too happy to don her coat and set out onto the slick pavement of the Heights with her sister. If Catharine were not here, she would feel desperately lonely. Together they trudge up Hicks to Montague, bending forward to protect themselves from a sharp wind. Harriet tells Catharine about the party at Sam Clemens's house, moving from that to her shock at seeing Isabella standing on the street in front of her home like some avenging angel, and then, to her chagrin, listening to the men on the train. She hears herself babbling on and on, and realizes how much she needs to talk.

Catharine doesn't comment on Isabella. She clucks over the men on the train. She too has listened to the conversations of the greedy bent on succeeding in the new world of commerce; all the talk is about making money and very little about spending it on education; witness the difficulties *she* always had getting funding for her schools.

"Your Mr. Clemens calls this the Gilded Age, doesn't he? I've read that somewhere. How did he put it? Something about how the great triumph of this age is that we are given chapter and verse on how thievery is done."

"They want to rob us of history, that's the worst."

"Mindless simpletons."

They walk on in mutual comfort, a force of two against change.

"I think this trial is part of it," Harriet says. "I can't understand why it is so popular. Why are people clamoring daily for tickets and reporters salivating over every detail? It's as if they're looking for moral decay. Why are they more willing to accept deceit than trust and civility?"

"I don't know, dear. Perhaps they're bored."

"They want to feed on us. Our family. Henry represents all that is good and pure, and they want to see him fall. Victoria Woodhull must be chortling every day."

Catharine smiles. "Well, at least we're not seeing much of her. I hear she isn't being called on for many speeches these days."

"Will she testify?"

"Tilton's lawyers will fight that, dear. There's more talk than ever hinting she had an intimate relationship with him."

"I certainly believe it."

"Have you been surprised yet?" Catharine asks.

"In the trial? Only by Henry's inept lawyers. As for the content, it is all lies."

"I must be some sort of simpleton, but I've been surprised at how long the effort to keep the scandal from becoming public went on."

"How do you mean?"

"Well, it's clear both Henry and Theodore wanted this kept quiet, I would say."

"Catharine, you can't believe those letters are true!"

"I'm not saying that. Although Henry did write some letters to Elizabeth, which he doesn't deny. I am saying that they appear to be at the heart of Tilton's case against Henry and—"

"Moulton wasn't a trusted friend trying to resolve this, he was working with Tilton to ensnare Henry!"

Catharine stops dead and gives her sister a puzzled look. "Hattie, I'm not declaring Henry guilty. You are reading far too much into my words."

They stand uncertainly for a moment, neither quite sure what to say.

"I'm sorry," Harriet says at last.

"It's all right, dear. We're all tense these days."

In awkward silence, they make their way back to the Beecher home, where even the flickering lights from the windows can't manage to exude an aura of warmth tonight. Harriet's exhausting, self-appointed job of scrubbing away contradictions is taking a toll. But not her belief that loyalty deserves no less.

The days inch by. Then the weeks, and the months. Harriet makes the commute between Hartford and Brooklyn so many times, she loses count. Dinners at home are tepid affairs, indifferently cooked, abstractly eaten. Her paint box remains closed and locked. Calvin resigns himself to his wife's gypsylike schedule, but she notices he doesn't ask her much about the trial.

"Don't you want to know what is going on?" she asks one morning.

He looks at her in surprise. "Hattie, I read the paper every day. I'd rather we talked about other things."

In Brooklyn the parade of witnesses continues, each one swaying sympathy toward either Henry or Theodore. One day an Irish housemaid claims that, on one of Henry's visits, she saw him passionately embracing Elizabeth. But Evarts handles this masterfully, saying slyly that, as everyone knows, the Irish are always drinking, so who could believe this woman's testimony? The court gets some good laughs out of this.

Then Theodore Tilton takes the stand, where he remains for fourteen days, slowly losing his image as the wronged husband. Harriet's faith in Henry's lawyers revives when she realizes their strategy is to attack Tilton at every turn in some very surprising ways.

"Evarts is proving *him* the adulterer," Harriet reports to Calvin triumphantly. "He'll be laughed out of town by the time this ends."

One morning Victoria Woodhull's housekeeper—a sturdy, motherly soul—testifies that Mr. Tilton frequently visited Mrs. Woodhull and once she had seen the two of them disappear into Mrs. Woodhull's bedroom. She blushes as she recounts this information.

And then there is the testimony about Tilton taking Victoria to Coney Island, where he went bathing with her in the ocean, at least twice. Oh, there is consternation in the Tilton camp over this! Harriet is delighted when he can't deny it, of course, because he is forced to admit it was true. And, demand Henry's lawyers, what was he doing spending an entire night with Mrs. Woodhull in September 1871, if there was nothing intimate between them?

Tilton insists he was only courting Victoria's "friendship" in order to placate her and buy her silence. He no longer slouches, world-weary, in the witness chair. He sits forward, querulous and defensive, explaining that he spent the night in Victoria's home only because it was late, and he was too exhausted to make his way home. Furthermore, he says, his voice rising, he deeply regrets having forged a friendship with such a volatile, godless woman.

Courtroom spectators chortle over this, enjoying his performance hugely. And when a reporter relays Tilton's testimony promptly to Victoria, the entire town's pleasure intensifies with her response.

"I believe Mr. Tilton would make quite a man if he should live to grow up," Victoria tells the reporter with her usual asperity.

There is high hilarity in the Beecher home that night over *that*.

One morning as Harriet makes her way into the courthouse, she sees two vendors fighting near the steps. Some kind of altercation seems to be happening every few days now, and the police are indifferent. According to the newspapers, the lurid quality of Henry's trial is changing the personality of Brooklyn. There is less decorum in general on the streets, crime is up, and everybody is in a hurry, shouting over the din of the hammers and saws of the construction crews. New buildings seem to be sprouting everywhere, changing the face of the city, each one taller than the last. It all fits together, according to the papers. It is as if the city—maybe even the nation— has loosened a corset and dropped it shamelessly to the floor, the better to enjoy the unprecedented spectacle of the Beecher trial.

A small crowd of people has gathered around, shouting, waving their fists and laughing.

"What's happening?" Harriet asks a bystander.

"Oh, that sly one with the plaid cap snuck in here early and stole the spot old Harry's nailed down for selling his fish cakes during this bloody trial," he says cheerily. "Nothing important."

Harriet sees the older man, almost apoplectic, trying to shove the younger and stronger one away. "It's his spot, isn't it?" she asks timidly. "Shouldn't someone speak up for him?"

The bystander looks at her more closely now. "You're a lady, ma'am, you needn't bother yourself with such things. It's a different world out here. Dog eat dog." Suddenly he laughs. "Although, I don't know, from what I'm hearing, it's not that much better in there!" He strolls away.

That night Henry and his lawyers are closeted in the parlor, the pocket doors pulled shut, not emerging even when the maid announces dinner. Catharine and Harriet sit with Eunice at the table, focused on their plates, trying to ignore the muffled sound of the arguing voices from across the hall. More than once, Harriet hears Elizabeth Tilton's name.

Just as Harriet pushes back from the table, the doors slide open and Henry strides out of the parlor, followed by Evarts and Porter. Henry's face is flushed, and he seems agitated, unlike the oddly serene demeanor he had exhibited through much of the early weeks of the trial. The two lawyers bow to the women and make gruff, hasty departures, clearly preparing to continue their discussion after they leave the house.

Henry sinks into a chair, wipes his brow, and grins at them all. "Don't misunderstand what's going on," he says, his amiable self again.

"Why were you discussing Elizabeth Tilton?" Eunice asks sharply.

"We are trying to decide whether or not to put her on the stand."

"How can you think of doing such a thing?" Eunice lays her fork down, looking alarmed.

"Well, she is denying any affair took place."

"But she has come down on both sides," Harriet says, as alarmed as her sister-in-law. "How can you trust her not to be swayed back again?"

Henry reaches for a platter of dinner rolls, his brow clear. "I have a plan," he says. "And I think I've convinced Evarts. I'll have to work on Porter a little longer." He winks. "My dear ladies, don't worry about this. All will be well."

⚜ CHAPTER FOURTEEN ⚜

Brooklyn
April 1875

Juror Five fell from his yellow chair onto the floor, face forward, on the first balmy day of spring. Afterward, the blame for emptying the courtroom that day was put on Juror Twelve. When the unfortunate Juror Five collapsed, Harriet's juror clutched his throat, jumped to his feet, and gasped in a hoarse voice, "I'm feeling poorly. Smallpox, I believe it is!"

His words swept the courtroom, causing an immediate scramble in the galleries. Women and men grabbed their lunch baskets and shoved and yelled at one another as they made for the doors. The more affluent crowd on the first floor put handkerchiefs to their noses, looking for guidance to the important lawyers in black serge, who sat frozen at their desks. They, in turn, were watching the judge, who banged his gavel.

"Court is adjourned, someone help that poor man up," he said and then quickly left the bench.

For two days, the vendors outside the courthouse hawk their wares in vain. The populace of New York and Brooklyn chooses to stay home.

And then Juror Five, William T. Jeffreys, grumps his way back into the jury box, complaining about the rumors that gifted him with smallpox, saying the air was so bad in the courtroom, he had suffered a bilious attack.

In that evening's paper, a relieved and helpful city official suggests cutting a hole in the courthouse roof and running a pipe through it to bring in clean air.

"That's absurd," Henry scoffs as he tosses the paper onto a table.

"Why do you say that? The air is fetid in that place. It smells of rot and mold, and I don't think rumors of the pox are bizarre." Instead of pressing her lips together and saying nothing, Eunice is snapping at her husband much more now.

Henry sighs, a long, slow exhalation carefully designed not to convey impatience. "I'm complaining about the tendency of the press to run with every crazed idea as if it makes sense," he says. "Surely you agree with *that*."

Eunice makes no reply. She simply folds her napkin in precise squares and puts it on top of her barely touched dinner, nodding to the maid to take it away.

Harriet and Catharine exchange glances. It is never easy in this house, but it is worse now, with Henry's yearnings to be elsewhere almost palpable. He checks his pocket watch constantly, sometimes insultingly, when earnest witnesses testify to his good character. There are days he doesn't show up at the courthouse.

"You are my warrior, my champion," he says to Harriet one evening after she protests. "If you're there, I know all will be well." His voice is neither confident nor exuberant, but thoughtful, almost ruminative. "I don't know what I would do without you, Hattie; you're the best friend I have. It's always been true, but never more than now. Don't think I don't realize what you are sacrificing by being there for me in that courtroom. You listen to everything; you miss nothing. If you were a man, by God, you'd be one of my lawyers."

Impulsively, she hugs him. Then he kisses her good night, and the next morning he leaves for the family's summer home in Peekskill to spend, he tells his family, "a few much-needed days alone."

Harriet doesn't feel much like a warrior. Her ability to stay angry, to keep the heat and bile high in her heart and head, is waning in the face of deadly dailiness. The only things worse are the lurches of comedy.

Susan Anthony is supposed to be called as a witness for the plaintiff; she was, after all, the first to hear the confession of adultery from Elizabeth Tilton. But there are uncomfortable aspects to putting her on the stand, the papers say. There is that unfortunate story about how she and Elizabeth were forced to hide behind a locked door to escape the wrath of Theodore. She might have things to say the prosecution won't like.

But then other news drifts out of Tilton's lawyers' discussions: Miss Anthony will be called to testify only if the defense tries to prove that she once sat on Theodore Tilton's knee.

Such chortling in the papers the next morning! Both sides are being laughed at now. Harriet feels no love for Susan, but—sitting on Theodore Tilton's knee? Had Henry's lawyers really been toying with such a preposterous charge?

"We're cheapened by this infernal trial," she says to Catharine one morning after breakfast. "What is becoming of us all? How do we stop this carnival?"

Catharine, busily knitting and reluctant to engage, only shakes her head. She knows what she has to do to survive. Harriet wishes she could employ the same discipline of detachment, but it is not in her nature.

Emma Moulton is the one who pauses the carnival, freezes it in place. The courthouse is jammed with eager spectators, even more than usual, the morning she takes her seat as a witness for the plaintiff. Harriet watches her folding her hands calmly in her lap, looking downward, long eyelashes brushing her fair skin. Her dark hair is pulled back into a bun and covered by a simple hat adorned with a wide silk ribbon. She seems neither flustered nor hurried, and Harriet feels a stab of fear.

The courtroom quiets down immediately. It is as if all recognize at the same time that here sits a woman of grace, dignity, and unquestionable virtue. Indeed, she is generally known as a wise woman who does not deal in idle gossip. Most disturbingly, Tilton's lawyers have the delighted looks of children on Christmas morning.

Mr. Morris begins the questioning. Emma Moulton, in an even, calm voice, testifies that Frank Moulton and Henry Beecher were close friends, seeing each other every day.

"And when did you become aware of what engrossed them both?" asks Morris. "When did you find out what tortured Mr. Beecher?"

"Henry said at one point to me, 'Do you know about this great sorrow of my life?' I said yes. He seemed greatly relieved."

"What did he say?"

"He said, 'I'm glad, then, that there is one woman in the world to whom I can talk without reserve on this great trouble which has come into my life.'"

She then tells of an evening in June 1873 when Henry, distraught and despairing, came to the Moulton home. "He told me he was contemplating suicide. He said he had a powder at home in his desk that would end it all."

A collective gasp sweeps the room.

"Why would he, a man of God, consider such a move?" asks Sam Morris in a shocked voice, as if all this was not carefully choreographed.

"He said he feared he couldn't keep Theodore Tilton quiet and he couldn't bear the strain any longer. He expressed to me his love for Elizabeth, and his great remorse and sorrow that she should have ever confessed to her husband, saying it would bring only ruin in the end to all. He walked up and down the room in a very excited manner, with the tears streaming down his cheeks, and said that he thought it was very hard, after a life of usefulness, that he should be brought to this fearful end."

"What did you say?"

"I said that it was very hard, and there was only one way out of it for him."

"And what was that?"

"Confessing."

Harriet wants to jump up and scream that this clear-voiced, demure woman in the witness chair is a masterful liar, and why can't everyone see that? Why isn't the judge banging his gavel and making her stop?

"Please tell us more, Mrs. Moulton." Morris's voice fairly purrs.

She continues in the soft, musical voice that now has the court mesmerized. "I put my hand on his shoulder and said, 'Mr. Beecher, if you will only go down to the church, Frank will go with you. He will stand by you through everything. And I will always be your friend if you will only confess. You have to take responsibility for yourself and suffer the penalty.' I told him he was living a lie."

Harriet looks at her brother. He is smiling at Eunice, leaning over to pass her a quickly scribbled note. He has become a hardened defendant, seemingly indifferent to being characterized from the witness stand, joining that corps of the accused who learn how to sit calmly through trials that become versions of hell, a skill no one learns in advance.

"And what was his reaction?" asks the lawyer.

"He said he could not confess, that his children would despise him, that he could never go back to his house. He said he had better go out of life than to remain a burden to his children and—" She pauses.

"And what, Mrs. Moulton?"

"And that he rather longed for death."

Morris lets this sink in, clearly enjoying the stir amongst the crowd. Henry Ward Beecher was so distraught, perhaps so guilty, he thought of killing himself? Could this be the despair of an innocent man?

"There was another evening, was there not, when you and Mr. Beecher talked about his troubles?" the lawyer says finally.

"Yes," Emma Moulton replies, her hands still resting calmly in her lap. "I told him in July of the following year that Mr. Tilton was going to sue, and that he planned on publishing Mr. Beecher's letter confessing to an affair."

"His response?"

"He was surprised. He said, 'How could he? He's already for-given his wife's sin.'"

"And what did you say?"

"I told him it wasn't too late to confess," she says evenly, casting a glance at Henry. Their eyes lock for the briefest of seconds. "But he said he could not."

"Was there anything else of significance said that evening?"

She sighs. "When Mr. Beecher was ready to leave, he took my hand and said something I could never forget. He said, 'You're the best friend I have. You bear with me knowing I am guilty. My own sisters bear with me because they think I am innocent.'"

"Thank you, Mrs. Moulton," says Morris. He turns to the bench. "That concludes this witness's testimony, Your Honor."

"Fine, then. Court is recessed until the afternoon," the judge says.

Harriet's vision blurs as Emma Moulton steps down from the witness chair. It isn't from tears; none are flowing at the moment. Her senses are shocked, so much so she can barely hear the noise of chairs being scraped back, loud voices calling to one another. She cannot hear; she cannot see.

"Hattie."

She looks up and blinks. Henry is standing over her, an expression of concern on his face. Her vision is clearing, and it strikes her how much his face has aged in the past few months. The lines are deeper, and the folds of flesh around his mouth have thickened. She blinks again. Is it her eyes? Strangely, his face itself seems blurred.

"Are you all right?" he asks.

Now the tears flow. "Is it true?" she whispers.

"No, Hattie. It is all a lie."

She waits for release from her fears. It will come, it will come. Just not right away.

Henry takes her hand, watching her closely. "Come join us for lunch," he urges.

She thinks fleetingly of sitting with the stone-faced Eunice after that testimony and decides she cannot do it. "No, thank you," she manages. "I'll be fine. I need a walk. I hope the cross-examination will be strong."

He smiles and squeezes her hand. "It will be devastating," he says.

The corridor outside the courtroom is almost empty by the time Harriet trusts herself enough to leave. She is determined not to run into anyone she knows, and so she makes her way to one of the back staircases. She needs to flee the building quickly. Fresh air, she tells herself; that's what I need, fresh air.

As she reaches the top of the stairs, she sees a man and a woman descending ahead of her, almost at the bottom. All she registers is the fact that the man has his arm around the woman's shoulders in what appears to be a comforting gesture.

Harriet slows her step, but she has been heard. The man raises his head and looks back briefly, a startled expression on his face. She squints, trying to see his face clearly. Is that Tom? No, it can't be. What would he be doing here today? He is supposed to be in New York. She starts to call out, but he disappears around a corner with his companion.

The cross-examination begins with the lawyerly, droning questions that always seem off the mark to Harriet. William Evarts questions Emma Moulton repeatedly about the exact dates when her supposed conversations with Henry took place, his voice skeptical as he tries to raise doubts about her memory. Was it the tenth or the twelfth? Ah, the thirteenth? Are you sure? Harriet is wondering why he is wasting time on such trivia when he changes direction.

"And where did you and Mr. Beecher meet on that vaguely identified June day in 1873?"

"In my home."

"I see. In the parlor?"

"No."

"And where exactly in your home did you talk?"

"In our bedroom," she replies serenely. "My husband was there for a short while."

"You and your husband make a practice of entertaining visitors in the room in which the two of you have your marital bed?"

"Yes, at times we do. It is furnished as a sitting room too."

"And you were there alone with Mr. Beecher after your husband left?"

"Yes."

"He was upset, distraught, you've said. What exactly transpired?"

"He paced in such distress, I had him lie down on the sofa and I covered him with an afghan and told him to rest."

"Then what?"

"I kissed him on his forehead."

Evarts stares at her, a look of joy in his eyes. "You *kissed* Mr. Beecher? Your *pastor*?"

A puzzled smile plays across Emma Moulton's lips. "The poor man was in great distress and I felt compassion for him," she says.

"A *kiss*."

Evarts stares now at the ceiling. He says the word slowly, sorrowfully, drawing out the single syllable, tongue to the roof of his mouth, making it both wondering and obscene. He has been handed a weapon, an old-fashioned one in this world of women yammering for rights, of course; more like a dagger than a revolver. Propriety is all, for it signals virtue. A woman who ignores proper behavior is a woman without character, and a woman without character can surely never be trusted. It is such a simple formula, and it has worked so well in the past.

The crowd stirs uneasily. Juror Twelve, the often sleepy Mr. Flate, pushes his chair back with a loud, scraping noise and is sitting ramrod straight, a properly shocked look on his face. Harriet, praying his reaction is contagious, tries not to show the gleam of hope in her heart. For the first time, a slight flush stains Emma Moulton's cheeks, but her eyes stay clear and steady.

"Ah, well." Evarts begins pacing, shoulders stooped. He seems saddened by the news, disinclined to attack. "A kiss." He shakes his head, as if to clear it, then looks directly at the jury.

"Here we have a wife, surely a loyal wife, braving this public exposure that no lady should be subjected to, and all because of her love for her husband." He raises his shoulders and spreads his arms wide. "She of course has the *right* to stand by him in this matter. Yes, she does," he repeats, nodding, as if the jury were disagreeing with him. His voice hardens. "She does—even though her loyalty were a poisoned dagger, poisoned not by her but by her husband, to drive straight through the heart of her pastor, from whom she has received the bread and wine which testify to the body and blood of the Savior!" Evarts pauses for a breath, then thunders, "This is her due, even if she really believed that *her unreturned kiss in the absence of her husband* was given to a confessed adulterer and a perjured hypocrite! This, for her *husband*? But we repeat—we do not question her right to such loyalty."

Evarts looks up at the judge, shrugs, and smiles. "Who can argue with a wife doing her husband's bidding, Your Honor? Any husband will understand *that*." He lets out an elaborate, pained sigh that all can hear. "But we do question the truth of her testimony. We have no further questions for this . . . witness, Your Honor."

Judge Neilson hits his gavel against his desk with a little more force than usual. "You may step down, Mrs. Moulton. Court is adjourned until tomorrow."

The muscles at the edges of Emma Moulton's mouth are trembling as her husband takes her hand and they exit the courtroom.

"We did good, we did good today," Henry says. Dinner was perfunctory, no one eating much, and the family has gathered in the parlor. Henry sits on the least comfortable chair, heavy thighs spread wide, leaning forward, clasping and unclasping his hands. He looks to Harriet as if he has a slight fever.

"Eunice, will you sit down?" His voice is uncharacteristically sharp.

His wife is by the window, making sure the shutters and drapes are tightly closed, a job that has obsessed her since the night a week ago when a reporter with a spyglass was discovered in a tree in front of the Beecher home. She had screamed in fury when she saw the man and talked wildly of painting the windows black until Harriet and Catharine managed to calm her down. The reporter was routed by the police, but everyone is more nervous now.

Eunice leaves her post reluctantly, grabbing at her shawl with tense, gnarled fingers, taking a seat on the piano bench. She keeps staring at the windows. Too many months have been spent in this pit of uncertainty and spite. Too many lies collide with one another. How long can any family's façade last under such scrutiny? There is no veil of piety around the Beechers now. They have been put on a revolving stage with nowhere to hide, and they must adapt or shrivel away.

Harriet looks around at her gathered family, seeing the changes. Henry walks with a heavy step most of the time now and complains about his aching knees. Edward seems bowed and haggard, and even Catharine's unflagging domestic energy is clearly spent. What would I see if I could look in a glass clearly, she asks herself.

"We did good today," Henry repeats. "Evarts knows human nature, doesn't he? I've been watching the jurors; the difference in their faces from the morning testimony was amazing. You could see Mrs. Moulton losing stature in their eyes, couldn't you, Hattie?" He turns to his sister with that familiar, endearing, imploring look.

"Yes," she says and starts to say more, but Edward interrupts.

"She's the most credible witness they've got," he says roughly. "And no matter how good Evarts was today, she still is."

Henry views him coldly. "What gives you that idea? Tell me."

"Gladly. There's too much unguarded talk going on, and none of us can rabbit on to the press, not even you, Henry. Especially you."

"What are you talking about?" Catharine asks. She rests her knitting in her lap.

Edward's face is darkening. "You know what I'm saying, Henry."

"I have no idea," Henry retorts. "And I don't like your belligerent tone."

Edward jumps up from his seat. "Well, then explain that quote in the evening paper about Mrs. Moulton's testimony, will you?"

"What quote?"

Harriet feels her stomach sink as Edward exits the room and returns quickly with a newspaper in his hand that he tosses to his brother. "Third page. The Reverend Henry Ward Beecher on Mrs. Moulton. Fresh from the steps of the courthouse."

Henry reads silently and passes the paper to Harriet without comment. She quickly scans the item:

> *Mr. Beecher was asked today about the veracity of Mrs. Moulton's*
> *extraordinarily vivid testimony, giving this strangely ambiguous*
> *answer: "There was foundation in truth, but in effect it was a lie."*
> *Which leaves all earnest searchers for the facts wondering: how*
> *indeed does a phantom edifice come from a foundation of truth?*

"Let me see that, please." Eunice has her hand out, and Harriet passes her the paper without a word.

"Henry was obviously misquoted," Eunice says a few seconds later, staring frostily at Edward.

"Is this true?" Edward asks. He has not sat down again and is standing by the doorway, arms folded, his brow furrowed.

"For God's sake, the newspapers distort everything," Henry replies with disgust. "I don't know what you are so worked up about."

"Did you say it?" Edward presses.

Harriet cannot lift her eyes from the carpet. She forces herself to focus on its swirling woven vines of green and purple wool as she waits for her brother's answer.

"And what if I did?" Henry explodes. "Does no one any longer understand that ambiguities are part of life? I had to say something compassionate! I'm not about to destroy her outside the courtroom, why would I do that? Let me repeat, for those who need to hear it again—I am the innocent party in this. I have said this defamation is a lie, and I say it again—*It is all a lie!* Why am I being questioned in my own home, by my own brother? Edward, what poison has infected you? I am your *brother*! Or have you forgotten?"

Edward, nonplussed, simply stares at Henry.

"Now if you don't mind, I am going to bed. Good night." Henry rises with some difficulty to his feet and strides from the room, brushing past Edward without a sideways glance.

The room is still. No one moves or says anything for a long moment until Edward breaks the silence.

"I'll be leaving now, Eunice," he says, his voice shaky. "Perhaps we are all under more strain that we realize." And then he too turns and departs.

Much later, after the house is still, Harriet walks in her nightshift to an upstairs window and stares out onto the deserted street. Without carriages and throngs of reporters, it is what it used to be, a quiet village scene. Beyond is a ribbon of darkness. That is the harbor, a dark strip of velvet that brings the ocean to Brooklyn's doorstep. To the right, she can barely make out the almost complete Brooklyn Tower, the hulking anchor of Mr. Roebling's ambitious project. It is a masterpiece of construction, and people are saying now, yes, there really is going to be a bridge. Perhaps. Directly in front of her, the trees seem less scrawny than they were a week or two ago. They are beginning to bud, and soon they will be fresh and green again; life will renew.

But change feels as if it is breathing hot and heavy everywhere, and coming with such raucous, uncontrollable speed. Politics seems to be one story of corruption and greed after another; workers are taking to the streets in city after city to protest working conditions; fires, riots, financial peril . . . It is too much.

How long has it been since the night of the snowfall, that lovely evening at the Clemens party when she and Calvin joked and laughed with their friends and played like children? Too long. She needs to remind herself to savor the small pleasures of life more. To lose from her brain and heart Father's admonition that pleasures enjoyed too much are sinful, that God exacts a cost for each one. Woe to those who love a child too much, he always said. Or a man, like dear Catharine, for love too fully enjoyed always meant loss in Father's view. Only when Henry blew those dark clouds away and made a loving God real did the heavy weight of Father's teachings begin to lift from them all. She must never forget that. She must always be grateful.

A sound. What is that sound?

She listens. It is at first like the mewl of a kitten, or a soft wind curling around a corner, but it is coming from Eunice and Henry's bedroom. Tiptoeing slowly, Harriet moves back toward her room. She stops at their door and hears the unmistakable sound of weeping, a dry, pathetic sound, filled with pain. A woman's pain. Eunice.

She puts a hand to her mouth and moves on.

⚜ CHAPTER FIFTEEN ⚜

Brooklyn Heights
May 1875

Henry descends the stairs with a heavy step the morning he is scheduled to take the stand to defend himself. His face is gray, as if he hasn't slept well. He slumps down at the breakfast table, ignoring the plate of six eggs put immediately before him.

When last was he his usual exuberant self? Harriet picks away at her own breakfast and tries to think back, alarmed at her inability to identify the turning point. Once her brother would have rhapsodized over everything on a sunny spring morning. The way he exuded joy over the simplest of God's blessings had always lifted the spirits of those around him.

"Are you feeling all right, dear?" Catharine asks gently.

He shoves the plate of eggs toward the center of the table. "I'm not hungry," he says. He seems to sink deeper into his chair. "Give me some coffee."

"Are you comfortable with the strategy for today?" Harriet asks.

He casts her a weary glance. "Strategy? Hattie, Hattie, it's going to be the same droning, burrowing, snuffling story that it has been since January. I can't stand this much longer. I am being unjustly treated."

Eunice picks up the coffeepot and fills her husband's cup with such force, splatters of the brew fly across the tablecloth. "Well, you'd better stiffen your resolve," she says briskly. "You've got the stand, so speak up for yourself. Tilton and the Moultons have sworn you did it. Today you prove them liars, or you lose your case."

Her sharp words pull Henry straighter in his chair. He looks up at her with the pained hurt of a child hoping to be consoled after a tantrum, but her expression is stern, so he picks up his cup without comment and takes a tentative sip. Then he looks at his wife and says in a meek voice, "I can do it."

Harriet's instinct has always been to comfort and protect her much loved baby brother, believing this the best way to nurture his exuberance and ambition. Perhaps he has needed something more, she wonders. Had he chosen a wife as flinty as this one because he lacked the strength to survive on his own? A wife who would stay sturdy as he embraced the world, and be there each time he chose to return?

His mood lifting, Henry reaches to the center of the table, plucks a small bouquet of violets out of its vase, and holds it aloft. "I will take these lovely blooms with me for luck. As well as these." He pulls from his pocket a handful of glittering precious stones—a small emerald, a diamond, a piece of jade—and shows them to the women with an almost happy smile. "These are my lucky charms," he says. "I always carry them."

Harriet's eyes widen in surprise. So this was why Henry seemed always to have his hand in his coat pocket. "Why?" she asks, wondering fleetingly if he made himself a target of robbers by carrying such valuables.

"Because they comfort me." He drops them back in his pocket, pulls the plate of eggs close, and begins eating with relish.

Harriet catches a look of satisfaction on Eunice's face as she watches her husband mopping up the remains of his breakfast with a piece of bread. Perhaps it is this simple. Power has been wielded; Eunice has done her job.

If anything, Henry seems too relaxed when he settles into the witness chair. He puts the small spray of violets next to his chair as the suave, mild-mannered William Fullerton begins the cross-examination. Mr. Evarts warned Henry last night not to be fooled by the man. "He looks meek, but he isn't," he said. "And he always cuts with a razor, never smashes with a club."

The questions are general at first, the usual repetitive, droning kind that Harriet realizes now are intended to lull unwary witnesses. Henry's answers are vague and filled with "I can't recollect" and "I don't remember," but Fullerton doesn't seem to mind.

Around ten-thirty, his questions sharpen.

"You made several apologies to Mr. Tilton that seem quite heartfelt to those of us reading them," Fullerton says. "Why did you do so if you had nothing to apologize *for*?"

Henry pauses to sniff his flowers before answering. "All I was doing was conveying to Mr. Tilton my deep regret at the developing scandal," he says. "And for the *appearance* of having done injury to him."

"*Appearance,* Mr. Beecher? You tell us you were not apologizing for soliciting the affections and love of his wife?"

"I had denied that charge explicitly through Moulton," Henry retorts.

"When, sir?"

"January 1871."

"In what words did you frame this denial?"

"I can't tell you exactly," Henry replies with a shrug. "I don't remember."

"Did you not tell me the other day that you did *not* send any such explicit denial at all?"

Henry looks annoyed. "I did not, in that sense. I spoke with Tilton in Moulton's bedroom, saying that insofar as I had unconsciously and unintentionally done any injury to his wife, and through her to him, I very heartily was sorry for it and asked his forgiveness for it."

"Which is worse, Mr. Beecher—undue solicitation of a woman's attention or the *winning* of another man's wife's affections?"

Henry is paying closer attention now. "The charge of making improper advances, insofar as it affected my relations to the church and to the community, would be about as bad as could be."

"Why didn't you renew your apology two days later? Why didn't you say to Mr. Tilton, 'Sir, as to the improper advances, this charge is completely untrue.' Why did you wait to have him repeat the charge?"

"As he didn't ask for my apology again, I paid no attention to it."

"Didn't Mr. Tilton say to Moulton, 'How can I speak to a man who has thus treated me?'"

Henry doesn't respond as quickly this time. "He may have said something of that kind in substance. I cannot give you his words."

"You say you don't remember that these words were used on direct examination of Mr. Tilton?"

Harriet cringes inside. Everyone in the courtroom probably remembers; how can Henry look so befuddled?

"Something like that," he says.

Fullerton turns slightly toward the gallery, rubbing his bald head with a puzzled gesture. "Can you now see anything prior to 1870 that should have warned you, put you on your guard, that Mrs. Tilton's conduct indicated she was placing her affections on you?"

"Not during our friendship prior to 1870."

"Nothing?"

"I ought to have seen many things that occurred in our conversations."

"Can you say what they were?"

Henry's hand is in his pocket now, deep inside. "I cannot give you words, only the substance. I spoke about her household as a place of peace and rest, where I was not run down as I was at home. I spoke to her about my books and letters, I spoke to her about some she had written, and a variety of things." His voice grows softer. "I was entering into her life, and in some sense, giving her an insight into mine."

Harriet blinks back sudden tears. Just that one response gives her a glimpse of her brother's lonely heart. Why would a man not accept warmth and comfort, when he couldn't find it at home? Why must

friendship be presumed to be sexual? But other questions are forming. What if that were Calvin on the stand, saying these words?
Would she be so understanding? Did her own husband ever feel
'run down' at home? She stirs in her seat, wishing it were
lunchtime. She needs to get out of this fetid, crowded place.

But Fullerton shows no signs of slowing down. He grills Henry
now on a compromise letter in his own handwriting to the church
committee, promising he and Tilton would settle their differences
and keep things quiet if the committee agreed. Fullerton begins to
press Henry, asking the same questions several times in different
ways.

"Did you know at the time you wrote that that you were going to
be charged with adultery?" the lawyer finally asks. "Did you think
this compromise you proposed would settle the matter?"

"I can't remember if I knew," Henry says. "And I didn't have
much confidence that the compromise would amount to anything."

"Why were you writing something in which you had no confidence?" Fullerton says with barely contained exasperation.

"It was contingent on the church committee approving what I
proposed, and I knew they wouldn't unless Tilton retracted his accusation."

"Stop evading the question!" Fullerton snaps.

Evarts jumps up. "My client is not evading the question," he
protests.

"Mr. Fullerton, you should not have used the term *evaded,*" Judge
Neilson says, obviously wishing the plaintiff's lawyer would hurry
up so he could leave the bench.

"I take the admonition, Your Honor," Fullerton says with a
slight bow in the judge's direction. "But I insist, I asked the question
three times and it has not been answered. I insist the question is
evaded."

"The counselor has great latitude, and the witness has solemn duties," Evarts interjects. "I think he should get on without this scuf-
fling."

Fullerton flashes a sly smile, winking at the gallery. "If those remarks are meant for the witness, I hope they will be profitable to him."

The gallery breaks into laughter, with some hoots at Henry's expense. "Don't be too hard on the old man!" yells one. The growing impatience for a break is spreading through the courtroom.

Suddenly Henry, with great dignity, rises to his feet. He seems to swell in presence, and all are reminded in an instant of just who the "old man" is.

"Your Honor, am I under the rebuke of the court?" he asks. His voice is full-throated, filling the courtroom as it has so often filled the stately confines of Plymouth Church.

"No, Mr. Beecher, the observation was intended to rest on Mr. Fullerton, not on you," replies the judge quickly.

"Then I will repeat my answer. I had lost faith that Tilton would agree to a compromise." After saying this, Henry sits down.

Fullerton must feel the sway of opinion in the courtroom going against him, for he grows more snappish and short-tempered as his questioning continues.

"You came to believe early in 1871 that somehow Tilton was going to abandon his charge of improper conduct. Now what single, solitary reason did you have for thinking that?" he says.

"Because he proposed to cooperate with me in business matters to help himself—proposed in a way which precluded pursuing his charge against me, unless, of course, he wanted to become infamous."

"Are you saying you were trying to bribe him into being quiet?"

"Not at all." Henry is calm, retaining his aura of dignity.

"Did you or did you not mortgage your house and pay him five thousand dollars in 1872?"

Henry is now unflappable. "I heard he needed money, and I was trying to help. I believe anyone who cared would have done the same."

Finally it is over, well past one o'clock. The moist fabric of Harriet's shirtwaist under her arms is chafing her; she'll have a rash to contend with tonight. She rises to escape, looking at Henry. He picks up the now limp bouquet of violets and, catching her eye, holds it aloft with a smile. She feels at that moment a swell of tenderness; a renewal of her lifelong desire to protect him. She has never loved him more.

By mid-May, everyone knows the trial is winding down. There is no more to say, on either side.

Tilton has sworn to his wife's confession; Henry has sworn she retracted it. Tilton has accused Henry of adultery; Henry has denied it. Frank Moulton has said he tried to broker a peaceful settlement between the two men. And both he and his wife have said Henry confessed his guilt to them—which Henry has also denied.

So who is lying and who is telling the truth? What happens with a muddle that gives no one side clear advantage? The talk now is of the possibility of a split verdict, one that will neither exonerate nor condemn the Reverend Henry Beecher.

Even the titillating testimony of a parade of minor characters has become boring. For the first few months, Judge Neilson on occasion barred women from the courtroom to protect their sensibilities. After a while, it didn't seem to matter. Words that had previously been only whispered or hinted at, acts that involved sexual proclivities never before talked about in mixed company, have lost their ability to shock.

There is a ripple or two when Stephen Pearl Andrews, a Woodhull disciple who introduced Tilton to Victoria, explains his views on free love. "People should be able to conjoin at will and separate at will," he declares to the court. "However the children and the inheritance of property and other economic questions should be taken cognizance of by the state."

Children an 'economic question'? There is a good deal of indignant response to *that*.

Through it all Elizabeth Tilton remains the floating, almost tragic figure at the center of the drama. She attends almost every day, this woman abandoned now by her husband, her wan, beautiful face sending countless reporters into rhapsodic conjecture about the woman of mystery who could set the entire matter to rest with the truth. But no one has heard her speak, and she refuses all requests for interviews.

It now seems clear she will not be put on the stand to testify, even though all the newspapers have clamored and pleaded for this to happen. Realizing this, reporters have lapsed into sullen resignation. Here she is in front of them every day, a dramatic story all to herself, and she might as well be cut from paper, like those cardboard dolls children play with so much these days.

But their hopes stir anew one soft, sunny morning around ten o'clock, while a paperhanger is testifying to seeing Henry exchange affectionate glances with Mrs. Tilton in her drawing room.

It is the seventy-seventh day of the trial.

Elizabeth Tilton rises from her seat and stands, swaying slightly. "Judge Neilson," she calls out. Her cheeks are flushed, and her voice is low and clear.

The judge's eyes widen in surprise. "Yes, Mrs. Tilton?"

"Your Honor, I have a communication which I hope Your Honor will read aloud." She holds aloft a white piece of paper, and all can see how her hand is trembling.

"I'm afraid I can't do that, but I will read it," the judge says, recovering from his surprise.

Mrs. Tilton makes her way up the aisle and stands before the bench, a tiny figure dwarfed by her surroundings. A clerk takes the note she offers and hands it up to the judge.

"Thank you," Judge Neilson says kindly.

She quickly returns to her seat, making her way past excited observers and reporters who can barely remain still in their chairs. Several are scribbling furiously. Tomorrow's papers will talk about "the terrible load under which she staggers and which she must bear alone to the last." But if any of them think Judge Neilson will give a hint about the contents of her note, they are disappointed.

Harriet glances expectantly at Henry, waiting for a clue as to what this is about. His lips turn up in a small, comfortable smile. She remembers then the night he argued with Evarts and Porters over the wisdom or danger of having Elizabeth testify, announcing afterward that he had a plan. Whatever it is, she suspects it is playing out now. May his lawyers this time know what they are doing, she prays.

At that point the judge raps his gavel and the court adjourns for lunch. She makes her way out of the courtroom and into the corridor, and sees Elizabeth standing by herself, staring out a window—for once, not surrounded by her protective friends.

Without thought, Harriet strides forward and taps her on the shoulder.

"What did you tell the judge?" she asks bluntly as Elizabeth whirls around. She can't think about her rudeness, not now. She has to know. "What did you say?" Even as she asks, she is startled to see how much more lined and aged Elizabeth's face appears up close than she expected.

"I exonerated him. What more do you want?" Elizabeth says in a little-girl whisper. Her eyes are as wide and suffering as those of a wounded animal. "I did my best. I don't enjoy being the mystery woman, you know. I wish I were invisible."

"Then why do you come every day?"

"It is my punishment, that's why. God will not forgive me if I try to flee. Now leave me alone. Please, leave me alone." She hurries away, leaving Harriet with another question on her lips, unspoken.

That night Elizabeth Tilton releases her statement to the press.

Harriet is up at dawn and snatches the paper from the stoop, scanning it quickly. Good, it is an unambiguous denial of adultery with Henry and a request to tell her story under oath.

> *I desire to say explicitly Mr. Beecher has never offered any improper*
> *solicitations, but has always treated me in a manner becoming a*
> *Christian and a gentleman. . . . I am innocent of the crime charged*
> *against me. I would like to tell my whole sad story truthfully—to*
> *acknowledge the frequent falsehoods wrung from me by*
> *compulsion—though at the same time unwilling to reveal the secrets*
> *of my married life, which only the vital importance of my position*

makes necessary. I assume the entire responsibility of this request,
unknown to friend or counsel of either side, and await Your Honor's
honorable decision.

The judge's reply, of course, makes the point that counsel on each side has the right to refrain from calling any particular witness. Furthermore, he says, the statute of 1867 "expressly declares the wife to be incompetent as a witness for or against the husband."

"You see?" a beaming Henry says as they gather around the Beecher dining table for breakfast. "It worked. We got her testimony without putting her on the witness stand. She stood up, spoke the truth, and the entire court heard her. So what if Judge Neilson won't read it out? That was a long shot, anyway. But I'll wager every juror knows today what she said."

"It was her statement, was it not?" Catharine asks unexpectedly.

"Well, of course," Henry says with a laugh.

Harriet agrees, it is a clever play. She continues to say so, even after the newspapers begin speculating that Elizabeth's letter was far too adroit and carefully constructed to have come from anywhere but Henry Beecher's defense lawyers. Skepticism bleeds through the coverage. Again the undertone: what is going to happen? On the one hand, there is enough evidence against Henry to make exoneration a problem. On the other hand, Theodore Tilton's true colors have emerged: he himself is an adulterer, a coarse, unethical bird. Why should anyone believe him?

One Saturday a group of men and women from Plymouth Church appear on the Beechers' front stoop, looking both grave and determined. Henry answers the door.

The leader, a stockbroker with puffy cheeks and a carefully trimmed mustache, clears his throat and speaks. "Reverend Beecher, we know you are the same man who has led us honorably and with great passion to a new understanding of God," he says. "Sir, we were among those who marched past this house to honor your twenty-fifth anniversary. We are glad you have maintained your presence as our pastor, and we are here now to reaffirm our respect and trust." He thrusts forward a lavish bouquet of flowers.

Henry thanks them graciously, accepting the bouquet, shaking hands with the men, hugging the women. He then bows and closes the door. And in that moment the strain of months spent mounting his podium to give careful sermons—revolving mostly around the virtue of forgiveness—never knowing for sure who among his congregation remain friends and how soon they might turn to enemies, overcomes him. With the door safely closed, Henry faces his sisters and wife and bursts into tears.

The day is gloomy, heavy with pounding rain. Tom, who visits less and less frequently now, collapses his black umbrella in the Beecher vestibule, shaking off the drops, seemingly oblivious to the puddles forming on Eunice's floor.

Harriet takes his coat, ignoring the puddles as well. There are enough reprimands and scoldings in this household, and she doesn't intend to add another one, even for the sake of the floor. Tom looks heavier than usual, but then, nobody looks quite the same as they did six months ago.

"I'm surprised you're still here," Tom says. "I thought you would be back in Hartford."

"We're so close to a verdict, I can't leave yet."

"Calvin must think you've moved permanently," Tom says with a grin.

Harriet responds defensively. "He is fully in support."

"Hattie, I know that. I'm sorry. I've been living this trial like everyone else, on the outside, judging freely. Walking through there"—he points to the front door—"puts me in your insular world." He looks around with a wary expression on his face. "I'm not sure I'm comfortable here."

"Well, accept it," she says tartly. "You can't change your heritage."

"I know that, and I wouldn't want to if I could, so let's not make that a challenge between us."

"Oh, Tom, I'm the one sorry now. All I can say is, this is a very hard time."

It is the waiting that chips away at her. The daily speculation in the papers, the glances of people on the street, the wary expressions on the faces of the baker, the florist, the cobbler—mostly, it is walking into a room that immediately goes silent upon her arrival. Oh, friends come by to voice their support, but there is something else in the air. It is as if people are holding their breath, waiting to see which way the ax will fall so they can decide where they stand.

"It should be over soon," Tom says. He sits down on a lower step of the staircase to the second floor, glancing around to make sure they are alone. He kneads his hands together, frowning. Harriet sees how raw and bitten his fingers are, remembering this as Tom's nervous habit as a child.

"How do you think it's going?" she asks anxiously.

"I don't know, though I don't think they'll find against him, and I don't know if that's right or wrong. Tilton is despicable, and I wouldn't be surprised if cooking up a case against Henry was a way of getting money from him. Tilton got at least five thousand. But then again—Henry is vulnerable on this. He embraces everybody, and if he embraced a woman or two along the line, the jury might go the other way. But I'll not condemn him."

"Yes, he's vulnerable, but not in the way you mean. Our whole family is vulnerable. There are people out there who want to see us disintegrate."

"Oh, probably some. But you're more protected in here than you think you are, Hattie. We are very privileged people."

She sits down next to him, determined to be firm. "Forgive me, Tom, but I'm tired of hearing that. We're being assaulted right and left, and I think half the country wants to see Henry sacrificed."

"And the other half?"

"His supporters stand behind him."

"So the entire country is involved? He's not that important, Hattie. None of us are."

Harriet wants to burst forth with her indignation but manages to hold her tongue. Not that important? Tom is shrugging off reality. No, more than reality. Responsibility. We are, she thinks, every one of us, under a family mandate to excel—over one another, a war not always acknowledged; over the rest of the world, always. It is our duty as the children of Lyman Beecher. Writing *Uncle Tom's Cabin* had been her God-given responsibility, and Henry emerging from hesitant beginnings to capture the nation's imagination with impassioned eloquence had been his. Catharine—establishing schools was hers. Isabella—she was the radical among them. Better not to think of her. Tom, Edward, the rest—all had the responsibility to live up to their obligations as the sons of Lyman Beecher. She struggles to sort her thoughts. Our roots are all tangled together, she tells herself. All of us, struggling for light and air.

Was Tom right? When had they become something other than they were separately? When had they become "The Beechers"?

"I truly wanted to be known," she says quietly.

"It isn't a sin, and you earned your acclaim. I wanted it too, for a while. But I saw how fame consumed Henry while leaving Catharine frustrated and on the sidelines. In any other family, *she* would have been the star."

"What about Bella?"

"The most frustrated of us all, I suspect."

"She chose her own path."

"I need to say something, Hattie."

Harriet waits as Tom, seemingly uneasy now, clears his throat. "First, you needn't worry so much about Henry. He'll survive, no matter how the verdict goes."

"How can you say that? If they find for Tilton, it will destroy him."

Tom shakes his head. "No, it won't. He'll re-create his sunny world, although it will be a bit smaller. And it will still revolve around *him*—not the other way around. Henry's armor is not easily pierced."

"What an unkind thing to say."

"Is it?" Tom sighs. "I don't mean it to be. I guess I'm saying, Henry is resilient. But Bella doesn't have the same protections."

Harriet looks at him sharply. "Were you in the courthouse the day of Emma Moulton's testimony?"

Tom nods.

"And the woman I saw you with was Bella?"

"Yes." He casts her a steady glance. "And don't give me some lecture about her betraying the family. I'm tired of that. We planned it carefully, and stayed near the back. In case you're worried, no one recognized her. She kept herself quite covered and plain."

Harriet's curiosity cannot be stemmed. "What did she think?"

He pauses, then speaks slowly. "When she heard that Henry had called Emma Moulton 'the best friend he had' for bearing with him even though he was guilty, she cried."

Harriet says nothing, struggling with the memory of her own pain during that testimony.

"Do you understand why?" he asks.

"If I believed Henry ever actually *said* that, I would guess she would have wanted that accolade for herself."

He nods, and they sit again in silence.

"Remember the night at your house when she came in with her apron filled with blackberries?" Tom finally says.

"Yes, I do—and she promptly threw them out when she felt criticized."

"Ah, Hattie, leave it be. I'll tell you what I remember. I remember her standing there, looking at us, from one to another, her hands holding up that apron—there was a brightness to her, an imploring brightness. It almost hurt my eyes."

"She was preparing to lift the banner for Victoria Woodhull."

"I think she was pleading for her place. With us."

"She burned the potatoes," Harriet whispers.

"For God's sake, Hattie. Let yourself love her, you always have. You've tried too long to be the family watchdog."

She gives up. She leans against Tom's sturdy shoulder and closes her eyes, letting the tears trickle through, making no effort to wipe them from her cheeks.

✂ CHAPTER SIXTEEN ✂

June 1875

HARRIET HEARS CHEERS in the street outside the Beecher home and jumps to her feet, running quickly to the door.

"What is happening?" she calls down to a laughing cluster of people walking rapidly toward the neighborhood of Fulton Ferry. The summations are to begin today, could something have altered that? Is it some kind of good news? She panics at the thought of not being in the courtroom. It has to be about the trial; everything is about the trial.

"The bridge tower opens today," yells a young boy. "We think maybe we can climb it! See all of New York and maybe most of the world!"

Tower? Harriet blinks; it takes her a second to realize he is talking about that huge obelisk that has been rising out of the harbor for what seems like an eternity.

"What is it?" Eunice is behind her, panting from running down the stairs. Splotches of cold cream dot her cheeks and nose.

"Nothing important, they're saying the tower is completed. I was alarmed when I heard the shouting."

"Is that all?" Eunice, suddenly conscious of the cream on her face, rubs at it furiously and remounts the stairs just as Catharine comes hurrying down, fully dressed. Eunice brushes past her without a word.

"And so we begin another day," Catharine says beneath her breath.

"It's my fault," Harriet says, quickly telling her what is happening.

"For heaven's sake, there is no fault. Although that idea is probably too radical for Eunice."

Harriet smiles a bit uncomfortably, for the family prejudice against Eunice has rules. Criticism is supposed to slide through in joking fashion, with a roll of the eyes or a shrug of the shoulders. But Catharine seems impatient with such protocol these days and is making increasingly snappish, acerbic comments. Her tolerance for niceties is diminishing as the trial drags on. Perhaps age makes her crankier, but she is also the one subjected to living here through this tedious, soul-draining time. Harriet can go back and forth from Hartford, choosing when she needs to breathe. She decides she must think a little more about her good fortune.

It is early June, and a beautiful morning. With summations about to begin, the crowds at the courthouse are increasing. According to the *Eagle,* over three thousand people will be turned away today. Given the escalating anticipation of a verdict, this is good news for the shops. Women are happily exploring the wares of Brooklyn Heights, bargaining with bonnet makers over the cost of feather boas and caressing the soft leathers of gloves and purses put forth by the merchants on Montague Street. There is an energy that quickens the step, and the restaurants are enjoying the chatter of throngs of customers. The neighborhood bars are too, which of course makes civic leaders a bit nervous. The bars draw the disreputable types, the men usually constrained to the saloons on the docks. A certain egalitarianism prevails—barristers in spectacles now sit holding beer steins shoulder to shoulder with dockworkers, sharing curiosity about the same question: Will Henry be found guilty or innocent? Everyone wants to know the verdict, but none of the shopkeepers or bartenders want this delightful burst of business to end.

"Hattie, let's do something right now," Catharine says. "Let's walk down and take a good look at this thing out in the water people are yelling about."

"But we have to get to the courthouse," Harriet says.

"Oh, hang the courthouse. We've seen nothing, thought of nothing, and done nothing but live this trial for months. Let's do this first; it will only take half an hour, if that. Look at the weather! Why should we bury ourselves in that place before we have to?"

Indeed, why? Harriet knows she thinks of nothing but the trial. When she is home in Hartford, it is an effort to talk with Calvin about the garden, the neighbors, the leak in the roof, his thoughts on the latest economic news. Their conversations are labored, with her constantly trying to corral her thoughts and pay attention. Calvin puts up with it because he knows her very well, which is disturbing. She can't hide obsession.

"All right," she says. "I hear it's two hundred and eighty feet high—who climbs first, you or me?"

After first putting on their oldest shoes for comfort, the two sisters follow the crowd gathering down at the dock, peering upward at the shaft that marks completion of the first stage of the new bridge. From the foot of Sands and Washington, the structure takes Harriet's breath away. Why hasn't she paid more attention as this was going up? It is indeed a massive edifice of masonry and brick, but it is also a thing of strange and splendid beauty. How can a structure be both hulking and graceful at the same time? Across the water, on the New York side, she sees the beginnings of the tower that will match this one. People are talking of huge cables of steel that will loop through the sky connecting the two towers, and she tries to imagine the finished bridge. What will it look like?

"See those staircases?" Catharine murmurs, pointing upward. "They look as frail as cobwebs. Who could be so brave as to climb *that*?"

"A few crazy people," says a man standing in front of them. He points upward too, and only then do Catharine and Harriet see tiny figures laboring up those staircases, that small first cadre willing to risk life and limb to see a view of the vast sweep of land and water never before possible.

"I wonder what they see," Harriet says, amazed by the possibilities. "Catharine, we'll be up there one day too—walking and riding across that bridge and seeing amazing sights."

"Perhaps you alone, dear," Catharine replies.

Harriet stops herself from glancing at her sister, not wanting to see the signs of age she knows are there. Catharine turns seventy-five this year.

"You must go up with me," she says. "How else can I enjoy the view?"

"I'd get too dizzy. And besides, the good Lord will provide a better view than *that*." Catharine turns away and starts back up the street, beckoning to Harriet. "Time to go, Hattie. We'll have a brisk walk up to the carriage and be the better for it. Exercise is good for us, remember? When we use our muscles, the heart receives blood faster and sends it to the lungs faster. Yes?"

Harriet smiles, remembering how adamantly Catharine emphasized this in the one book they wrote together, *The American Woman's Home*. "And the heart sends the blood more quickly through the arteries to the capillaries, where decaying matter is drawn off and the stomach calls for more food to nourish the blood," she recites.

"Ah, good memory. Well, it's true."

"I know it is, I'm just playing. We can do that, can't we?"

Catharine tucks her sister's arm into the crook of her elbow. "We were good collaborators, Hattie. We told women important things about their bodies, if they would only pay attention."

There are indeed at least three thousand shouting, frustrated people milling around the courthouse who have been refused entry. Some of those lucky enough to have tickets are hawking them on the steps for as much as five and ten dollars each as Harriet and Catharine push their way through.

Please let this be one of the last times I have to be here, Harriet thinks as she takes her seat. She glances to her right. Yes, Elizabeth Tilton is in her usual place, her face today shrouded in the veiling of a particularly large black hat. She is seated not far from her estranged husband. In all the months of the trial, Harriet has never seen

Theodore and Elizabeth exchange even a glance. More than once she's wondered how they both manage such discipline. Everything about this trial involves passion and treachery and pain, and yet, to all appearances, this husband and wife might never have known each other.

William Beach, a striking figure with long, silver hair tucked behind his ears, begins the summation for the plaintiff at ten o'clock sharp. His reputation for oratory is legendary, and the papers have all proclaimed this will be his hour.

"Gentlemen of the jury," he begins. "I beg you, do not be taken in by the Reverend Beecher's reputation and bearing. Do not be taken in by your natural hunger to believe in a man who presents himself as innocent, no matter how pious he may appear. You must dig beneath the surface of appearances with tools of reason. You must induce the truth from the clues presented, and follow them wherever they lead. The message they have given us is this: *Moral virtue is not always what it appears to be.*"

For the rest of the afternoon, Beach paces the courtroom, pushing back damp strands of hair from his forehead as he builds his case against Henry, utilizing every ounce of skepticism from his audience, inviting them to laugh again with him over the absurdity of Henry's supposed acts of virtue.

"Mr. Beecher told us at one point that he and Tilton decided to put this scandal—which he denies was taking place—to rest four years ago," Beach declares. "Do you remember the words he used that made us all laugh? I will repeat them. 'When we arose,' Mr. Beecher said, 'I kissed him and he kissed me, and I kissed his wife and she kissed me, and I believe they kissed each other.' Well now"—he makes a comic face—"is this farce or tragedy?"

The room titters as Henry stares straight ahead.

It is not over that day, nor the next. Harriet watches her juror obsessively, trying to discern which way he is leaning. Why has Flate shaved his mustache? He shows up each day now with ruddy cheeks as smooth as apples, which makes him look younger. Is this a good sign or a bad sign? Does youth make him more skeptical, more able to accept the scenario of hypocrisy Beach is trying to build?

By the time Beach is finished, he has the crowd in his hand. Murmurs of appreciation ripple through the room: the man makes sense; he has hit the nail on the head. Harriet tries not to listen.

When the defense summation begins, it is the flamboyant Mr. Porter, a man of legendary lung capacity, who steps onto the floor beneath Judge Neilson's bench. Scorning any warm-up, his voice booms forth at full velocity, and all present immediately snap straight in their chairs.

"Gentlemen of the jury, each of you is one hundred and thirty-five days older this morning than when this trial commenced, and those one hundred and thirty-five days of your life have been taken from your business, from your families, from your domestic occupations, in the interest of an adulterer, who brings this suit for the purpose of establishing by your verdict that he *slept for four years with an adulterous wife!*" He pauses and draws in a deep breath. "You have been pressed for five months of your lives *into the service of Theodore Tilton,* in the forms of law, bound by a mandate you were bound to obey for the discharge of a duty from which you could not shirk!"

"Yes," murmurs someone behind Harriet.

"Make no mistake about it, this trial, this charge is an attack on all we hold dear," Porter says. "It is an attack that says the favored, approved, tried, best results of this social scheme of ours, which includes marriage, and of this religious faith of ours, which adopts Christianity, *is false to the core.* Do we believe that? Do we?"

"No," comes the murmur from behind Harriet.

She closes her eyes in relief, then looks at Samuel Flate. What does she see this time? He has uncrossed his legs and is sitting like a student in a classroom. Is that a good sign? Does he realize how brilliantly Porter is performing?

Porter and Evarts take turns over the next few days demolishing Tilton's case. Harriet becomes convinced Henry is winning and is delighted that Catharine shares her feelings. How could he not be, given how persuasively Henry's lawyers are taking the high moral ground? They are lifting the trial out of the mud and reaffirming the right values, and almost one hundred members of Plymouth Church who manage to squeeze in for these last encouraging orations burst into spontaneous applause when they finish.

Finally both sides are done. There is nothing more to be said. All the words have been spoken as the final day comes to an end. Accusations, insinuations, jeers, defenses, rebuttals—all finished. Exhausted. Spewed out. Tossed to the air. That night Harriet leans out the window of her bedroom and counts stars, feeling a strange peace settling in.

June 28, 1875

For the first time, the galleries are not full, and the courtroom has the look of a dismantled and almost deserted fortress. The members of the jury file in and settle with wiggles and sighs into their yellow chairs. Samuel Flate slouches back in his chair, joking with William Jeffreys, the man who triggered the smallpox scare. All Harriet knows about him is that he is some kind of a broker living in a rooming house. He has sharp, aquiline features and is always fiddling with the lapels of his jacket. The jury chairs are all out of line this morning, and none seems in any mood to straighten them. The jurors have seemed sullen since the Kings County board of supervisors turned down a proposal to pay them each an extra five dollars a day. The trial had gone on too long, they claimed. They deserved more money. Although the argument hasn't worked, it is clear this body of twelve men doesn't expect to be here much longer. Release, of a sort, is coming.

Judge Neilson walks with a ponderous gait into the room and takes his seat. Glancing up at the gallery, he smiles and pounds his gavel. "Court is in session, ladies and gentlemen," he declares. "Although I can see not many were interested in coming here today." He clears his throat. "Gentlemen of the jury, final arguments have been concluded. You will now retire to reach a verdict. And I instruct you to reach that verdict calmly and dispassionately. You have heard the testimony and you have seen the evidence, and I urge you to reach your verdict solely on the basis of that testimony and evidence. The bailiff will now escort you to the jury room."

Harriet isn't prepared for it to happen so fast. Reporters scramble to exit the courtroom, and she can hear them shouting the news out in the corridor. Catharine leans close and whispers, "It might be all done in an hour, Hattie. Now we just pray."

The day drags on interminably. The judge retires to his chambers, but Harriet and Catharine cannot bring themselves to move from the courthouse, even when Henry and Eunice leave for lunch. Sitting outside the courtroom, they see an anxious-looking Theodore Tilton wandering in and out of the judge's chambers, talking to clerks and reporters. The rumors are that the costs of the trial are bankrupting Tilton. The same would be true for Henry, except for the fact that Plymouth Church, fully loyal to its pastor, has raised one hundred thousand dollars for his defense. Eunice wept in relief the night that news came.

By late afternoon the jury moves to a room on the third floor, with deputy sheriffs and police officers guarding every avenue of approach. Harriet wanders outside and sees reporters with spyglasses trained on the windows of the room in which the twelve men are deliberating. People stand in clusters, arguing over what they think will transpire.

"How can they find Beecher guilty?" says one man with a bald head and large ears. "It's Tilton that's lying. Why would a man stay with an adulterous wife for four years?"

"You must be joking," argues another man. "Beecher exudes guilt from his pores."

Harriet hurries back into the courthouse, trying to calm her breathing.

At five in the evening, the judge goes home.

"If he can go home, so can we," Catharine says, carefully positioning her favorite leghorn hat, somewhat shabby but with new fancy braid, on the top of her head. "Come now, Hattie."

As they walk to their carriage, Harriet looks back and sees lights flickering in the third-floor windows of the courthouse. She tries to imagine what those twelve men are doing. Are they sitting around a table in their shirtsleeves, arguing with one another? Have they already voted, and are they swapping stories and waiting for supper before emerging? Or are they dozing, pacing, yawning?

What a futile exercise this is—as hard as imagining herself standing two hundred and eighty feet above the world as she knows it and seeing everything to the horizon.

The weather grows very hot the second day. Clerks and reporters are loosening their collars and looking for shade but not wandering too far from the spotters in the trees.

A shout goes up around one in the afternoon—there is movement! A juror leans out of the window in the jury room, scanning the crowd below. His body seems to sag with fatigue.

"What's going on?" shouts a reporter. "Got a verdict yet?"

The man shakes his head as he pulls a white cloth out of his pocket and mops his brow. Is it a signal? People look at one another with confusion; reporters eye one another suspiciously. Has someone struck a deal with a juror for advance notice of the results of the deliberations? But nothing happens. No reporter suddenly scuttles away to file an exclusive. The man in the window flops partway out, inhaling deeply, mopping his brow and blowing his nose. Then he pulls back inside and disappears.

"They must be frying in there," marvels one observer.

"Good. Maybe if they're hot enough, they'll hurry up and make a decision," mutters a reporter for the *Chicago Tribune*.

Two women collapse in the hall outside the courtroom on the third day. The heat is unbearable inside, and people afraid of not being nearby when the jury reaches its decision are sleeping on the grass in front of the courthouse at night.

Tilton looks more anxious each time Harriet sees him, but Henry stays seemingly serene. Eunice keeps dabbing at her face with a handkerchief, but when the newspapers report she has been crying, she angrily objects that she is simply wiping away perspiration. No one thought the juror hanging out the window was crying, did they? Then they should know the same is true of her.

Still no news from the jurors on the fourth day, which Harriet feels in her bones cannot be good news. She watches with unease as the scene in and around the courthouse degenerates into a tawdry circus. Hawkers of food and drink pick their way through crowds huddled under the few shade trees, arguing with customers who accuse them of hiking their prices higher with each passing day. Several drunks from nearby bars face off against one another on the lawn, bringing policemen swinging nightsticks to arrest them for brawling. Mothers warn their children to stay away from the scene.

By day five, the press is calling the jury the "Imperturbable Twelve" and complaining in print of their own excruciating plight as they try to work under the blazing chandeliers of the courthouse pressroom.

That night there is great gloom in the Beecher home, in part because Edward insists on talking through every detail of the trial, probing for weaknesses in the defense summation, talking on and on until Henry abruptly stands.

"I don't want to hear any more!" he shouts, tossing his napkin onto the dinner table. "How long is this going to take? How much more is a man supposed to endure?"

Day six comes and goes, and time begins to blur for Harriet.

Then the seventh day, which is more hot and humid than ever. At five o'clock, Harriet walks back alone from the courthouse. She doesn't have the energy to speak to anyone, not even Catharine. Her bodice is drenched in sweat. She imagines she can actually see drops of water suspended in the air as she blinks to clear her vision. She yearns for a basin of cool water and a cloth as she turns onto Henry's block. Ahead of her, sitting on the stoop, is the figure of a man. She blinks again, trying to see who it is.

"Hello, Hattie."

Calvin. He sits with his hands clasped, a quiet grin on his face. He is almost bald now, and the wisps of white hair curling around his ears under the yarmulke he is fond of wearing are limp in the heat. His collar is slightly askew, but then he doesn't think much about such small details when she isn't around to remind him. She quickens her pace. By the time she reaches the stoop, he is standing. She puts out her arms wordlessly, and he wraps her in his embrace. Until this instant, she hasn't understood how much she misses him. How can she have become so hermetically sealed? Has she so divorced herself from her own life?

"Well, that answers my first question," he says, kissing her on the forehead and holding her at arm's length. "Your old rabbi is welcome, it seems."

"You are more than welcome," she says, tears in her eyes.

"So then, my second question. How are you doing?"

"It's the waiting. It's knowing Henry's future depends on those men up on the third floor of the courthouse."

"And they are in no hurry, I understand."

"I lie awake at night and try to imagine their arguings. And then I can't sleep until early in the morning. Everyone is tense, and it's miserable here, and I want to go home." Her voice trembles. "Tom didn't help. He was here several days ago and told me I was too harsh on Bella. He said I try to be the family watchdog and I should give it up."

Calvin gently takes her hand, and they sit back down on the steps. A boy and a girl pushing a hoop down the sidewalk go clattering by, whooping and hollering; together they watch the children skip to the end of the block and vanish around the corner.

"I want to feel happy and free like that again," Harriet says.

"Hattie, I do have news of your sister."

Harriet stiffens slightly and waits.

"Her daughter Mary's husband has barred her from seeing her grandchild."

"Oh, my goodness. Why?"

"He says she's shamed the family by not supporting Henry."

"Oh no, Calvin," she says impulsively. "That's so harsh. Bella loves that child." She cannot help but feel the injustice: Isabella, a scattered but loving mother to her two daughters and son over the years, has had uneasy relationships with Mary's and Alice's husbands. Especially Mary's husband, Eugene Burton. Harriet has never liked Eugene, and this convinces her he is a cruel man.

Calvin says nothing, letting her words hang in the air.

"Are you thinking I'm like that? Is that why you are silent?"

"Hattie, my love, where does righteous certitude lead us?"

"We need to stand up for our values," she says, remembering Porter's stirring summation.

"True, but perpetual banishment must take a great deal of energy. Is it worth the cost?"

Again they sit in silence.

"Is Henry guilty?" she whispers the question.

"I don't know," he says slowly. "But I think you should consider that, if there is a guilty verdict, it may be a true one."

The next morning, after breakfast, Harriet makes her way to the library and closes the doors. She sits at Henry's desk, staring at the richly polished surface, remembering her brother's pride the day it was delivered. "Solid Honduran mahogany," he boasted. "The best there is." Henry's pleasure with every new possession is like a child's with a new toy, one of the many things about him she loves. It is the artless side of him, the side that shows how impossible it is to think of him as deceitful or false.

She opens a drawer and pulls from it a sheet of paper. Everything is arranged quite neatly, which must be Eunice's doing. A pen? In the center drawer. Get this done, she tells herself.

"Dear Bella," she writes and then stops, staring at the words. What can she say? She will reach out carefully, offering forgiveness. No, just a step toward reconciliation. First she will decry the action by Bella's son-in-law. The pen moves across the paper sluggishly: "I am sorry to hear . . ."

A furious banging at the front door stops her hand in midsentence. Shouts, more banging. She tosses the pen into the drawer, folds the paper into a square, and tucks it in her sleeve before running out to the hall.

Henry has reached the door first and thrown it open.

"There's a verdict!" yells the young boy, a courthouse clerk. He is red-faced from running and is gulping air. "Hurry! Judge Neilson said to get you!"

They run to the waiting carriage, all of them, including Catharine, huffing and puffing and trying to keep her hat from flying off her head. Calvin grabs Harriet's hand and squeezes it tight on the fast, bumpy ride to the courthouse and then again as they fight their way through the shouting, disorderly crowd to the courtroom.

Judge Neilson takes the bench and pounds his gavel for order. No one pays much attention until the jury begins to file in, and then the courtroom goes completely silent. Not a cough, not a rustle, not a whisper.

"Gentlemen, have you agreed on a verdict?"

The foreman, a man named Carpenter, stands. He hesitates under the gaze of the hundreds of observers looking now only at him, clutching the railing before him with white-knuckled fingers.

Harriet keeps her eyes on Henry, grateful to the core for her husband's comforting hand in hers.

"Well? I ask again—do you have a verdict?"

"No, Your Honor, we have not. I regret to say."

The judge's face shows dismay. "I'm sorry to hear that, but you must go back and try again."

"I'm sorry, Your Honor. We cannot." Carpenter looks around at his fellow jurors and speaks with heavy weariness. "It is a question of fact, a question of the veracity of witnesses on which we do not agree, Your Honor. We ask to be discharged."

"How are you divided?"

"Nine for the defendant, Your Honor. And three for the plaintiff."

Henry stares at the jury, looking stunned, as if he expects to hear more. Theodore Tilton shrugs William Beach's hand off his shoulder and swears loudly.

"Are you certain?" presses the judge.

"Yes, Your Honor. As certain as I am about anything."

Harriet's gaze flies to Samuel Flate. He looks defiant, that naked, rosy chin of his thrust forward with heavy lips pulled tight. She knows viscerally that he voted against Henry, and she hates him. He has failed her personally.

"If that is your final judgment and you cannot reach a verdict, then I have no choice but to declare this a mistrial. I thank you for your efforts. You are dismissed." The judge slams down his gavel with unnecessary force, throwing into the motion all the disgust and irritation that months of presiding over this melodrama have produced.

A roar goes up from the press as Judge Neilson leaves the bench. Reporters knock over chairs and stumble over one another as they lunge for the jurors, shouting their questions.

"Calvin, have we won or lost?" Harriet says, bewildered.

"It's what you want it to be," he says quietly.

It doesn't take long for the story of what happened to sweep through the courthouse, out onto the crowded lawn, down to the Fulton Ferry, up the street into the Heights, over the water to New York, and from there to Chicago and San Francisco. The nine jurors for Henry declare to any who will listen what happened: it was the three non-family men, non-property owners, non-religious men who voted against Henry. It was Flate, the roofer; Jeffreys, the itinerant broker; and that small gnome of a man named Davis, who carried his real estate office in his hat. Jeffreys was "covert and sly from the first," declares one indignant juror. And Flate? A clown. He had so little respect for deliberations, he would jump on the table, flap his arms as if they were wings, and give an imitation of a rooster. "He crows capitally," says the juror.

The worst of it, the worst of it, they all declare, was that these three renegades had finally—by the seventh day—*agreed to find for Henry.* And then, in an appalling reversal, they *changed their minds.*

A reporter for the *Eagle* catches Flate on the run from the courthouse on Myrtle Avenue near Fulton and tries to get him to talk about what happened.

"I won't tell you for a hundred dollars!" Flate yells and then makes his escape.

But the *Eagle* pieces it together from other sources. The jury was ready to call the judge on the night of the seventh day with a unanimous decision, but then one of Henry's supporters made a "disparaging remark" to Flate. Flate got mad and the others stood with him, and the verdict was split irrevocably.

"What was said?" yells Edward, back at the house. Again the blinds are drawn, the shutters closed, the Beechers in seclusion. "What bloody thing was said to make those three men abandon the truth?"

"It doesn't matter," Henry says. He sits on the sofa, sunk deep into the pillows, his collar loosened. "I was not cleared."

"Henry, your congregation is gathering at the church," Harriet pleads. "They're expecting you to come preach tonight."

"I can't. I don't want to see anyone."

Eunice, who has been keeping her usual vigil at the window, whirls around and faces her husband. "Who are you, Henry Beecher?" she demands.

Startled, he looks up at her as she walks to him, kneels down, and takes his hand. "We have *won*, Henry," she says in as firm and gentle a tone as Harriet has ever heard from her. "You have not been found guilty of anything, and you are *free to be who you are*. Your enemies cannot and will not try such perfidy again. You have *won*, I'm telling you. Now go and reclaim your world."

The room falls silent as Henry absorbs his wife's words.

"You are right," he says, straightening. "Yes."

Plymouth Church is jammed, every pew filled to overflowing with men, women, and children. Henry decides not to go first to the vestry but instead to walk in by the front doors and pass through the gathered crowd.

The message travels quickly, among those assembled. "He's coming through the main door," people whisper to one another. Harriet is behind Henry as he steps inside the church and sees all faces turn in his direction. For months now, he has spoken each Sunday to them under a cloud, hewing stubbornly to his basic image of a loving, forgiving God. She sees smiles and hears whisperings, sensing a hovering anxiety, an anticipation—a waiting.

Henry stands straight and tall and strides into the church, reaching out to the people in the back pews. "Thank you for your support, my friends," he says with a big smile. Someone holds up her baby. Solemnly, the Reverend Beecher kisses the child's hand, and the child laughs, a sweet, caroling sound.

It is as if a mass exhalation of breath has swept the building.

"Congratulations, Mr. Beecher!" yells someone from the middle of a pew. Henry reaches out for the man's hand, hugging a woman in the next row, and begins slowly to make his way down the aisle, hugging, crying, slapping another man on the back. There are more congratulatory shouts, then clapping, then cheering. By the time Henry mounts the podium, his hair rumpled, his face ruddy with pleasure, the entire church is in an exuberant, celebratory uproar.

He stretches his arms to the sky, and the crowd instantly goes quiet.

"My dear and loyal friends," the Reverend Beecher says, tears running down his cheeks. "I thank you. *We have won!*"

Later that night, as Harriet undresses for bed, the piece of notepaper with the beginnings of her letter falls from her sleeve. She leans down and picks it up, reading the few words she wrote before the verdict came in. A lifetime ago. Her world is straight again, and she no longer feels imperiled. She glances over at her sleeping husband, and then back down to the note. Watching Henry walk up the aisle to reclaim his rightful moral place was one of the high moments of her life.

She stares at the letter and then crumples it in her fist.

Not now, she tells herself. Not now.

PART FOUR

✣ CHAPTER SEVENTEEN ✣

Brooklyn Heights
March 7, 1887, 6:00 p.m.

H ARRIET GLANCES OUT the parlor window just as Isabella begins ascending the steps, and a weary anger swells in her throat. This is what she was expecting, what she had braced herself for, hoping she would be wrong. Bella is staging a scene, thinking only of herself, courting rejection to get the attention of the reporters. Why is she like this? Did nothing change?

But as she looks closer, Harriet feels less sure. Bella is smiling; why is she smiling? Her eyes are bright, her step almost jaunty, her small gloved hands skimming lightly over the railing. Her demeanor seems natural, her motions unorchestrated. On the contrary, she looks as if she expects a welcome. How can that be? She knows better.

Their eyes lock. Harriet has not seen her sister's face so alive and hopeful in years. Something is going on that she doesn't understand, and she feels confused. What sort of reception is Bella expecting? A reflexive need to protect spills out, unbidden.

"Go back, go back," she mouths through the window, waving her hand in warning. But Isabella is now almost to the top of the stairs.

Harriet is moving toward the door, with some vague thought of heading her sister off, when a figure rushes past her and blocks the way.

"Stay back, please," Eunice says. "I've waited for this and I shall not be denied." Her cheeks are stained with purple blotches as she takes both hands and flings open the door. She is breathing hard.

Eunice's screeched denunciation is shocking, but the sound of the slammed door is what sends Harriet stumbling backward. She hastens back to the window in time to see Bella look up like a wounded animal, her eyes wide and glazed with tears. Harriet presses her forehead against the glass, wanting Isabella to see her, wanting her to know this is not her doing. But Isabella's gaze slides away. She turns her head and starts slowly down to the sidewalk, her feet swaying perilously on the edge of each step. Harriet scans the faces looking up. She sees one reporter nudge another in the arm and roll his eyes up at Isabella. The two men laugh; others grin. Her own cheeks begin burning with humiliation, her sister's humiliation. Bella is all alone out there.

She runs for the door.

"Don't you touch that door," Eunice says calmly. "No more installments to this Beecher drama, thank you."

Harriet freezes in midmotion. From the corner of her eye, she sees the cook peeking out from the dining room and suddenly puts it together.

"You tricked her into coming," she says to Eunice. "You deliberately planned this so you could shame and humiliate Bella."

Eunice nods, her hands clasped tightly in front of her. "Yes, I certainly did, and I have no apologies. No one has been more shamed and humiliated than I, and I don't care what you think. I learned long ago not to care. Your sister triggered the worst humiliation of our lives, do you hear me? I have sat through days, weeks, no, months of being described in an open courtroom as cold and sexless, and I had to pretend it didn't hurt. Henry suffered, our children suffered. None of that would have happened if it hadn't been for Isabella." Her voice breaks, and tears appear in her eyes. "None of it."

Harriet's hand goes to her mouth. Words are forming in her throat that she must hold back. She has done too much to keep peace in this house, and she can't stop compromising now. Henry lies dying upstairs; she has no choice.

Just two more steps. Isabella pauses again and this time lifts her head high. She will not dissolve, she will not give this hungry crowd the satisfaction of seeing her crumble into pieces.

"Isabella." She turns at the sound of her name and sees Puckett at the bottom of the stairs, a look of consternation on his face. "I'm sorry," he says.

She brushes past him and strides into the crowd, forcing her way through and not looking back. She imagines herself encased in a shell of iron, and suddenly feels freed from it all. They can clamor after her, yell at her, laugh at her. But they can do nothing more to her than what has just been done.

"What did I see you give Mrs. Beecher? It was a note, wasn't it? Was it from Mrs. Hooker?"

Harriet has the cook backed up against the stove in the kitchen.

Miserable, wringing her hands, praying not for the first time for release from these volatile Beechers, the cook nods.

"Who was it for?"

"I was going to give it to your sister, Mrs. Perkins, but Mrs. Beecher made me give it to her."

"Who sent it?"

"Mr. Puckett."

"Who is he?"

"An *Eagle* reporter."

"I want to see him."

"Yes, ma'am. I'll find him."

Anna Smith appears suddenly at the kitchen door, her jaw set. The cook shoots her an alarmed glance, the glance of a servant communicating in code.

"Your sister is in the rooming house across the street, three doors down," Anna says, ignoring the cook. "I tried to warn her when I found out about this trickery, but she had already left." Her voice holds a distant precision that Harriet has never heard before.

"You don't think I had anything to do with this, do you?"

Anna lifts her chin, gazing at Harriet with a troubled expression. "I hope not, Mrs. Stowe."

Harriet is shocked. Does Anna actually think she would stoop so low? This friend, her truest since Charley's death, had seen something in her that raised doubts. And she has suddenly become Mrs. Stowe. How could it come to this?

"I would never do such a thing," she says.

Anna nods, a crisp motion, as crisp as her ironed collar, and when she speaks it is as if from a great distance. "This isn't a kind household," she says.

"Anna, you know me."

"All I know is that your sister has been up there staring at her family going in and out of this house, hoping for an invitation and being humiliated instead. She's in a room on the third floor, in case you're interested."

"Anna?"

But Anna leaves the room, quickly followed by the cook.

A man's voice from behind Harriet spins her around. Standing in the doorway is Eunice's son Harry, arms folded, a scowl on his face. She has always thought him a pale replica of his father, a boy who never quite grew up, a man a little too much like his mother.

"It wasn't the kindest thing to do, I'll grant you that," Harry says in a flat voice. "But to my mind, Mother was entitled."

"No one is entitled to such a calculated act of cruelty," she says.

"Lofty words, Aunt Hattie." His eyes have a cheerless look. "But you waste them on me. Everyone knows what you think of Mother. It all is still raw, isn't it? Father was never truly vindicated, and Mother was never given the respect she was due." His voice is calm, almost as if he welcomes the opportunity to speak.

"Harry, I don't hate your mother," Harriet says wearily. "I am sad and heartsick over your father, and I think everyone in this house is under terrible stress right now. Don't say things that can't be taken back."

"Oh, don't worry about that. I've thought about them too long, and they must be said. I've read the letters you wrote before the trial."

"That was over twelve years ago. We were all frantic then. I was focused only on saving your father."

"And blaming Mother for his needing to reach out to other women was fair? Saying she was too cold to hold him?"

The story has whiplashed. Harriet pushes down the urge to protest, to say nothing like that ever happened. She wants to believe it. She searches her memory, both avoiding and remembering snatches of the fevered letters that went back and forth among her and her brothers and sisters during that time. Had she implied that?

"Things are said at times of terrible pressure . . ." She falters.

He leans back against the doorframe, suddenly drained of the will for battle. "This is a crazy family, it runs in the blood," he mutters.

Harriet needs to reach him, to convince him it isn't true. "I'm sorry, Harry," she says.

"For what? Tell me for what."

She throws herself verbally prone. "For anything I have done to hurt you and your mother."

"So it is permissible that Mother slammed the door on your sister?"

"You play with me."

"I'm just asking you a logical question. You're supposed to be the peacemaker in the family, I understand. Which I find rather humorous."

"What do you want to goad me to do, Harry? Or do you even know?"

Still leaning against the doorframe, he closes his eyes. "I want things to be clear, not always muddied. It doesn't matter, I want nothing from you."

"Do you want me to leave this house?"

He smiles faintly. "It wouldn't change anything, that's the rub." He turns and walks out of the kitchen.

"Isabella, stop." Puckett is running to keep up with her.

"Don't talk to me," she says over her shoulder, barely registering that he has called her by her first name.

"Whatever you want, but will you stop? Nobody is following, just me."

She glances around, wary. "I thought they would be on my heels."

"You looked too fierce for our motley crew of predators."

"Fierce?" She can hardly see him through her tears.

"A bad joke; I'm sorry. I gave your note to the cook, but it was too late to warn you when she told me Eunice intercepted it. I don't think either of your sisters ever saw it."

"Hattie was at the window—"

"Laughing? Urging you on? Think about it—I saw her too."

"No." Isabella is confused. That welcoming glimpse of Hattie's face—had she been beckoning? Or warning her off? The palm of her hand, thrust up to the window—

"She was trying to make me go back."

"That's what I think. Your only enemy in that house is Eunice."

She manages a smile at that. "That isn't likely, Mr. Puckett, but thank you for wanting to believe it. At least you've given me reason to think Hattie wasn't complicit."

They fall into step, with Puckett glancing back frequently to make sure no one breaks from the crowd around the Beecher house to follow them. A few expletives to his colleagues stemmed the initial rush, but he knows it won't last.

Isabella feels calmer now, able to think through what she must do. She thinks longingly of John's quiet presence, of the library where he reads to her in the evenings, reminding herself that there is a place where she is loved and safe. She will give up this quixotic idea of reunion with her brother or anyone else in that cold, rejecting house. Hattie might not have orchestrated her humiliation, but she did nothing to help her either. Let them all turn their backs to her, she doesn't care anymore. She will go home.

"The newspapers tomorrow will detail every step you took up and down your brother's stoop. I hope you're prepared for that," Puckett says.

"No, but I know it's going to happen."

He shakes his head. "Your sister-in-law single-handedly put the spotlight on you and took it off Henry. I know it's hard for you to appreciate the irony, but I'm saying it now, in hopes you will think about it later."

"What did you think would happen?"

"I thought your sister would be at the door and let you in and I'd have a great story about the Beecher clan reuniting."

"So you've still got a good story—a better one for the newspapers."

He says nothing, yanks his hat low on his forehead, and shoves his hands into his pockets as they walk. "Oh, it's a good one," he says finally.

"So why aren't you running to your typewriter to tell the world? Isn't that what you're supposed to be doing? Or are you just getting more material, running after me?"

He barely lifts his head as they round a corner, out of eyesight of the crowd behind them. "I already know all I need to know about you."

He says it so flatly, Isabella hesitates, holding back a rejoinder.

"You were brave going to see Woodhull at the Tombs," he says unexpectedly.

"I was a fool."

"I didn't say you weren't foolhardy, I said you were brave. How many people would have stood up for that crazy woman, even if they thought she was right? You did, nobody else, and you caught hell for it."

She slows her step, and fumbles for a handkerchief.

"I don't think much of your brother, but it's not just that he's made of jelly, it's for his treachery. It's for what he did to you."

"I don't want to hear this—"

"Well, you're going to. It was his idea to send Tilton up to your home to blackmail you into silence." He lets out a harsh snort. "What a pair those two made!"

Her heart jumps a beat. "You know about that?"

"I had something at stake myself, as you might remember."

She flushes. "Did Tilton threaten you too?"

"It wouldn't have done them any good if he had."

"It was Tilton who was most responsible, not Henry. They hated each other."

"Your brother was desperate to shut you up. I'm sorry, that's the fact of it. Why you can still believe in him is beyond me."

Impulsively, she tells him the truth. "I wanted us to have the chance to apologize to each other. I think it would have happened. You don't know all that we shared, all the roots—" She can't go on.

He shoots her a look of disbelief and then simply shakes his head. "I think you really believe that."

Yes, she does. Broken families do mend; they do make repairs, some shakier than others, but there has to be someone who thinks it can happen. Each side must give up something, some part of the story, to find wholeness again. Miracles do come from love. Yes, she has to believe that.

They walk along in silence, finding themselves shortly at the bottom of the hill, staring up at the Brooklyn Tower. The day is waning, and the tower looms above them, shrouded in thin, gray fog. Two young women in proper flowered hats and reddened lips pedal by on their bicycles, giggling and calling out to each other, enjoying the freedom of their evening ride. Perhaps at home they still must sit quietly at tables headed by fathers in muttonchop whiskers, but here they are New Women, down on the dock to take a peek at the future.

"You've tried to help me, and I thank you," Isabella says finally.

"I wish it had worked. For your sake."

"You've done it more than once," she adds, glancing at him. Not a handsome man, exactly, but there is an unusual clarity to his eyes. Had she noticed that before?

"There's something else I want to say, Mrs. Hooker—"

"My Christian name is fine."

He smiles. "Isabella. That night back at the convention? When I brought you your lost speech?"

"Yes—"

"Truth was, I was somewhat smitten."

She smiles faintly. She had been nothing more than a middle-aged woman in a state of panic that night. It was not a moment for the tiny coquettish mannerisms of social life that women employed reflexively, always, of course, within the boundaries of convention. Had she signaled otherwise?

"I must have looked insane. If you hadn't found my speech, I would have lost all credibility with my suffragist friends, and I was very grateful."

"You're wondering if you invited my reaction. No, I'm just stating a fact."

"You're so blunt."

He sighs. "And you're smart and strong. You're better than you think you are."

His words jolt her; how does he know what she thinks of herself? "I have to go now," she adds. "I have to say goodbye."

"I can walk you back to the boardinghouse—"

"No, I can get there on my own, I need to settle with the landlady. I'm going home in the morning."

"Well, goodbye then." He grins at her, a sudden awkwardness in his voice.

Impulsively, she reaches out a hand. He takes it, and she feels comforted by the strength of his grip. Then she turns and begins walking back up Washington Street.

"Isabella?"

She stops and turns again.

"I would have lingered if I'd been invited—not to offend you."

She shakes her head, smiles, and starts back again up the hill. Ahead of her, she sees that the girls on bicycles have stopped next to a cluster of young men and the giggling and laughing have intensified.

She feels a tenderness for them, a touch of wistfulness for their casual liberty as she walks past. Could she have been tempted? She will never know.

The servants are scurrying from room to room, talking in whispers, avoiding direct contact with family members as much as possible. Tom and Mary hurry down from their vigil in Henry's bedroom at the sound of the slamming door and witness Harriet's encounter with Eunice. Mary covers her face and sits on the steps. Tom, his face dark with anger, eyes going back and forth between his sister and sister-in-law, turns and stomps back upstairs. Harry Beecher's small children, who are sitting at the dining room table reading picture books, tumble from their chairs and settle themselves in a far corner, watching the adults with wide eyes.

There is a heavy knock on the front door.

Harriet emerges from her encounter with Harry in the kitchen to see Eunice has vanished, and clearly no servant wants to go near the door. Her heart heavy, she takes on the duty herself.

"Mrs. Stowe, I presume?" A stolid, white-haired older man tips his black fedora with careful formality. "Reverend Charles Hall, pastor of Holy Trinity."

It takes a second to remember. Yes, this is the rival clergyman who, at the dark moment when Henry had been under the most suspicion, saw him at the back of Trinity and immediately marched down the aisle to take him by the hand and bring him forward as a guest of honor in his church.

"Reverend Hall." Eunice appears, brushing past Harriet. "Come in, come in, dear friend." She guides him in, ignoring introductions, as he murmurs his good wishes to her.

"May I visit him, madame?" he asks.

"You're one of the most loyal friends of his life," Eunice says quietly. "Of course you may. Come with me." Together they mount the stairs.

Harriet stares after them, feeling invisible.

"Mrs. Stowe?"

The cook is looking at her from the kitchen door.

"Mr. Puckett is in the back," she whispers, looking around to make sure she is not heard.

Harriet follows her into the kitchen, annoyed by her surreptitious manner but looking around herself all the same.

The angular man standing in the kitchen has his hands shoved deep into his pockets. He is dressed better than most of the reporters Harriet sees and does not bother to remove his hat. The set of his jaw shows impatience as well as a hint of scorn.

"Hello, Mrs. Stowe. I don't know why you wanted to see me, but here I am."

"You know my sister?"

"I know her from years ago. An admirable woman, in my estimation. Which probably ends our conversation." He turns as if to go.

"No, please. You brought a note from her—"

"It wasn't for you, it was for her sister Mary."

"Not for both of us?" The words simply spill out.

He shrugs. "She knew you wouldn't pay any attention."

"What did she say?"

"I didn't see it, Mrs. Beecher, I just delivered it. But I know she was asking Mrs. Perkins to help her see her brother one last time. A simple request, right? Just not for the Beechers."

He isn't impatient, he is angry. Everyone is angry; she herself has been angry for years. A sudden perception of the cost hits her, a realization of the uselessness of fanning flames that should have died long ago. And now a new cost—Bella had counted on kindness from Mary, not herself.

"Is Bella all right?" she asks, almost timidly.

"I think so," he says. And then, more to himself, "I hope so."

"I will send her a note. Will you take it for me?"

He pauses a moment, considering. "No, I'm sorry. I'm not going to do that. I don't see the point, frankly. Either help your sister or don't, but do it yourself." He flashes her a cold smile. "Now I know I'm dismissed. Good day, Mrs. Stowe."

He starts out the door and turns. "She's going back to Hartford tomorrow morning. You know where she is?"

"Yes, I do."

"Goodbye, then. See you at old Henry's funeral."

She winces. Yes, anger is hard to put away.

The hour is late, somewhere past ten o'clock. Tom has shut himself in his room, his eyes red and his face haggard. Harriet and her sister eat alone in the dining room, taking some comfort from each other's presence. They speak only a little, aware of the hum of reporters' voices outside and the quick steps of Eunice's sons going up and down the stairs. The doctor comes, staying with Henry for an hour, then clicks his black bag closed and leaves silently, pausing only to speak to Eunice at the door.

"It won't be long," he says. "A good man, one who will be sorely missed."

Hearing this, Mary puts down her fork and stares at her plate. "Dear God," she says softly. "It's upon us."

Eunice pauses on the threshold. "Harry and I are working on the obituary," she says in a wavering voice. "Is there anything you think should be in it that we might have forgotten?"

"The editorials he wrote fighting slavery," says Harriet.

"His bravery during the 1836 riots after James Birney's press was destroyed," says Mary.

"When he poured lead into molds and made bullets to defend us all," Harriet finishes.

"It's all in there," Eunice says. She seems frail this evening, drained of fight.

"That he loved his wife and was faithful to the last." Harriet's words are calm and firm.

A hint of a smile passes over Eunice's face. "Thank you," she says.

"Eunice—"

"No, Hattie, she can't come. Nor is she welcome at the funeral. There will be guards there, watching for her. I'm sorry. I'm tired too, but don't ask me to bend on this. I'm too old; I've lost too much. Maybe, somehow—somehow it all ends."

"But not with forgiveness?" Mary says unexpectedly.

"Please understand, I cannot."

No one wants to be far from Henry's room that night. They take turns holding vigil, ready to warn the others if his rasping breathing ceases. Harriet finishes her stint around two in the morning and rises to cede her place to Tom. He gives her a hug as she stands. "We all just do our best," he says brokenly.

She didn't realize how hard it would be to move back into the hallway and down to her own room. One fragile thread of life remains, and soon it will break. She felt the same last year as she was losing Calvin, wanting to hold on, hold on. And the same with dear Catharine, her anchor and sounding board during the trial, gone now nine years. But this thread too will fray, and her grasp will hold nothing.

She takes from her bureau drawer a small velvet carrying bag and sits on the bed. After smoothing out its creases and untying the strings, she allows its contents to slide out onto her lap.

The bracelet is an ungainly object, in truth. But it gives her pleasure to finger each link and slowly read each inscription. She holds it up and slides it onto her wrist, willing herself to remember why it has always been both her most cherished and most intimidating possession. It is simple, really. A feeling of peace envelops her; she knows what she is going to do.

❖ CHAPTER EIGHTEEN ❖

March 8, 1887

I᷈T IS NOT YET FIVE in the morning when Harriet rises from her bed, dresses quickly, and makes her way to Henry's room. Mary is slumped in the chair, dozing.

"Mary?" Harriet touches her sister's arm.

Mary's eyes fly open, her pupils round and staring.

"It's all right," Harriet whispers. She moves to Henry's bed and lightly touches his cheek. His breathing hasn't changed.

"Why are you dressed so early?" Mary is still scrambling for wakefulness.

"I'm going out, and I want to leave before anyone is up to ask questions."

"Where—" Mary stops herself. "Hattie, dear, is this wise?" she says. "At this time?"

Harriet gives her a quick kiss. "I can't choose the timing," she says. "I won't be long."

She leaves the room without waiting for an answer and descends the stairs as quietly as she can. Carefully she extracts her coat from the tree at the foot of the stairs, wary of knocking the entire structure over if she moves too quickly. She glances out the parlor window—so far, only a handful of reporters stand huddled in the cold on the sidewalk. The night crew, sleepy and ready to be relieved. She will exit through the kitchen back door.

But the kitchen isn't empty. Anna is there, lifting a tray of fresh-baked biscuits from the stove just as Harriet enters. She turns with it in her hands as she hears Harriet's step.

"You are up very early," she says calmly.

"So are you," Harriet replies.

"The cook doesn't come in until six, and I couldn't sleep."

"Neither could I."

"How is he?"

"Still alive. The doctor doesn't think he'll live out the day."

"Again, so soon."

Yes, so soon. Anna mourned with her for Calvin, but her words echo far back to the past, back to Charley. And now they stand with this strange awkwardness separating them. Harriet blinks and keeps her voice steady. "Please don't tell anyone you saw me," she says. She pulls on her gloves and buttons her coat, not looking directly at Anna. When she finally looks up, Anna has placed the tray down on the counter and is wrapping two biscuits in a soft cloth.

"Here," she says, holding them out to Harriet. There is the wisp of a smile on her face. "One for you. And one for her."

Harriet takes the biscuits and tucks them into a pocket, then hesitates as she opens the back door. "How did you know?" she asks.

"Why do you think I am in the kitchen?" Anna says it softly—so softly, Harriet isn't at first sure she hears her words right.

The morning is cold, with a sharp wind blowing up from the water. Harriet makes her way through the back alley, emerging cautiously onto Hicks Street on the far side of Isabella's boardinghouse. She looks up at the weathered frame structure, suddenly nervous. Bella is on the third floor, Anna said. But which is her window? She can't shout, that would alert everybody.

She bends down and scoops up some pebbles, then stares upward. It has to be a front window, if Bella has a side view of Henry's house. The windows to the left and right are dark. Only the center one shows a flicker of light. Could Bella too be unable to sleep? Harriet takes one pebble in her right hand, a large one, and throws. It hits the side of the house, below the windowsill. She bites her lip and glances down the block to the small group of sleepy reporters, but no one has noticed her yet.

She takes off her right glove and heaves a second pebble. It hits the window with a sharp *ping,* sharp enough to echo in the silent morning air. Surely that will get a response, she tells herself. And if anyone but Bella comes to the window, she will simply duck her head and hurry on down the block. Please, Bella, hear me. Please.

The window opens, and she sees Bella standing with one hand on the sash, staring down at her.

"Hattie?"

Harriet nods, afraid to speak too loudly. "May I come up?" she asks.

Isabella is clinging to the window, still staring. "Come up?"

"Please."

Nothing, for a long moment. Then, to her great relief, Isabella speaks again.

"Come to the back entrance," she says.

Isabella hitches up her flannel gown, runs down the stairs, through a still-dark kitchen and pushes open the door. Yes, it is, it really is Hattie, her small frame engulfed in a long coat, one glove missing, her nose and cheeks red with cold. Too stunned to speak, Isabella realizes they have not stood this close to each other in over fifteen years.

"Will you see me?" Harriet asks.

"Of course," Isabella manages.

"So much lost time." Harriet's face looks worn and tired and she has tears in her eyes.

"It's all right." Still stunned, Isabella reaches out to her sister, hardly aware of what she is saying. "It's all right," she repeats.

Harriet raises her arms in an almost imploring gesture, and the two women come together in a fierce embrace.

*   *   *

"How long have you been here?" Harriet asks, looking around at the sparse furnishings as Isabella leads her into the rented room.

"Since the day before yesterday. It's not the most pleasant place, but it brings me close to Henry's house."

Harriet walks over to the window and looks out, wondering how it has felt for Bella to stand here and watch family members come and go. She leans forward, sees the reporters, and pulls back.

"Have to be careful about that," Isabella says with a tentative smile. "I didn't want any of them to see me, but one did."

"Mr. Puckett?"

"Yes, how did you know?"

"I talked to him last night. He made it very clear where his loyalties lie." It is Harriet's turn to smile. "And they aren't with the rest of us in that house." The tortoiseshell mirror on the chest catches her eye. "Oh my, Bella, you still have that mirror I gave you for your fifteenth birthday."

"My first grown-up gift? I would never part with it."

"You treasure old things better than I," Harriet says, almost sadly.

Isabella isn't sure how to answer. She is still getting used to the fact that Hattie is actually here with her in this forlorn little room. She fears if she says or does the wrong thing, somehow her sister will disappear.

How do they put a conversation together again, these two sisters who have said no more than a few words to each other in fifteen years? For a moment they hesitate, each fearful she sees only a stranger. How to find common ground? They are indeed strangers, but strangers who remember the warmth of each other's hands, the sound of each other's laughter, the jokes, the play, the confidences shared. Now they must grope for connection, beset with remembered intimacy and the awkwardness of years apart.

Harriet speaks first. "I don't know how to blunder through this, but I'll try. What Eunice did was cruel. When I saw you walking down those stairs—I couldn't bear it. I don't think I realized until that moment the destructiveness of all the bitterness—" Her voice falters. "I've committed the sin of pride, Bella. Self-righteousness. I'm sorry."

"If anybody's going to talk about blundering, it should be me. Hattie, I blundered badly. I was impossibly naïve. Why I ever thought I would be welcomed in that house by anybody is—" Isabella stops.

"You can finish that thought, it's true. I was afraid you'd cause a terrible ruckus. That you would be thinking more of yourself than of Henry. The way you did things before." Harriet hesitates, but if she doesn't speak plain now, there will be no more opportunities. "I don't want to rip open old wounds, I just have to say what was wrong. I know you love Henry, and I believe you didn't want to hurt him. It was Victoria Woodhull who gained ascendancy over your mind—"

"Don't blame her. I believed Henry should tell the truth, and I would have felt that no matter what Victoria did."

"I have to think you were misled—"

"Hattie, I've thought about this many, many times. It's the denial that gave this scandal its fuel—"

"It was that crazy woman—"

"No, it was Henry not owning up to his own behavior." This is so hard, Isabella is having trouble breathing. "And this prideful family—no one could admit anything that would sully the family name. I became the pariah—"

"I know, I know. But you were smitten by that woman, admit it, please admit it." Harriet's voice is breaking, and Isabella realizes she too is breathing raggedly.

"I thought she brought fresh air and courage to the suffrage movement. Yes, I admired her."

"Do you now? If she lied about your role, how could you? *She* betrayed *you,* didn't she? You were willing to condemn your own brother for falsehood but not her?"

"I *didn't* condemn Henry, and I *didn't* betray my family. I didn't betray anyone; I told the truth." There, she has done it; said too much, ruined this precious opportunity. She gulps air, sure now her sharp words will send her sister back down the stairs. Please don't leave, she prays. Please don't leave.

Harriet lets out a low moan and sits down heavily on the sagging, aromatic mattress. "Bella, Bella, can we do this?" she pleads. "Can we do it?"

There is no sound in the room, only the twittering of a sleepy bird in the tree outside the window. How clear it all seemed before to Isabella. How hard it was to dig down through the layers and examine it all once again—to see that strong principle has its own perverse seductiveness. Yes, it feels clean and pure. But why *didn't* she protest more against Victoria's treachery? She should have. Was she as blind to the costs of stubborn loyalty as Harriet?

"I made rash decisions; I made things worse," she says haltingly. "There is much I would change if I could." It isn't enough. Where are the right words?

Harriet is groping too. She must give back more. But she is devoid of guideposts, and longs for Calvin to give her counsel. The truth is, they can't argue this out. There is no final resolution, the only ultimate is the fact of Henry dying. She is here to reclaim her relationship with this troublesome, maddening sister, because she finally knows the pain of the ostracism she inflicted on her. I love her, she realizes. Tom is right. I didn't realize how much.

"I'm tired of all this," she says finally. "I've been stubborn and cruel, and I suspect neither of us owns the truth, and in a few years, we are both gone; all the Beechers are gone, and no one will care about our battles."

Isabella sits down beside her, her added weight taking the bedsprings almost to the floor. An invisible clamp across her chest is unlocking; she feels anxiety flowing away. "I feel the same way," she says and reaches for her sister's hand.

They sit in silence, side by side.

"We had good times, Hattie. I used to think you knew everything," Isabella says. "You were like a mother to me when I was a child, and I loved being with you."

Harriet thinks back to that time when the bright-eyed Bella

seemed always at her side, chattering away, and how sometimes her presence was more of an annoyance than a pleasure. "I didn't always welcome taking care of you," she admits.

"Oh, I knew that, but you did. Remember on the wharf? The day the slave ship came through? I was terrified when I was separated from you, all because I was trying to keep my hat on my head. Those people in chains, and that little girl on the ship—I've never gotten them out of my mind. I really thought someone might shove me onto the ship too."

Harriet hesitates. "It was my fault, that day. You didn't let go of *me,* Bella. I let go of *you.*"

"You did? But I thought—"

"I saw a friend from school and let go of your hand to wave, and when I reached for you again, you were gone. I thought you had fallen in the water, and I wanted to die. And when I found you, you were crying and saying you were sorry, and I let you think it was your fault."

Isabella takes a moment to absorb this. "So we were both terrified," she says.

"That's a kind way to put it."

They sit in silence for a moment, and then Harriet reaches into her coat pocket and pulls out the velvet bag holding the slave bracelet, shaking it out onto her lap.

"Remember this?" she asks.

"Of course. How many times did we march off to the engraver together?"

Harriet makes a show of slowly counting the links. "Five times," she says. "The last was Missouri—a free state in 'sixty-five."

"Why did you bring it?"

"I want you to have it if I die first."

Isabella puts her hands to her mouth. "Me? Why?"

"I want it to be a symbol for us. I want it to help us put the past to rest."

"How do you mean?"

Harriet isn't sure if she can explain; every word is an exploration.

"It was supposed to reward courage, but I've never felt comfortable with that mantle. I've never felt courageous. Bella . . . you know, I wanted the world to read my story, but I didn't want to be criticized for it. Bravery is a muddle, isn't it? It only emerges when one is sorely tested. I did more than I thought I did at the time, but I was less willing to endure the results of my test than you were."

"You don't need to do this," Isabella says with some alarm. "I don't need a symbol of reconciliation, Hattie. It's your bracelet. It has nothing to do with me—I didn't write *Uncle Tom's Cabin*. You did."

"Well, unfortunately, dear Bella, God won't let me take it with me."

"What about your children?"

"To you first. And then to them. Here, hold it in your hands. Deserving isn't the point. I'm acknowledging something—" She loses the words.

Isabella takes the bracelet and stares at the soft, weathered gold.

"If I take it, I warn you, I will have one more link engraved," she says quietly. She runs a finger down the inside of one of the blank links. "This one should have your name on it."

A smile hovers on Harriet's lips. "With the date of my death, of course."

"A date many years yet in the future," Isabella says promptly.

"That leaves one empty link." Harriet's voice lightens. "If the cause of freedom is advanced by some future event, I hereby give you permission to engrave it."

But Isabella responds seriously. "I think the last link is too important. I think it should be left blank, as a token of—"

"Possibility?"

"Yes." Isabella carefully hands the bracelet back to her sister. "I promise you, I will cherish this."

This time they say nothing, for a long time. The birds are beginning to twitter in the trees outside, and daylight is weakening the night shadows. Isabella feels a strange resignation, then a sense of peace.

"I'm not going to be allowed to see him, am I," she says. It isn't a question.

"No. Eunice is implacable. I doubt if any of us dare cross her now."

"She must be suffering—"

"How can you feel generous toward her?"

Isabella shrugs. "It isn't really that. It's all the sadness and tiredness—mine, hers, yours."

"Actually, I wonder how you can feel generous toward *me*." Harriet raises a finger to her sister's lips as Isabella starts to speak. "Don't, Bella, you didn't have to let me come up here. I wish I could help you see Henry before he dies. I'm sorry."

"Thank you."

So it is not to happen in this life. But Isabella feels a stirring inside of her, a different kind of hope. There is a way to reach her brother, or at least it is possible— But she can't talk to Hattie about it. It would only make her wonder again if her little sister is crazed, influenced, whatever pejorative might fit. The last thing she can ever say to Hattie is that she still believes the living communicate with the dead. To speak of this would only raise memories of the painful, embarrassing séance led by Victoria. But perhaps she will be able to reach Henry after he passes beyond . . . perhaps.

"It will most likely happen very soon," Harriet says softly.

"How will I know when he's dead?"

"All the church bells will ring, starting with Plymouth Church."

This time Bella covers her entire face with her hands. Her farewell will have to come from the confines of this mean little room, a whispered goodbye sent out on the pealing bells. And that means she cannot go home yet; not until she hears the bells. Perhaps they will release her.

"I've brought you something else, Bella. Breakfast for you, from Anna."

Isabella opens her eyes as Harriet gently deposits the still-warm biscuit in her lap. "So now you know there's one more person in that house wishing you well," she says. "And it isn't Eunice's cook."

"From Anna?"

"She is another friend of Isabella Beecher Hooker, you know."

"And she doesn't want either of us to starve," Isabella says with a smile. She is amazed that she actually feels hunger as she takes a bite.

Harriet watches her sister with troubled eyes. "It isn't just a matter of visiting Henry on his deathbed," she says as gently as possible. "Eunice has banned you from the funeral too. She plans to have guards posted to stop you if you try to attend."

For a moment, Isabella looks like a lost little girl. "Even that?" she says.

"Even that."

Isabella nods, saying nothing.

Harriet continues to watch Isabella as she resumes eating, convinced now that keeping her away from the house was terribly wrong. Henry would not have agreed, she is sure of it. Given his warm nature, would he not have wanted to see his youngest sister? There is the inconvenient realization that not once in the twelve years since the trial has he reached out to Bella, not once has he relented in his demand for total loyalty. She must puzzle now whether that iron determination caught her in a tangled web.

It is too much. Surely he would have changed his stance if he knew he were dying. Now it is too late. She might have managed to soften Eunice's anger if she had not been so stubborn herself, but there is nothing to do about it at this point, and that is the truth.

The first glow of morning light is breaking through a scattering of clouds as Harriet makes her way back to the Beecher kitchen door. She can hear stirrings upstairs and has the sudden, panicked fear that Henry has died. She hurries through the empty kitchen, pulling off her coat, and is just managing to hang it back up and start up the stairs when she sees Harry Beecher standing at the top rising, staring down at her.

"Is he dead?" she asks, her voice quavering. Please, not when she was gone from the house.

"Not yet. Have you been out?"

He is staring now at her damp shoes, but a knocking on the front door saves her from answering.

James Pond, one of Henry's oldest friends, stands there, hat in hand. His face is distraught.

"Come in, Mr. Pond," says Harry. "I'm glad you got our message. The doctor says it will be very soon now, and the family and his friends are gathering in Father's room." He glances once again at Harriet's shoes. "At least you made it back in time," he says flatly.

The air in Henry's room grows heavier as more people gather. James Pond stands by the window next to two other longtime friends of Henry's, all three men with their heads bowed. Tom stands slightly apart from them, holding his wife's hand. The doctor, in his black vest and shirtsleeves, is at the head of the bed, a stethoscope around his neck, waiting to do his duty. A runner is posted at the front door to take the news to Plymouth Church when the moment of death arrives.

Harriet and Mary are together at the foot of the bed as Eunice and her children pull chairs close to Henry, taking turns holding his hands. Such strong, expressive hands, Harriet thinks. How can they lie so still? They are meant to gesticulate, to embrace, to reach out in gestures of comfort and caring— She is having trouble seeing.

The doctor leans down and presses his stethoscope to Henry's chest, frowning. He straightens, pinching his lips together, not stating the obvious.

Henry's breath has become shallower, quicker. Harriet watches her brother's chest rise and fall, each breath moving higher toward his throat.

"Henry, Henry," moans Eunice. She begins squeezing his hand with sharp, rhythmic motions, as if somehow she can stop the inevitable.

His face—that strong, noble face—is losing color, taking on the pallor of death. The breaths are quicker now. Then one deep, rasping breath, let out. After that, nothing. For an instant, there is not a sound in the room.

The doctor bends down once again with his stethoscope to Henry's chest, and once again he straightens. "The Reverend Beecher has gone to the Lord," he announces solemnly.

"My baby brother," Mary whispers. Her plump, lined face folds into itself, and great tears begin coursing down her cheeks. Harriet puts her arms around her sister, glad that she is here to mourn with her for the young Henry, the Henry no one else in this room has known—the little boy who tried to dig to the opposite side of the world to find his dead mother, the young man who barely stumbled his way through school and yet somehow managed brilliantly to transcend a religion of despair to preach a religion of love.

Eunice leans close and kisses Henry on the cheek, then pulls the blanket over his face. After a moment she stands and sweeps all in the room with her gaze. "Henry has a horror of black, therefore there will be no black drapings in this house," she announces.

"Mother," Harry says quietly. "All will abide by your wishes, don't worry."

Eunice begins to cry, a dry, hiccuping cry, as Harry leads her gently from the room.

The bells have already begun to peal. Someone opens the window, and the doleful cadence of the chimes of Plymouth Church fills the room. Harriet thinks of Isabella, alone in that horrid rooming house, hearing them too.

"I'm sorry, Bella." She whispers the words, letting them float out from this place of death and sadness to the cleaner air outside.

By early afternoon, white satin runners flow from a wreath of pink and white roses on the front door of the Beecher home. Messages of condolence are coming from all over the world, with the clapper on the door hardly ever still. Harriet busies herself welcoming people she vaguely knows, listening to them, finding herself consoling them, saying the same comforting words, over and over, as they decry the injustice of the Reverend Henry Beecher's departure from the world.

Telegrams come. She stacks them on the buffet in the dining

room for Eunice, opening only the one from John Hooker. "My wife and I grieve for you and your family," it reads. No more. No mention of Isabella's now notorious presence in Brooklyn Heights, blaringly documented in the morning papers. Harriet feels a surge of warmth for the quiet man her sister married. He always supported Bella, she thought. She isn't alone, even if he isn't here.

Sometime around midday, Harriet loses count of the number of people trooping through the house: the undertaker, the embalmer, the florist, church members, clergymen, officeholders. It is as if some grand production has been unleashed, and all the players waiting in the wings are marching onstage. Eunice is the general, assigning jobs and roles to each member of the household, holding court in a businesslike manner, her face carved deep with lines of exhaustion. She accepts embraces, even from Harriet. How bony and stiff she feels, Harriet thinks. And yet how fragile.

The casket brought into the house is a brilliant thing of polished brass and mahogany. By late afternoon it sits in the parlor, still empty, its presence both reducing the space and muting the voices of those still gathering to convey their sadness and regret.

Henry's body is brought down that night and placed inside. A panel of clear glass allows a view of his head as the lid is gently closed.

Harriet, joined by Tom and Mary, waits until the rest of the family leave the parlor to approach the casket for their last private moment with Henry. Part of each of them lies there too, for a piece of the whole has died. Their collective identity as Beechers has weakened, a realization impossible to convey in words. They ask one another with their eyes: Was he the linchpin, the true center of the family? Perhaps the time is not far off when if anybody asks who were those Beechers anyhow, there will be no one left to answer. Is the glory gone?

Henry's long, gray hair has been parted in the middle and pulled back from the high, bold brow, giving him a strangely severe look. No stranger to death, Harriet still finds this disturbing. She wants him to look as he was.

"He was my hero as a child," Tom says haltingly. "I had this image of him when he was a young preacher on the Indiana frontier—I could see him on some long-boned, fast-walking sorrel, with well-worn saddlebags, riding hundreds of miles to take care of his people. It made me proud to be his brother."

He bows his head, and Harriet sees suddenly how white his beard has grown. Tom has suffered too. Years of strain with Henry since the trial have taken their toll on him, perhaps the most gentle member of the Beecher clan. He never wanted to become a preacher. He was forced in that direction by Father, but he had the knack of injecting common sense into dogma, a skill that has brought him much respect. He isn't a person who wears high principle as a mantle, as she does at times. After all, he not only stayed loving toward Bella, but managed to reconcile with Henry. I take him for granted, she tells herself sadly. Will the realizations of her failure to understand ever stop coming?

"I need to tell you both, I will bear witness through the funeral trappings of the next few days," he says to the others. His eyes are wet. "But I'm not going to the cemetery. I'm not going to traipse all over Brooklyn behind a corpse just because I'm supposed to as a Beecher."

"Eunice will be upset," Mary ventures.

"She won't miss me," Tom replies, then turning to Harriet. "You saw Bella?" he asks.

So he knows about her visit. "Yes."

"High time, Hattie."

"I know."

"Where is she?"

"In a rooming house, down three houses in the next block."

"What can we do?"

Harriet wants to cry but can't. "I don't know."

"Perhaps she has gone home," Mary says quietly.

"Perhaps," Harriet replies. But she doubts it.

Later that night Harriet slips out of the house and walks up the block, breathing in the deep night air, grateful for relief from the heavy, sweet odor of the thousands of flowers filling the house.

She stops and looks up at Isabella's window. Will it be dark? No, light still flickers inside. It seems fitting that Bella is holding vigil too. She stands in place for a long time, staring upward, wondering about Tom's question.

Isabella is lying in bed, staring at the ceiling. She faintly hears the sound of receding footsteps outside, but she wants no further part of this dismal day. She is remembering the kind brother who made a rod for her and took her fishing and did not scold when she stumbled and lost it in the water. The brother with the warm grin who gave her textbooks to read when she had to leave school, and did not laugh when she had to ask him how to spell unfamiliar words. "That's how you learn, Bella," he would say. "I'll never laugh at you." She remembers him teaching her how to ride a horse, gently, patiently. She remembers how he listened to her when she was a child—and how he listened to her when she was an overwhelmed young mother. "You loved me," she whispers into the air of the barren room of flickering shadows. And then, on this day of final separation, she descends into the labyrinth of wondering if she could have done it all differently.

The private funeral takes place at the house on the tenth of March, with thirty-five friends and family members present. Red and white roses fill every available space, and a quartet of musicians stationed at the head of the casket plays "Nearer, My God, to Thee" and "Beyond the Smiling and Weeping." Reverend Hall offers a eulogy, praising Henry for his "great soul," saying, "I was drawn to him because I hate shams and believe that politeness is often too full of insincerity. He was a man of transparent sincerity."

It is all quite brisk and fast, but that is because Eunice has worked out a schedule that must be followed with careful efficiency. Harriet glances out the parlor window and sees the guard of honor, eight sergeants from the Thirteenth Regiment, ascending the front steps of the house, facing one another, standing at attention. She looks back toward the casket as aides spread a blanket of lilies of the valley and maidenhair fern, bound with smilax, across the bier. She feels a stab of pain as the eight pallbearers lift the casket onto their shoulders. It is over; Henry is leaving his home.

Eunice walks to the front door and opens it wide. The guard of honor presents arms, and the haunting tones of a bugle lift into the air. Harriet looks out past the steps and sees a silent crowd representing all classes filling the street. Men from the docks whip faded caps off their heads, and lawyers and merchants remove fur hats braided in silk cord as the bugler plays. Moving slowly, the pallbearers carry the casket down the steps and out to the sidewalk, walking a few steps to the waiting hearse.

Harriet and the rest of the family follow. She cannot help marveling at the sobriety of the reporters clustered around the stoop, most of whom have removed their hats too. She spots Mr. Puckett, who is gazing at her soberly. She acknowledges his gaze, accepts what it says to her. They bear witness, each of them, to more than a funeral.

Police officers line the street on both sides, their duty obviously to hold back the crowds. A young girl runs to pick up flowers that drop from the bier; one officer rushes forward and whacks her on the head with his club. The crowd murmurs, but the girl runs back to the curb, crying, into the arms of a woman who appears to be her mother. The woman glares at the officer, but not even she will do anything to disturb the solemn elegance of Henry's last journey.

The hearse moves slowly away for the short journey to Plymouth Church with the throngs following, and all sound is muted, save that of muffled drums. People wipe their eyes as Henry's body passes by.

At the church, the pallbearers lift the flower-covered bier and, to the somber tones of Beethoven's Third Symphony, carry it down the center aisle.

Harriet is amazed at the sight that greets her. The entire church is covered in flowers; asparagus fern, tea and Cook roses, an abundance of varieties hangs from the gallery railings to the gas stands on either side of the organ. She looks up as she walks up the aisle and sees Henry's Bible on the lectern stand, surrounded by white roses and lilies. Her brother will never again open that Bible and thrill his congregation with his words.

Enough, she tells herself. She needs the quiet of her room. The soldiers will guard Henry's body in shifts through this day and through the night; there is no reason to be here now until the church funeral in the morning. She makes her way to a side entrance, glancing back only once, and walks slowly up Hicks Street. She squints into the light, feeling that strange chill to the spirit brought by a cold winter sun. Henry is gone; Calvin is gone. If her dear husband had lived, he would be at her side now, giving her strength and easing her loneliness. But she has found Bella again; she has that. It won't be easy; it will never be as simple and pure a bond as they had so long ago. The price of their reunion will be regret for time lost.

Harriet walks now burdened with an empty sense of waste—all those years and energy given to active estrangement, what had it been for? Why was it easier to stay hostile than to give up anger? And there it is, that stab of truth that clarifies so piteously. No one wants to acknowledge wasting time.

And then, finally, Harriet allows her mind to rest on the question she has worked hardest to avoid. Had Henry indeed fallen prey to his lusts? Asking it of herself is like staring straight into the sun. It violates faith. It means facing the possibility that in the constrained, insular world of her family, loyalty had been the easy way out. There were few moments when she had allowed herself to doubt Henry, and she had pushed them away. Offering loyalty as proof of love had never seemed an unreasonable bargain. But had that been simply a way to avoid uncertainty? If so, she had sacrificed her own integrity to protect her brother. She had committed an immoral act.

The thought is jolting, stopping her in her tracks. For a long moment Harriet stays still, mulling this over, before she continues walking.

She has just said goodbye to a brother she loved with all her heart. Was that a false love if she entertains thoughts like these? She cannot accept that. And love does carry responsibilities. Perhaps it demands loyalty, and she was right all along. How tempted she is at this moment to pick up her shield of self-righteousness, to run for safe ground, to rely solely on faith. She can almost hear the deep baritone of her father's voice, laying out the rules imposed on a Beecher, narrowing the walls of belief and behavior for all his children.

No. She will live without an answer.

She reaches the house and finds Anna waiting for her at the front door. "I saw you coming," Anna says quietly. "There's hot tea and biscuits waiting for you upstairs."

Harriet stares at this unassuming woman she has counted as her friend for all these years. Has it really been an equal relationship? Anna has been a source of comfort, a person she has taken for granted—a friend with whom the unspoken pact was that she would not change. She would be there through hard times and good, always supportive, valued for her loyalty.

"If I hadn't gone to see Bella, were you going to call me Mrs. Stowe for the rest of my life?" she asks.

"And beyond," Anna says.

Harriet smiles faintly. "Will you come share the tea with me?"

"There are two cups on the tray."

The two women link arms, and together they mount the stairs to the second floor.

The doors to Plymouth Church open on March 11 at nine in the morning to a crowd so great, the police initially are almost overwhelmed. All of Orange Street, from Hicks to Henry, is closed to the public, and only those with tickets are allowed to pass through the line. Afraid of being barred, people jostle and shove one another as they thrust their tickets at the guards and make their way into the church.

They are confronted just inside the door by a huge pillow of roses and carnations with the inscription, "The Friend and Champion of the Slave," a tribute sent, people tell each other, by a group of colored clergymen. A few whisper the scandalous rumor that a group of prominent Congregationalist ministers who haven't forgiven Henry for his trans-

gressions with Elizabeth Tilton have refused to send their condolences to Eunice.

The church is filling with generals, senators, clergymen, friends, family. The service begins at thirty-five minutes after ten, and Reverend Hall, all later agree, delivers an impassioned, eloquent eulogy.

But it is Henry's brother, Tom Beecher, who brings tears to the eyes of the many mourners with his description of Henry's true role in life.

"He was a watchman," Tom says, "and, seeing the first turn of the tide, shouted discovery. Men thought him the cause of great movements, but he never so esteemed himself. 'The man that sees the streak in the east is not the cause of the sunrise,' he said. And that is how I will always remember him—a man of great gifts and of great humility."

At the back of the church, a woman in a heavy veil is heard to weep at these words, causing curious reporters to ask one of their own if this might be the elusive Isabella Hooker. "God, no," replies Brady Puckett with a disdainful shrug. "Don't you think I would have checked her out, first thing? She's gone."

After the service, the front doors are opened to those who wish to file by Henry's coffin to pay their respects. The crowd outside blocks all avenues to the church, and it is only with great effort that the police are able to form it into a line that goes down Henry Street to Fulton, and down Fulton as far as the Brooklyn Eagle office. White and black, Irish, Chinese, Germans; people in silk and sealskin; all wait patiently for their turn as hucksters weave through the line selling pictures of Henry.

Around ten that night, some fifty thousand people have made their way past Henry Ward Beecher's coffin, peering under the engulfing flowers to catch a glimpse of his face. The doors are soon to be closed. Knowing that, many give up and leave.

But here, coming up the center aisle, are two women, one quite slight with dark hair and a determined chin, and the other shrouded in a veil. They are holding hands. As if by some tacit consent, the line breaks to let them by. They reach the bier. The smaller of the two women, in a somewhat daring manner, sweeps clusters of flowers away from the lid of the coffin and steps back, beckoning to the other. The taller woman steps forward and removes her veil as she gazes downward.

People gasp. One guard moves forward, but Harriet steps between him and her sister and it is clear to all, by the determined look on her face, that she intends to stand fast.

Isabella Beecher Hooker looks down at her brother's face, and traces with her finger the line of his chin on the cold glass.

"Goodbye, my dear brother," she says. It is too late to hold his hand, to kiss that cheek, to reconcile. Too late to say just the right words that would give each back to the other, linking them again to a happier past. She must bow to the fact that fate is indifferent to grievance. Death comes, passions fade.

Onlookers strain to hear more. But there is now in Plymouth Church only the dull, echoing sound of shuffling footsteps punctuated by the occasional sob.

AUTHOR'S NOTE

A few years ago I was circling around the idea of writing a novel about Harriet Beecher Stowe but couldn't quite get a grasp on the story I wanted to tell. Her life as a writer? Her role in her famous family? Her relationships with her brothers and sisters? What? I wanted something tangible that would vault me into her life.

Then I read an account of that memorable night in London when the Duchess of Sutherland presented Harriet with a bracelet shaped of gold slave fetters. There it was, something real. But where was the bracelet now?

I soon learned Harriet had planned to give it to her daughter, Georgiana, but she had preceded her mother in death. After that, no mention of it, and I wondered if it had been lost. It finally emerged as part of the contents of a box of Beecher papers at the Schlesinger Library at Harvard. Upon inquiry, I was told the bracelet had been recently transferred to the Harriet Beecher Stowe Center in Hartford, Connecticut.

I went to Hartford. With the kind permission of the Stowe Center curator, Dawn Adiletta, I was able briefly to slip that bracelet over my gloved wrist. The gold links glowed under the lights of the room. It was unexpectedly large, with no elaborate design hiding the plainness of what it was intended to be.

Staring at it, I tried to imagine how Harriet must have felt when she first slipped it on *her* wrist, for it was no ordinary gift. Each link of this remarkable bracelet would record an important date in the fight against slavery in the United States. The duchess had inscribed British abolition dates on three of the links—from there on, she said, it was

Harriet's responsibility. Harriet took this charge very seriously, and the slave bracelet became one of her most cherished possessions.

I handed it back and watched as it was carefully repacked and put away, wondering what stories that bracelet could tell about the woman who wrote a book so impassioned, it forced a nation into facing the truth about its shameful history. *Uncle Tom's Cabin* is one of those books that used to pop up regularly on school "required reading" lists, and so I was sure I had read it. I certainly knew all about Eliza fleeing across the frozen river and little Eva's soul wafting toward heaven, and understood very early the intended scorn when someone was referred to as an Uncle Tom. Which meant I knew nothing about the book, and certainly nothing about Harriet. When I finally picked it up, not only did I realize I *never* had read it but I was not prepared for its strength and power. And here, getting tucked back into its box, was a tangible symbol of that achievement. Where did it take her? Did it come to represent both triumph and burden? What was her life like in the aftermath of celebrity?

Curiosity soon drew me into the lives of the entire Beecher clan, and it was only a step from there until I found myself immersed in the ups and downs and scandals of this extraordinarily influential American family. The Beechers were the Kennedys of the nineteenth century, a family of high achievers who lived much of their lives in the glare of public scrutiny. Reading their letters at the Stowe Center and at the Schlesinger Library brought them jumping out of the pages of history.

Especially Isabella.

Here she was, Harriet's much-loved younger sister, a prominent feminist, a key player in the biggest scandal of the nineteenth century, and I had never heard of her. She remains a vague historical figure, mostly known as just one of the Beecher sisters. But when I read of the angry split between Isabella and Harriet over the guilt or innocence of their brother Henry, I knew I had my story. This was going to be a book about the painful struggle between family loyalty and opposing views of truth.

When it came to writing about Henry's trial, I was lucky to discover a rich lode of information in the archives of the *Brooklyn Daily Eagle,* which covered the 1875 scandal in great color and detail. Reading those daily accounts was like sitting in the courtroom—I could smell the damp wool and the acrid air and see the onlookers chomping away on their lunches as they watched Tilton and Beecher do the best they could to destroy each other. It was all dutifully reported. I have used some of the actual testimony in the chapters on the trial, and I am deeply grateful to the Brooklyn Public Library for providing access to these archives online.

Using a novelist's license, a few dates and details have been merged. For example, Brooklyn Heights had several names into the nineteenth century; I have used only the one with which the reader—and the Beechers—would be most familiar.

Although the framework of my book is based on history, I want to stress first and foremost that this is a story of the imagination. There is, for example, no direct evidence that Harriet attended Henry's trial, but given her strong support of her favorite brother, some historians presume she did. I think she would have done her best to be there. I like the way E. L. Doctorow describes the novelist's necessary pact with readers when using historical figures or events. He says it very simply: "This is my rendering."

But some things did happen.

The episode on the dock where slaves were herded onto the steamboat *Emigrant* is based on an 1853 first-person account by Thomas Brainerd, editor of the *Cincinnati Journal,* expressing his shock at what he saw.

And Calvin Stowe, on the triumphant trip he and Harriet took to England after the success of *Uncle Tom's Cabin,* did scold the British for continuing to buy cotton from the South.

Mark Twain's house still stands only a few dozen yards away from Harriet's house at Nook Farm in Hartford. She was a frequent visitor at his parties and was called upon often to relate the story about finding a slave's ear in her mail.

Elizabeth Cady Stanton and Susan B. Anthony knew the Tiltons and the Beechers, and were involved in the unfolding scandal. The tale about Susan Anthony and Elizabeth Tilton hiding behind a locked door with an irate Theodore banging on the other side to be let in is reported in the *Brooklyn Eagle* and in several historical accounts.

Victoria Woodhull was indeed imprisoned in the Tombs on a trumped-up charge after denouncing Henry, and Isabella rashly spoke up in her defense. When Henry was dying, Isabella did try to see her brother, only to have Eunice slam the door in her face. And, yes, there was an eventual reconciliation between Harriet and Isabella.

So, to the question readers may wonder most about: Was Henry indeed guilty of adultery?

I asked that question of two board members of Henry's much-loved Plymouth Church, which thrives to this day as a place of worship and a vibrant source of community services in Brooklyn Heights. There was a slight hesitation before each answered, just long enough for me to realize how sensitive that question remains to them after more than 130 years.

Both then said they believe Henry was innocent—perhaps a man with a roving eye and in a profession subject to much temptation, but done in by a vindictive Victoria Woodhull. As for myself, it took reading Henry's letters to sway me to the opposite view. All his letters brim with warmth and appetite, but nothing quite matches the great sensual relish he once used to describe his breakfast eggs. He saw them as quivering on the plate, "red bosoms framed with white" looking like "buxom rustic beauties ruffled for a holiday." Any man who can describe eggs like that probably has a fair amount of happy lust in his heart.

For those interested in pursuing the saga of the Beechers, there are many fine nonfiction accounts. The ones I found most valuable are listed in the Suggested Reading List. I am particularly grateful to the Brooklyn Historical Society, the Schlesinger Library at the Radcliffe Institute, Harvard University, and the Harriet Beecher Stowe Center Library—which, by the way, is housed in Harriet's meticulously kept home and well worth a visit—for giving me access to their Beecher materials.

I can't thank enough the friends who patiently endured multiple drafts to give me their opinions and suggestions: Linda Cashdan, Ellen Goodman, Laurel Laidlaw, Margaret Power, Mary Thaler Dillon, Judith Viorst, and Irene Wurtzel. My agent, Esther Newberg, has always been there with encouragement and full support. Trish Todd, my editor, has given me the great comfort of her intelligence, enthusiasm, and ideas.

Finally, thank you, Frank—husband, trusted editor, and dearest friend. Without you . . . Oh, we all know how that sentence ends.

SUGGESTED READING LIST

Applegate, Debby. *The Most Famous Man in America*. New York: Doubleday, 2006.

Beecher, Catharine and Harriet Beecher Stowe. *The American Woman's Home*. New Brunswick, New Jersey: Rutgers University Press, 2002.

Beecher, Charles. *Harriet Beecher Stowe in Europe*. Hartford, Connecticut: The Stowe-Day Foundation, 1986.

———. *Life of Harriet Beecher Stowe*. Honolulu, Hawaii: University Press of the Pacific, 2004. (Reprinted from the 1890 edition.)

Fox, Richard Wightman. *Trials of Intimacy: Love and Loss in the Beecher-Tilton Scandal*. Chicago: The University of Chicago Press, 1999.

Goldsmith, Barbara. *Other Powers: The Age of Suffrage, Spiritualism, and the Scandalous Victoria Woodhull*. New York: Alfred A. Knopf, Inc., 1998.

Hedrick, Joan D. *Harriet Beecher Stowe: A Life*. New York: Oxford University Press, 1994.

Hibben, Paxton. *Henry Ward Beecher: An American Portrait*. New York: George H. Doran Company, 1927.

Rugoff, Milton. *The Beechers: An American Family in the Nineteenth Century*. New York: Harper & Row, 1981.

Schreiner, Jr., Samuel A. *The Passionate Beechers*. Hoboken, New Jersey: John Wiley & Sons, Inc., 2003.

Sherr, Lynn. *Failure Is Impossible: Susan B. Anthony in Her Own Words.* New York: Crown Publishing, 1995.

White, Barbara A. *The Beecher Sisters.* New Haven: Yale University Press, 2003.

Wilson, Forrest. *Crusader In Crinoline: The Life of Harriet Beecher Stowe.* New York: J.B. Lippincott Company, 1941.

Harriet and Isabella

Discussion Points

1. On page 10, Harriet tells a young Isabella that hypocrisy is the enemy of truth, the coward's way out. What circumstances prompt this moral proclamation, and how deeply does it affect Isabella?

2. Discuss Harriet's and Isabella's opinions of each other as each reflects on the past while Henry lies dying.

3. After seeing a woman struck by her disapproving husband at Anna Dickinson's speech in Hartford, Isabella realizes how closely paralleled are slavery and the treatment of women, especially underprivileged women. What similarities do you see in the abolition and women's suffrage movements and their philosophies as described in this novel? Do you agree that the situation of the slave and that of the nineteenth-century woman is similar? Why or why not?

4. Mary Beecher points out to Harriet that betrayal is never simple. Consider those characters accused of betrayal in this novel, such as Isabella, Frank Moulton, Elizabeth Tilton, and Victoria Woodhull. Why do you think these characters did what they did?

5. Henry is furious with Isabella, yet Harriet is the one who leads the family in ostracizing her. How much of Isabella's supposed betrayal does Harriet take personally? What clues tell you that Harriet's outrage and hurt may be more about Harriet herself than on Henry's behalf?

6. How does Isabella's role as the "baby" of the family affect how she leads her life? How much do you think it influences her commitment to the suffrage movement and to Victoria Woodhull?

7. When Isabella confronts Henry about his supposed affair with Elizabeth Tilton on page 125, why is she so sure that he's lying? What does she mean when she says that the contempt in his voice is so telling?

8. In addition to the belief that Isabella's pleading note to Henry only adds to the public appearance of his guilt, the Beecher siblings seem to feel that the very idea Isabella proposes—to admit his guilt and ask forgiveness of his congregation—is insane. What do you think? Is Isabella naïve to think that Henry's admission would really end the scandal and promote healing?

9. In a private moment of honesty, Tom Beecher tells Isabella that he believes that Henry has slippery doctrines of expediency. What do you think drove Victoria to attack him? How much do her motives influence how her actions are judged? How much *should* her motives matter?

10. Why isn't it enough for the Beechers that Isabella promises that she'll say nothing about the matter for the rest of her life? What are they more upset about—Victoria's claim that Isabella confirmed Henry's guilt to her in private, or that Isabella thinks Henry actually *is* guilty?

11. Why is Isabella so adamant in refusing to defend her brother when she does not, in fact, know that he is guilty? Why is she more will-

ing to believe the rumor mill and Victoria Woodhull than her own brother?

12. Isabella has a vivid imagination. What do you think her dreams described on pages 165 and 172 symbolize?

13. On page 184, Harriet becomes irritated by the organization of jurors' chairs, saying that she "wants symmetry." What does this reveal about her personality? Does it give you insight into her actions?

14. Why is Isabella unable to convince her sisters of the importance of supporting the women's suffrage movement? As members of an esteemed family, do you think privilege keeps the Beecher women from understanding the plight of the ordinary wife? How else does being privileged affect how the Beechers see and interact with the world?

15. In the wake of Henry's death, Harriet wonders if her loyalty has been less a moral choice and more a way to avoid uncertainty. What do you think? Were both sisters "blind to the costs of stubborn loyalty," as Isabella puts it? Does loyalty take precedence over truth? Would the truth in this situation have precluded Harriet's and the other Beechers' ability to be loyal to Henry?

Enhance Your Book Club Experience

1. Throughout the novel, there are references to many important political and social events that occurred during the mid- to late-nineteenth century, a rich time in American history. Do some research on any historical figure or event from 1852 to 1887, from the abolitionist, women's suffrage, spiritualist, or labor reform movements, to share with your book club.

2. Harriet Beecher Stowe's novel, *Uncle Tom's Cabin*, is credited with single-handedly waking America up to the evils of slavery and fueling the abolitionist movement. Today, many Hollywood versions are available, including the acclaimed 1987 made-for-TV movie starring Avery Brooks, Samuel L. Jackson and Phylicia Rashad. Rent one of these versions and watch it with your book club or on your own prior to your next meeting.

3. The Beecher family has been called the "Kennedys of their time." Do a little research about the members of the Beecher clan and see how the historical information available lends credence (or contradicts) the fictional accounts given in Harriet and Isabella.

Author Q&A

1. *This is your second novel imagining the relationships between famous figures in American history. Can you tell us a little about your process for writing* Harriet and Isabella? *Was it different than the process that gave birth to* The Glory Cloak?

The most important part of the process at the beginning this time was deciding what to discard. The Beecher saga is incredibly rich, and picking one route into the lives of Harriet and her brothers and sisters meant walking away from other, equally tantalizing paths. But that's what a novelist has to do.

What stayed the same was my being drawn into the lives of these people through something tangible that made them real to me. In *The Glory Cloak*, it was running across an obscure account of Louisa May Alcott's work as a Civil War nurse and reading about the discovery of Clara Barton's long-forgotten Missing Soldiers office in downtown Washington. Visiting those rooms was like stepping into a time capsule and I had a feeling that I could talk to Clara.

In *Harriet and Isabella*, it was the gold slave bracelet given to Harriet by the Duchess of Sutherland. I had the great satisfaction not only of tracking it down on the Internet in the listed contents of boxes from different Beecher repositories, but of briefly slipping it over my wrist and wondering how Harriet felt the night it was placed on hers. That gave me the connection to her that I needed.

2. *You now have two historical novels under your belt. Have you written other types of fiction or nonfiction? What are some of the special challenges of writing historical fiction?*

I've written several contemporary novels and three nonfiction books on women, marriage, and friendship. I love writing historical fiction, in part because it lifts me out of my world and demands immersion in another period of history. It takes me out of myself. The challenge of bringing the people of a particular time alive means researching with an eye to balancing fact and imagination, always remembering that—when a choice must be made—the story comes first and the historical detail second. A novelist isn't writing biography. The most helpful piece of advice I've heard about writing historical fiction came from Thomas Mallon at a seminar a few years ago: read less *about* a period and more *from* a period—especially newspapers of the time. That took me to the papers that covered the Beecher trial, especially the *Brooklyn Eagle,* which was a major help in writing *Harriet and Isabella.*

3. *This novel covers several significant eras in American history, such as the growth and success of the abolitionist movement, women's suffrage, spiritualism, labor reform, and of course, perhaps the first tabloid-worthy "Trial of the Century." Were you already interested in writing about this time period before you discovered the story of the Beecher family?*
   Yes, I was actually reluctant to leave the nineteenth century after finishing *The Glory Cloak*. I was learning too much to let it go, and I still feel that way.

4. *The historical details that form the foundation of this novel are well known. What inspired you to imagine the Beechers' personal lives in this way?*
   I was curious about how a scandal as scorching as this one affected the lives of what was essentially a religious, tightly connected family. Harriet and her brothers and sisters were no strangers to criticism, but Henry's trial must have exacted a high cost. What was it like to live day-to-day in public view, with nothing sacred or private? What did it do to them? Of course, celebrities live in that kind of culture full-time now.

5. Harriet and Isabella *concerns many historical figures and scenes as well as those you invented in order to tell a rich, realistic story. What cues helped direct you in weaving this novel together?*

I wanted the spine of the story to be factual, and from there, to explore the inner lives of my characters, real and fictional. I looked for cues in their lives that have universal meaning. I think, for example, that the estrangement between Harriet and Isabella—which not much is known about—underscores the irony and sadness of relationships between people who love each other but do not understand each other. So they judge and condemn. Self-righteousness takes over. People can beome so invested in anger, reconciliation becomes impossible—because it means admitting they might have been wrong all along.

Another important part of weaving the past into my story was walking the streets of Brooklyn Heights, especially on a snowy night when it's easier to imagine carriages clattering down the streets and gaslight flickering behind the windows of the brownstones. Being on the site where history happened anchors imagination.

6. *You wrote* Harriet and Isabella *from the sisters' alternating points of view. Why did you choose to begin with Isabella's?*
Because she was the prodigal child, the one cast out, the one hurting the most. Or so I imagined her. I wanted to establish what Isabella was yearning for, to pose questions that would keep the reader intrigued: Will Isabella succeed in seeing her brother again—or not? Will she reconcile with her sister—or not? Framing a future question allowed me to dip back into the past and fill in the blanks as the story moved along.

7. *There are several items in the novel that serve as a kind of "lucky charm," such as Isabella's hand mirror, Harriet's gold bracelet, and Henry's pocketful of gemstones. Do you believe in charms? Do you have any of your own?*
Hmmm, I don't think so.

8. *The Beecher siblings are an imposing unit, but behind the well-constructed façade there are a variety of complicated relationships. Do you have any siblings? If so, did your relationship with them inspire or give you insight into your characters' actions?*

I have one sister, but I don't see us in the relationship between Harriet and Isabella. Fortunately, we've never been estranged.

9. *You treat all your characters with such sensitivity and understanding—even Eunice, who for the most part has a rather off-putting personality. Were you able to get a good idea of these people's temperaments from your research, or did you do a lot of filling in the blanks? What facts helped you shape your characters?*

I think their letters were the biggest help. Many of them are crammed with the kind of detail that tells volumes about a person; I filled in the blanks. For example, Harriet's loving but scattered approach to her children was evident in the worries and complaints she voiced in letters to her sisters. Isabella's energy and fierce desire to be known came through in her letters and diaries, and Henry's warmth and exuberance spilled out of his. I also tried to read (as many of us often do) between the lines of those letters, especially during the period before the charges against Henry became public.

As for Eunice, I began by not liking her very much, but eventually came to feel a good deal of sympathy for her. I tried to imagine being in her shoes. She really had the hardest, most demanding role to play in the Beecher drama. What was it like to be laughed at and described publicly as cold and sexless? How did she manage to hold together in such stoic fashion through that trial? Sometimes I wanted to sit next to her at the trial and whisper, "Eunice, he's asking too much of you. Go get a massage."

10. *Many of the characters in this novel are historical figures, such as Susan B. Anthony, Victoria Woodhull, Harriet Beecher Stowe and, of course, Henry Ward Beecher. What was it like to delve into the more personal side of these famous and important figures?*

Intimidating, at first. I read everything I could find and then just thought about them for a while. I tried to walk each character through an imagined day—what they did when they woke up, what they wore, what made them cranky or gave them pleasure, who they saw. When it came to Harriet (the most intimidating of all), it was reading her account of the death of her son Charley that brought her personal life alive. She wrote with such anguish about her loss it made me cry.

11. *Throughout Henry's trial, the Beechers are aghast at the way the press and public impose on and feel entitled to their private lives. Why do you think the trial sparked the beginning of what we today refer to as the "carrion press"?*

It was inevitable that it would happen in that era of changing moral attitudes, especially given the ease by which information could finally be sped via wire or telephone by a clamoring, competitive press. But Henry was the most famous preacher in America, and his trial was a terrific story that needed to be covered. So I am of two minds when it comes to blaming this all on the "carrion press." As a former newspaper reporter, I believe that public people who thrive on celebrity cannot at the same time demand, on their own terms, complete privacy. Still the Beecher trial was our first major example of how journalistic excess can cheapen the legitimate job of reporting an important story. That doesn't bode well for us in this era of instant global communication via the Internet. Things can't get much faster—or can they?

12. *In your Author's Note, you mention interviewing two board members of Henry's Plymouth Church, still an active congregation in Brooklyn today. Can you tell us a little more about that conversation?*

I was struck with how they talked about Henry as if he were in the next room or at least in the building. I had the sense that he wasn't just a statue in the courtyard to them. They projected an attitude of "knowing" Henry, describing him the way a novelist thinks of a character: living, breathing, walking around. It was intriguing to see how much this amazing man's personality still permeated their imaginations.

13. *After immersing yourself in the historical documents pertaining to the Henry Ward Beecher trial, you must have formed an opinion. What do you think: Did Henry commit adultery with Elizabeth Tilton? Why or why not?*

I think the likelihood that a man like Henry could resist the temptations of adultery are very low, given his charismatic personality, his celebrity, and his unhappy home life. Certainly many people suspected as much well before the trial, and he was linked by gossip to several other women. Still he was a man of innovative ideas and immense eloquence and an important figure of his time. The fact that he was not fully exonerated (and, by the way, the story of the three balky jurors comes directly from stories published in the *Brooklyn Eagle*) leaves a question mark over history's judgment. It isn't so much his guilt or innocence that shows his flaws, it is more how he responded—especially to Isabella and Elizabeth Tilton—when under seige.

14. *In a sense, at the heart of this story is an examination of the frailty of great people—that even the most brilliant icons are still only human, with human failings. What do you hope readers will take away from this story?*

I hope in an era where sound bites pass for wisdom and where certitude is somehow a virtue that readers will reflect a little on the ambiguities of the human heart. In real life, it isn't always easy to know what is the "right" thing to do. Motives can be mixed, truth can be murky, and loyalty can be blind. It's not just about the frailty of great people. It's about all of us.